A Twist of Fate

TINA DISON

ISBN: 978-1-968970-75-8 (sc)
ISBN: 978-1-968970-76-5 (e)

Rev. date: 09/15/2025

In loving memory of

Kerri Whitter

My wonderful friend

I miss you dearly every single day

Contents

Preface

It didn't matter that I had been beaten most of my life or that my body was covered in all kinds of abrasions and large scars.

It didn't matter that I had been abducted by some random stranger who had so conceivably tricked me into believing a lie, and then nearly ended my life.

It was only now, right here in the cover of the trees beside the ocean that mattered.

I stood a ways from this dangerous predator, staring him in the eyes. They were now wild with thirst and jet black. Even as he was sitting on a tree that had fallen over his body formed into a crouch, simply waiting for me to make the wrong move.

I didn't care that my body was rigid as a plank or that my hands were balled into fists at my sides, my breathing erratic.

It didn't matter that the monster side of him threatened to attack. The only thing that did matter to me more than anything was I knew the man trapped inside the stone, cold body of this monster loved me.

He loved *me*.

Unusual Circumstances

My father has hit me for the last time! The only light I had to see to pack my backpack with was the moonlight casting through the curtain of my only bedroom window. While tossing what I could fit in it, which wasn't much, I thought sourly; I carefully considered my options of where I could go. As much as I hated admitting it I knew there really wasn't any. No matter how well I managed to hide from my father his cop buddy Troy Kensley would find me.

It wasn't until I picked up the money I'd saved the last few months it occurred to me the only option I had for an escape was to leave town. I pondered over the idea for a long moment. My eighteenth birthday was still three months away so I'd have to go somewhere that I wouldn't stick out. Though it was just the beginning of May I had already graduated with a small class, which included my best friend Jennifer Collins, in January as the new semester was just getting under way. Even though I was seventeen I still wouldn't be able to apply for a job anywhere till August to be sure I could remain safely hidden. That means I would have to make what money I have last.

Could it last three months? Probably not.

You could wait just a bit longer, I told myself. Your letter from Juilliard could show up anytime now. Or not, I argued. I have been waiting for that audition letter since January ----- haven't seen it, yet. I had been envious of Jen since summer has started. She had gotten a job at one of our many gas stations while I was forced to clean up my father's alcohol messes, and drag his drunken body out of bars. If I want any kind of life at all it's time to let go of the hope I'll ever see that letter.

Once I had everything I could fit in the bag I tossed the strap over my shoulder, and then crept to the bedroom doorway. The house was still dark and quiet, with the exception of my father's snores. I could hear them drifting out of his room. I tiptoed through the living room and opened the door as quietly as possible. After walking out on the porch I turned, taking the time to carefully pull the door closed.

I walked the dark, quiet streets watching and listening for any police cruisers. Even that didn't keep me distracted enough not to think about the money hidden in my bag and my dilemma. I was sure I had more than enough money to buy a plane ticket to just about anywhere. The only problems I saw with that plan was I didn't know anyone anywhere other than here, and more importantly how would I even get to Kansas City?

It was at that exact moment Jen reentered my mind. I could ask her, I said to myself. She clearly wouldn't say a word about my whereabouts to anyone *if* they should ask. She will be discouraged by your idea and fight to make you stay, I told myself. At that I frowned. Although, the real problem would more likely be her trying to force me into going to the emergency room. Even as I tried not to dwell on the injuries I knew I had, I could feel my left eye swelling. My vision was becoming blurry.

When the darkness began to fade, becoming lit from the bright street lights I had gone as far as I could staying hidden. I didn't hear much traffic on Broadway, but I knew I couldn't stay in the open too long. I still had no answer to my resolve and knowing I had to act fast I ran across the open road to Walmart's parking lot. They were the only place, besides a couple of gas stations that was open this time of night. And, they were also one of the last places to still have a payphone.

I entered the building, heading straight for the phone. My hand shook uncontrollably when I tried reaching into my pocket for the only change I had. I closed my eyes, breathing deeply through my nose and began calming myself. After a few long seconds I felt my body relax. I opened my eyes, pulled out the change, and then picked up the receiver.

All or nothing ----- I thought.

I dropped the money in the slot and dialed Jen's number. The line rang three times before a sleepy voice answered.

"Hello?" Jen's soft voice asked.

"Hey, Jen," I answered quietly.

"Angel?" Her voice suddenly went from soft and sleepy to instant alarm.

"I'm sorry to call so late," I quickly apologized. "I need to talk to you."

"Did something happen to your dad again?"

"No, he's fine."

Now she was confused. "Then why do you need to talk at this hour? What time is it, anyway?"

"It's just after two am. If you come meet me I'll explain everything," I promised.

"At your house?"

"No, Walmart."

"Why are you there?" Her tone went from calm to frantic in less than a second.

"Just come meet me," I nearly pleaded.

There was a long pause. The same instant I began to panic her voice came through the phone.

"All right," she finally agreed. "You'll have to give me at least ten minutes. I have to redress."

"That's fine," I said, reassuringly. "Oh, and, Jen?"

"Yes?" she asked, her tone sounding uncertain.

"You can calm down, everything is okay. I'll be waiting for you in front of the doors."

"I'll be there soon." She hung up.

I leaned against the building, nervously watching each vehicle that pulled into the parking lot, as well as, the people passing by me. I was sure Scott (my father) was looking for me or at the very least, Troy was. There weren't many people out shopping, but the ones who noticed me stared hard at my face as they walked inside. I could hear them whispering to each other. I soon regretted not grabbing my hooded jacket before I left the house. It was May for crying out loud!

Finally, Jen's white Mazda turned into the parking lot, slowing as it pulled up in front of me. I quickly walked to it, opened the passenger door and climbed in.

"Hey," Jen greeted me, keeping her eyes straight ahead. She slowly rolled the car to the nearest stall, and then put the car in park. She turned the car off then turned her eyes on me.

"Hey." I tried to smile at her, but the pain in my lip was nearly unbearable. Jennifer's face suddenly became horrorstruck.

"Oh my gosh! Angel, what happened?"

"Scott's drunk again," I stated, hatefully.

"Did you call the cops?"

"For what?" I snorted. "So Troy can lecture Scott over knocking around his teenage daughter? You know Scott's friends with most of our police department, therefore they're not going to do anything. They never do."

Jen leaned back against her seat, listening while I went on about how I didn't have anyone to help, not even my mother. I hadn't seen or heard from her in seven years. Even though Jen knew all of this she still let me rant.

"So what are you wanting to do?" she asked when I was quiet.

"That's why I wanted to talk to you. I need a ride to the airport. I have money I can give you for gas," I quickly added when she looked at me.

Her eyes were wide with shock. "You're going to leave state?" she gasped.

"Jen," I sighed, deeply. "I know this may be difficult for you to understand, but I have to get out of here."

"And just *where* are you gonna go?" she asked in disbelief.

That was a good question. It was also one I still hadn't been able to answer for myself. Now that fear and adrenaline were no longer pulsing through me I was starting to fully feel my injuries. Just simply turning in my seat to face Jen caused me to wince.

"My mom used to talk a lot about Nevada. There's bound to be a number of places where I can get a job," I laughed.

"Doing what?" she demanded. "Dancing around half-naked in a casino? Get serious, Angel," she snarled.

The look on her face made me laugh a little harder, causing my battered ribs to protest. Jennifer clearly didn't see the amusement in my response.

"Calm down," I grumbled. "I was only kidding."

"If you leave what are you going to do about Juilliard?" she asked, completely ignoring me.

"I haven't heard from them since they came here last December," I informed her.

"Ms. Lewis told you they probably wouldn't contact you again until sometime this summer," she reminded me. "They're like every other school, their classes start in the fall."

"Maybe," I hedged. "Do you really think Scott will let me go to New York?" I paused, pointing to my face. "And just how well do you think they'd react *if* I were to show up looking like this?"

"What if I talk to Mom about you staying with us? At least until you get your letter for the initial audition."

"What a great idea," I said sarcastically. I tossed my hands in the air. "No one would think to look there so it's a perfect place to hide."

"All right, you've made your point," Jen growled. "It's just ... you're destine to be a concert pianist, Angel. I don't want to see your dreams fall short of becoming reality."

"I understand that," I said, feeling much calmer now. "I truly do. However, at this point in my life waiting for a letter is not an option I have."

"Okay," she stated, her tone disapproving. "so then go to New York."

I slowly shook my head back and forth. "Their prices for places are too high, I don't have enough money to even keep something a month. I was actually thinking ..." I paused, picking out a name as it came to mind. "... maybe Salt Lake City, Utah."

"*Salt Lake City*," she repeated in disbelief. "It might be warm here right now, but they haven't caught up with our temperatures, yet."

I shrugged. "Yeah, so?"

She frowned impatiently at me. "Need I remind you how big the city is? You're going to have the same problem."

"Maybe not," I disagreed. "I vaguely remember my mother speaking often of a brother she has there. *If* I can find him then I'll have a place to stay till I figure things out."

"Angel," Jen pronounced my name carefully, seeming to struggle to choose her words. "*If* you're really that interested in finding family why not look for your mom?"

Now I understood why she was so careful. Talks of my mother were always tough topics.

"I don't know where she is." I released a repressed sigh. "Besides, even if I did I wouldn't know what to say or do. Would you look for someone who abandoned you?"

She answered without even considering my question. "If I wanted answers I would."

I glared at her. "Jennifer, I understand your concern, however I'm not particularity fond over the idea of being rejected a second time."

Jen sighed, heavily, and then laid her head against the headrest, her eyes focused on my face.

"Angel, are you really sure she left you?" Her voice suddenly trailed off. There must have been something on my face warning her to choose her words lightly. "I mean," she began again. "can *you* really be sure Scott had no part in her decisions?"

"Oh, I'm sorry," I hissed. "I forgot, you've met my mother!"

"How much money do you have, exactly?" she suddenly asked, completely changing the subject.

"Five hundred," I stated icily, fighting to calm the irritation pulsing through me. "Why?"

"I'm going to be perfectly honest, I don't like your plan." She saw I was about to argue, and raised a hand, stopping me. "I also think you should let a doctor look at your face to be sure none of the bones have been broken or fractured."

I was shaking my head before she finished.

"However," she grumbled, the word almost unintelligent. "I know you won't. I'm going to drive you to Kansas City only because I know you need to get out of this place, but -----" she paused, pointing her index finger at me. "----- you're going to take the extra money I give you without a fight."

Totally unexpected. I was just simply asking for the ride.

"Jen," I whined. She cut me off.

"Look, Angel," she stated flatly. "This is by far the hardest thing you've ever asked from me, and even as I know how important it is that you get away from this town it doesn't make this decision any easier. All I'm simply asking you to do for *me* in return is to take the extra money so I have peace of mind knowing you'll be all right a little bit longer."

I opened my mouth but couldn't find a way to really argue. I closed it and silently surrendered. Seeming to be satisfied with my silence she started the car, and pulled out of the parking lot.

The ride to the airport was quiet. Jen didn't seem to have anything more she wanted to say. My heart was fallen into pieces as I thought about what I was doing and how it was affecting Jennifer. We had talked a lot about my leaving for New York, that was exciting. But this ----- this was a plan neither of us could be sure of. And what if things don't work out? I asked myself. What will you do then? I quickly banished those kinds of thoughts out of my head; scolding myself for even thinking that way.

I don't know what I expected when we got to the airport, but it wasn't Jen parking and going inside with me. Though secretly I was grateful she did. I couldn't be sure I'd stay in that big place by myself. We walked side by side in silence to the ticket counter. An older lady stood behind it, patiently waiting for us to reach her. She had a smile on her face, which I watched her fight to keep when we got closer.

"How may I help you?" she asked politely.

"I'd like a ticket to Salt Lake City, Utah, please," I answered softly.

She stared at me for a long second, and then she turned to the computer, typing in my request.

"I have a couple of open seats, the wait for departure is three hours," she stated, looking back at me.

"It's quite a wait, but it's the best I've got."

The idea of not having to look over my shoulder entered my mind, and for the first time all night I relaxed. Why rush? I thought to myself. I set my bag on the counter and unzipped it.

"I only need one seat, and that's okay. I'm in no rush. How much do I owe?"

"Do you have any luggage?" she asked earnestly.

"No ma'am," I said, pointing to the bag. "this is all I have with me."

"Okay then," she smiled warmly.

I was suddenly anxious for a long second, I thought she was going to ask to see my driver's license.

"A one way ticket to Salt Lake City, Utah in coach with tax included is two hundred dollars." She paused, turning her eyes back on me. "Is there anything else I can do for you?"

She kept looking back and forth from me to Jennifer, seeming to be uncomfortable with how my face looked. I really had no idea what anyone saw, I never stood in front of a mirror to see myself. When you're hit nearly every day you stop looking, and anyways, as soon as I was sure Scott had passed out I went straight into my room and began packing.

"No. Thank you," I said, politely.

I counted the money out, and then handed it to her. She carefully took it, and cashed out the transaction while the ticket printed.

When it was finished she handed the ticket to me, told me the gate number and the time for boarding. I kindly thanked her, and then turned and walked away. Jen had been quiet the entire time I bought my ticket and was remaining quiet. A deeper guilt then I've ever felt was beginning to course through me.

"Jen, are you okay?" I felt like an idiot for asking when her face clearly stated she wasn't.

"I'm really worried about you," she answered softly. "and, I can't help thinking this is the last time I'll ever see you."

I had to swallow a large lump I hadn't noticed formed in the back of my throat. I could feel tears swelling up, I blinked wildly, fighting to hold them in.

"We'll see each other again," I said, trying to sound reassuring. "I'm just going to need time to get things figured out and hopefully get a job."

"I know," she sighed. "I would like for you to call now and then to let me know you're all right."

"I'll do my best," I promised.

She nodded her head, letting me know she understood, and then dropped it, staring at the floor.

Suddenly feeling desperate for a change in our conversations I pretended to put an interest in the airport. If only there was a way to take her mind off my obviously horrible looking face and my leaving. And then there it was, the answer to my resolve. A sign for the restrooms. I can at least clean up my face.

"I'm going to stop and use the bathroom," I informed her. "How about afterwards we get some coffee?"

Jen instantly snapped her head up, her eyes wide with shock. I suddenly felt anxious about my decision, unsure if it was because of the way she was looking at me or if it was my offer. We were at the restrooms now. I took a deep breath, and then slowly walked into the woman's bathroom.

I took my time walking over to stand in front of the mirror. When my face wasn't battered my complexion is clear. I've never had any kind of moles or even acne, though I do have a few freckles along my nose and across my cheeks. I also had a small scar just above my left eye, a result from one of Scott's drunken rages. He threw a bottle at me, it hit me, cutting open my eyebrow. It took fifteen stitches to close the wound.

I was ivory-skinned with an oval shaped face. My hair was long, naturally curly and reddish-blond. I've heard people refer it as strawberry-blond but truthfully, it's more red than blond. My eyes were an unusual color; emerald green. I was slender, seeming to somehow be softer, more fragile than everyone else.

But however tonight, when I looked at my face all I saw was a very swollen eye that's close to looking like a rotting tomato, a cut on my bottom lip that is scabbed over, and cuts across my right cheek from Scott backhanding me and his ring cut the skin. I stood staring at my reflection for what seemed like forever. I felt my knees begin to shake as my body wanted to collapse against the floor and cry. Figuring it would only make things worse I forced myself to focus on just simply cleaning up.

I took a long breath, and then began pulling paper towels out of the dispenser and turned on the water. I carefully wiped around my left eye then ran the wet towel over my cheeks. I cringed from the sting, but kept going. Finally, all the dried blood disappeared. Aside from the eye, my face didn't look quite so bad.

I glanced over my reflection one last time, tossed the towels in the waste basket, and then walked out of the bathroom.

My short time in the bathroom didn't appear to change anything. Jen and I seemed to pick up right where we left off. We were once again walking side by side in silence. By the time we reached Starbucks the silence had grown eerie. I so badly wanted to say something but I didn't know how to start a conversation that wouldn't wrap around the current situation. So I bought our coffee and followed Jen to a table.

"Are you sure you want to go to Utah instead of New York?" Jen asked as we sat down.

I took my time sitting down, letting her question turn over in my mind. I knew what point she was making without saying it. I didn't know anybody out there, nor did I know the uncle my mother claimed long ago lived in Salt Lake City.

"I've already bought the ticket," I stated. "so it's too late to change my mind. And anyways, I believe something good will come from my plans."

Jen sat quiet for a long moment, staring at her cup. "You know I'm always here for you, right?" she said in almost a whisper. Then she lifted her head to look at me. I could see the tears swelling in her eyes.

"You get stuck out there," she continued. "or even simply just run out of money, you call me."

"Yes, I know," I blurted out automatically. "You have been my best friend ----- my only friend and you've stood by my side through everything. I will never forget that or *you*."

She nodded her head at me, slowly, and then finally our conversations changed to brighter topics.

Once we began to really talk time seemed to pass quickly. At one point Jen looked down at her watch. It was then we noticed I only had thirty minutes to get to the gate. Jen walked with me to my designation, pulled me into a vice-tight hug, and then walked away. I could feel my heart sink as I stood there watching her get further and further away from me. Barely putting one foot in front of the other I walked over and sat in a chair.

As I waited to board the plane flashbacks of my life ran through my mind. I couldn't help wondering why my life ever got to this point. Thanks to the earlier argument with Jen thoughts of my mother passed through my head. Those were always the ones that bothered me the most. When I was eleven she dropped me off at Scott's house, promising to return for me. I *never* saw or heard from her again.

The lady at the ticket counter finally called for boarding and I stood from the chair. While I walked over to stand in line I couldn't help wondering if this would be the first and last time I'd say goodbye to Kansas.

I landed in Salt Lake City a few hours later. I was bumped into many times after getting off the plane as people buzzed to get past me. Many of them had loved ones waiting for them. I don't really think I've ever been envious too often in my life, but in those moments I felt envy swirl through me like the winds of a tornado. I readjusted my backpack, put on a brave face and walked to the exit.

The sun was already bright and I could feel the temperature rising with each passing minute. Even though I wasn't wearing a jacket I had on a long sleeved shirt. I had so many scars on my arms it made me feel embarrassed to wear any other kinds of shirts or blouses. I was starting to think Jen may have been wrong about the temperatures here.

The glare from the sunlight casting off the cars began to hurt my eyes. I cupped my hands around them to try and block some of it. I took a couple of steps and suddenly a shadow fell across my face. I bumped into it before my mind had time to process someone was standing there.

"Sorry ma'am," a soft voice apologized. "I didn't realize I was so close."

"It's all right," I blushed. "I should be the one to apologize, I ran into you."

Now that my hands were no longer covering my face I was able to see the man standing next to me. He was dark-skinned, medium build with short blond hair. His eyes were slightly larger than average and blue.

"Are you heading into town?" he asked.

"Yes," I answered shyly.

A slight, yet friendly smile appeared on his face. "My cab is right here," he said, pointing an index finger over his shoulder. "I'd be more than happy to drive you."

I couldn't understand why but at that moment alarms began to sound off inside my head.

"It is kind of you to offer," I replied politely. "but I'm not quite sure where I'm going. I think the bus would be more helpful to me."

"C'mon," he countered, his voice pleading. "I nearly ran you over, it's the least I can do."

I slowly shook my head back and forth. "I'm sorry."

I'm not sure why, but I waited a long second for his reply. When he didn't answer I turned away from him and started walking.

"What if I don't charge you the fare?" he suddenly called out.

I stopped walking, turning slowly, almost unwillingly to face him. "I'm afraid I wouldn't feel right not paying you. Thank you, Mr. ..." My voice trailed off. It was in that second I realized I didn't know his name.

If he noticed my hesitation he didn't show it.

"Tony," he stated matter-of-factly. "My name is Tony."

"Okay, Tony," I said, feeling uneasy. The shuttle bus had just arrived and I was suddenly desperate to get to it. "I really must be on my way."

"Don't you think it would be easier to look for any certain place in a car?" he asked, quickly. "A bus can't stop in front of just anywhere."

I thought that through for a long minute before sighing in defeat.

"You're right," I said softly. "A car would make all this easier."

A strange distinctive light flashed through his eyes when I turned my body toward his car.

I froze.

"Excellent," he said, becoming enthusiastic. "You haven't told me your name."

I wasn't sure it would be a good idea if I told him, of course I was raised that when someone asked you answered.

"Angel," I said, warily.

"What a pretty, yet unusual name," he mused. "Well anyway, Angel. Are you ready?"

"As ready as I'll ever be," I said. My voice wavered as I struggled to sound confident.

He smiled at me, nodded his head, and then turned on his heels and walked to his car. He opened the back passenger door, continuing to stand there, waiting for me. I took a deep breath, readjusted the strap on my shoulder and slowly walked to the car.

Tony waited till I was settled in the seat to close my door. While he walked around to get in his seat I looked around at the inside of the cab. It was difficult to see well with one eye close to being sealed shut and the other was still slightly blurry. Tony was already in the driver's seat and starting the car before I got my right eye in focus enough that I could see.

Only then was I able to see that there was a panel of glass dividing the back from the front, there was no meter, no handles on the back doors, and there wasn't any way to roll the windows down. Paranoia suddenly swept over me.

"Tony, what happened to the door handles?" I asked. My voice shook with every ounce of fear I felt.

He slightly turned his head and reached up, placing his hand on the small window. "It's all right, Angel. Just sit back and enjoy the ride." He closed the window.

His tone wasn't harsh or bitter but I could hear the tenor behind it. I now understood I had gotten myself in a very dangerous situation. I wrapped my arms tightly around my backpack, pressing it against my chest and leaned back on the seat.

It took several minutes for Tony to reach the exit. There were a large number of people walking in the crosswalk to wait for the next shuttle bus. I could see security guards standing on the sidewalk watching as people came and went. I thought for a brief moment of screaming out to them for help. I couldn't be sure they would hear me since the windows were rolled up, and even if they did Tony would accelerate to make our escape. I couldn't live with myself if someone were hurt because of my actions. I refrained from trying to get their attention.

I stared out the window, watching the unfamiliar city pass by me. The longer we drove, the hotter the air had become. Tony had the front windows rolled down, though it didn't do much for the back with the window shut, and the seat was leather. It seemed to hold in the heat.

"It's hot as *hell* out here," Tony's soft voice suddenly stated, breaking the long silence. "I think we'll make a short stop somewhere for a drink."

I hadn't been aware he opened the window and the sound of his sudden voice startled me. I flashed my eyes forward to see he was looking at me through the rearview mirror. It was then I could see we were stopped at a light. I looked around and saw restaurants lined on both sides of the street. In that moment, for the first time since meeting Tony, my pulse began to race as the thought of getting free from him entered my mind.

"I think we'll stop at Sonic," Tony's voice began when the light changed. "I advise that *you* just sit back there very quietly."

I felt my heart sink to the pit of my stomach at his words. His eyes briefly flashed to my face, he seemed to waiting for a response. I barely nodded my head. He turned into Sonic's parking lot, slowly pulling into a shaded stall. He left the car running while he pushed the button on the menu board and ordered our drinks.

A few long minutes later a girl on roller skates came to the car carrying our drinks. Tony flirted with her, keeping her attention on *him*. The few brief times her eyes flashed to mine I dropped my head. I knew eye contact would create a dangerous situation for both of us. This was something I'd learned in the years I had spent with Scott.

When she rolled away Tony leaned forward, pulling something from the compartment under the stereo. He sat up, and after a second he handed a tall cup to me through the window. I leaned forward, carefully taking it from his waiting hand. I thanked him, and then leaned back against the seat. He closed the window and put the car in gear. As he eased his way out of the stall, and then out into the traffic I took small sips from the cup, keeping my eyes on it. I no longer cared much about the world around me.

I had a very deep feeling I was dead. Because, though my body felt like it had been submerged under water, I could hear angels calling out somewhere close by. Even as beautiful as they sounded ----- as ghastly as anything I'd ever heard; there was also a deep, wild menacing roar. My mind seemed dazed and slow, ultimately strange.

I couldn't understand why, but there was both a sharp impatience and fear in the angel's voices. That made me feel frustrated, it didn't make any sense to me. Why would angels have fear? I tried to focus on their voices.

And then something cold touched my cheek with the softest pressure imaginable.

It was then the feeling of the water began to fade, ----- my body suddenly felt stiff like I hadn't moved for hours. I squeezed my eyes shut tighter, struggling through the confusion, completely unaware that I was becoming alert. And again that cold sensation touched my face.

"Stay with me," an angel's voice spoke softly.

Behind it was another noise ---- the sound of someone crying out in pain, followed by a roar of fury that was so loud my mind tried to shy away from it.

"Sean," another soft, stern voice called out. "you need to get her aroused before we can safely move her."

"I know, I'm trying."

Suddenly everything felt so surreal, but then I realized it all somehow felt real, too. With a heavy sigh, I slowly wrenched back my eyelids.

"Oh!" I gasped, and my eyes opened widely.

Clearly my imagination had gone too far this time. There was no way anyone's eyes could possibly be *that* shade of blue. This unfamiliar figment my imagination had conjured-up watched my expressions change, eventually his becoming alarmed. It took less than a second for me to realize I was staring at nothing more than a hallucination ----- my mind had finally snapped.

"I'm sorry if I frightened you." His voice was low and anxious.

I blinked rapidly for a moment, desperately trying to remember the last thing I could recall was real. Tony had just handed me a cup and we were once again driving amongst the Salt Lake City traffic. I stared at this perfect face while I scrambled together a puzzle that was missing pieces. His irises were pitch-black, with what looked like bruises under them. My mind was simply too perplexed.

I shut my eyes again, briefly, a hundred percent sure I had truly gone insane. I used the time to concentrate on breathing before opening them. He was somehow still there, his angelic face just inches from mine.

"Am I dead?" I croaked. My throat felt thick with cotton.

"No." His short-lived smile faded, the corners of his lips turning into a frown. "Do you feel pain anywhere?"

"No..." I said automatically, then my voice trailed off. It wasn't till he asked I thought about it, I wasn't absolutely sure. "... no, I don't feel anything."

I tried to sit up, but his cold hand pushed against my shoulder.

"Just lay here and relax for a moment."

"But whatever I'm lying on is wet and I'm cold," I complained. It surprised me when his face relaxed and he chuckled.

"Who are you?" I instantly blurted out.

I watched as the humor disappeared and his expression turned hard.

"All you need to be concerned with is that we're the good guys," he said sternly.

His voice was so low I barely caught the key word 'we're'. I opened my mouth to ask, never to get the chance. A voice suddenly came from somewhere in the room.

"Sean, it's important we go now," a male voice stated. "Is she stable enough to move her?"

Sean stared at me for less than a half a second. "I believe so."

"Then let's be on our way."

Sean stretched out his arm, moving it toward my head. I moved involuntarily, shying away from him.

"I won't hurt you." He unleashed the power of his eyes on me, the blue in them blazed. "*Trust me.*"

He waited till I was completely relaxed before reaching out to me again. He carefully tucked his arm under my head, and in one fluid move was on his feet with me cradled tightly against his chest.

When he turned I was finally able to see where I was. Just moments ago I had been lying on a mattress; it looked like it was soaked in water. This now made sense to why I had felt as though I was under water.

The room itself was dark, preventing me from seeing anything well. This included my rescuers. I knew Sean was wearing a long-sleeved sweater, yet I could feel coldness radiate through it, as though I was resting on a freezer. And, because I was already cold I shivered involuntarily, my teeth started chattering.

Sean walked to what I could now see was an open window. There was a man and a woman standing in front of it. When Sean climbed through it they moved aside. We weren't outside long when I felt a hand gently stroke my hair.

"Poor girl," the woman's voice cooed. "We really should be getting her to the hospital."

"I know," Sean replied bleakly. "Where is Kelsey and Luke?"

The stern male voice I'd heard earlier answered. "They'll join us shortly. The girls' heart is beginning to falter again, we must go."

I didn't have the slightest idea what that meant. What was wrong with my heart? I nearly opened my mouth to ask, but my eyelids were suddenly feeling heavy and starting to droop. I knew I was supposed to feel terrified, or something close to it, and yet all I felt was safe. I relaxed in Sean's arms, letting my eyes close without a fight.

And then something sank in. My eyes instantly flew open, flashing to Sean's face. I was immediately startled when I saw his eyes were already on my face.

I tried to swallow a large lump that had just formed in the back of my throat. "Where's Tony?" I asked weakly. My voice sounded very strange to me.

"Don't worry about him," he said, almost a growl. "right now you just need to focus on keeping your heart beating."

And again I didn't understand what he was talking about.

"Sean," I whispered, nearly inaudible.

His eyes narrowed into slits, his brows burrowed. "Yes?"

And then something in my mind snapped. Everything went black.

I must have been slowly regaining consciousness because the next thing I became aware of was hands touching me. First on top of my ribs, and then down my sides, pressing lightly. And then I became aware of voices. None of which were familiar. At first everything seemed dreamlike ----- a very colorful nightmare just swirling around inside my head. The clearest part of it all was the horror in Salt Lake City. It was the unusual blue eyes that was the dream.

This was the part I struggled with. Had I *really* seen such a strange thing or had something gone horribly wrong after all? As my mind became more alert, I slowly began to focus on reality. I couldn't be sure, but I had a strong sense I was surrounded by people, who were waiting for some sort of response.

I inhaled deeply, slowly opening my eyes.

"Dr. McKnight," a female voice called out. "I believe she's coming around."

The lights overhead were extremely bright. I lifted my hands to my face, trying to cover it. It was then I felt a small tug and a sharp pain run through my hand. Becoming alarmed I lowered my hands, searching for the source. Suddenly a pair of warm hands caught mine, holding them firmly.

"It's all right," a voice stated softly. "it is only an IV."

I turned my head a fraction to the right and saw a pair of unfamiliar eyes. I took a long minute to stare back at them, giving my mind a chance to catch up. It wasn't hard to figure out he was a doctor by the collar of his white coat. He had a handsome face, sandy brown hair that was cut short, with hazel, almost blue eyes. His wire-rimmed glasses were a deep blue.

Since I was now much calmer he released my hands and stepped back from the bed.

"How are feeling, Angelia?" he asked politely.

How does he know my name?

"Angel," I mumbled. My throat was so dry, my voice so hoarse. It felt like I had swallowed a bunch of feathers.

"I'm sorry," the doctor apologized, sounding confused.

"My name is Angel," I repeated.

"All right, Angel." He enunciated each word as if he were speaking to someone mentally incompetent. Though in that moment I might have been.

"My name is Dr. Alexander McKnight," he continued. "Since you're finally alert enough to talk I need for you to tell me if you're experiencing any pain."

How long have I been out? I nearly asked, but my throat hurt too badly.

"Just in my throat." I tried to swallow and moaned instead. "I feel as though I haven't had anything to drink in days."

"You're extremely dehydrated, Angel," he informed me. "That's why I had an IV put in your hand. I've ordered for X-rays to be taken to see if there's any fractures. Your ribs have me deeply concerned. I'm also requesting one to be done on your head on the chance you may have a concussion. Aside from those things, is there anything else you think I should look for?"

My mind was still slow and dazed, it took several long minutes for me to think before I finally moved my head slowly back and forth. "I don't think so."

Dr. McKnight just simply nodded his head at me. "I'll see you soon."

He handed the nurse my chart, turned on his heels and walked out.

The doctor was only gone a few minutes when an orderly came in to wheel me away. There turned out to be nothing wrong with my ribs, I didn't even have a concussion. I wasn't so much surprised about the ribs as I was my head. As hard as Scott hit me I expected the concussion. The orderly wheeled me back to the ER, reassuring me I would be free to go once the doctor looked at my X-rays.

This was where I was thankful none of this was new to me. With all the previous trips I've made to the ER over the years I knew I'd be here for several more hours before the doctor returns.

After the orderly walked out I looked around the room, taking notice of it for the first time. It looked the same as any other; it was lined with beds shielded by the long pastel curtains. And as usual, I was the only person occupying it.

A headache began to surface behind my eyes. I considered for a second about calling the nurses station and ask for some Tylenol, but I knew they would tell me I have to wait till I saw the doctor. I decided to close my eyes instead, and just listen for sounds of someone's footfalls.

I'm not sure how much time had passed. I must have fallen asleep because when a soft voice shattered the silence I nearly jumped off the bed.

"Okay, Angel," the doctor stated. "your X-rays are good. However, I am concerned about your blood work. The lab found traces of drugs."

Drugs? I thought, confused. Why would there be drugs in my blood? I carefully turned my head to look at the doctor. My stomach was feeling queasy, I didn't want him to see any nausea and keep me here any longer.

"Drugs?" I repeated. This was the hardest part for me to concept.

Dr. McKnight looked at me with an odd expression for a long second. "Do you have any medical problems that require you to take narcotics?"

Great, I thought sourly. He thinks I'm an addict. "No," I said, suddenly realizing this looked bad.

He continued to stand across the room, staring at me, his eyes penetrating before finally relaxing enough to walk toward me and speak, again.

"You have been held captive," he mused, seeming to believe me. "Other than the dehydration you seem to be in good health."

This was good news to my ears. "Can I go?"

The doctor seemed reluctant to answer. "Yes, Angel, you can. Though I am concerned about where you'll go as I'm told you don't have any family here."

Of course he would think that, I said to myself. He clearly knows my name somehow, so clearly my last name wouldn't match my uncles. I opened my mouth to correct his confusion when images of those unusual eyes, and trees entered my mind. I closed my mouth, becoming deeply confused. I didn't remember seeing any trees like that in Salt Lake City.

It was now that I really began to feel nervous.

"I'm not even sure where I am," I said, my voice low.

I wasn't aware the doctor had heard me till he answered my unspoken question.

"You're in Newport, Oregon, Angel. You were brought in hours ago completely unconscious. Do you remember anything that happened to you?"

I remember being locked in Tony's car, I thought bitterly. His accounts of my state when I was taken to the hospital made me realize that anything I had thought I saw was in fact nothing more than a colorful dream ---- a hallucination. That helped to me relax a little bit. Then something he said sank in.

"Newport, Oregon?" I gasped. "When did I leave Salt Lake City?"

My sudden reaction made Dr. McKnight nervous, he spoke quickly. "Since you're still dehydrated, though not as bad, I could sign you in for the night. We can help you get things straightened out later."

"No, no! I'll be fine," I insisted, sitting up quickly.

Much too quickly ----- Dr. McKnight had to move fast to catch my arm before I fell of the side of the bed.

"Angel, I really think..." His voice trailed off when I shook my head.

"I'll be fine," I repeated.

He scowled at me while he held on to me a moment longer to be sure I was steady before releasing me.

"I'm going to make a couple of calls and I'll be back."

He stepped back away from me, and then handed my chart to the nurse, who was now standing beside him. "I'll need a few minutes," he said turning to her.

She took the chart, nodding her head, silently letting him know she understood.

All I could do was moan.

A few minutes had passed after the doctor walked out when another lady entered the room. She didn't look much older than me. I thought nothing of her presence, as I figured she was sent in to assist the nurse, and then she walked to the end of my bed.

"Hi, Angel," she said shyly. She stood at the end of the bed, her nervous fingers running over the bottom of the blanket. It wasn't hard to figure out she was a shy person. She had long, dark blond hair that seemed to protect a round face. Her eyes were a deep brown, and like the doctor she wore glasses.

She looked to be an inch taller than my five-feet-two.

"My name is Bobbie Mason," she finally continued. "Dr. McKnight is deeply concerned about you. As we speak he's on the phone trying to find somewhere safe for you to stay."

The nurse suddenly appeared next to me, pulling a tray. When she lifted my right hand my stomach instantly became nauseous again. I flashed my eyes back to Bobbie, desperately fighting to keep from watching the needle get removed. The doctor must have found something for me.

"I'm sure this will sound strange," Bobbie said when she noticed I was looking at her. "but I have an extra bedroom you can use."

The expression on her face made it clear to me it was difficult for her to offer a complete stranger access to her home. I couldn't blame her; I'm not sure I could have, either. While she talked I thought about turning down her offer. I also knew if I did I'd probably be forced to stay in the hospital, and truthfully I had nowhere else to go. This was at least an offer for a shower, which I was now starting to notice I was in desperate need of, and a place to sleep.

It was only now when I looked down at myself that I noticed I was wearing a hospital gown.

"I appreciate your offer, Bobbie," I said, warily. "Would it be possible to get my clothes back? I'd feel extremely embarrassed *if* I have to walk out of here like this."

And before she could answer a soft, musical voice appeared behind her.

"I'm afraid your clothes are unavailable. I'm sure if you saw them you certainly wouldn't want them back."

Bobbie whirled around quickly at the sound.

"I'm sorry to frighten you, Bobbie," the voice apologized.

"It's all right, Sean," she answered weakly. "I wasn't expecting anyone to come in."

I had forgotten the nurse was still there till the disruption from the person I could hear but couldn't see.

Bobbie's body blocked my view of the doorway. The nurse didn't say a word, she finished bandaging my hand, and then quickly exited the room.

"I almost didn't come," Sean admitted. "I thought maybe *she* would like a clean, dry set of clothes."

I scowled at the way he said 'she'. He made it sound like I was something contagious. I considered for a second to say something awful, but I'm a coward. I just sat there quiet, instead.

"Okay," Bobbie said, her voice sounding stunned. She turned, flashing her eyes back to my face. "It's still a while before my shift is over," she informed me. "I'll come back and check in with you when I'm finished. *If* you're still interested in my offer I'll be more than happy to drive you home."

"Okay, thank you." I couldn't help feeling awkward.

She sent me a shy smile then walked away, quickening her steps to pass Sean.

It was than I could clearly the person with the soft voice. He was quite tall, his hair was mahogany, curling over his brow. His skin was pale, somehow even paler than mine. He wasn't someone I recognized, yet there was something familiar about his sky-blue colored eyes.

"I didn't mean to interrupt," he said after Bobbie was gone.

It took several long minutes for me to answer, I was searching through the scattered puzzle my mind had become, trying to understand the familiarity. It might have been the voice; then again maybe not. His didn't sound anxious when he spoke.

"We were just discussing my placement," I finally answered.

The words were already out before I could process them. Then they made me sound like a kid being placed in a foster home.

His brows burrowed, the blue in his eyes began to blaze. "Truthfully we're all concerned about that."

"Yeah, I suppose you would be," I sighed. "Especially since I'm clearly in the wrong place."

"Yes, well ..." His voice trailed off. He seemed to be at a loss for words.

He made an effort to step in the room, still keeping his distance from me.

"I brought you some warm, dry clothes. They might be too big, but they'll beat that awful gown," he said with a chuckle.

I threw him a quick scowl, and then climbed off the bed. And then it hit me; the sound of his laugh!

This was my hallucination! There wasn't any profound blackness in his eyes, but the bruising under them was still clear. What I saw had been *real*.

He must have guessed by my reaction that I recognized him because when I tried to stand next to him he took a step from me, his jaw clenched.

"Could I ask you a question?" I asked.

"Bobbie's shift will be ending soon and you need to be ready," he said through his teeth.

I stared at him in a state of shock. His unfriendliness was so sudden it intimidated me. My words barely came out audible. "I owe you ..."

"Nothing," he said quickly, cutting me off.

His single word was cold and cutting. I flinched from it. He looked at me for a half a second, and then held the clothes out to me.

"Just take the clothes and when you walk out of here try a little harder to keep yourself safe."

When I didn't make the effort to reach out he thrust the clothes at me, careful not to touch his skin to mine. As result of instinct my arms wrapped around the clothes to prevent them from falling to the floor.

Sean wasted no time turning on his heels, and disappearing from the room.

I was so distraught, it took me a few minutes before I could will my body to move. When I finally could walk, I slowly made my way to the bed and dropped the clothes. My tear ducts began to sting from the tears I felt swelling up. That only added to my frustration. I wasn't going to cry just because someone was rude. Maybe I'd been wrong about *him* being my dream. The face I saw then had been friendly.

I stood there staring at the gray sweats for several minutes before carefully putting them on. Once I was dressed I sat on the bed and waited for Bobbie.

Introduction To A Wet World

Bobbie and I drove in silence, I was lost in my thoughts, not really in the mood for chitchat. The rain falling on the windshield had sent my mind and my mood back to the time when I felt like I was drowning in a pool of water. Those same thoughts had also reminded me of my backpack.

While I sat on the bed in the ER waiting for Bobbie I remembered my bag. I found my way to the nurse's station and asked about it. The nurse searched her area for nearly five minutes, and then left me standing there to find other nurses and ask them. In the end I was informed the bag never arrived with me.

Even as I was dressed in clean clothes, my hair was matted, my skin was covered in dirt and I smelled of filth and stale water. Bobbie hadn't made any obvious faces while we were confined in her little car, nor had she said anything to make me uncomfortable. Yet, I knew if I could smell myself clearly she could, too.

Eventually we made it to her house. It was the usual white framed two story house. The only thing I found odd about it was the choice of color on the shutters around the windows and the trim of the porch; they had been done in black. It didn't look bad, just different.

When Bobbie opened her door, I followed. After getting out I closed it as soundlessly as possible. This was one of the many habits I'd learned to have through my years with Scott. He *always* had hangovers, anytime I made too much noise it only made him angry.

Bobbie jogged to the porch to get out of the rain. I would have, instead of walking what probably looked like turtle speed, but my body didn't have the energy jogging required. So much for dry clothes, I thought sourly.

She had the door unlocked and opened by the time I reached her side. She walked inside, and again I followed, closing the door. While she hung her jacket on a hook and tossed her keys in a bowl sitting on a small table beside the door I looked around. We stood in a small foyer, directly in front of me was narrow staircase leading to the second floor. There were doorways on the left and on the right.

Bobbie turned to the doorway on the right, disappearing through it. I took an extra couple of minutes to calm my nerves and focused on just simply breathing normally. I closed my eyes briefly on a prayer for the courage to be in a stranger's home. A half a second later I opened them and walked in the direction I'd seen Bobbie go.

She was standing in front of the refrigerator, pulling a package from the shelf. While she was distracted I looked around at what I now knew was her kitchen.

A small table with three unmatching chairs sat in front of a large window. My body sighed at the idea of sitting in one of the chairs, but I couldn't will myself to walk over and sit in them. I knew it was silly to act like that, I couldn't help it. I was feeling more self-conscious then I ever had in my life.

"Angel?" Bobbie's soft voice called, breaking my reverie.

I snapped out of my thoughts to look at her. She was now standing next to a counter, tearing open the package she'd taken out of the refrigerator.

"Is that all right with you?"

Apparently there was some sort of conversation taking place I hadn't been aware of.

"I'm sorry," I replied, embarrassed. "Is *what* all right with me?"

She continued the conversation, as if I'd never missed a thing.

"If you'd like to clean up before breakfast you're more than welcome to. The bathroom is the door straight across from the stairs."

"That would be great," I said, hesitantly. "Since my bag is missing I'm afraid I don't have anything to change into."

She stopped tearing at what I now saw was bacon to stare at me. "Well ..." she began, slowly. "... you're awfully skinny, but I might just have something you can fit." She picked up a dishtowel lying beside the sink and began drying off her hands. "C'mon, we'll go up and look through my closet."

She passed me and entered the foyer.

"I don't want to be too much trouble," I said, weakly.

She turned, frowning at me. "It's not any trouble at all. *If* I do find something then it means they no longer fit me."

What was I to say to that? I sighed in defeat, nodded my head at her, and then followed her up the stairs.

I stood inside Bobbie's bedroom doorway while she was searching through her closet. Her walls were painted mint green, she had pictures of her and what I assumed were members of her family hanging everywhere.

A canopy bed, covered in red and green bedding sat in the middle of the room, made up. It wasn't hard for me to figure out green was her favorite color.

"Ah ha," she suddenly squealed. She stepped out of the closet a second later with a pair of jeans and a blue t-shirt in her hands. "These should fit nicely." She walked to me, stopping a few inches away and held them out at me. "If you go into the other bedroom you should find an unopen pack of underwear in the top drawer of the dresser."

I hesitantly took the clothes from her waiting hands. "You sure are doing a lot for someone you just met," I noted.

"I suppose I am," she laughed, the sound nervous. "but on the bright side the clothes are finally getting some use. Now, you go on and get cleaned up, meanwhile I'll finish getting breakfast ready."

She gave me an encouraging smile, and then walked down the stairs.

The room she had called *extra* looked like it was waiting for its former resident to return. A double bed, with a turquoise quilt folded neatly at the foot, sat in the center of the room. The walls in here were painted white. A small table sat next to the bed and held a large number alarm clock. There was only one window and it was covered by a pale blue curtain. In the corner beside it stood an old upright oak dresser.

To my right along the wall was another small table, with a computer chair pushed under it.

I crossed the room to the dresser and opened the top drawer. Just as Bobbie had said, there was an unopened pack of underwear. I reached inside, took out the package, and after a short struggle to open it, pulled out the first pair. I resealed the package, placed it back in the drawer, closed it and walked out.

The bathroom was small, yet somehow there was plenty of space between everything. Behind the door was a small cabinet, each shelf was covered with towels, washcloths, shampoos and body soaps. An endless selection of lotions covered the entire bottom shelf. I pulled out a towel, closed the door, and then took it along with my fresh clothes and set them on the back of the toilet.

I turned on the water in the shower without giving much attention to the temperature. I let it run while I got undressed. By the time I climbed in the drugs in my system was completely worn off and exhaustion had taken over. I didn't notice I was freezing till the water hit my skin, the streams beat against my skin a while before I realized there was too much hot water. I rested my head on the shower wall and readjusted it.

I stood under the steady streams even after I finished washing, letting it work out the knots in my sore muscles. When my legs began to shake I shut the water off. This was one of the times I would have loved to let it run cold, under these circumstances it would have resorted into another trip to the emergency room. I wasn't quite ready to face that experience again.

It took all the energy I had just to dry off and dress in the clothes Bobbie had given me. I waited till I was completely dressed to stand in front of the steamy mirror. I wanted to be sure my legs were steady before I tried to stand a while longer. *If* I'm being honest with myself it was because I was trying to mentally prepare myself for the shock I was curtain I'd feel when I looked at my face.

I leaned up against the sink and used the towel to wipe the steam from the mirror. I looked away, giving myself another minute and tossed the towel into a laundry basket. I took a huge breath, slowly turning my face back to the mirror.

I was instantly shocked at what I saw. The cuts on my cheek and lip were healed. My once swollen eye was normal, with the exception of the light shade of yellow under it. I turned my head from side to side, examining my face closely. I couldn't understand why my eye looked almost healed; it usually took a couple of weeks for it to look like this. I stared at my reflection so long I didn't notice tears had swelled up till a single one slowly rolled down my cheek. I quickly wiped it away, turning from the mirror. I picked up the borrowed sweats and walked out of the bathroom.

Unsure what to with them I balled them up and tossed them inside the empty bedroom doorway. It was now the frustration of not having a toothbrush to brush my teeth with or even simply a hair brush began to weigh on me. I would have been happy just simply having a straightener. The chaos that was my hair was so tangled my fingers couldn't get through it. I finally gave up, pulling it over my shoulder and braided what I could.

I hadn't been aware I was hungry until the aroma of Bobbie's breakfast caught my attention as I came down the stairs. My stomach growled in delight. Bobbie already had two plates on the table when I entered the kitchen.

"Could I do something to help?" I asked.

"No, everything's already done." Bobbie had two coffee cups sitting on the counter in front of her. She was adding sugar to them.

"I hope you don't mind bacon and eggs. I haven't had time to really shop." She paused, turning to look at me. "It's probably too late to ask now, do you take anything in your coffee?"

I had just pulled out a chair and was sitting down. "Milk and sugar is fine." Then I looked over the plate in front of me. "These will do fine."

Bobbie was now setting the cups on the table. She had a confused expression on her face when she looked at me. "What?"

"Breakfast," I said suddenly feeling uneasy and pointed to the plate. "It looks and smells great."

"Oh," she blushed. "Thanks."

She pulled out the chair across from me and sat down.

I felt awkward after embarrassing myself and began racking my brain for something to get her talking that wouldn't be personal. I had to admit there weren't too many topics to choose from.

"In case I don't get the chance to thank you later I'd like to do so now. I don't know what I would have done without your kindness."

She shrugged, as if this was an ordinary day. "You're welcome. I believe in the pay it forward philosophy. I would want someone to do it for me."

I certainly would ----- I thought.

"And anyways," she continued. "it's nice having the company. Mom moved to Washington a couple of years ago to be with my brother and sister. It's been just me ever since."

So much for *not* sharing anything personal.

I did however feel bad for her, knowing all too well what that loneliness was like. The conversation had ended again. I took another bite of the eggs, trying to figure out how to get the chatter going again. It had been a long time since I'd had this much interaction with anyone. Jennifer was really the only person I'd spent a lot of time with. Since graduation there hadn't been too much time for us to talk.

"Do you have other family here?" I suddenly blurted.

She nodded her head then took a drink from her cup. "I have an aunt and a couple of cousins."

"I guess that beats being completely alone," I stated dryly.

She knit her brows and I instantly feared she was going to start asking me personal questions. I braced myself for it ... then she didn't.

"You were pretty out of it when you were brought to the hospital," she said, changing the subject. "I'm willing to bet you could use some more sleep. If you'd like you can sleep in the spare room."

"Thanks," I sighed. I was relieved from the change of topics and at the thought of sleeping. "I feel extremely exhausted."

Bobbie looked embarrassed when she responded. "I wasn't going to say anything because you've had a rough day but ... you do look bad."

"Gee, thanks a lot," I grumbled.

She laughed.

I stood from the chair, picked up my dishes and crossed the room.

I set the dishes in the basin, excused myself, and then walked into the foyer and up the stairs.

I laid on the bed and stared at the window. Even as exhaustion took its claim on my body my mind didn't seem to slow, nor would my eyes close. There were a large number of things I couldn't remember and that frightened me. But more than that, I knew this would involve the police. They'll soon learn, *if* they haven't already, I'm only seventeen. That means they'll end up sending me back to Scott. I felt my face turn into a scowl. As soon as I get my strength back I have to do something. There's no way I'm going back to the house of *hell*!

If I wanted any chance of sleep I had to rid my body of all stress. I banished the thoughts from my mind and looked away from the window. I searched the room for a distraction to help me relax. It was then I looked at the ceiling and saw some designs. I tried to concentrate on them, picking out shapes I knew I imagined. It took a long time, but eventually worked. I fell into a deep sleep.

I had the sense I'd slept for days. My body felt stiff and was starting to tremble like I was cold. I knew my mind was becoming alert because I could hear the wind blowing and the rain falling outside the window. I could also hear footsteps on the bedroom floor, they seemed to be pacing. I squeezed my eyes tighter, wrapping the blanket around me. I tried ignoring the sounds that surrounded me. And then I realized there was a real sense to my coldness and the noises.

I wrenched upright in the bed, my eyes flashed to the window. It was open, the curtain moving with the breeze. Instantly horrified I climbed out of the bed, nearly running to the window. There wasn't a single thing in Bobbie's very large backyard. A tall wooden fence closed the yard off from the forest behind it.

A hundred percent sure I heard something I leaned out the window, trying to see if anyone was standing next to the house.

Nothing.

My pulse finally began to slow as I closed the window. It was then I noticed the green-gray cast had darkened ----- letting me know I'd slept most of the day. At least now it made sense to why I felt so stiff and sore. It was also time to go.

I picked up my borrowed clothes and opened the door. I didn't quite feel right about taking them but since I no longer had a bag or any other clothes I was going to need something to change into. I immediately noticed Bobbie's bedroom door was open. Maybe it was her I heard in the room, I told myself. When I walked out in the hall I didn't bother looking in her room. I made my way down the stairs, instead.

I didn't hear any noises when I reached the bottom of the stairs. Figuring Bobbie was in the kitchen I entered the room. It was empty. I searched briefly for a bag and after finding one I tossed the clothes in it. I nearly walked out when I saw a pen and a pad of paper lying on the table.

I sat in a chair and picked up the pen, scrawling out a quick thank you note to Bobbie. I didn't feel right leaving without saying goodbye after all she had done for me. I tossed the pen on the paper, and then stood from the chair.

I tucked the bag under my arm and opened the door. It was still raining, though lightly. You've walked through the rain before, Angel, I reminded myself while pulling the door closed. You won't melt. When I turned around a tall man dressed in a cop uniform was walking to the porch. My heart thudded, stammered then picked up in double time.

"Angelia Johanson, right?" he asked, a smile crossing his lips.

His voice was friendly, but it certainly didn't lessen my heart rate any. *He* was still a cop. I sucked in a deep breath, releasing it slowly in hopes my voice would be strong.

"Yes," I replied. My voice broke anyway.

"I apologize for having to do this after what you've been through but I have a few questions I need answered."

He walked up on the porch, eyeing the bag under my arm. "I'm afraid you're going to have to stick around a while," he continued.

He looked young, aside from the crow's-feet around his eyes and the crinkles in his skin when he smiled. He had a mustache, his face looked like he hadn't shaved for a least three days. His hair was cut Army style and dark, with dull blue eyes. His skin was a deep bronze like he'd spent months in the sun rather than in a place where it rained.

"How longs a while, officer? I don't exactly have anywhere to stay."

He shook his head at me and chuckled. "I'm the sheriff." He held his right hand out to me. "The name's Mike Jacobs."

I reluctantly reached out to shake it. Very reluctantly.

"I'm sure Bobbie would be more than happy to let you stay as long as you need. I'm also sure you being here gives her something to look forward to."

Is it every cop's duty to offer what isn't theirs to give?

"What kind of questions do you have for me?" I was sure I already knew the answer. You were very lucky, Angel, and this must suck for you but it's back home you go.

"I think it would be more comfortable if we talk at the station. Are you up for a ride?"

Do I have a choice? I thought sourly.

"Right behind you," I sighed in defeat.

When he turned and walked down the stairs I followed.

I sat quietly in the front seat as we drove to the police station. Even though it was a short ride, it felt like the longest one in my life. Sheriff Jacobs parked his car in front of the building. I scanned the parking lot as I was getting out. There was only one other sheriff car, beside it was a black sedan.

I slowly followed the sheriff to the door. When he opened it, letting me enter first I caught the smell of stale coffee and a bad choice of air freshener. The inside didn't appear to be very large. There were only a few desks, no one was sitting at and even fewer file cabinets. In the back of the room was a long counter, with a coffee pot, a stack of Styrofoam cups and what looked to be a stack of empty donut boxes.

"Angelia?" the sheriff's voice called.

Completely unaware there was some sort of conversation taking place I turned to look at him. It was then I saw the deputy officer standing next to him. This is where my mind really became perplexed; I *never* saw anyone other than the sheriff when I walked in. I felt the blood fill my cheeks, instantly becoming embarrassed.

"I'm sorry," I mumbled. "What?"

"I'd like to introduce you to one of my officers." He paused, placing a hand on the man's shoulder.

"This is Deputy Callenger."

Deputy Callenger looked like he should have been a model instead of an officer. His hair was short, golden brown, with green eyes. He looked very young, his skin tone was a chalky pale. His pupils were dilated, deep purple bruise-like shadows lined the skin under them, making him look as though he hadn't slept in days. I waited for him to offer his hand like the sheriff had, he didn't. He seemed to want to avoid making contact with me, shoving them in his pockets, instead.

"It's nice to see our rangers weren't too late," deputy Callenger said, filling the now awkward silence.

At first I didn't quite understand what he said. Then it hit me, like a ton of bricks falling down around me. He was the stern, yet frustrated voice I'd heard. My body instantly turned rigid as a plank.

"You were one of the angels ... I mean, in the rescue." I further embarrassed myself when I called him an angel. Of course, his facial expressions at my words only seemed to intensify the embarrassment. My cheeks suddenly felt like balls of flames.

"I'm afraid that is incorrect," he disagreed. "I'm sure this is very confusing to you, I assure you I had no part in rescuing you."

I looked at his concerned, innocent expression and was disoriented. Am I wrong about what I saw and heard?

"You were there," I argued, though I suddenly felt uncertain. "I heard you."

His expression turned hard. "No, I wasn't."

I continued to stare at him, my mind becoming clouded.

"Well, Angelia," the sheriff said, sounding nervous. "we should get started. If you'll have a seat at my desk deputy Callenger can take your statement as we talk."

"Angel," I corrected.

"I'm sorry," the sheriff apologized, his voice sounding confused.

I looked away from deputy Callenger to look at him. "I prefer to be called Angel," I explained.

"Angel," he repeated slowly. "All right, Angel, shall we begin?"

He stretched his arm out, indicating me to take a seat beside his desk. I stared at it for a long second, noticing the back faced deputy Callenger. After my brief chat with him I couldn't have been more grateful. I didn't understand why he was denying rescuing me, I don't think I could have talked with the sheriff *if* I saw him looking at me. Once I sat down Sheriff Jacobs walked around the desk and sat in the chair behind it.

"Okay," he said, leaning back in the chair. "I need for you to tell me how you ended up with this man.

Starting from the top."

I bit down on my bottom lip, staring at my hands. I really had no idea just where to start. I twisted and untwisted my fingers as I opened my mouth, slowly telling my story. His questions were endless; did I know I was being held captive in a hunter's cabin? Was there any details I could remember about the room and the condition the mattress in which I laid on was in? How much time did I spend with Tony while I was conscious and more importantly had I been aware he was slipping me drugs?

I answered each one to the best I could remember. Sheriff Jacobs eventually laid my driver's license on the desk. He was now curious why I left Kansas. Anytime I was hesitant with my answers brought on more questions. After being exhausted with all his questions I finally broke down, giving him the answers he was looking for.

"Well, Angel," he finally stated. "the man you know as *Tony* is really Jeremy Corbin. He's wanted in a number of states for kidnapping, sexual assault, murder and the list goes on. He's been smart enough to stay one step ahead of the authorities."

Murder? I could feel the sudden shock on my face before I heard it in my voice.

"Until now," I said, nearly inaudible.

"Until now," sheriff Jacobs agreed. "I have one last question and we'll be finished."

"What?" I asked, carefully. I still hadn't recovered from his last statement. The thought of knowing Jeremy intended to kill me had my mind in a state of shock and my body shivering.

"Did he tell you anything about the other girl?"

Other girl!? I thought, horrified. He got someone else the way he had me?

"I'm sorry, sheriff," I said, confused. "I wasn't aware there had been anyone other than me. I have a lot of blanks in my memory of the last twenty-four hours. So I don't remember much of anything after Sonic."

Sheriff Jacobs was silent for a long second, staring at me with an unfathomable expression.

"Angel," he pronounced my name with care. "do you even know what month you're in or the date?"

His question only added to the confusion. My body tensed, with stress.

"May sixth," I answered, suddenly feeling unsure.

He leaned over the desk and stretched out his arm, turning a small calendar near the edge towards me.

"It's the twentieth, Angel," he informed me. I heard the deep concern color his tone.

This is not happening! I lost two weeks? It was now my face flashed through my mind. I clearly understood why it was nearly healed.

"Angel," the sheriff's voice suddenly called out. Even though we were sitting close to each other his voice sounded like he was a distance away.

I barely lifted my head to look at him. "Yes?"

"I'm going to let you go back to Bobbie's. This is the part where you have to give me your word I won't catch you trying to leave again."

"I'll stay," I nearly whispered. And then something I feared more than this entered my mind. "Are you going to send me back to my father when this is over?"

He leaned back in his chair, his eyes took on a knowing look. "It may take a couple of months to resolve this matter. Mostly because as I said earlier, there are other states involved. I'm sure by then you'll be a legal adult."

For the first time since waking up in the hospital the tightness in my chest, threatening to cut off my air supply relaxed. Sheriff Jacobs leaned over his chair, picked my bag up from the floor and handed it to me.

"Stay close." He paused, locking his eyes on mine. "I'll be in touch soon."

I nodded my head, picked up my driver's license and stuffed it in a pocket on the bag, and then stood from the chair. Without even a glance at deputy Callenger, I hurried to the door.

It wasn't till after I walked out of the station and seen it was raining heavily, I realized I didn't know my way to Bobbie's. Frustrated over this realization I turned to go back inside. I was seconds from pulling open the door when the sound of tires on wet pavement caught my attention. I turned back to see a white, four door Ford F-150 King cab stop in front. The windows were covered in a dark tent, preventing me from being able to see inside the truck. My heart started to pound and I made no effort to move.

Suddenly the passenger door opened, though no light came on.

"Are you just going to stand there in the rain?" an irritated voice asked.

Without a conscious decision to do so my legs carried me toward the truck. Sean was sitting upright in the driver's seat, his eyes on my face. The fear I had pulsing through me instantly disappeared and I climbed in the truck.

"I figured you wouldn't know your way to Bobbie's," he spoke, his voice now soft as velvet.

"How did you even know I was here?" I asked as I pulled my door closed.

"Don't all victims have to speak with authorities after an ordeal like yours?"

I scowled at his choice of words. "I suppose so." Then it occurred to me I was still carrying the clothes he had brought me. I held the bag out to him. "Would you like your clothes back?"

He eyed the bag for a half a second then looked at me. "You should probably keep them, you'll most likely need them again."

I set the bag on my lap and pulled the seat belt across my body. Sean let the truck roll forward before finally driving out of the parking lot.

"I also wanted a chance to apologize," he said after a long silence.

"I'm not sure I'd understand what the apology is for," I admitted.

"I may have been too harsh when we spoke at the hospital."

"May have been?" I snorted. "You were a complete jerk."

Sean laughed.

"I suppose *if* you mean it," I sighed, heavily. "then I accept it."

"Angel," he said, serious now. "I never say anything I don't truly mean."

I hadn't been aware he knew my name and when he said it I was taken by surprise.

"How do you know my name?" I asked, my voice stunned.

He looked at me, his brows burrowed in confusion. "I heard it mentioned at the hospital. Would you prefer Angelia?"

"No," I blurted out quickly. "Angel is fine ----- great actually. It's just ... everyone, aside from Bobbie has called me Angelia."

His mention of the hospital brought back the suspicion I had when I spoke with deputy Callenger. I knew I was right about them being there and he was going to admit it.

"Why is it a big secret that you and deputy Callenger rescued me?"

"Angel, I'm sure you're confused from all you've been through, but I assure you we were not there."

Right then my suspicion was confirmed. They are hiding something; the question is, why?

"I will admit I'm missing pieces of my life from the last two weeks. I *do* clearly remember what I heard and saw. I saw *you*. I will keep your secret, Sean, I just want to know the truth."

He looked at me, unleashing the power of his blue eyes on me, as if to cloud my mind.

"*Please*, Angel," he whispered. "Please, for me."

"Please, what?" I demanded.

"You've got to trust me."

I was so obsessed with getting him to tell me the truth I forgot to pay attention to where we were going. And then, suddenly the truck slowed and stopped.

"If you run you can keep from getting soaked."

"What?" I asked, instantly confused.

His face lost all expressions as he pointed his index finger past me. "You *are* staying here with Bobbie?"

I looked away from his face, my gaze following where he was pointing. We were now sitting in front of Bobbie's house.

"Yeah," I breathed. "Yeah, I suppose I am."

Sean lowered his arm and was quiet, seeming to be waiting for me to get out.

"Well ..." I paused, suddenly needing to clear a lump from my throat. "... thanks for the ride."

"You're welcome," he said softly.

I squeezed the handle, slowly cracking open the door. I hadn't noticed my knees were shaking till I climbed out of the truck. I held onto the door, giving myself a minute to pull it together. When I was sure I could move without falling on my face I closed the door, making my way to the porch. I turned just before the stairs in time to watch his taillights disappear from sight. I turned back to the stairs and walked up on the porch.

It took two taps on the door before a voice called out. I caught Bobbie in the middle of unpacking grocery bags.

"Angel," she said, her voice sounding relieved. "I'm so glad you came back."

"It looks like I have to hang around a while."

"Good," she said cheerfully. "After I found your note I began to worry about what was going to happen to you."

"You and everyone else," I mumbled. I set my backpack and the bag with Sean's clothes in it on the table and went to the counter where she had a bag sitting. "Could I do something to help?"

"Sure, all the boxes go in the cabinet next to the stove."

I picked up the bag and crossed the room.

"Angel," Bobbie called. I could hear uncertainty in her tone and started to worry a little about what she was going to say.

I answered without turning around. "Yeah?"

"I don't want to pry in your business, but where are you from?"

I finished putting the boxes in the cabinet, closed the door, and then slowly turned to face her.

"Pittsburg, Kansas," I answered carefully.

"Really, I've never met anyone from Kansas," she laughed, the sound nervous. "What brings you to Newport?"

My near death, I thought sourly. I quickly banished it from my mind before she could read anything on my face. I've always been easy for people to read just from the expressions on my face. This was why I was always such a bad lair.

"Weren't you told why I was in your hospital?" It stumped me that she didn't already know the answer to her question. Everyone else did.

She just shook her head.

I picked up the paper bag, folding it while I crossed the room and sat down at the table. Bobbie was now carrying an arm load of groceries to the refrigerator.

"This is going to sound like a Hollywood horror movie," I warned. "but sadly, it's true. I went to Salt Lake City, Utah to meet family and met a man who tricked me into believing he was a cab driver. The next thing I remember is waking up in your hospital."

I can't be a hundred percent sure of *what* I actually saw in the cabin, yet I couldn't quite forget, either. Sean and deputy Callenger seem desperate to keep their part a secret. So I guess I'll do my part.

I never noticed while I was answering Bobbie's question that she had stopped moving to stare at me. I suddenly felt uneasy.

"W-o-w," she said, exaggerating the word into three syllables. "You're right, that does sound like a horror movie." I pushed my bag to the center of the table, catching her attention. "I see your bag was found."

"Yes," I sighed, relieved. "I have at least one other set of clean clothes." And a hairbrush, I said to myself. "It turned out the sheriff had it in his possession."

"That is wonderful," she stated, delighted. "Is that the only luggage you took with you to Salt Lake City?"

She finally finished putting the food in the refrigerator, and then closed the door.

I used the time while she was distracted to think of a way to answer her question without having to reveal too much. I decided to go with part of the truth, only because I was never good at lying and one look at my face she would clearly know I wasn't being honest.

"Yes, unfortunately," I sighed. "I had to leave in such a rush I didn't really have time to pack a suitcase."

Her facial expression turned calculating. "So all you have for clothes besides the ones in your bag is what's on your body now?"

I slightly nodded my head. "I'm afraid so."

Bobbie tossed the paper bag, still in her hand on the table and looked up at the clock on the wall. "Again, I don't want to sound nosey, but do you have any money left from your travel?"

That was a question I couldn't answer. Until she mentioned it I had forgotten I even had money. *If* it was even still in my bag.

"I don't know," I said, uncertain.

I turned to my bag and unzipped it. I had sewn a pocket in the bottom years ago and is where I hid money from Scott. I pulled everything out, lying them on the table, and then slid my fingers into the small pocket. A sudden rush of relief pulsed through me when I felt the bills.

I carefully pulled it out and took my time to count it.

Twice.

Every bit of the five hundred was there. I was suddenly grateful for the extra two hundred Jennifer forced me to take. She argued anything less would result in me running out of money before two days passed. I may not have needed it for a place to live or food, but I certainly would for clothes.

"It's all here," I said, sounding surprised. Even to me.

"Awesome," she squealed.

I raised my brows at her.

"I still have a few hours," she continued, ignoring my facial expressions. "If you would like we can go to Walmart."

"Isn't this the time you need to sleep?" I would have felt guilty if we left and she hadn't slept.

I watched as a confused expression crossed her face.

"I went to bed shortly after you did. I got up a little earlier than usual to shop. I didn't want my guest to go hungry," she laughed.

"Oh." The word seemed inadequate, but I couldn't think of a better response.

Bobbie laughed.

"I suppose having sleepwear would be more comfortable at bedtime," I mused.

Bobbie stretched her arm out, grabbing her purse strap, and lifted it up from the table. "Then let's go shopping."

She was already at the door and opening it by the time I stood from the chair and stuffed my money into my front pocket. I quicken my steps to her side, following her out the door.

I paid better attention this time. It didn't take me long to figure out I was in a small town. This was where being raised in a small town gave me advantage. *If* I was going to be stuck here for three months I wouldn't have any trouble finding my way around. There is nothing worse than having to ask someone for a ride. And, since Bobbie worked the night shift I wouldn't have to feel guilty each time she had to drive me somewhere instead of sleeping. The only hope I had now was feeling some sort of normalcy while we shopped. I needed that more than anything.

When we finally got to Walmart the rain had turned to a drizzle. For this I was thankful; I wasn't used to this much rain at once and since I didn't have a jacket I was still fighting off the shivers from being soaked earlier.

Once we got inside Bobbie grabbed a cart and we headed for the junior's section. I left her to scan the racks and went to look over the sleepwear options. I wasn't sure what I wanted, the only thing I was sure of, it had to have sleeves. Even though no one had noticed or said anything about the long, nasty scar running along my forearm, I wasn't comfortable having it exposed.

"What do you think of this, Angel?" Bobbie suddenly called out.

I swirled around in time to see her pushing the cart in my direction. She had a blue, short-sleeved shirt covered in rhinestones hanging from her free hand.

"Think of what?" I asked, confused.

If the confusion was on my face she didn't seem to notice. She lifted her arm, dangling the shirt in the air. "This shirt."

"It's pretty," I stated carefully. "I like it."

"Do you think it suits me?" she asked with a laugh. She stopped the cart inches from me and held the shirt against her body.

"I do," I agreed. "It might be blinding to everyone when the sun's out."

She wrinkled her nose in disgust. "Then I guess it's a good thing we don't have too many." She leaned over the cart and hung the shirt on the side of the basket.

Now I was really confused. "What do you mean?"

"I guess you know as much about Oregon as I know of Kansas," she laughed. "This is what is called the Olympic Peninsula, Angel. It's rains more in this region than anywhere else in the country."

"So... you're saying there's *never* any sun?" I was appalled.

"There is," she countered. "just not often."

At least now I understood the impending gloom I'd been facing. It was still hard to believe it could rain so much.

"Oh," was all I could manage.

I turned back to the rack full of sleepwear. It was then I saw a powder blue pajama set, a single sheep on the top. I took it down, examining the sleeves.

"Angel, did you meet Mike before you left the hospital?" Bobbie suddenly asked.

Her voice wasn't harsh or bitter, I could clearly hear curiosity in the tenor. It didn't stop me from cringing.

"No, I met him after I had gone to your house. Why?"

"Mmm .... I've never seen Sean visit anyone at the hospital before. Come to think of it, I've never seen Sean visit anybody, with the exception of his family."

"Okay," I said weakly.

"If you didn't meet Mike or deputy Callenger at the hospital then how did Sean know you didn't have clothes?"

"I don't know," I lied. I was thankful my back was still facing her, if it wasn't she would have known from my expression my answer was a lie.

"You were brought in by a forest ranger," she mused. "maybe he told Mike about the condition of your clothes."

A forest ranger? Maybe that wasn't a lie after all, I said to myself. Then why the need to lie?

"Maybe," I hedged. "I'm sure he called it into the sheriff's station as he was transporting me to the hospital."

"You're probably right."

She was silent for a long moment and I figured this conversation was over.

"Of course, deputy Callenger is Sean's dad." Or not.

I was just placing the pajama set in the basket when she made her statement. My hand shook causing the clothes to fall. If Bobbie saw my sudden nervousness she didn't show it. Instead, she turned the cart, walking to a shelf lined with jeans.

"Deputy Callenger doesn't look old enough to have a son Sean's age," I said, tentatively.

"I know," Bobbie giggled. "Jonah is in his early thirties, maybe and his wife is too, I think. He has a daughter, Kelsey, and his wife Becca is also the mayor's secretary. She has hosted a lot of fundraisers for different things over the years. A couple of years ago she held one to raise money for cancer treatments the hospital didn't offer."

I hadn't ever really noticed a difference in the accents till I stood, listening to her talk. Sean and deputy Callenger sounded Southern, whereas Bobbie didn't. There was a big difference in skin color, too. Bobbie's skin was brown like she had been in the sun all day, they looked albino, without the pink eyes.

"Are they native like you?" I asked when she was finished.

"No." She paused, pulling a pair of jeans from the shelf and walked to the mirror. "Jonah and Mrs. Callenger moved here eight years ago from somewhere in Maine."

"Deputy Callenger and Sean are … nice-looking." I got the sense she somehow didn't notice what I thought was a clear difference between her and them.

"Yes!" Bobbie laughed. She moved from the mirror and tossed the jeans into the cart. "Just to warn you, don't give too much of your attention to Sean. He's a nice guy, he simply doesn't date. Not that I've ever seen anyway."

Most girls would have been bitter and resentful over that idea; it didn't seem to bother Bobbie.

"Honestly, I wasn't planning to."

Bobbie's eyebrows raised a fraction at my tone. I waited for her to say something, instead the conversation turned into another topic and we continued our shopping. I couldn't have been more relieved.

After what seemed like hours we finished our shopping. We each checked out, and then walked out of the store.

"How long will you be staying in Newport?" Bobbie asked as we walked to her car. Because I wasn't expecting this question I threw her a quick glance. "Not that I'm in a hurry for you to leave," she added, as if that made her question sound friendlier.

"Your sheriff says it could be a couple of months," I answered, warily.

Her face lit with excitement. "That's great news for me! I get to have your company a while longer." She paused, flashing her eyes to my face. "Though it might be bad news for you."

"Why is that?" I asked, my mind suddenly perplexed.

Her expression turned apologetic and she held up the bags in her hands. "It means we'll have to shop again soon."

I mumbled unintelligibly as I stalked forward and Bobbie laughed.

We were at the car now. Bobbie stopped at the back, I walked on, eventually opening the passenger door.

"Angel, it'll be less hassle getting the bags out if we put them in the trunk." She pushed up the lid, setting the bags in her hands inside.

"Okay," I shrugged.

I left the door open and walked to the back, stopping next to her. I set one bag inside the trunk and a sudden wave of images of being placed in a trunk flashed through my mind. In that instant I could clearly see a girl lying beside me. Her dark hair was spilled out away from her head, gray duct tape was wrapped around her wrist, a long piece was across her mouth.

My chest tightened, threating to cut off my air supply. I dropped the rest of the bags and tried to step back. My legs felt, as if they were stuck in a mound of cement.

"Angel!" Bobbie screamed, frantic.

It wasn't even a second later and she was grabbing my arm.

"Honey, you're white as a ghost. Are you all right?"

"I'm fine." I sounded like I was choking.

She didn't buy it. "C'mon," she said, pulling me backwards from the car. "we're going to get you in the car."

I had no problem obliging, especially since my legs felt like mush. Just simply trying to put one foot in front of the other on my own was a difficult process. After I was settled in the seat Bobbie walked away.

I pulled my legs to my chest, wrapped my arms around them, and then laid my head against my knees. I wasn't like that long when I heard Bobbie's door open then close.

"Are you sure you're all right?" she asked. Her tone was much calmer, though I could still hear the fear behind her words. "Should I take you to the hospital?"

"No, I'll be fine," I answered, hazily. "I just need a minute."

"What happened back there?"

That was a question I couldn't answer for myself. I also couldn't be sure if the images I saw were even real. I took a long second to answer, the last thing I wanted was to tell her the truth. She would do more than panic and I had no interest in seeing Dr. McKnight again.

"I'm not sure," I finally stated. "I guess maybe I'm still worn out."

"Okay, when you're ready we can go home."

"Kay," was all I could say.

A few long minutes later the tightness in my chest relaxed, allowing me to breathe slow, deep breaths.

Moving very slowly, I turned in the seat and pulled the door closed. I laid my head back, closing my eyes and felt the car move forward.

Once we were back at the house, Bobbie made me take her keys and unlock the door while she got all the bags out of the trunk. She wasn't wanting to witness another attack. I waited on the porch then took some of the bags before we entered the house and helped carry them upstairs. After taking what I had of hers she scurried to her room to get ready for work.

When I finished putting the clothes away I carried the empty bags downstairs to put them in the trash. I figured Bobbie would have been down there already, she wasn't. I poured myself a cup of coffee and stuck it in the microwave. I was about to lean against the counter when another room caught my attention. I crossed the room, slowly entering the other.

After turning on the light I realized it was an enclosed porch. There was a wash machine and dryer sitting side by side against one wall, with a shelf nailed above, containing a bottle of bleach and laundry soap. A built-in pantry was on the opposite side. There was a door at the far end, figuring it was the back door I turned out the light and walked back in the kitchen.

The microwave dinged, I pulled my cup out and began adding sugar to it.

"Angel?" Bobbie suddenly called out.

"In here," I called back.

She entered the room dressed in her scrubs. "I was thinking while I was getting ready I'd like you to think of this as home. You're welcome to anything you need."

"Thank you," I said, shyly. "Would you mind if I used the phone? I have a friend back home who is probably worried sick by now."

Bobbie was grabbing things out of the refrigerator and tossing them in her lunch bag.

"I don't mind," she stated. "I hope you don't think I'm being nosey, again, but how long has it been since you left Kansas?"

"According to your sheriff, two weeks."

"Oh my," she said, her tone shocked. She quickly flashed her eyes to my face. "You go on and make that call. I'm sure your family is worried."

I suddenly felt too cowardly to admit I didn't actually have a family.

"All right," she continued. "I have to get going. If you have any problems or questions call the hospital, otherwise I'll see you in the morning."

"I'm sure I'll be fine," I assured her.

"Okay." She seemed to be hesitant about leaving me alone. "Try and get some sleep, Angel."

Translation ----- you look like *hell*. I smiled, shaking my head "I will."

She returned the smile, and then disappeared into the foyer.

After she walked out the door I took the phone from the wall and walked to the table to sit down. I knew when Jen answered the phone this would be the longest call in my life. My hands trembled as I dialed her number. While the line was ringing I took a huge, deep breath.

"Hello," came a very anxious voice.

"Hey, Jen," I answered carefully.

"Angel!" she gasped. "I'm so glad you called, I've been going out of my mind with worry."

Her voice seemed to become more frantic with each word.

"Calm down," I said, trying to make my voice sound soothing. "I'm fine."

"Good," she replied, taking a deep breath. "Do you need money, a plane ticket home or anything?"

"No, I still have money and I certainly don't need to come back."

"Okay, how do you like Salt Lake City?" I couldn't be sure if it was me or if she really sounded disappointed.

I had no idea just how to answer, especially since I never really saw Salt Lake City. I finally decided to go with the truth. She knew me well enough that she'd know I was lying. That would only bring on more questions I didn't want to answer. I already didn't want to tell her what I'd been through.

"I'm afraid I'm not in Salt Lake City."

"Then where are you?" she asked confused.

I took a deep breath, already regretting this question. "Oregon."

"*Oregon?*" she repeated in disbelief. "How did you get there?"

"It's a story you probably wouldn't believe if I told you. My father hasn't bothered you or your mom has he?"

"No, I hadn't even seen him till yesterday when I was in Dillon's. I don't think he saw me."

Even though I was deeply grateful to be away from him and Troy I couldn't stop the hope that he cared even a little bit from diminishing. I knew he was always too drunk to feel anything, doesn't it even bother him in the least that I'm missing?

"That's great," I said, fighting to keep from sounding distraught. "I've been hoping he wouldn't give anyone any trouble."

"Yeah," she sighed. "Mom never did like Scott so it would have definitely caused problems."

Leslie Collins was the only person who knew what was happening to me. Of course, every time she tried to turn it in it didn't help. Troy could make anything disappear.

"Does she know I left?"

"Yes, though I didn't tell her *I* had any part in it."

"Great," I said, relieved. "the less anyone knows the better. I'm sure there's more you want to know, but this is long distance on someone's phone and it's late, I'm extremely tired. I wanted you to know I'm all right."

"I'm glad you did, now I can tell Mom you're okay."

"Kay, I'll call again soon," I promised.

"Take care of you, I'll be waiting for your next call."

"I will, bye, Jen."

"Bye, Angel." She hung up the phone.

I returned the phone to the wall, turned off the light and walked up the stairs to my room. My legs felt as heavy as my heart. I had tears falling down my cheeks before I reached the top. When I entered my room I heard the rain falling and thought it was ironic. My mother used to tell me when I was younger that whenever we suffer from a broken heart angels cry for us. I know it sounded silly, yet in that moment it didn't seem so far from the mark.

New Friends

That first week was probably my longest one yet. Figuring since I didn't know anyone besides Bobbie I stayed in her tiny living room, watching TV. That was a bad idea, every news station seemed to be following the story.

CNN was the first to break the news. In the beginning it was nothing more than a few sentences, followed with one grainy picture.

"Jeremy Thomas Corbin, suspected serial rapist and murderer wanted in the states of Louisiana and New Mexico was apprehended two nights ago inside a cabin just a few miles in the Suislaw National Forest. Corbin was found unconscious along with two of his victims. Officials are unable to say at this time whether he will continue to be held in Oregon or be extradited to New Orleans or Santa Fe to stand trial."

I stared at his picture longer than I should have. He had more facial hair than I remembered, but those piercing blue eyes had that same look of evil in them. My body trembled in fear as I remembered being face-to-face with those eyes. They hadn't released any pictures or the names of his *victims*, yet I feared since the story was now all over CNN it had gotten to Pittsburg.

I shut the TV off and called Jen. I tried to be crafty while I fished for information and luck seemed to be on my side; at least for the moment. They had heard nothing about any abductions, just shootings in California. I began to relax and ended the conversation.

Though only a little.

The days to follow became more in-depth. It was now that all the news stations were covering the story as they began showing pictures of Jeremy's unfortunate victim; Amanda Raines. They talked a lot about her family's loss and what officials were hoping would come next for Jeremy. Even Newport's newspaper New Times was beginning to cover the story locally. It was hard to miss the headline on the front page:

ONE GIRL DEAD, ANOTHER BARELY RECOVERED, POLICE FEAR THERE MAY BE MORE.

I tried not to see the names on the page, but they jumped out from the rest of the print. There were at least four names of missing girls listed, along with mine and one other that really stuck out at me; Amanda Raines.

When I'd seen her picture flash across the TV screen my heart sank to the pit of my stomach. She was the image I'd seen lying in a trunk covered with gray tape. Her picture was like that of any other; very much alive, her long dark hair hung effortlessly over her shoulders and her face was full of dreams and promises. A heedless smile on her lips, her cornflower colored eyes full of mischief.

It wasn't until her picture was broadcasted I learned Jeremy had taken her from Santa Fe, New Mexico.

She was already in the trunk of his cab when he tricked me in Salt Lake City. I couldn't help but wonder if he had gotten her the same as he had me.

The lives of the other girls had been considered over, their families were in mourning now. It was difficult for me to know this, only because I appeared to have been the first and last to survive, yet I couldn't stop myself from reading the names. Cassandra Nichols, Stephanie Miller, Ava Hunter, Sally

Henderson. Teenagers who'd had parents, siblings, pets and maybe even boyfriends ----- girls who had hopes and dreams for their future ...

"Angel, you've got to stop reading this before you drive yourself mad," Bobbie scolded me. "It isn't going to help you move on in your own life."

She snatched the paper off the table and tossed it in the trash can.

"I know," I whispered, half to myself. "I can't help feeling guilty for surviving and Amanda didn't."

Bobbie sat down at the table, reaching across it for my hand. "I can't imagine what you're going through so I won't pretend I do. But I do know this, when Jeremy is finally convicted whether it's here or somewhere else the other families will get their justice and Amanda will be allowed to rest in peace."

"I know," I whispered again.

She squeezed my hand gently then released it, sitting upright in her chair.

"I think you're spending way too much of your time alone."

"Is there really another choice?" I asked, grumpily.

I was used to being alone, it was always the outcome from being raised by an alcoholic.

"Actually, there is," she said as a smile crossed her lips.

I suddenly became deeply suspicious. "What?"

"Remember the aunt I told you about?"

"Yes," I answered carefully.

"Well ----- I spoke with her this morning and it turns out she needs another waitress." Her voice was so full of enthusiasm I wasn't sure if I should have been grateful or worried.

"I really appreciate your generosity, but I'm afraid I don't know anything about waitressing."

She frowned at me before standing from the chair. "It's not hard." She held up her hand when she could see that I was about to argue. "Just give it a chance."

"Fine," I muttered in disgust.

"Good, I'll see you in the morning." She tossed the strap of her lunch bag over her shoulder and walked out.

I didn't sleep well that night, even after turning up the volume on the clock radio to drown out the constant whooshing sound of the wind and the rain. I couldn't shake the near hyperventilation I felt whenever I thought about what Bobbie wanted me to do. I've never been good with meeting new people.

I either don't say things that make sense or I just simply trip over my own two feet.

The next morning I sat at the table, barley drinking the coffee in front of me, examining Bobbie's small kitchen, with its bright walls, mint green cabinets and green and white linoleum floor. I knew the handkerchief-sized living room needed to be picked up. The old Afghan that usually hung over the back of the sofa needed to be folded and replaced. Over the small fireplace where a row of pictures sat needed wiped down.

I talked myself out of getting up from the chair to clean up, I didn't want Bobbie to be upset that I never made it to meet her aunt. I didn't want to be too early to the diner, either, but *if* I continued to sit there I'd never make it out the door. I donned in my raincoat and headed out into the thick fog.

It wasn't till I turned from locking the door I realized it was raining. It was just a drizzle, not enough to soak me, still I wondered if I would be by the time I got to the restaurant.

I stared at the small rectangular building as I walked across the gravel driveway. A faded yellow sign was on top, indicating it as Kloe's Diner. There in bubble letters beside it was the words Coca-Cola. It may not have seemed like much, it had my stomach full of butterflies.

I felt my breath gradually creep toward hyperventilation as I approached the building. I held my breath when two girls in raincoats exited through the door. I quickly caught it before it closed and walked inside.

I was nervous because I'd never met Bobbie's aunt and had no idea who I was even looking for.

I did a quick scan of the tidy dining room, noticing it was brightly colored, with the warm feeling of home. A cast of different colors covered the walls, sea life photos hung all around. I had barely gotten my nerve to walk to the counter when a tall, slender girl with dark hair covered in blond highlights approached me.

"You're Angelia Johanson, right?" She seemed to be the up-beat, over eager type.

"Angel," I corrected. Everyone with-in ten feet of us turned to look at me. I instantly felt my face turn tomato red.

"Awesome," she laughed. "Sorry I got your name wrong, it's what I've heard on the news. Mom's been expecting you."

I fought to keep from cringing when she mentioned the news. She never noticed my discomfort, turning her body slightly, instead and pointed in the direction of the counter.

"The lady with her back to us is who you're looking for." Yep, definitely over eager. "By the way, I'm Brandi," she added. She held her hand out at me. "Bobbie talks about you a lot."

I shook her hand, seconds later she walked away.

I made my way to the counter, the short, thin brunette still had her back facing me and was talking to what I assumed was the cook through the window. The second his eyes met mine he pointed a finger my direction deflecting her attention to me. She turned a fraction of a second later, a smile instantly crossing her lips.

"Hi, you must be Angel," she said, her voice cheerful. "I wasn't expecting you for at least another hour."

If I hadn't been so anxious I might have remembered Bobbie telling me the restaurant was only three blocks from her house. There was no point in dwelling on that, I reminded myself.

"I know," I replied, embarrassed. "I wanted to be sure where I was going and that I got here on time."

"I can understand that," she said, approvingly. "Bobbie is very worried about you and tells me you could use a job."

"She doesn't really need to worry about me, Mrs. Hallsworth. I'm afraid she's right on the job, I could use one."

"Have you done this kind of work before?"

I slightly shook my head back and forth. "No, ma'am. My first and only job was babysitting." I wasn't sure why exactly, but at that second I felt like an idiot.

Mrs. Hallsworth stared at me for a long second while she crossed her arms over her chest then suddenly shrugged her shoulders. "I have faith you'll learn quickly enough. Are you interested in starting today?"

"Yes, ma'am," I said shyly.

She smiled, slowly shaking her head. "Please, just call me Kloe." She paused, dropping her arms and walked to the end of the counter. "Come along, I'll show you around, and then get you a uniform."

I followed her to the kitchen, listening as she droned on about everything. When the sound of a bell suddenly rang out, I jumped, my head quickly snapping in the direction it had come from. It was then I saw the gangly boy Kloe had been talking to when I arrived. All I could really see was the way his dark blond hair nearly touched the collar on his shirt.

I never noticed my legs were still carrying me forward till I ran into Kloe. My cheeks felt like they were on fire as she stopped and turned to look at me. I fought to keep from hanging my head.

"Sorry," I mumbled.

"It's quite all right," she laughed.

I saw from the corner of my eye the boy walk toward us. He stopped inches from me and crossed his arms behind his back.

"This is Kyle Hesner," Kloe's soft voice stated. "He's the morning and afternoon cook. Kyle, this is Angel."

"Hi, Angel," he said warmly.

"Hi," I answered weakly.

"If I hadn't seen the news or read the papers I'd think you came from California. You're just as pretty as Julia Roberts."

Instinctively my hand went to my head. "We have the same hair anyway." My face turned red.

"You don't look very tan for someone who comes from the land of sunlight," he chuckled.

"My parents kept me locked in a dark tower."

Kyle stared at me with an odd expression and I feared he didn't get sarcasm, and then suddenly he laughed.

"That's a good one. Imagine that, she's beautiful and funny."

The blush in my cheeks darkened.

"Kyle," Kloe stated scornfully. "you're embarrassing her."

"Sorry," he apologized. His tone didn't sound like he meant it. "It's nice meeting you, Angel."

"You, too." My voice shook.

Kyle flashed me a grin, and then turned on his heels and walked away.

"I'm sorry about that," Kloe suddenly apologized. "He really is a nice guy."

"Don't worry about it," I said, dismissively. "I've been told worse."

We walked to the back of the kitchen as she pointed out a few more things before coming to a stop in front of the office. She stepped inside long enough to pick up the pink and white dress lying on the desk.

"When you finish changing look for Brandi," she said as she handed the dress to me. "Today should stay slow so you will be able to keep up." She seemed to have more faith in me then I did.

I smiled at her vaguely and walked away.

The rest of the day passed in almost the same fashion. There was always someone braver than others to speak to me. They would introduce themselves then ask what I thought of Newport. I wasn't honestly able to answer since I kept myself locked in Bobbie's house so I lied, a lot.

When business died down Kloe allowed us to sit in the kitchen for our breaks. I sat at the table next to Brandi while she carried on conversations with the other waitresses who's names I forgot as soon as they said them. It was in those moments I felt sorry for Kyle. He was the only male in the entire building.

It was the same every day after that. I slowly learned to remember the names of the other waitresses.

One of them constantly reminded me that her name was Catlyn. She was Brandi's sister, Kloe's youngest daughter. She was shy, just like me.

Kyle quickly became a nuisance. If he wasn't staring at me he was trying to help me at every open opportunity. I hadn't ever gotten attention like this in Pittsburg and wasn't too sure I didn't still prefer it.

I'm sure other girls would have loved the chance to have a cute, brown-eyed boy offering to be their beck and call boy, but not me. I found it unnecessary and even a little irritating.

When I walked to the diner on Saturday afternoon I caught the sound of faint footsteps. I stopped to look many times, never to see anyone. Paranoia swept over me and I walked faster. My heart pounded so hard I could hear it behind my ears.

I caught Catlyn and Kloe in the middle of a discussion as I entered the diner. Catlyn was wiping down tables while her mother stood behind the counter looking over papers. The conversation continued, completely unaware I was there.

"Why can't Brandi work tonight?" Catlyn complained. "It wouldn't kill her. She has a car and Angel doesn't, leaving her to walk alone after dark."

"Catlyn," Kloe said scornfully. "Derek has a show tonight, therefore

I had no choice but to put Angel on the night shift. I don't like it any better than you do."

"What is she going to do *if* he gets signed to some label?"

"I don't know," Kloe sighed. "I suppose we'll have to cross that bridge when we get to it."

Kloe looked up, finally catching sight of me. I was trying to slip past them without interrupting their conversation, even as it was about me.

"Hi, Angel," she said in a brighter tone.

"Hi." I stopped next to her long enough to grab an apron then turned to walk away.

"You're early," she noted.

I stopped walking turning to look at her. "Actually, I'm not." I pointed to the clock on the wall. "I only have five minutes."

Her expression was stunned as she turned her head to look at the clock. "I guess it's later than I thought."

The opportunity of an escape emerged, I took it without hesitation.

The night seemed to just drag on. I was grateful when Anna Tisdale came in, replacing Catlyn. Even as daylight began to fade out she couldn't let it go that I was working late, instead of Brandi.

Anna was tiny, she was somehow several inches shorter than my five feet two inches. She kept her long dark hair pinned up in a bun on the back of her head. She prattled a lot, and because I didn't know much about her topics I smiled and nodded often. I didn't try to keep up.

Sheriff Jacobs came in as diner rush was getting under way. I watched him closely when he passed in front of the counter, eventually seating himself in a booth in the corner. I finished with a customer sitting at the counter and was making my way to the end when suddenly Deputy Callenger came through the door.

I froze.

My mind was so focused on the corner booth I didn't notice Anna was now standing next to me till her concerned voice was suddenly in my ear.

"Angel, are you all right?"

"Yes, I'm fine," I said in almost a faint voice.

"Okay." She didn't look convinced when I finally tore my attention from the town's law enforcers. She kept her eyes on me as she picked up a menu.

"Here," she said, shoving it in my hand when I made no effort to take it. "A customer just walked in so you can wait on Mike while I seat him."

She turned and headed to the door.

Get it together, Angel ----- I scolded myself. I tightened my hand around the menu and walked to the end of the counter. Try as I might, I couldn't get my legs to move quickly to the booth Mike occupied.

The men seemed to be engaged in a deep conversation. I stayed a few feet away from them, letting them continue without any interruptions from me.

"Hey, Angel," Mike suddenly called out after he noticed me. "I had no idea Kloe give you a job."

"I've been here a couple of weeks."

Deputy Callenger stepped aside, giving me room to stand next to the table. I very slowly extended my arm and handed Mike the menu.

"Great!" Mike said enthusiastically. "So, does this mean you'll stick around once I get matters resolved?"

"I don't know, Sheriff," I breathed. "I'm just simply taking one day at a time."

And before he could respond Deputy Callenger coughed to hide a laugh. His eyes were closer to black then green, he also had dark shadows under them ----- purplish, bruise-like shadows. It was as if he were suffering from sleepless nights.

"I'm sorry," he said, apologetically. "Mike, I'm going to head back to the station."

"All right, Jonah," Mike answered, agreeably. "As soon as I finish my dinner I'll be in."

"Take your time," Jonah said, condescendingly. "I'll probably stop by City Hall on the way." He looked over at me and nodded his head. "Angel."

I felt a chill flow down my spine when I heard the way his voice caressed around my name. I kept my eyes on Mike as he walked away. He returned to our conversation as if there hadn't been another.

"Anyway," he continued. "I'd like it if you just called me Mike and I'd also like it if you do stay here.

It isn't often we get new faces."

That didn't sound right to me. Especially since I learned Newport is a tourist town.

"I don't believe that," I said, nonchalantly. "You get tourist all the time."

"You're right," he agreed. "they're usually just passing through or on vacation. Most of the folks here are from generations that have lived here their whole lives."

"Oh." I knew the word was inadequate, but I lacked a better response.

Mike laughed, his hands snaked out, catching mine. "You never know, Angel," he cooed. "we may have something special, just for you."

Like what, the Callengers, I thought bitterly. I held back the shiver I felt trying to run through me and pulled my hand free of Mike's grip.

"What do you say we take this day by day?" I suggested. Mike laughed.

When I walked away with his order I had to fight the urge I had to hang my head and run.

Finally, it came time for me to clock out and leave. And as usual, I walked to Bobbie's constantly looking over my shoulder. Jennifer had never mentioned during our conversations hearing anything about me, yet I was sure Scott and Troy knew where I was by now. Troy Kensley *is* a cop, a crooked one without a doubt, but still a cop. He has to know something.

I was lost in thought but not enough to keep me from hearing the faint footsteps somewhere behind me.

I started to walk faster like all the other times when something in my mind stopped me. For reasons I couldn't fathom I stopped walking, turning to the sound. Noticing it had stopped, too.

"I know you're there," I called out nervously.

It was silent for a long time, and then suddenly Sean stepped out of the shadows. I held my breath to keep from screaming from being both scared and relieved to see his horribly familiar face.

"How did you know I was here?" He was stunned.

"I heard your footsteps," I breathed. I slowly released the breath I was holding before my lungs could burn.

"People can't hear when the earth slightly moves," he contradicted.

"Well, I can ----- *if* it's quiet enough. I hear the way we see; when I see a butterfly I don't just see it, I can also hear the wind whooshing from its wings."

He was staring at me with an unfathomable expression.

"What?" I asked, suddenly feeling self-conscious.

"It's nothing."

"Okay," I said uneasy. "if you're finished trying to scare me to death I'd like to get to Bobbie's."

"I never meant to frighten you, Angel." He wasn't standing close enough that I could clearly see his facial expressions but his voice sounded sincere.

"Fine." I turned away from him and walked away. "Have a good night, Sean," I called over my shoulder.

Since I no longer felt scared I walked with my head up, veering off to the right, toward the turn at the end of the street. Something suddenly caught my jacket, yanking me back.

"You really think I'm just going to stand here and let you walk alone?" he asked outraged. He was gripping a fistful of my jacket in one hand, carefully pulling me backwards until I was standing next to him.

I was confused. "Is there something I should be afraid of?"

"No, but with the luck you appear to have you could be incapacitated by a simple crack in the sidewalk," he chuckled.

"Hey," I hissed. That only seemed to add to his humor.

I walked next to him for a while, not saying anything. Then for reasons unknown to me, I thought about when I'd seen Deputy Callenger earlier in the evening. It was odd how these two show up in just a few short hours of one another.

"Since we're alone could we discuss something?" I asked, causally.

"What about?" His tone was calm so I figured it might be safe to bring up a subject that really mattered to me.

"I guess I'm still waiting for that day when you're finally going to tell me the truth."

"I don't know what you're talking about," he stated matter-of-factly.

I shook my head and stopped walking. "You're *really* going to do this?"

"Do what?" he asked innocently.

I balled my hands into fists at my side so I wouldn't do anything rash. I was determined to have this conversation calmly.

"Sean," I pronounced his name carefully. "we both know I've been lying to everyone, including Mike.

I just want to know why. I've *never* asked you for anything, I'm asking now for the truth."

"What do you think is the truth?" he snapped.

My response came out in a rush.

"I saw you in the cabin, I clearly remember talking to you. Just as I clearly remember hearing Deputy Callenger instructing you. One moment I was lying on a mattress soaked in water, the next I was in your arms and slipping out an open window."

While ranting I could hear how crazy the story sounded. Even as I was angry and was fighting to demand answers I ran out of steam.

"Look, I'm well aware of the fact that I sound crazy. Maybe in some ways I am ----- I know what I saw and heard."

He was staring at me incredulously, yet his face was tense, defensive.

"You really believe I carried you out of that cabin?" I knew he was questioning my sanity, but I held my ground.

"Yes."

He continued to stare at me unrepentant. The longer I stared back at his perfect face I was losing my anger.

"Sean, please," I nearly pleaded.

"Even if I were to tell you what you want to hear, no one will ever believe you," he suddenly blurted.

"I have no intentions of telling anyone," I said slowly, carefully choosing my words. "I don't know if you've even bothered to notice, but I've kept my silence, flawlessly."

"Angel," he groaned in exasperation. "It really is best you let this go." The black fire suddenly blazing in his eyes made it nearly impossible to doubt his words.

I could only stare at him, bewildered.

"Since you're trying so desperately to drag this out aren't you even going to thank me?" he snarled.

For a fraction of a second I considered saying the words, and then decided not to. If he wasn't going to give me what I wanted ----- what I needed then there was no need for saying the words. I squared my shoulders and walked past him with a resigned sigh. I only had a block to go before I was at Bobbie's, surely I could get that far without arguing with *him.*

"Is that a no?" he called after me. His voice was alluring.

I said nothing.

It wasn't even a second later and he was at my side, easily keeping pace. I kept my eyes straight ahead, completely ignoring him. I knew it was childish for me to behave in this manner, but for the first time in my life I didn't care.

Sean walked me to the entrance of Bobbie's yard and stopped. I kept going, not bothering to look back or simply say goodbye. Even after I was on the porch and had the door unlocked and opened I still never looked back.

The next afternoon I was sleep deprived and fought to get through the work day without thinking about the night before or being grumpy. Thankfully the diner was busy enough my plan had been successful.

When my share of the day was over I clocked out, fighting the urge not to run out the door.

I got a big surprise once I walked through the door. It was raining, (not just a drizzle, it was a downpour), I had forgotten through my haze this morning to grab my lime green raincoat before I left the house. In truth I think it was because of the color; who wants to be seen in lime green?

"Don't worry so much, Angel," came a friendly voice behind me. "you'll get used to it and remember."

I quickly turned around, Brandi was standing next to the door, stuffing her hair inside the hood of her jacket.

"I'd be more than happy to give you a ride," she continued.

"That would be great," I said somberly.

"How fast can you run?" she asked with a laugh.

I looked up at the sky and scowled. This certainly wasn't helping my bad mood. "Probably not fast enough to keep from getting soaked."

Brandi walked up next to me still laughing. "On the count of three we run, okay?"

"Which car is yours?" I scanned the parking lot suddenly fearing the worst.

She pointed to the direction of the long line of cars in front of us. "Do you see the brown one next to the jeep?"

"Yes," I answered hesitantly.

"That's' our designation."

Her answer was much worse than I feared. Her car was parked at the far end of the lot.

"Great," I grumbled. "I won't have even one dry spot."

Brandi broke into a laugh and grabbed my arm. "C'mon, Angel, we can do it."

She sprint out into the rain, nearly dragging me. I had to put forth the effort to match her pace to keep from getting my arm ripped off.

When we reached the back of her car she released my arm. I was soaked, as I knew I would be, butcontinued to run to the passenger door. We climbed in at the same time.

"Wasn't that fun?" Brandi laughed.

"Sure," I glowered, pulling the door closed. "I never knew summer rain could be so cold."

She adjusted the heater then pushed her hood back, using the heat to dry the front of her hair.

"You get used to it," she said with a shrug. "Does it rain much in Kansas?"

I wasn't surprised she knew where I was really from. The news had said I was from Salt Lake City and everyone but Mike believed it. I knew the moment I told her cousin ----- my roommate the truth it wouldn't take long for it to get around. Gossip is very vital in small towns.

The water dripping down my back was beginning to soak the seat so I pulled what was once a braid over my shoulder.

"It might for a couple of days then turn into weeks of the sun. Summers there are hot and sunny."

Brandi turned off the heater and pushed her long hair over her shoulder.

"I know you doubt our days of the summer sun, but I promise we do have them." She put the car in drive and slowly drove out of the parking lot.

"I know, Bobbie has told me the same thing. Honestly, I'm looking forward to seeing that bright cast of yellow, although I don't know why. It's only the beginning of June and I'm still wearing jeans."

"I know what you mean," she sighed. "I always carry a pair of shorts in my bag that way when the sun does come out I can change."

"Crafty idea," I stated. I pondered her thought for a second then released a long sigh. "I probably wouldn't remember to do that. I still haven't gotten the concept of grabbing my raincoat before I leave the house."

We were at Bobbie's now. Brandi pulled behind her red Ford Escort and stopped.

"Enjoy your day off tomorrow. I'll see you again on Tuesday."

I was opening the door when she uttered her statement. It caught me off guard and I looked back at her.

"Tuesday?" I was confused.

"Derek has gigs in Portland tomorrow night so I won't be back till sometime Monday," she explained.

"Okay," I said slowly. My tone almost made me sound like a moron. "Thanks again for the ride, Brandi. And, could you tell Derek I wish him luck?"

I hadn't gotten the chance to meet Derek but from the chatter I'd heard around the diner he appeared to be on his way to fame. I wouldn't have felt right if I didn't at least cast my support.

"You bet I will!" she stated eagerly.

I pushed open the door and got out, half running to the porch. Brandi was already driving away before I got the door open. I heard movement in the kitchen as I entered the foyer.

"Hey," I called.

"I'm in here," Bobbie called back.

She was standing beside the stove, staring into the open cabinet.

"Are you waiting for something to jump out at you?" I teased.

"No," she laughed. "I can't decide on what to make for dinner." She lost interest in the cabinet and turned to face me. "You look like a drowned rat," she noted.

I pursed my lips. "I feel like one. Do we have tortilla shells and hamburger?"

I watched as a confused expression crossed her face. "I think so."

"Great." I clapped my hands together and turned for the foyer. "I'm going to take a quick shower then I'll be down to start dinner."

"Could I ask what you have in mind?" She was stunned.

I leaned around the wall and looked at her. "Beef enchiladas."

"Mexican!" she squealed enthusiastically. "My favorite."

I rolled my eyes and headed up the stairs.

Kyle and Catlyn greeted me when I walked in Monday afternoon. It was then I learned I was working the night shift with Mark Dawson and Marisa Hadley. I had only worked with them a couple of times and quickly learned why everyone complained about Marisa.

Mark wasn't so bad, he was more of the quiet type. He was in his mid-forties, maybe; he was tiny for a man, his hair was short and turning gray, with dark eyes. He had been the newcomer from somewhere east until I came along.

Marisa was the exact opposite. She was tall, and had the figure every girl would kill for; even herself.

She looked like she should have been a contestant in a beauty pageant. Her hair was a sliver-blond, gently hanging to the middle of her back. She was determined to get in the modeling world and she wasn't afraid to make sure we all knew she was only working for Kloe till she got the call of a lifetime.

I always felt intimidated whenever I was around her and was deeply grateful Catlyn was working the late shift, too. At least now I had someone friendly to talk to.

Kyle left after Mark came in and dinner rush was soon under way. We were busier than usual and I couldn't have been more grateful. Marisa didn't have time to stand around, glaring at me.

When things finally slowed down enough we could breathe and clean up a bit Catlyn and I carried arm loads of dishes to the dishwasher. I pulled clean silverware out then took them upfront to be rolled in napkins and eventually laid in the tray.

"We're finally slow," Catlyn stated when I entered the dining room.

"I hope the late crowd is easier on us," I sighed heavily. I laid the silverware on the counter and grabbed a stack of napkins. "I don't know if I have any energy left to run like that again."

I never minded working in the evenings, I absolutely *despised* the late hours. The diner was open till midnight during the week, on the weekends we were open till three. Those were the times when everyone came in from the local bar and they were usually drunk.

"I don't know why you're complaining, Angel," Marisa said hastily. "The after hour group always prefers you, anyway."

"Marisa, don't be like that," Catlyn said scornfully. "You know, if *you* bothered to be nice like Angel is then maybe they wouldn't complain to Mom about you or refuse your service."

"Whatever, Catlyn," she snarled. Marisa picked an empty tray up from the counter and stalked off to the kitchen.

"Don't let her get to you, Angel," Catlyn said thoughtfully. "She's just mad because no one's called her for an audition."

"I'm not worried about it," I lied.

The conversation ended after that. I stood behind the counter, quiet and rolled the silverware.

We stayed slow all night. A little before close I headed to the kitchen to start cleaning up. I wasn't in there long when I heard the doorbell chime. Figuring it was someone who usually turns down Marisa I set the broom next to the wall, resting the handle on it and walked to the front.

"Are you still opening the hall on Saturday?" I heard Marisa ask.

"Yes," a deep voice answered.

"Brandi, I have a million things still left to do," Catlyn growled. "Why are you even here?"

"Mom asked me to stop by and make sure you remember to put the inventory in the computer," she nearly snarled. "And, if it's any concern to you Derek wanted to stop in and say hi since he hasn't seen you lately."

"Whatever," Catlyn grumbled. She walked to the register and pushed in a bunch of numbers.

Brandi was standing by the counter with her arm snaked around the waist of the boy next to her. His face was toward her so I couldn't see what he looked like. He was much taller than Brandi, his hair was cut short and dark. He was dressed in a rock-n-roll t-shirt and a pair of jeans.

"So, Catlyn," Derek began carefully. "are you still dating that Billy kid?"

"Billy Reynolds?" she asked, her tone mortified. "Heavens no, did Brandi tell you what he did?"

"All she said was something about another girl."

Catlyn pulled the money out of the register and pushed the drawer closed. "I found out he was only dating me to make another girl jealous. I'm not putting up with that."

Derek laughed.

"Are you going for the whole weekend Derek or just Saturday?" Marisa asked.

"I was thinking about doing it all weekend," Derek answered. His tone sounded annoyed. I pressed my lips together , fighting a laugh. "But, Brandi has to work Friday and I have some things to take care of."

Because I now knew it was Brandi and clearly her boyfriend I turned around to walk back to the kitchen. Derek owned a place everyone called the hall, it was where he would get his band together and play for the town. I wasn't interested in hearing them discuss the show planned for the upcoming weekend.

"Angel!" Brandi suddenly squealed, sinking that plan.

She ran to me and took my hand, dragging me over where everyone stood. I fought a cringe when I caught Marisa's glare.

"I'd like you to meet someone," she continued. "Derek, this is Angel."

We came to a stop next to him. I tried to take a step back, Brandi firmly held me in place. "Angel, this is Derek Woods, my boyfriend."

He looked at me, his stormy gray eyes were full of curiosity. A grin spread across his face as he held his hand out at me.

"It is so nice to finally meet you. Brandi speaks of you often."

I made the effort to shake his waiting hand. "It's nice meeting you, too," I blushed.

"Will you be joining us on Saturday?" he asked.

Suddenly feeling awkward I pulled my hand free of his grasp.

"I'm not sure," I said weakly.

"Angel, you have to," Brandi cut in. Her voice sounded almost like a sulky child. "I just know you'll enjoy it."

"Do you have a favorite song, Angel?" Derek suddenly asked.

"Not really," I nearly whispered.

"That's too bad." He was disappointed. "I'm sure I can come up with something special just for you."

"Awe," Brandi cooed. She flashed her powder blue eyes to my face. "Now you have to come."

I didn't need to see Marisa's face to know what her expression was. I could feel her stare boring into my back.

"Fine," I said exhausted. "I'll go. Now, will you get out of here so we can close? I'm ready to go home."

"Yes!" Brandi agreed with a giggle. She caught me up in a vice-tight hug, and then she and Derek walked out the door.

I never looked toward the counter as I passed it to see any expressions on the other girls' faces. I headed to the kitchen, instead.

Catlyn finished before I did and stood by the door waiting for me. Thankfully, Marisa had already left.

"Do you want a ride home?" Catlyn asked as we walked outside.

I looked at the sky before answering. "No, I really need the fresh air."

"Okay, have a good night." She turned on her heels and walked away.

I was already near the edge of the parking lot when I noticed a dark sedan sitting there. I instantly recognized it, it was the one I had seen the day Mike took me to the police station. Paranoia swept over me and it was now I began to wish I'd taken Catlyn's offer.

Familiar Strangers

My heart hammered in my chest so hard I thought it was either going to jump out of the skin or explode. I tried keeping my eyes forward as I passed the dark colored car. I didn't see anyone despite the street light, but suddenly the passenger door opened.

"Hello, Angel," Deputy Callenger's soft voice greeted me. A second later he stepped in the light shining from the open door.

"Hello, Dep ----- Deputy Callenger," I stuttered. This wasn't helping to calm my rapidly beating heart.

"Please, call me Jonah," he said in a polite voice. "Could I offer you a ride?"

Talk your way out of this, Angel, I demanded myself. Quickly.

"Thank you." I paused to swallow a lump that had suddenly formed in my throat. "It's such a nice night and honestly, I don't have far to go."

There, I thought smugly, I was friendly and honest. But, no matter how friendly or polite my dismissal was made him scowl.

"It's late to be walking alone and I would really like to speak with you."

I hadn't gotten the chance to get far, yet I doubted very much I was *alone.* I was about ninety percent sure Sean was out there somewhere. I opened my mouth to point that out, but the sudden intensity burning in Jonah's eyes made me close it.

My heart was now pounding rabbit jumps against my rib cage as I walked to the open door. Jonah waited till I was settled in the seat to close the door and walk around to the driver's side. My hands were shaking uncontrollably by the time he was in his seat.

"Thank you for agreeing to speak with me," he said. A second later he was starting the car, it hummed soundlessly as he pulled out of the lot. "I want to say first that I'm aware of the fact you're afraid of myself and my son. I can assure you there is no reason to fear us."

I stared out the window the whole time he spoke. If I was lucky enough to fool him with my voice, I wouldn't *if* he saw my face. I felt his eyes on me and knew he was waiting for a response.

"I'm not actually afraid," I breathed.

"Angelia." His tone was disapproving.

"Okay," I said in defeat. "I am."

"That's better," he approved. "May I ask why?"

I don't know, maybe because your son stalks me, I thought bitterly. I knew it was probably better to keep that to myself.

"I don't know, Jonah," I lied. "I don't exactly trust anyone."

"I know Sean has been following you when you're out after dark and I also know you're questioning our motives about your rescue."

My eyes widened in shock with his admittance, my heart pounded wildly, again. I stared at the door handle contemplating pulling it and jumping out.

"Just settle down, Angel," he demanded me. "you're completely safe. I can say this with sincerity, we won't hurt you."

There was a part of me that believe him, my being alive was proof. Yet still, there was an even bigger part of me that knew something about him and Sean was dangerously wrong.

I took another minute to control my facial expressions, and then slowly turned my head to look at him.

It was dark in the car, making it difficult to see his face. For that I was thankful, his face was already etched in my mind so I didn't need to see it clearly.

"I don't mean to question you," I said. My voice was shaky and breathless despite my efforts to control it. "I'm just simply trying to figure what is real and what isn't."

He looked at me with a skeptical expression. "I believe there's more to it than that. I know things are confusing as I'm sure different memories are beginning to surface in your mind."

Paranoia swept over me again. Was he wanting me to tell him what I remember? I decided it was probably safer to play dense. Scott had reminded me, almost daily that I was. Maybe now was the time to use it as my best defense. I looked down at my hands so I could hide my face.

"I'm not sure I'm following you," I lied.

"Angel," he glowered. His voice disapproving. "We both know what you've lived through for a number of years. I also know why you never got any help with the situation."

His mentioning of my past had my head snapping back up.

"You talked to the cops?" I shrieked.

"I did no such thing," he stated matter-of-factly. "I spoke with the hospital. I knew *if* the accounts you gave to Mike were true talking with the local authorities would only put you in more danger. The nurse I spoke with is very fond of you, therefore she had no problems filling me in about officer Troy Kensley."

That name had me frozen in the seat.

We were at Bobbie's now and Jonah seemed to pick up on my sudden distress. He stopped the car in Bobbie's spot and put it in park. Then he turned those green eyes on me.

"Angel, I don't want you to just know what I'm about to say but *understand.* You no longer need to fear, you have my word you will not be harmed again."

"But Troy -----." My voice was full of sheer fear.

"Will never get to you," he said confidently. "Now, we need to discuss you're reactions to *my* presence."

My mind was so horrified I couldn't find my voice. All I could do was stare at Jonah, helpless.

"You're extremely intelligent," he began when I said nothing. "and, it's been brought to my attention you have unusual hearing for a person. With just knowing that, I truly believe you pick up on what others never notice."

I waited a few more seconds to answer so my voice ----- if I still had one ----- would be strong, strong enough at least.

"Jonah." I paused, listening closely as his name came out. It was shaky, but I didn't no longer hear any fear. "I apologize if I cause any discomfort to you or Sean. I understand better than anyone how important secrets are. I have no intentions of telling anyone what I do remember from that night in the woods."

Jonah laughed.

The sound was creepy and I fought to keep from cringing.

"I'm not concerned with you discussing the matter with anyone. I'm just concerned with the fear you have in my presence. I know you're simply avoiding telling me why, I would very much like an answer."

I wasn't a hundred percent sure what was wrong about him, therefore I wasn't going to admit to any theories, either. I felt for that moment it was safer for *me* to speak the obvious.

"You're a cop," I said warily. "I'm sure since you've spoken with the hospital you can understand."

"You didn't appear to have any discomfort with Mike a few afternoons ago," he noted.

He had me there, dang it! I dropped my face to hide my expressions.

Jonah suddenly reached out and placed a long, cold finger under my chin, lifting my face so I was looking at him.

"I cannot say I'm convinced with your answer. However, for what it's worth, you're in the safest place you will ever find."

I was until you make that call, I said to myself.

"Let us prove you have no reason to fear," he continued.

"O-okay," I stammered. "I'll give it my best effort."

He stared at my eyes a few seconds longer then dropped his hand. I sucked in a quiet breath to fill my lungs as they were starting to feel deprived of oxygen.

"Get inside, Angel," he ordered me. "Keep the door locked and get a good night's rest. You look like you could use it."

Sure, I thought sourly. Make the noises stop and I'll sleep better than a baby.

I squeezed the handle on the door and opened it. The night air had cooled off and after being in Jonah's stuffy car I felt grateful when it brushed across my face.

"Thank you for the ride, Jonah," I said politely.

"Good night, Angel."

I walked to the porch in a daze. There was something about Jonah and Sean's eyes that could cloud my mind. I unlocked the door and entered the house thankful Bobbie wasn't home. I didn't know what my facial expressions were, yet I was sure they would have alerted her something was wrong.

I tossed the keys in the bowl then suddenly my skin felt like it was freezing. I headed up the stairs, I had high hopes a hot shower would somehow ease the trembles now running through me.

And again, I didn't sleep well. I heard sounds through the empty house. They weren't loud, they were simple sounds, like someone was having a restless night and pacing around downstairs. There was a moment when I thought I heard the computer chair roll across the floor. I wrenched upright in the bed, instantly turning on the lamp and scanned the room.

Nothing.

I flopped back on the bed, my heart was racing, as if I'd just ran for miles. It took hours for me to fall asleep again, this time the light stayed on.

The next morning I saw a magazine lying on the table. I didn't think anything about it and walked to the coffee pot. After I made up a cup I went to the table and sat down. I looked over the cover of the magazine, and then it suddenly seemed strange for it to be there. I've never seen Bobbie read this kind of stuff. I picked it up and began looking it over.

It wasn't very interesting so I started to close it, and then there in the back was an unusual article:

NEW ORLEANS PREPARES FOR ANNUAL FESTIVAL.

As I read the print I saw it was about a festival being held to honor *vampires*. At first I thought it was crazy and nearly turned the page when the words "casket girls" caught my attention.

New Orleans held the festivities every year between the dates of October thirtieth and November second. It went on to say the town would dress as vampires and spend each night awake, waiting for the creatures to emerge from the darkness.

It described them to be pale and gaunt, with deep red eyes. They were believed to have extreme speeds and unbelievable strength. Anyone who trespassed on the grounds of the old convent were found laid out on the porch the next morning with two puncture holes in their necks and missing most of their blood.

While reading the article I thought about Jonah and Sean. I knew it was crazy to compare them to the theory, but my sub-conscious had already made its own conclusions long before this magazine appeared. Their eyes clearly didn't match what I read, yet other similarities seem to fit.

They were pale and gaunt, even as tall as they were they made little noise. I could only hear Sean as he followed me when there wasn't any other sounds. Jonah's skin felt like smooth marble and was extremely cold for a human. Especially since it's not cold, just rainy. Jonah's articulation sounds like that of another century. It was also interesting to me how he had a Southern sound to his tone.

Could it be possible?

I had two theories instantly come to mind.

Theory one: This is why they're not being forth coming about being in the cabin that night. It could also be the reason Jonah wanted to talk to me last night since Sean has clearly told him about my unusual hearing, as Jonah called it and that I was questioning their secrets. They're worried I've figured out *who* they are and my knowledge would be dangerous for them *if* I told anyone.

Possible.

Theory two: I've lost my mind. The few books I've ever read about the *undead* states one very obvious thing; they can't come out in the daylight. The books have also stated their eyes are blood red and they have fangs. They're supposed to resemble that of a vampire bat just without the fur.

Sean nor Jonah appeared to have fangs and they certainly didn't look like bats. They look like everyone else ----- well, almost like everyone else. They are inhumanly perfect and beautiful. So am I just plan crazy?

Probable. Maybe even likely.

I closed the magazine before it cost me my sanity (though it probably already had) and picked up the coffee cup. If I was going to get through this day at all I needed the caffeine to fight off the tiredness. I haven't had this many sleepless nights in my life.

I glanced up at the clock suddenly realizing the time I'd lost while daydreaming. I jumped out of the chair, nearly running to place my cup in the sink. I donned in my raincoat and rushed out the door.

I hadn't noticed anyone on the porch till the figure stood up. I'd never seen him in the daylight, the clarity of his face took my breath away. I got an eerie feeling as it was strange to see him after reading that article. I couldn't believe the rush of emotions suddenly pulsing through me.

"Good morning, Angel," he greeted me, his voice soft. His lips formed a half smile, taking away my ability to think or speak. "I don't mean to frighten you. I've been trying to convince myself to knock on the door, I'm not really even sure I should be here."

Despite my loss of thoughts I had to force myself to remember how to breathe so I could speak.

"It's all right, Sean," I finally managed.

I made myself look away from him and focus on putting one foot in front of the other. Sean stepped back from the stairs, allowing me to pass him without any chance of skin contact. My knees shook the entire time I walked down the stairs causing a simple action to become difficult.

"You're probably starting to think of this as a Callenger invasion," he suddenly stated.

"The thought did cross my mind," I admitted.

"I promise it's not."

I looked up at the sky with its dark clouds, promising to dump buckets of water down on us at any time, secretly wishing he would go away. It wasn't even a second later and he was next to me, matching my pace.

"My father didn't frighten you last night, did he?" he asked. His voice was soft, his question was genuine.

"No more than usual," I said, artlessly. "What do I owe the pleasure for this visit?"

I may have kept my eyes off his face, I could clearly hear the frown in his voice when he responded.

"You don't owe me anything."

Since I was now in control of myself I stopped walking and looked up at him. I instantly began to regret it. His sky-colored eyes were glowing, a strand of his mahogany hair was curled over his brow. His pale face was twisted in a scowl. I had to remind myself to exhale.

"You usually follow me from a distance at night. There has to be a reason for you to be here now."

"It isn't uncommon for friends to show up at each other's homes," he mused, dubious.

"*Friends?*" I repeated, doubtful. "In what universe?"

I knew if I wanted to get to work on time I had to start walking now. I looked away from him, concentrating on keeping my legs moving without stumbling. The last thing I wanted was to look like an idiot in front of him. It was a slow process, but I was successful in putting one foot in front of the other.

"I don't want this to sound rude, but I really have to be on my way. I'm already late."

"I've gone this far with you," he stated as though I didn't already know that. "Do you mind if I walk the rest of the way?"

His response caught me off guard and I looked up at him. He was smiling at me.

"Sure, I guess," I said hesitantly. Despite the deep purple shadows under his eyes his smile caused my heart to skip a few beats. "Did you honestly drive over here just to walk me three blocks?"

Now he laughed. "I didn't know you had to work until you came running out the door."

"Right," I mumbled.

I looked away to concentrate on where I was going.

"I would have offered you a ride, but you walked away before I could ask."

"I would have turned you down, anyway," I admitted, sheepishly. "It's not that long of a walk."

"Is that really the reason or are you afraid if you get in the truck I'll drive away with you?"

The tenor in his voice had my head turning sharply his direction.

We were at the diner now. I knew I needed to give him a simple goodbye and walk away, yet I couldn't. There was something in his eyes that wouldn't allow me to look away.

"Well," he began, his tone indifferent. "I suppose our journey is over."

I opened my mouth to answer then suddenly his blue eyes were hypnotic. My heart began to pound so hard I could hear it behind my ears. The longer his eyes held mine my mind began to cloud, my thoughts scrambled and eventually disappeared.

"I guess it has," I said enunciating each word carefully. I was still fighting to regain control of my mind. "And thank you," I tacked on. I didn't want to give in to what I believed he was waiting for, yet I couldn't continue with being rude about it. He did save my life whether he admitted it or not.

His eyes released their hold as I watched a puzzled expression cross his face. "You don't need to thank me for walking with you."

"For my life," was all I could say.

"Oh." He looked down, and then glanced up at me from under long lashes. "You're welcome."

I smiled at him and walked away.

Brandi was standing behind the counter, staring at the door and was practically bouncing in agitation. I knew right then she had seen us. I reluctantly walked past her, hoping to avoid the string of questions I was sure she had. I tried taking my time in the kitchen before having to return to the front. She waited till I finally entered the dining room to pounce.

"Is there something you'd like to tell me?" she asked. Suspicion colored her tone.

"No," I spoke slowly. "I don't think so."

She crossed her arms over her chest, her lips puckered in disappointment. "So you're just going to leave me to wonder how you got Sean to walk you to work?"

Maybe I should have called off for the day or at least told Sean no when he asked to join me. I could have told her some lie, like I bumped into him and he wanted to talk. I decided to go with the truth, instead.

"He was on Bobbie's porch when I walked out of the house."

She glared at me with stiff skepticism. "Sean Callenger, Angel," she stated, disgusted. "Sean freaking Callenger."

Marisa had just entered when Brandi said his name the second time. She walked towards us, wearing a confused expression on her face. "What about him?" she asked.

Brandi answered her without ever taking her eyes off my face. "He walked Angel to work today."

"Of course he did," Marisa said hatefully.

I grabbed a spray bottle full of sanitation water and a rag and headed to a dirty table. I suddenly needed to get away from what was becoming a hostile situation. Brandi followed a few steps behind.

"You are beautiful," she snorted. "it's not surprising he noticed."

I rolled my eyes while shaking my head, sadly. "I really doubt it's like that, Brandi."

She walked around me and her hands flew up, palms towards me, like she was stopping traffic. "Just stop right there. You clearly don't seem to understand something."

"I already know he's not the dating type," I informed her. I tried to step around her and she blocked my escape.

"Then you know he's never looked at any of us. You've got him paying attention to *you*, Angel. It means something."

I pondered asking her if she was one of the many admires he turned down. She didn't sound bitter about it so I changed my mind.

"Brandi," I glowered. "you're letting your imagination get the best of you."

Her eyes narrowed at me. "I saw the way he was looking at you. Like it or not he's hooked, line and sinker."

I tried stepping around her again, this time she let me pass.

"Are you going to see him again?" she asked. Her question was out of pure curiosity, I could clearly hear the hope in her tone.

I finally reached the table. I sprayed it and began running the rag across it. "We live in the same town so we're bound to bump into each other."

"That's not what I meant," she growled. "Will we see you with *him* again?"

"I doubt it." Hoped was more like it.

A customer entered before she could say anything else. I breathe a sigh of relief when she walked away.

The morning passed in a blur. Lunch rush kept us busy enough I was able to avoid Brandi's interrogations and Marisa's hateful glares. I couldn't help wondering if *she* was one of the many Sean had refused.

Things finally slowed down enough I could go to the cooler in the kitchen for another tray of dressing cups. Kyle and Catlyn were in the middle of a serious conversation. I tried not to hear any of it as I passed. It sounded like they were making plans for Saturday.

I stood inside the cooler, enjoying the cold air. My poor body was so drenched in sweat I could feel it as it ran down my back. I pulled a tray down from the shelf and used the other hand to move the others around.

"Angel," Kyle said, inches behind me.

He instantly startled me and I nearly dropped the tray. "Jeez, Kyle, don't do that!"

With both hands now tightened in a death grip around the tray I turned around.

"Sorry, here -----." He reached out to take the tray from my hands. I fought against him for a second, and then let go. I was already fighting to calm my rapidly beating heart.

"What do you need, Kyle?"

He didn't answer. I waited, almost impatiently for his response. The seconds ticked by.

"It doesn't have anything to do with work," he informed me. His cheeks flushed red.

"And?" I prompted.

"I was wondering if you wanted to go with me. You know, to the hall Saturday?"

"Weren't you just making plans with Catlyn?" I was confused.

"She did ask," he admitted. "but I told her I'd think about it."

I looked down to make sure my hands hadn't balled into fists and fight to keep my voice warm while I answered. "Why would you do that?"

"I wanted to ask you first." His tone sounded like he didn't see my response coming.

I slowly lifted my head to look at him. "It's really sweet of you to ask, Kyle. You should go with Catlyn. I'm sure you guys will have fun."

His face was bright red as he looked away from me. "I guess you've already been asked by someone else."

His guess was off ----- way off, but it didn't lessen the sudden irritation pulsing through me. I snatched the tray out of his hands.

"I'm afraid you're wrong. I'm not going with anyone."

He carefully lifted his eyes back to my face. "I don't know if you've noticed, Angel, but I really like you."

"I'm the shiny new toy, what's not to like." My tone was much sharper then I wanted it. I softened it and smiled warmly at him. "I would like for you to simply return to the crush you had before me. I'm not looking for anything more than friendships. So go tell Catlyn you'll go with her."

"You're right, I should," he mumbled, and then turned and walked away.

I stood there another minute and hung my head. Even as what I told him was the truth I felt a horrible guilt for dismissing him that way. I sucked in one long, deep breath and walked out of the cooler.

"There you are," Brandi called out at me. "I've been looking all over for you."

"Why?" I was confused.

A sly smile slowly crossed her lips. "You have a gorgeous guy waiting for you."

It wasn't hard to figure out who she was taking about since that was the same look and tone she had this morning.

"Sean's here?" I nearly shrieked.

"Yes," she laughed.

The tray in my hands began to shake, the quake so bad the cups were on the verge of falling off. I carefully walked to the table and set it down. "Why?"

"I don't know," she grumbled. "He came in and asked if you were still here."

I felt the blood rush to my head causing me to suddenly feel dizzy. Brandi walked to me and picked up the tray of dressing cups.

"It's time for you to go, anyway," she said, not seeming to notice my reaction. "So go on and have fun with Mr. Dreamy."

My mind was so clouded I walked to the time clock, punching my numbers in mechanically. It still hadn't cleared by the time I headed to the dining room or even after I entered. Sean was standing by the door with his hands shoved in his pockets. His eyes flashed to my face, a smile slowly spreading across his face.

"Angel, don't forget your raincoat."

I stopped walking, turning toward the sound. It was only then I saw Brandi running at me with my raincoat in her hand.

"See you on Friday," she said as she handed it to me.

"Thanks," I said nearly breathless. I turned away from her and walked to Sean's side.

"Hello." His voice was velvet soft.

"Hi," I answered, faintly.

He pushed open the door, allowing me to exit first. That first hit of the cool air helped to clear my head and calm my nerves. It was raining heavily and I stopped under the roof's overhang, pulling on the raincoat.

"Why are you here?" I asked when the door closed.

He looked at me with a sour expression. "It's raining so I thought you would like a ride."

Please, oh please let him not keep finding reasons to complicate my life!

"I could have waited for Brandi." I finished stuffing my hair inside the hood and fastened the top button on the raincoat.

"Now you're being absurd," he growled. "Just wait here while I get the truck."

I watched him jog across the parking lot. I thought about the article I read this morning, again, comparing Sean's movements to it. His speed was no faster than the average person's, though his run looked more effortless.

It wasn't but a minute later and the long, white truck was pulling up in front of me. When the passenger door opened I ran to it and climbed inside. I suddenly had a rush of guilt wash over me for my rudeness.

"I'm sorry for sounding rude," I apologized. I closed the door, and then reached for the seatbelt. "I do appreciate the ride."

"You're welcome," he replied, his tone was still bitter. "It just so happens that not all of us are bad guys, Angel."

I sank in the seat, full of more than just guilt. "I've never said you were a bad guy," I said, ashamed.

He looked over at me, his brow creased angrily. "It's not so much what you say, it's the way you act. I have no intention of biting you."

He suddenly laughed and turned his eyes back to the windshield. I apparently missed the joke somehow.

"Would you prefer I stay away from you?" he asked, serious now.

It boggled my mind how he could change from one emotion to another so quickly.

"No," I answered quietly. It surprised me when the word escaped my lips. It was also scary to know I really felt that way. "I just need time to adjust, everything has been overwhelming for me."

"What's the general timeline here, Angel? How long do you need?" His voice was full of frustration. For reasons I couldn't fathom that bothered me.

We were at Bobbie's now. He parked behind her car and left the truck running.

"I don't know, Sean," I sighed, exasperated. "I've been told you don't pay special attention to anyone, so why me?"

He laid his head against the seat and stared at the ceiling. "I've never met anyone like you."

I waited for him to say something that made more sense. The seconds simply ticked by.

"I don't know what that means so I'm not sure if that was a complement or an insult," I stated, dryly.

Sean laughed.

"Since we're bringing this up, why do you follow me at night?"

"I have this …" His voice trailed off as he seemed to struggle for words. "I don't know why but I have a deep need to protect you."

"Protect me?" I repeated. "Why would you need to protect me?"

He rolled his head my direction, his eyes smoldering. "Were you *really* too drugged to remember what you've been through?"

Oops, opened the wrong can! His eyes were difficult to look away from, yet somehow I managed. I may have felt an odd sense of safety when I was with him, in no way did I feel safe enough or even comfortable enough to answer his question. Especially after my brief encounter with Jonah.

"I – I don't know," I stammered. "Thanks for the ride."

I squeezed the door handle and pushed it open.

"Angel?" he asked, his tone indifferent.

I slowly turned in the seat to face him. "Yes?"

"Do you think you will ever trust me?" His eyes were still doing that smoldering thing and I turned away.

"I already do," I said in a faint voice.

I jumped out the open door before he could find a way to keep me there longer. I fought to keep from looking back as I ran to the house. I caught Sean's taillights as they disappeared in the pouring rain. I closed the door and walked quietly up the stairs to my room.

Friday turned out to be a very long, very slow day. It rained heavily, preventing us from being busy. Every conversation I heard centered around the hall as everyone shared their excitement. I found a way to do something that wasn't standing around or engaging in their pleasures. When asked for my opinion I tried to be diplomatic, but I mostly just avoided it.

The next afternoon I worked around the house and washed my laundry. I found out the magazine on the table wasn't Bobbie's. She had seen it and thought I picked up from somewhere, very strange. I tossed it in the trash can and tried not to think any more about it. Kloe gave me the day off, she thought I needed the time to prepare myself for all the people she knew I'd meet.

Bobbie entered the kitchen as I took the last of my clothes out of the dryer.

"Hi," she greeted me cheerfully.

"Hi." I closed the dryer door, picked up the basket and walked into the kitchen.

"Are you excited about tonight?" she asked.

I fought a groan. "I don't know if *excited* is the right word."

Bobbie carried a glass to the refrigerator as I went to the table and set the basket down.

"It really will be a lot of fun. Derek and his band plays for the crowd, he even has a live DJ. Derek is truly amazing."

"Why hasn't he been signed with a label?"

Bobbie replaced the tea pitcher on the shelf then closed the door. "I think it's because of Brandi."

I watched her cross the room, and then sit down at the table. Her statement completely confused me.

"How does she have anything to do with it?"

"They have been a couple since they were in the eighth grade. He was there when Uncle Gregg died, he's what helped pull her through. I believe he's afraid if he gets signed and has to be gone more than he already is, it might end things between them."

Gregg Hallsworth was a contractor everyone in town thought very highly of. He had been involved in creating many of the buildings around town. He'd lived in Newport his entire life; he had met Kloe while they attended Washington State, and almost immediately they fell in love. They married not long after graduation, Kloe majored in business, allowing her to work anywhere. Gregg wanted to go back home and Kloe thought it would be a great place to raise their children and agreed without hesitation. They opened the diner two years before Brandi was born.

One cold, rainy night five years ago he was on his way back from Portland when his car slid off the road. It was dark, the road was slick and he made a turn too sharp. His car slid down an embankment, crashing into a tree. He died instantly as result of a broken neck.

"That does make sense," I mused. I knew how hard it was for Bobbie and her family whenever someone mentioned Gregg. It was time to change the subject. "What time does the show start?"

"The doors get unlocked at seven," she said, her voice perking up again. "Do you want to go to Walmart?"

"For what?" I was confused.

"So we can shop for clothes," she stated slowly. I must have sounded like an idiot.

"Just to go to a dance hall?" I made a face of mock horror.

"It's what we're supposed to do," Bobbie said with a laugh. "It's part of being a girl."

"Right," I mumbled.

She stood from the chair and headed for the foyer. "C'mon, it'll be fun."

I could only sigh in defeat as I picked up the basket of clothes and followed her up the stairs.

The shopping trip took longer than expected. Bobbie made at least a dozen trips to the dressing room. She wouldn't like what she tried on and then would look for something else. I settled with a blue long-sleeved shirt and a pair of jeans. I couldn't see getting dressed up just to listen to music while being surrounded by a crowd of people.

Finally, she decided on a beaded khaki skirt, with a white sleeveless blouse. She drove home faster than usual home. We still had to dress and she didn't want to be late and have to stand in a long line. I thought she was crazy, but kept it to myself.

We were late, anyway. It was a little after seven and people were already lined at the door. Since it wasn't raining the crowds covered the sidewalk and the street. It was several long minutes before Bobbie found a place to park.

It turned out the dance hall was an old warehouse. Directly behind it was a boat dock, (no longer in use) an open bay of water sparkled from the lights casting over it. I stayed close to Bobbie while we stood in the long line then eventually inside. I noticed a sign on the door indicating no alcohol was served. That helped to ease some of the tension I felt, though very little.

The inside was incredible! There were tables lined along the walls and all the way to the stage. A massive hardwood floor took up the center and two drink stations, maybe thirty feet apart were on each side. The girls working them were dressed in a white, long-sleeved shirt, with dark colored pants. Bobbie led me to the closest one.

"I'll have a Mountain Dew," she said. "Angel, what would you like?"

I tore my eyes away from the room and looked at the board hanging on a chain from the ceiling. It was then I knew they served more than drinks. I hadn't eaten anything since this morning and pondered whether or not to order a small nacho. My stomach was fluttering from butterflies, badly … better not.

"Um … a Pepsi is fine," I finally answered.

The girl reached above her head and took down two glasses hanging upside down. I had never seen any place use beer taps for soda and was mesmerized. I so was drawn to watching the glasses fill I was unaware we were being approached.

"What do you think?" Brandi asked from behind us.

The sudden sound of her voice had me spinning towards her. Once it registered in my mind it was Brandi my heart began to slow.

"It's bigger than I thought," I said warily.

"Derek doesn't believe in small crowds," she said with a laugh.

"It definitely looks that way."

"You should see the crowds when he *really* performs."

"Maybe sometime I will." I smiled tentatively.

She pointed her index finger at me and chuckled. "I'm gonna hold you to that. Well, have fun guys."

"See ya around," Bobbie answered before I could respond.

When Brandi walked away I turned back to the bar and held out money to the girl behind it. She waved me off, telling me my drink was already paid for. I stuffed it back in my pocket, picked up the glass and turned around to face the crowd.

It was then I noticed Bobbie looking around, like she was waiting for someone. I watched her in complete awe. She's such a shy person and it was fascinating to see her scanning the room in anticipation. Then suddenly a gangly boy with blond hair was walking toward us.

"Hi, Bobbie," he said when he reached us.

There were deep dimples in his cheeks when he smiled at her. His blond hair was in disarray, his eyes were a bright blue. I now understood why Bobbie had been so fussy over her clothes. Her cheeks were flushed with red.

"Hi, Josh," she answered shyly.

He stared at her a second longer then turned his eyes on me. "Hello, Angel," he said politely. "You're looking much better."

"I feel much better," I said, sheepishly. I wasn't sure why but I suddenly felt nervous.

"Do you remember me?" he asked earnestly.

I barely shook my head back and forth. "No, I don't."

He slowly extended his arm, offering me his hand. "I'm Josh McClaine. I was the person that took you for your X-rays the night you were brought to the hospital."

I carefully reached out to shake his waiting hand.

"She doesn't remember much of that night," Bobbie suddenly interjected. It was comforting to know she knew me well enough to know when I was uncomfortable.

"Sorry, Angel," he said, apologetically. He released his hold on my hand. "I don't mean to make you uncomfortable."

"I'm getting used to it."

He laughed, though it was humorless. "It's good to see you just the same."

"Yeah," I said unemotional. "you, too."

Just then a slow song came through the speakers from somewhere overhead.

"Would you like to dance, Bobbie?" Josh asked.

Her cheeks went red again. "Sure."

He reached for her hand and she flashed her eyes to me. I only smiled while nodding my head in encouragement. A half a second later he was pulling her toward the dance floor.

I took a drink from my glass and my eyes scanned the room, coming to a stop at the stage.

"Hello, Angel," came a soft voice.

My head instantly snapped to my left. There beside me was a girl I'd never seen before. She was somehow, strangely familiar. She was just a few inches taller than me, her dark hair barely hung over the collar of her jacket. Her face was pale, with butterscotch colored eyes. The jacket she wore was covered in rhinestones, instantly bringing a biker's jacket to mind. The flashing lights overhead seemed react strangely against her skin.

"Hello," I nearly whispered. My pulse reacted badly to her presence.

"I know we haven't had the chance to officially meet," she said, enthusiastically. "I'm Kelsey Callenger."

I could feel my face turn to shock then to horror. Now I understood why there was a familiarity to her; aside from the color of her eyes she looked a lot like Sean. I had to force myself to speak.

"It's nice to meet you," I nearly croaked.

She laughed, the sound dark. "With how hard your heart is beating I doubt you mean that."

Did she just say she can hear my heart? No ----- that's crazy. She probably guessed it by my reaction.

"I've heard you remember Sean and my dad from the night in the woods," she continued. "I'm really not supposed to tell you anything, but what you saw is *real*. They were in the cabin ... in fact, we all were."

If she wanted me to relax then she shouldn't have said that. My heart beat rabbit jumps against my ribs, my chest tightened, threatening to cut off my air supply.

"Oh, clam down, Angel," she glowered. "I'm clearly not here to hurt you."

I tried to take a breath so my voice would be strong when I responded. "Then what do you want?" My voice broke anyway.

She looked at me with a sour expression. "Sean says you're a reader yet you've never gone in the library. I figured if you weren't going to come to me then I'd come to you."

The horror I felt only intensified. How did Sean know I read?

"*You're* the librarian?" I nearly shrieked.

Her face was incredulous, with a hint of anger. "You make it sound like something dangerous. And, would you relax? Are you this touchy with Sean?"

"Sometimes," I admitted. "Why have you been waiting for me?"

"Are you kidding," she laughed. The tenor in her laugh was just as creepy as the others. "You're a popular topic in my house. My brother used to be boring until you came along."

"How did I change anything?" While she was talking I took deep breaths, slowly calming my beating heart. It seemed to help, a little.

She leaned closer to me, keeping her voice low. "Come see me sometime and I'll tell you. It might be too early to say this now, but I'd like to be your friend."

Yep, she's right ----- way too early. There is definitely something off with this family and I wasn't too sure I wanted to get close enough to find out just exactly what it was.

"Are you sure your dad would approve of you telling me anything?"

Kelsey puckered her lips. "What's he going to do, put me in jail? You're clearly trustworthy, seeming how you've never spoken a word of anything to anyone, Mike included. I personally don't see the point of lying to you, especially since you remember some things."

The song overhead stopped and Kelsey became uneasy, edgy. "I'll catch up with you later, Angel," she suddenly stated. "Don't forget to come by the library."

"You don't have to leave, Kelsey," I said. My words surprised her and I both.

"Actually, I do," she disagreed.

"Okay, then," I said, bewildered.

"I'll see you soon." She winked at me and less than a second later she was gone.

I turned to the bar as Derek's voice spilled out of the overhead speakers.

"Could I have everyone's attention, please?" he asked. "Thank you," he tacked on after every pair of eyes looked at him. "I've recently had the pleasure of meeting a new face our town is very fortunate to have. I'd like for each of you to help me welcome her as my band and I play a special song just for *her*."

My cheeks instantly flushed hot when everyone close to me turned their heads to look at me.

"I really had to think about this," Derek laughed. "Despite my asking her myself she doesn't seem to have anything in particular she likes so I had to come up with something on my own. I found some old stuff my dad had lying around and there, I found the perfect song. Angelia, this one's for you."

I could feel my eyes widen in horror when the first note of the song played. Richard Marx's Angelia couldn't have been his worst choice. I never listened to Pop music; I mostly preferred Beethoven's symphonies or country, but I knew this particular song. I had been tormented by a number of kids as they would blurt it out when I passed them in the halls at school.

Everyone was staring at me, not able to stand it any longer I set my glass on the bar and nearly pushed my way past them. I walked very quickly toward the direction I hoped was the bathrooms. Because I was nearly running, as I felt eyes the entire way, I wasn't paying attention to where I was going and slammed into a body. His hands quickly caught my shoulders before the impact knocked me down.

"Well, hello, Angel," Dr. McKnight said with a laugh.

He held on a moment longer to be sure I wouldn't fall before releasing me.

"Sorry, Dr. McKnight," I apologized, awkwardly. I didn't expect to see him in a place that every teenager and young adult liked to hang out.

"Please, call me Alex," he chuckled. "and, it's all right."

I smiled at him and walked away.

"Has anyone asked you to dance?" he called out.

I stopped walking, nearly mortified. "Dance?" I croaked. My body turned slowly, almost unwilling to face him.

He laughed and took a step closer to me. "It is *your* special song," he reminded me. "Could I interest you in a dance with an old guy?"

I was going to give him an absolute no, but the expression on his face made me feel guilty for even considering it. And anyways, I kind of owed it to him, I did try to knock him over.

"Sure," I said, reluctantly. Very reluctantly.

He laughed again and took my hand, pulling me closer to him. I tried to fight off the hyperventilation I felt when his arms slipped around my waist. I couldn't help feeling tiny and awkward as we swayed side to side. It was comforting to know he didn't dance any better than I did ... but still.

I kept my eyes away from him, focusing on the activities going on around us. I saw Bobbie with Josh and Catlyn was dancing with Kyle. I briefly saw Marisa as she was dancing with a dark haired boy. It was nice to see, no matter how brief it was, her attention focused on someone else.

"Thank you for allowing me to dance with you, Angel," Alex suddenly said, calling my attention back to him.

"Aren't you worried your wife might get upset?"

"I'm not married." His tone was martyred, yet I couldn't tell if it was because he was ashamed or just disappointed. "And, before you ask, there's no girlfriend, either."

Now I was the one disappointed. "How is that even possible?"

"I'm flattered by your notions, Angel," he said, his voice sounding slightly embarrassed. "I've had a number of ladies tell me they can't compete with the hospital."

I pulled back so I could look at him. "Keep your head up, I believe you'll find the one meant for you."

That made him smile. "You really are a sweet girl, Angel."

"Sure," I said, uncertain. The song ended and I abruptly freed myself of his arms. "Thank you for the dance, Alex."

"You're welcome," he replied, softly.

He lifted my left hand to his lips, gently kissing it. He glanced up at me from under long lashes and smiled. He then straightened himself, dropped my hand, and then turned on his heels, walking back to where I ran into him. I stared at his back, completely stunned.

"So you're the famous Angel," a male voice stated.

I turned to see a cute, baby-faced boy, his short, black as oil, hair was gelled neatly in place. It took me a moment to realize this was the boy I'd seen Marisa dancing with just moments ago. He was smiling at me.

"That would be me," I said, forcing a smile.

"I'm John."

"Hi, John."

"Could I buy you a drink?"

I usually would have said no, but I was heading to the bar, anyway. "Sure, why not?"

He was quite the chatter as we walked. He lived in Portland all his life, but came here around this time to spend the fourth of July with his grandfather. I could barely contain my horror when he admitted his grandfather was Mayor Wilkins.

Most of his family was political and wanted him to follow in granddad's footsteps. He went into criminal law, instead. His dream was to one day be the head DA in the prosecutions office. He sounded a bit conceited, at least he's goal oriented, I thought.

It wasn't long after he bought my drink when he was approached and eventually dragged away by a girl desperate for his attention. I didn't try to stop her.

The rest of the night passed in nearly the same fashion. Derek never called any more attention to me, though it didn't stop anyone from approaching me just the same. I met new faces and became reacquainted with others. There were many offers to dance and I quickly turned them down. I may have been great on a piano, not so much on my two feet. I wasn't blessed with coordination or balance, so it was safer for everyone around me that I simply didn't try.

Boyfriend? I Don't Think So

The next three weeks were probably the best since this nightmare started. Sean hadn't made another appearance at the diner and for some strange reason the noises in the house during the night had stopped. I slept better than a baby.

Even as Sean didn't come back my days at work didn't improve. It wasn't long before John Wilkins learned I worked for Kloe and began coming in regularly. At first, he would sit at any of the tables, watching me, by the end of the week he only sat at the tables I worked. I intercepted many unfriendly glances from Marisa.

The fourth of July turned out to be a very warm, very sunny day. It was the first one Newport had had in nearly three months. Everyone was filled with excitement as they set up a local park for the festival and made promises of fireworks after dark.

It had been more than month since that fateful night I was recused. It was also the same amount of time since Jonah talked to anyone in Pittsburg, yet I still looked over my shoulder whenever I was out. Jonah may have believed I was safe, I believed differently. No matter how many times someone promises not to say anything, they eventually tell Troy anything he wants to know; I knew Troy Kensley.

I was content just staying in the house and watch the fireworks from the kitchen window. To my dismay Bobbie and Brandi talked me into going with them. I stayed next to their side as we walked through the park, though it didn't ease any of the tension. I still watched each person when they passed, even the ones who appeared to lurk behind the trees.

Mike and two of his deputies were amongst the many faces, dressed in their uniforms. Even as I could clearly see the gun belt wrapped around their waist I didn't relax. I was still nervous whenever I saw Jonah, but I couldn't stop myself from looking around the park for him and his family. Despite my efforts, I didn't see them anywhere. I asked the girls' and was told they simply didn't participate in this event.

How odd.

A couple of days later the rain returned. I couldn't stand the paranoia anymore and went to the police station to cast my pleas for freedom with Mike. Despite my efforts he wouldn't agree to clear me to leave until Jeremy was convicted or until my birthday. I argued to no prevail.

"I don't know what the big deal is, Angel. You only have a month left then I can no longer legally hold you here. Surely, you can wait that long," he had said.

I turned to Jonah, hoping he would see I was right to fear and help me convince Mike. He just simply shrugged his shoulders at me. I groaned in frustration and stormed out of the station.

After losing my debate with Mike I kept myself busy so I couldn't have time to think about my fears. I tried to call Jennifer often, secretly keeping a close watch on Troy, though sometimes when I got home I was so tired I'd take a shower and go to bed. She would get impatient if she didn't hear from me and call. Sometimes she'd complain, but mostly she was curious how I was doing and *if* I'd met anyone special.

I lied a lot about my entrapment, leading her to believe everything was fine. There wasn't anyone I was interested in and as I tried convincing her of that (although it was the truth) I promised *if* I did she'd be the first to know.

Someone had informed Bobbie I had a driver's license and she managed to find a clever way of convincing me to use the car while she slept. It bothered her I walked everywhere, especially when it rains, which was a lot. I didn't feel comfortable with it, though I didn't watch everything around me, as often.

And another week passed.

I sat at the table on Monday reading one of Bobbie's romance novels while enjoying a cup of coffee. It was my day off and I knew I should have slept in, yet the rain falling on the roof had my eyes open. I lost interest in the book, closing it and laid it on the table when Bobbie walked in. Her face was weary, sleep burned heavily in her brown eyes.

"Morning," she said as she walked to the counter.

"Morning."

"You're up early," she noted.

"I have an alarm clock for a brain," I teased.

I watched as she unpacked her lunch bag and carry the untouched food to the refrigerator. It seemed to take a great deal of effort for her to walk back to the counter.

"It looks to me like Aunt Kloe made an early bird out of you," she laughed. "She does tend to do that, just ask her daughters."

"I figured once school was out I wouldn't have to be up before daylight … then I ended up here."

Bobbie was now joining me at the table with her own cup of coffee. "Ending up here has nothing to do with it," she said with a laugh. "I got a glitch in my brain and made you meet Kloe."

"True," I agreed. "I swear she's always in the diner when it opens and usually again before close. Does she ever make time to sleep?"

Bobbie sluggishly shrugged her shoulders. "She used to until Gregg died. After that she threw herself into the diner and her garden."

While she talked I racked my bran for a different topic. She seemed to mirror my thoughts, changing the subject herself.

"Do you have anything planned for the long day you're in for?"

"I don't know," I said with a shrug. "I've been thinking about wandering down by the shore."

"Today is a good day for it," she approved. "There's no sun, but we're catching a break in between rain falls."

"I realize I've only been here for nearly two months and even *I* know the time lapse between them isn't going to be very long." I pretended to be disgusted.

"You're right," she laughed. "the good news is you will be in the car for most of it."

I picked up my cup as I shook my head. "I'm going to walk today. My legs are desperate for a stretch."

"How do you plan to shield yourself when it rains heavily?" She sounded appalled.

"I've walked in it before," I reminded her. "and isn't that the reason I have a raincoat?"

"It's a bit of a ways from here to the water, so it may not help much."

I frowned impatiently at her. "You make this town sound bigger than it really is."

"All right," she surrendered. She stood from her chair and walked to the counter.

The thought of being paranoid again suddenly washed over me.

"Do you have something I could take with me to listen to as I walk?" I asked before she could exit the room. Maybe if my ears were occupied I wouldn't listen for footsteps or worry about what was behind me instead of enjoying my surroundings.

"Somewhere in my room," she answered.

I couldn't help laughing at her facial expressions as she made her statement. She walked out a second later.

I could hear her moving things around before I reached the top of the stairs. I entered my bedroom and headed for the dresser. I knew it was silly to consider a shower before leaving when there was hundred percent chance I'd be caught in the rain. I couldn't help it.

It wasn't but a few minutes later and Bobbie was knocking on the open door. She had a portable CD player in one hand and a stack of CD's in the other.

"I have a variety of music," she said as she handed them to me. "I've heard what station you're listening to so I grabbed what you might like."

"Thank you," I replied. I set them on the end of the bed and turned back to the dresser.

Bobbie watched me pick up my clothes, and then walked to the door. "You're welcome," she said over her shoulder. "I'm going to bed, have fun trying to stay dry."

When I reached Bay Boulevard I changed my mind about walking along the harbor and the tourist shops. I took a detour and walked across Newport's beautiful Yaquina Bay bridge. The arch in the center fascinated me, the view of Yaquina Bay was both mesmerizing and breathtaking from there.

I stopped in the middle of the sidewalk and pulled off the headphones while watching the seagulls as they glided over the bay. Even they were enjoying the break from the rain. It was unusual for there not to be much traffic, yet for a moment it felt as though time had been frozen.

"You're not considering jumping, are you?" came a musical voice.

His voice wasn't loud, but I still jumped at the sound, my head turning sharply in his direction. My eyes instantly traced over his pale white features; the square of his jaw, the curve of his lips ---- twisted up into a cocky grin, seeming to be amused. They continued on to the straight line of his nose, the sharp angle of his cheekbones, to the smooth span of his forehead and finally his dark, damp hair, curling over his brow.

"Not hardly," I snorted. "I don't have a death wish."

"Good," he stated, smugly. "This bridge is well known for its number of deaths and I'm not up for the swim."

I rolled my eyes as I turned back to look out at the water. "What would my jumping have to do with you?"

"What kind of person would I be if I didn't go in after you?" I could hear the smirk in his voice. "And, anyways the water is colder than usual today."

"Well, thank you Captain Obvious," I said, sarcastically. "Had you not informed me of that I wouldn't have known."

Sean laughed.

I saw from the corner of my eye when he stepped closer to me. My heart skipped a beat with each step he took.

"Was there something you wanted, Sean?" I felt a thrill go through me when I said his name and hated it. I fought against myself to keep from looking at him.

"I've heard you're trying to convince Mike to let you leave."

"Not that it's any of your business," I answered bitterly. "but yes."

"Why?" He was confused.

"I left Kansas for a reason. I know they will eventually show up here."

"Ever the pessimist," he growled.

"Yeah, well better a live pessimist than a dead optimist." I tried to mock his growl, though mine didn't sound as fierce as his.

My response surprised him. "Do you even know what the means?"

"Not really," I admitted. "but it seemed like a good answer. Did you honestly follow me just to ask me why I wanted to leave?"

"No, there actually was a reason I stopped when I saw you," he said, serious now. "I have done a lot of thinking about a number of things and I wanted to talk to you."

"About?" I prompted.

I heard him sigh, deeply. "I want to start by apologizing for not being around these past few weeks."

"Why are you so concerned that I might actually care?"

"My," he laughed, the sound almost a roar. "don't we have quite the temperament today."

I gave him a dirty look. "Obviously you don't bring out the best in me. I don't know if you've bothered to notice, but I'm *not* lost when you're not around."

My life is nearly peaceful when I don't see you, I thought to myself. I instantly banished the thought before he saw something on my face and misinterpreted it.

"Angel, I know I said I feel protective of you and you think I'm a hero," he said in a flat voice. "but there's ..." His voice suddenly trailed off as he seemed to struggle for words.

"Too late for misinterpretations," I murmured.

I was usually a nonviolent person ----- seeming how I grew up surrounded with violence, yet in that moment his words sparked my anger. It suddenly felt as though it would burn me from the inside out. I balled my hands tightly around the bars of the bridge.

"I'm glad you know what I think," I said, between my teeth. "I believe I've already said thank you and let it go."

"That is true, you did," he agreed.

"Then why act like I'm an obsessed girl?"

"I'm not," he snapped. His teeth made an audible sound causing me to jump. "I just simply want to tell you we shouldn't be friends, as well as the reason why."

His face was cold, expressionless, even though his voice burned with regret. I wasn't exactly sure what his feeling of regret was for. Did he regret saving my life or did he regret standing here now? He did sound like he was trying to convince himself more than me. I released the bars, turning my body so I could look up at him. It was then I noticed the clouds had gone dark ... rain was minutes away.

"Sean, may I ask you a question?" I asked, calmly.

"Depends on what you want to know." His tone was still harsh.

"Fair enough," I agreed. "Who approached who just now?"

"I did." He looked confused at my question. I didn't let that stop me from getting to my point.

"And who follows who?"

He was still clearly confused. "Again, me."

"Now that I've pointed this out why are you trying so hard to convince *me*?"

He let out a deep breath, the sound was unsteady. "I don't want you taking anything personally when after today I don't speak to you or come near you."

I hadn't ever noticed until now he had a Southern tone or perfect articulation. What century is this family from? I closed my eyes, inhaling deeply through my nose.

"I can promise you I won't lose any sleep over it!"

When I was sure I could keep my voice calm again I opened my eyes. Anger instantly flashed in his, his voice became dark.

"*Dammit*, Angel. I need you to understand how important it is to me that you keep yourself safe."

I felt my blood start to boil again and walked past him with a resigned sigh to keep from doing anything rash.

"Where are you going?" His voice was still angry and bitingly sarcastic.

"Home," I said over my shoulder. "It's going to rain again soon and I'm not going to stand in it, arguing with you."

Since I was no longer looking at him it helped to calm my irritation. I continued to walk, grabbing the headphones and pulled them over my ears.

"Angel, wait," he called out. His voice was velvet soft now.

Despite the effort I was putting into walking away, my legs began to slow without a conscious decision to do so. How does he have this power over me? I forced them to keep moving, suddenly he was next to me, easily keeping pace.

"I'm sorry," he apologized. "*Please*, Angel."

"Please, what?" I growled.

"Try to understand my choices. You have no idea how important you are to me."

I stopped walking and turned my face up so I could look at him. And, I instantly regretted it. His eyes burned with sincerity and for reasons I couldn't fathom, I got the sudden urge to reach up and stroke my fingers through his curly, windblown hair. I fought against it, balling my hands into fist at my sides.

"Have a good day, Sean," I said. I was trying for hateful, but his eyes had my mind spinning, I failed. "I would say I'll see you around, yet somehow I get the feeling I won't."

His eyes widened, staring at me, appearing to be dumbfounded. I looked away, pushed the play button on the CD player and walked away.

When I got home I decided to make potato soup from scratch. It would be a long process, giving me something I could take my frustration out on. This was always therapeutic anytime I had a moment when I couldn't control the situation. It not only helped, but there's no trouble to get into for butchering up vegetables.

I tried concentrating while I cut the potatoes and eventually the vegetables; I didn't want to take a trip to the emergency room. I didn't want *him* thinking I was looking for another way to get his attention since he was no longer going to follow me everywhere. But try as I might, my head was spinning, trying to analyze the conversation and the words Sean said that didn't make much sense then and still didn't.

How can you tell someone they're important to you but you can't be friends? He must believe if he continues being around I will become absorbed over his presence and not focus on my own life. What a crazy gesture! I mean, sure he's gorgeous and aside from that extra-large ego, he's nearly perfect. Even *if* there is something dangerous about him.

Well, either way he clearly isn't interested in trying to continue a friendship with me, I thought sourly.

Of course he wouldn't be interested, I told myself. He already got the thank you he was waiting for and he obviously believes I'm no longer in danger, as Jonah does. I couldn't necessarily blame him, he doesn't know the people I was raised around. Also, I wasn't planning to stay in his precious little town so what would be the point of sparking a friendship?

That was fine! He wants left alone and forgotten, I could easily do that. I wasn't continuing to stay here for him anyway! I would just get through my impending sentence, and then hopefully have quite a bit of money saved by my birthday to get out of here.

Bobbie entered the kitchen as I was pulling the crock pot out of a cabinet.

"You're dry," she said, playfully. "Have you been home long?"

I laughed, though it was without humor. "I got in just before the rain started. I've been here almost two hours." My voice still had a hint of frustration in it.

"I see," she mused. "What are you cooking?"

She stood at the sink, watching as I dumped the potatoes in the pot.

"Potato soup," I answered, hoping I sounded friendlier. "it's an old family recipe."

"Really?" she asked, her tone becoming enthusiastic. "I don't know what I'm going to do if you ever decide to move out."

I carried the cutting board full of chopped vegetables to the pot and dumped them in.

"Why would you say something like that?"

"I haven't had meals like yours since Mom left. If you leave I'll have no choice but to go back to eating sandwiches with macaroni and cheese."

"Didn't she teach you how to cook?" I asked, flabbergasted. I rinsed off the cutting board, and then washed my hands.

Bobbie walked to a cabinet, took out a couple of glasses then went to the refrigerator. "Not this kind of stuff," she admitted. "Since we're discussing food, would you happen to have something in mind for tonight?"

I picked up a dish towel and dried off my hands while pretending to think about it. "How about hamburgers with macaroni and cheese?" I asked with a laugh.

She closed the refrigerator door and walked to me, handing me a glass. "Okay."

Bobbie helped me clean up the kitchen after dinner. She washed the dishes while I cleaned the counter. I figured it was my place to do it since I was the one to butcher potatoes and vegetables all over it. I was headed to the table when three faint knocks came on the door.

"Were you expecting someone?" I asked.

"No," Bobbie answered. She was just as confused as I was. She grabbed the dish towel, drying her

hands as she walked to the door.

I tossed the rag in my hand on the table then pulled out a chair so I could thoroughly wipe down the table.

"It's for you," Bobbie stated as she entered the room.

"Who is it?" The words got stuck in my throat when I looked up. Sean entered a second after Bobbie walked to the sink. "Wh ----- what are you doing here?" I stammered.

My legs suddenly shook so badly I collapsed in the chair to keep from falling to the floor.

There was tension on his face and in his eyes when he spoke. "I wanted to apologize for my previous behavior."

"Angel," Bobbie's soft voice cut in. "would the two of you like some privacy?"

Sean answered for me. "Yes. Thank you."

He flashed her a gleaming smile when she looked at him, dazing her momentarily.

"Okay," she nearly whispered.

Her cheeks were stained with red when she turned away from us. She quickly walked into the foyer and up the stairs. Sean stood motionless till we heard the latch on her door click.

"Do you mind if I sit?" he asked, thawing out.

I hadn't collected myself enough to answer, I only shook my head.

"Thank you." He pulled the chair in front of him out and sat down. "I was trying to explain something when you became difficult and walked away. I would like to give you my reasons for the things I said."

I began to thaw out now, becoming irritated that he called *me* difficult.

"You don't owe me any explanations."

"Will you please allow me to finish?" he asked, sounding annoyed.

I sighed. "Fine then."

"Thank you," he grumbled. "I know you probably think I'm being rude without reason, I assure you I am not. I'm choosing to leave you alone for your own good."

"Why is everyone convinced they know what's best for me?" I growled.

Sean misunderstood the direction of my question, blurting out his own.

"What more do you want from me, Angel?" His voice turned sharp.

"Nothing!" I snapped. "I don't want a *damn* thing. I'm not planning to stay much longer, so I expect nothing more than what you've already done. I've thanked you for what you did despite the fact you still deny it. Now please, let this chapter of our lives close."

Anger flashed in his tawny eyes, his voice came low and harsh. "I really wish things could be that simple!"

A sudden need to hit something came over me and I stood from the chair, grabbing the rag, rubbing it over the table with more force than necessary.

"They can, *if* you allow them to be. You have made your point that you're not interested in a friendship or being anywhere near me, so you're free to go. Honestly, I've got no reason to hold on to you or even simply the need to want to."

He all but jumped out of the chair and forcibly pushed it in. His pretty blue eyes had changed to jet black. How is that even possible?

"You're absurd," he snarled. "I came here to apologize and make things right between us. You're dismissing everything as though nothing these past few weeks have meant a thing to either of us."

Us? Where did he get the idea there is anything between us?

The color of his eyes frightened me a little. I was in no way going to give him the pleasure of knowing it. What is it with this guy, anyway? I just told him I'm not staying around so why can't he leave me alone? I let out a long hiss of a breath. Obviously the man's head was as thick as his accent.

"You keep assuming I want something from you, well I don't. I think the real problem is you want me to give something back, though you don't seem to know what that is or how to ask for it."

"Give it a rest, Angel," he growled. "What could I possibly get from you?"

"I don't know, Sean." I said exhausted. "That's for you to figure out."

He looked down for a moment, and then glanced up from under his lashes with troubled eyes. They were still black, yet they kept me from breathing.

"I suppose neither of us will ever know." His voice was husky. "I've taken enough of your time. I'll just see myself out."

He turned abruptly and walked to the door.

I sank in the chair, unaware I was still holding my breath. My lungs began to burn from going without for so long and I slowly released it as a wave of guilt passed through me. I had barely gotten control of myself when Bobbie walked in.

"Are you all right?" she asked. Concern colored her tone.

"Yes," I breathed.

"Were you with Sean today?" She walked to the sink and picked up the dishes she hadn't gotten rinsed, putting them back in the water.

And the gossip continues. I shook my head, sadly and stood from the chair. "Not the way you're thinking," I amended. "but he did show himself this afternoon."

She gave me an odd expression while she added water to the sink. Great ----- she thinks there's something going on between us. I finished wiping down the table, and then walked to her side.

"You've got to be the luckiest person I know," she mused.

"What makes you say that?"

"You have two of Oregon's finest men so interested in you they're stumbling over their own feet. When you finally stop making them chase you and decide on one them, pick Sean."

"And why would I do that?" I grumbled.

"You are the first person Sean's ever gone through the trouble to see. I mean, sure he's always been friendly. He once helped an old lady by changing her flat tire. For him to just show up here out of the blue, you're clearly important to him, Angel."

"Well ...." I rinsed out the rag I nearly forgot was still in my hand then laid it over the counter to dry.

"... I doubt it's true now. He wasn't very happy with me when he left."

Bobbie's brows were knit in confusion. "That's not what I saw when he looked at you," she disagreed. "He may not have been happy, but feelings like that don't fade away because someone says something you don't like. How did the two of you end up in a heated argument, anyway?"

"He has a multiple personality disorder," I said, flatly.

Bobbie laughed.

I helped finish with the dishes and after lying the last plate on the towel I picked up the dish towel, drying off my hands.

"Angel, would you like my opinion?" Bobbie suddenly asked. She pulled the plug from the sink and began rinsing it out.

"Sure," I said, hoping to placate her.

I knew she would tell me even if I'd said no, so why not encourage her and get it over with? I tossed the towel next to the sink, and then walked to the table and sat down.

Bobbie shut the water off, picked up the discarded towel and began drying off her hands while she walked over to join me. She tossed it over her shoulder as she sat down.

"You may not want to believe me, it was pretty clear from the expression on Sean's face you mean something to him ..."

I groaned.

"Just hear me out," she continued. "Brandi tells me John comes in the diner nearly every day for you. Sean wants your attention for himself and I think the problem is he's not sure how to get it."

Oh, he knows how to get my attention, I said to myself, bitterly.

"When someone is important to you, you don't show up, telling them you can't be friends," I laughed. "Besides, he's got the wrong idea *if* he thinks John is any kind of competition. It is true that I end up serving him more than anyone else, but giving him food is as far as it goes."

"You may not see it as competition, but I bet Sean does. As I've said before, he's never been personal with anyone in the years he has been here, other than you. Therefore, jealousy can blind a person from seeing what is actually real."

"Maybe," I said, sluggishly.

"I don't believe having Sean as a boyfriend is a bad idea, Angel," she grumbled.

"That may be true," I said frostily. "I'm not interested in dating him or John."

She shook her head at me, frustrated. "You're really going to deny yourself the best part of life?" This was the first time I think she's ever been so disappointed with me.

"Since we're discussing relationships," I said. I was desperate to change the direction of the conversation. She was wrong about Sean, I was exhausted trying to explain it. "When are you going to date Josh?"

Her cheeks instantly flushed red and she quickly dropped her head. "It's not like that."

"Really?" I pretended to be shocked. "I saw the way you looked at him a few weeks ago. He appeared to return your interest."

"I guess I'm too shy to say anything." I could hear the embarrassment in her tone.

"You'll figure it out," I said, encouragingly. "Who knows, Josh might get tired of waiting and ask you."

She looked up at me, her expression horrified. I laughed and stood from the chair.

"I'm going to bed. Have fun tonight and stay safe."

The next afternoon I was greeted by Anna and Mark. Marisa had traded shifts with Catlyn so I didn't have to dodge her comments or her glares. I couldn't have been more grateful; nothing was worse than working with someone that had so much dislike for me.

John came in as dinner rush had packed every table, except one. Anna was the only waitress with an open table. I found it odd that he was dressed differently than usual, despite the fact he had his briefcase in his hand. He was dressed in a deep blue, Polo shirt, a pair of denim jeans and tennis shoes. I was close enough to hear the conversation when Anna reached him and tried not to listen. I failed in my attempts ... miserably.

"Welcome, John," Anna said politely. "if you'll follow me I'll seat you at a table."

"Thank you, Anna," he answered, mocking her tone. "If it's all the same to you I'd like to be at one of Angel's tables."

"Angel's tables are booked," she informed him. "It could be quite a wait."

"I don't mind the wait," he said, dismissively.

"Well, all right then. There's a spot open at the counter if you want to have a seat while you wait."

I couldn't believe what I heard. She knew I was working the counter, as well as the tables. I fought a cringe when he passed me and sat down at the end of the counter. I finished taking a customer's order and had no choice but to walk around the counter to put the ticket in the window for Mark.

"Angel," John said as I walked in front of him. Every person sitting there turned their heads toward him. "Are you sure I can't buy you a car? Anything you want it's yours."

I forced my lips to smile. "No. Thank you, Mr. Wilkins, I'm doing great with what I have. Could I get you a drink?"

I tacked the ticket to the window, and then turned back to face him.

"I'll take an Iced Tea while I'm waiting. How about an afternoon in Paris? It is beautiful this time of year."

I finished filling the glass and placed it on the counter in front of him. I tried racking my brain for something to say that would let him down easy. I decided to go with the truth.

"I'm afraid I'm obligated to stay in Newport."

His facial expression was discouraged. "I'm a pretty likable guy." He paused, his hand snaked out, grabbing my left wrist as I turned to walk away. "I promise you'll like me if you gave me a chance."

I tried to pull free of his grasp, he wouldn't allow it. "You must really like yourself."

Now he laughed. "It's all about confidence, Angel. You should have that in yourself."

"I'll see what I can do," I said, artlessly.

He winked at me and released my wrist.

I quickly walked away before he could offer me anything else.

Finally, things slowed down, allowing me to move John to a table. It had been nerve racking with him sitting at the counter, watching my every move. His conversations with his neighbors always centered around me.

"I'm sorry for your long wait, Mr. Wilkins," I stated apologetically. "If you're ready I have a table open."

"I'm ready." He picked up his glass and followed behind me.

I immediately took his order and walked away. I couldn't see the point in lingering near his table when he had kept me edgy all this time.

I walked in the kitchen for a couple more pies and heard a conversation between Anna and Catlyn, they were evidently unaware I was there.

"Did you hear the offer John gave to Angel?" Anna asked.

"Yes, I did," Catlyn answered, sourly.

"Wasn't that something?" Anna was stunned.

Catlyn shrugged, lazily. "John's an all right guy, I suppose. I think she would be better off with Sean. I think they would be a cute couple."

"Sean hasn't been around here in a while," Anna noted. "Angel is one lucky person, she's got two handsome guys falling over themselves for her."

I fought off a moan, as I thought about Bobbie saying that very same thing the night before and slipped past them, heading to the cooler.

"True," Catlyn agreed. "but you know how John is. If it wasn't for the fact that he's trying to get Angel he would have already been gone. Because she's practically family, I don't want her treated that way. I truly believe Sean would treat her better."

They never noticed me and despite the fact they were talking about me I walked out. I knew it was cowardly, I couldn't help it. It really bothered me that everyone was convinced I needed a boyfriend. I was content --- -- better than content ----- I was happy with the way things were.

I noticed empty dishes were stacked on John's table. I wasn't sure I wanted to return to it, especially after his actions at the counter and the fact I heard Anna and Catlyn's conversation.

Stop being a coward, Angel ----- I demanded myself. I held my head up and slowly approached his table.

"Would you like for me to take these?" I asked.

He looked up from the papers he was reading, surprised to see me. "Sure," he said with a smile.

I reached out for the dishes, and suddenly he held up a bill folded in half.

"What's that for?" I was confused.

"Just a small appreciation for the work you do."

"It's my job," I murmured, softly. I hesitantly took it and stuffed it in the pocket on my apron. "Thank you. Please, let me know if I can get you anything else."

"As a matter-of-fact, there is something." He smiled widely at me.

"Of course." I automatically reached in the apron and pulled out a pad of paper and a pen.

"I'd like you to have dinner with me."

My head snapped up, I stared at him in awe. "Excuse me?"

"Since you've gone through the trouble of pulling out that pad of paper," he laughed. "I'd like you to write down your address. It is extremely helpful to know where to pick up a date."

"I'm sorry, Mr. Wilkins, it's not considered professional for me to socialize with my customers. It's very kind of you to ask."

I knew it was crazy to put it like that yet I couldn't think of anything except to get myself out of this situation.

"My name is John," he stated firmly. He wasn't happy with my dismissal. "and it's not about kindness, Angel. It's just simply two people having dinner. I'm sure your boss wouldn't mind that."

I quickly shoved the paper back in my apron and reached for the empty dishes.

"I'll give it some consideration," I said tactfully.

"Take all the time you need." He winked at me.

I turned away, fighting the urge not to run as fast as I could.

When John finally approached the counter Anna and I were rolling silverware.

"I've spoken with Kloe," he informed me. He handed his ticket and credit card to Anna. "She says you're free on Saturday and has no problem with you socializing with me."

He called my bluff; *dang it*! I heard Anna snicker as she walked away.

"I'm sorry, John," I said slowly. "it really is sweet of you to ask, but Saturday is my only day off. I have a number of things I have to get done at home." I was annoyed ----- he obviously wasn't getting the point I simply wasn't interested.

"No is not an option, Angel," he warned.

This could not be happening.

"I'll pick you up at seven," he continued.

"I haven't told you my address." My voice sounded sharper than I was aiming for. He had already used up my patience for the day.

He shrugged. "That's all right, Kloe told me that, too."

And before I could respond Anna handed him his card and he walked to the door. I could feel the shock on my face.

"You're extremely lucky, Angel," Anna sighed, her voice dreamy.

"Some luck," I grumbled.

Anna laughed. "I saw him tip you earlier. How generous was he?"

I had forgotten all about it. "I have no idea."

I reached into the pocket of the apron, pulling out the only bill I had that was folded neatly. Anna's eyes widened in surprise when I unfolded it.

"Fifty dollars!" she exclaimed. "I usually have to wait on three or four tables to make that. Angel, I don't want to pry into your business or tell you what to do, but you're going to have to get to choosing one of them. And, soon."

All I could think was August twentieth wasn't going to get here fast enough.

Changing Faces

I woke later than usual Saturday morning still disgusted. I was in no way thrilled over the idea of what was in store for me. I had spent the last few days trying to find a way out of the awful mess I'd gotten into. The only idea I could come up with was to fake an illness. I would have been ratted out if I even tried it.

It didn't take long for word about my date to spread around the diner. I worked the morning shift with Brandi the next day, that only made things worse. Catlyn had told her what John had done and she had no problem expressing her disappointment I wasn't going to dinner with Sean. However, she was thrilled to know I was finally going out on a date.

"You've been here for two months, Angel," she had said. "I think it's time you allowed yourself to have some fun."

"Brandi," I grumbled. "I'm not interested in dating."

She scowled at me. "It's not every day the most rich, eligible bachelors ask girls like us to dinner. Be fair about it, let him take you somewhere fancy. All you have to do is smile and have fun."

I rolled my eyes, annoyed. "If it's so important to you then *you* go to dinner with John."

"He didn't ask me," she laughed. "besides, I couldn't anyway. *I* have a boyfriend."

"Technically, he didn't ask, he demanded."

She shook her head at me. "What would you whether do; go to dinner somewhere close or take a private jet to Paris?"

My mouth fell open at the thought of knowing how much she knew. I closed it, glaring at her while trying to think of something awful to say. Nothing entered my mind so I turned and stomped away.

Just remembering that day had my face twisting into a scowl. I pushed back the blanket, slowly rolling onto my back. I stared at the ceiling for a long second, and then sat up, swinging my legs over the edge of the bed. I caught the sound of the rain as it began to fall.

"Maybe it'll rain enough to flood out the roads and he'll have no choice but to cancel," I grumbled to the empty room.

I walked to the dresser and opened the top drawer. Maybe if I take a hot shower it will relax the knots in my body and improve my mood.

I was in the middle of making a cup of coffee when the phone rang, shattering the silence.

"Hello?" I asked, warily.

"Good morning, Angel," Brandi's cheerful voice greeted me. "I was hoping you were up."

"No thanks to anxiety," I said, grumpily.

She completely ignored my tone.

"Bobbie told me you don't own any dresses so I'm wondering what you are planning to wear tonight."

I felt my face twist into another scowl. So much for trying to relax.

"She's right," I confirmed. "I don't. Honestly, I haven't given it much thought."

"Angel," she groaned. "you're going to dinner with the mayor's grandson. You can't wear just anything!"

"I know *who* my date is with," I growled. "I may not have a dress, but I do have a couple of nice things I can wear."

"Ugh!" she moaned. "This is going to be much worse than I thought. I have to shop anyways, so I'll see what I can find then bring it by."

"Brandi," I grumbled.

I was too late, she had already hung up.

I mumbled unintelligently to the empty room as I place the phone back on the wall. I picked up my cup and stalked off to the living room.

When the afternoon finally rolled around I had already cleaned the entire downstairs. It helped to keep me from thinking, which would have led to panicking about tonight. Especially, since I now knew Brandi was planning something for me to wear. Now there was a reason to panic. I've seen her dressed up a few times and knew the kind of dresses she considered appropriate for these kind of occasions.

I flopped down on the couch and picked up the remote. I wasn't in the mood to actually watch TV, but I couldn't do anything upstairs while Bobbie was sleeping. My laundry was done and I didn't feel like reading another one of Bobbie's books. I was wound up and anxious enough without any more romantic gestures being put in my head. I considered calling Jennifer to check on Troy and complain about my problems, but then I realized she would already be at work.

I stared at the TV for I don't know how long, trying to figure out something that would ease both my mind and my body. Maybe I could pick out my own dress. Maybe if I already had one then I could call Brandi and tell her not to worry about it. I thought over that a while longer, and then finally decided it was a great idea. I turned off the TV and stood from the couch, and then headed up the stairs.

I grabbed my purse and jacket out of the closet, shoving my arms through the sleeves as I went down the stairs. I stopped in the foyer long enough to grab the keys out of the bowl then flew out the door.

The parking lot of Walmart was nearly empty. This was great. It meant I could park close enough that the dress wouldn't have a chance to get wet before I was able to wear it.

Getting out of the car the toe of my shoe got caught on the pavement. I stumbled, falling forward, then suddenly out of nowhere a pale white arm caught me around the waist.

"I'd hate to see you mess up that pretty face before you got to go on your date," he snickered.

My body instantly snapped upright and I twisted to get free of his arm.

"Messing up my face is my business," I hissed. "so you shouldn't concern yourself with it. How do you know about it, anyway?"

No matter how I twisted or struggled Sean wouldn't free me. Figuring all I was doing was wearing myself out I stopped moving. It was then he carefully released me and stepped back. I turned to face him.

"I believe everyone knows as it has become talk of the town. It isn't difficult for me to hear anything that goes on in the mayor's family when my mom is the mayor's secretary."

That's right, dang it!

"I seriously doubt you've come here to shop or to try giving me dating advice, so what do you want?"

His expressions turned innocent, his sky-colored eyes lightened. "Why would you think I wantsomething?"

I was now skeptical. "Because you say you're important to me, but we can't be friends so stay away, yet you show up the next time with demands."

"Got me there," he agreed. "I'm surprised you were actually listening to me. And, you're right, there is something I'd like you to do for me."

"And the truth shall set you free," I said sarcastically.

Sean ignored the sarcasm. "If we're going for truth then you should turn around right now and walk away from me."

"Oh, right," I glowered. "like you're going to let that happen. I try that nearly every time I see you, yet somehow I still end up talking to you."

He grinned, suddenly amused. "I know you don't care to admit it, but you wouldn't if you didn't like me."

"Ugh!" I groaned. "What do you want, Sean?"

It was starting to rain again. I was losing my patience and much rather preferred not to get wet. The smile on his face faded, a stunned expression twisting his features. He just continued to stare at me.

I shook my head, fully aware of the stubborn set of my chin. "I'm walking away now."

I turned, sloshing angrily through the water puddles to the building.

"I don't want you going out on that date tonight," he suddenly called out.

It was one thing for me not to want to, it was a wholly other for *him* to show up and try making me cancel it. I stopped walking, whirling around to face him.

"Why does it even concern you?" I asked, irked.

"John Wilkins isn't the kind of person a girl like you should spend time with."

"A girl like me?" I hissed, between clenched teeth. "I don't know what that's supposed to mean, but I'm a big girl. Therefore, I go where I please and with whom I please. If you think I'm going to break a date because some overbearing pinhead doesn't want me to go, think again!"

Sean took a few steps towards me then stopped. "Angel, you don't know him like I do. I don't want you to get hurt."

"Wow, this is just a bit out of your character," I laughed, bitterly. "The big, untouchable Sean Callenger is jealous."

"Not jealous," he corrected. His tone was bitingly sarcastic. "Concerned."

"Well, whatever it is you don't need to worry over it. I can take care of myself."

I pushed out my chin and turned on my heels. I meant to sweep dramatically across the parking lot, but I tripped over a piece of the pavement I didn't see was sticking up from the ground. I swiftly straightened myself and stalked off to the building without looking back.

There weren't many dresses hanging on the racks to choose from. They were all some sort of polka dots or stripes. I wasn't fond of either. Of course, I really couldn't concentrate on anything as my mind was still spinning around Sean.

Because he wasn't the first to cast a warning about John I couldn't help wondering if I should fake an illness and cancel. Don't be a coward, Angel, I demanded myself. It was one date, surely you can get through this one night. Since I was now too frustrated I gave up looking through the slim selection and walked away. It looks like I'm stuck with Brandi's dress after all.

The dress Brandi brought for me to wear was worse than any nightmare I've ever had and much worse than anything I feared. It was made of silk and red; a form-fitting glitter of flame. The slit on the side went all the way up to my hip, two skinny straps on the shoulders so thin, if they were to get caught on something they'd tear, easily. The front went to almost the neck, the back dipped much lower causing quite the complaints from me.

"Is this really necessary?" I grumbled. "It's only dinner and no matter what happens tonight there won't be a second time."

"You're supposed to dress fancy when you're going to dinner. It's exceptionally important to dress this way when your date is rich."

I groaned.

Brandi pulled me up the stairs and into the bathroom. I stared helplessly at the counter, Bobbie had covered it in every beauty product she had.

She pushed me down on the toilet and picked up the straightener.

"Wouldn't the natural curls of my hair look better?"

"Have you looked at this dress?" she glowered.

"Okay," I mumbled.

When my hair was as straight as it could possibly be Brandi moved on to mask, buff, and polish every part of my exposed skin.

Once we were back downstairs Brandi made me stand on a stool while she fiddled with the bottom of the dress. As it got closer to time for John to arrive I became fidgety.

"Could you stand still?" Brandi growled. "I can't keep the hemline straight with you moving."

"I'm sorry," I sputtered. "I'm nervous and I feel ridiculous."

"I'm not going to lie by saying I should be dressing you for Sean," she said, her voice dreamy. "but going on a date isn't ridiculous, Angel. It's what people are meant to do."

"I agree this should be Sean picking her up," Bobbie said.

Brandi and I snapped our heads up at the sound of her voice. She was standing in the doorway with a pair of high heel straps hanging off her index finger.

"I don't think I'll ever get the way he looked at her out of my head," she continued.

"You saw that, too?" Brandi asked.

"The day he stopped by to see her. I've never seen him look that way at anyone."

The conversation I had with him flashed through my mind. I felt my face twist into an angry scowl.

"You're both reading too much into it. And, Bobbie didn't you tell me on my first day he's not the dating type?"

"Apparently he isn't interested in us the way he is you."

"Have either of you seen him around since?" I fumed.

Bobbie entered the room, heading to the chair. "Sadly, no."

She placed the shoes on the floor beside the chair and walked over to flop down on the couch.

"All right then," I said, feeling smug. "let it go now."

Brandi finished with the dress and stood up, her eyes looked me over.

"John Wilkins is in for the night of his life," she smirked. "Too bad you're not interested in seeing anything through."

"She's definitely going to make him regret all the womanizing he does," Bobbie laughed. "Angel's the only person of interest he can't promise the world to then sleep with and never be heard from again."

I sat down in the chair, listening as Bobbie talked. Now that I understood why everyone spoke so poorly of John, I thought back to Sean's pleas for me to stop this. Was this what he was trying to tell me? I grabbed the shoes I was sure would send me to the emergency room with a broken neck and put them on.

"I'm only seeing this through so he won't make any more demands on me, as well as get one thing sunk into his head ----- I have no interest in dating him. No matter what he thinks he'll get from this clearly isn't going to happen. It's time for him to return to Portland and remain there."

I stood from the chair for a practice walk around the living room. I stumbled and Brandi caught me before I could fall on my face. Once she was sure I was stable again she released me. She walked next to me so she wouldn't have to run across the room to stop me from crashing to the floor.

"Angel, he's known for making his move on the first date. Just be careful tonight," Bobbie stated.

"I know the type," I informed her. I thought back to Troy Kensley and the way I'd seen him treat the women he dated. "No matter what he tries or how smooth he talks he hasn't got a chance."

I suddenly secretly hoped tonight would be one of the nights Sean would follow me. *If* John tries anything it would be sure to end badly.

There was a brisk tapping on the front door.

"I'll get it," Brandi announced. She half ran to the door.

"Angel, you look ... amazing," came a stunned voice.

I stopped concentrating (it wasn't helping me to walk any better) on trying to walk and turned, slowly to look at him. John was dressed in a deep gray, three-pieced suit, his tie was stripped with light and dark gray. His short black hair was combed neatly, he didn't appear to have any gel in it.

"Thanks," I blushed. "You look nice yourself."

"Are you ready to go?" he asked, earnestly.

"As ready as I'll ever be." I tried to sound confident, though it didn't quite come across that way.

John turned his body sideways, holding his left elbow out at me. "May I escort you out?"

I was beginning to understand why girls fall for him. He was quite charming and was full of manners, still I wasn't going to fall for it. Under normal circumstances the answer would have been no. I didn't want to take the chance of walking alone and end up on my face. Though it would definitely get me out of this date, I mused. It was tempting but I wouldn't be able to stand the humiliation.

"Sure," I said, hesitantly.

I walked slowly to him and looped my arm through his.

"Bobbie ... Brandi," John said, politely. "it was nice seeing you again."

"You, too," they giggled in unison.

I rolled my eyes as I fought the urge to shake my head.

John appraised me after he got in the driver's seat of his Ferrari.

"You really look extravagant tonight. I've made reservations at a little place in Toledo."

"You want to drive the extra twelve minutes just to have dinner?" I was confused.

"They have a place perfect for a night like this." He started the car and drove away from the house.

I was quiet on the ride. I couldn't get the brief encounter with Sean out of my head. It wasn't the conversation that had my heart pounding now or my thoughts spinning. It was the way my heart had raced wildly to his touch, the way his arm had slipped effortlessly around my waist. I'd fit perfectly in the contours of his arm like we were corresponding pieces of a puzzle made to match up to each other.

I felt the car slow and looked up. John was pulling in the parking lot of the waterfront restaurant. I saw the cobblestone sidewalk and tried not to think of the horror I faced as I walked it in heels. John opened my door and offered me his hand. I was hesitant, but I placed mine in it, letting him help me out. The walk to the door was a slow pace.

The restaurant wasn't crowed, but it was busy. The host was a pale blond female and I was suddenly aware she knew John as her eyes assessed him. She welcomed him with a little more excitement than necessary.

John gave his name to her as though she didn't already know it. I figured it was probably for my benefit, trying to make a good impression. I held my head still so it wouldn't shake involuntarily and forced a smile on my lips when he looked at me.

"Your table is ready, Mr. Wilkins. If you'll just follow me."

She picked up two menus and led us around a small ring of booths to an upper level where only a few tables sat ----- all of them empty. She placed the menus on the table.

"Your server will be with you shortly." She walked away.

"I think you have an admirer," I said as I sat down.

"When everyone knows who you are it comes with the territory." His voice was unemotional.

And then our server arrived. The look in her eyes when she looked at John was the same as the hostess's had been. I couldn't help wondering how many women he'd fooled into believing they were the *one*.

"Hello. My name is Carly and I'll be your sever tonight. What can I get you to drink?" It was hard to miss that she was only speaking to him. Her eyes never flashed to me, I was apparently invisible.

John looked at me. I guess I wasn't invisible to him.

"I'll have an Iced Tea," I said.

"Two Iced Teas," he said.

"I'll be right back with those," she said. She tucked a piece of her dark hair behind her ear and walked away.

I pretended to have an appetite, studying the menu while secretly trying to slip out of my shoes. The straps were tightened too much and wouldn't allow me to kick them off. John had chosen the only table that looked out over the water. The only activity around us was the candlelight flickering against the walls.

"Why do you give someone a hard time when they ask you out to dinner or anything in particular?" John asked.

"I don't mean to," I lied. "I have no intention of making Newport a permanent place for me. I'd much whether nobody gets attached."

"I think you are much too late for that."

Our server returned before I could respond. And again, her focus was on him.

"Do you know what you would like?" she asked after she set our glasses on the table.

John pushed my glass to me. "Angel, have you decided on anything?" He completely ignored her.

"I think I'll just have the chicken strips and a bowl of cottage cheese."

She had no choice but to look at me now. "Would you like shrimp added to your cottage cheese?"

"No, thank you." I closed my menu and pushed it towards John.

"What about you?" She eagerly turned her attention back to him.

"I think I'll have the steak and shrimp dinner. Could you please be sure the steak is medium-rare?" He picked up our menus and handed them to her.

"I sure will." She smiled widely at John and walked away.

"Is there a reason you're not interested in the sleepy little town?" He kept his eyes locked on my face while he picked up his glass.

"No," I laughed. "I grew up in a small town so that doesn't bother me. How about you ----- what's it like growing up in Portland?"

My reasons for not wanting to stay was none of his business and I wasn't giving him fuel to deepen his interest in me. He chatted endlessly; he told me about the travels during the summers of his youth. He gave me glimpses of London, France and parts of Europe. It was much to my surprise impossible not to relax, not to be charmed by him. Even as he grew up surrounded by riches and politics. He didn't, as most people like him often did, talk constantly of it.

When my thoughts drifted back to Sean I doubled my determination to enjoy myself. I wasn't giving him anymore of my thoughts or my time.

"I feel like I'm talking about myself too much," John laughed.

The waitress approached us and placed our dishes on the table in front of us.

"Could I get you anything else?"

"I believe this is fine," John replied. He never bothered to look at her.

"Enjoy your dinner," she said as she walked away.

John returned to our conversation as though she had never been there.

"I'd like to thank you for a delightful dinner."

"You're welcome." I reached out for my glass and took a long drink. "I can't say I understand your insistence."

"I wanted a chance to get to know you. What better way to do that then dinner. I hope you don't mind."

I didn't answer.

We lapsed in silence for a while, neither of us having much to say. I just wanted to get through dinner and get back home before it got too late. I was scheduled for the morning rush. Brandi was going to be there and I had hopes of getting through the day without her interrogations. John managed to find a topic to discuss that didn't cater to our lives. I hoped my lack of interest in personal discussions would finally sink in his head that nothing would ever spark between us.

Our server returned again to remove the empty dishes. This time she didn't try to linger or try to get John's attention.

"Could I interest you in dessert?" he asked before she walked away.

"I'm afraid I'll have to pass. It's getting late and I have to work early in the morning."

He waved her off and looked at his watch. "You're right," he agreed. "it is much later than I thought. I still have a few things to do before I leave tomorrow. I have to be in court Monday morning."

We stood from our chairs and walked to the counter. I stood next to the door while he paid our bill then we walked out of the restaurant. Once again, I held on to his arm for dear life as we walked to his car.

He did most of the chatting on the way back to Newport. His topics were general, he spoke of his trip back to Portland, the things that were in store for him the rest of the week and his hopes of being able to return to Newport for the weekend. Despite my efforts of discouraging him, he didn't have to say why he wanted to return. I already had a good idea.

When we pulled up in front of Bobbie's house he parked and walked me to the door. I expected to see the curtains move as Bobbie tried to spy on us. The kitchen light was the only one burning, the curtain never moved.

"Angel, I hope this doesn't come across as pushy, but I'd like to see you when I get back," John said as I opened the door.

"John, I -----"

"Nothing special this time," he said, a charming smile crossing his lips. "We'll make it very casual, a movie perhaps."

"I don't think so," I said tactfully. "I have a very busy schedule."

"What if I call on Friday to see what the weekend is like for you?" He sounded desperate.

"Are you aware that I'm only seventeen?" I asked.

"I have been informed of that," he confirmed. "I've also been informed that your eighteenth birthday isn't far off so there's nothing illegal here. Grandad says Mike is only forcing you to stay until it is determined on what is going to happen with Jeremy."

So he's known all along? Wonderful.

"Well … thank you for the dinner." I was the one who was desperate now.

"So, Friday?" he asked again.

I couldn't answer and he certainly didn't give me the chance. He slowly leaned in toward my face, his eyes closely watching me. It took a few seconds for me to understand what he was doing. When it finally sank in he was going to kiss me I quickly turned my head and his lips touched my cheek, instead.

"Again, thank you," I said in a rush and stepped inside the open door before he could try kissing me again.

I closed the door then walked in the kitchen.

"Did you have a good time?" Bobbie asked. She was sitting at the table writing on a pad of paper.

I shrugged. "It wasn't as bad as I thought it would be. He's practically begging to see me again."

She looked up, her eyes wide with shock. "That's a first," she sputtered. "Are you going to go out with him again?"

I shook my head back and forth. "No. I'm not interested in him so what would be the point in leading him to believe something that isn't real? And anyways, tonight felt ... awkward."

Bobbie laughed at my reluctance. "Dating for the first time usually does feel awkward."

"I suppose so. Well, I'm going to shower so I can wash this stuff off then go to bed."

"Okay, good night."

I turned and trudged up the stairs.

I awoke early Monday morning to the sound of the rain pinging against the bedroom window. For the first time in a week I woke up with a feeling of relief. It was my day off and I didn't have to live through anymore embarrassment from my friends. Brandi was the worst; she waited in the empty dining room, pouncing the second I walked in. She was shocked when I told her about John nearly begging for me to go out with him again over the weekend. Apparently he never sees the same girl twice.

I pushed back the blanket and climbed out of bed. I opened my door and carefully crept across the floor and down the stairs. I went into the kitchen and headed straight for the coffee pot, pulling the coffee can out of the cabinet. Once I had the pot set to brew I replaced the coffee can, and then took out a bowl and a box of cereal. It was then I noticed the cabinet was low on food, it was my turn to buy.

I poured milk in my bowl and walked to the table. It was raining heavily now so I wasn't in a hurry. I ate the cereal one piece at a time while staring mindlessly out the kitchen window. When I was finished I rinsed out the bowl, placed it upside down on the towel, and then poured myself a cup of coffee. I grabbed a pen and a pad of paper from a drawer under the counter and took them to the table.

I made out the grocery list, left it on the table and returned to my room so I could dress and get my jacket and purse. It wasn't easy keeping the stairs from making noise while I walked up and down them, but somehow I had success. I donned in the jacket and place the strap of the purse over my head as I entered the kitchen for the list, and then headed out the door.

The parking lot of the Thriftway was nearly full, forcing me to park at the far end. It had stopped raining and I had hopes it would wait till I was back home to start again. Getting out of the car I instantly stepped in a water puddle. Of course, I thought sourly.

I pulled the list out of my purse while I walked beside the car. It wasn't even a second later and a small gust of wind blew across the lot, taking the paper out of my hand. I turned, watching helplessly as it landed in the puddle of water next to the car. Could this day be any better?

I pondered leaving it and going on, but my noble side reminded me that if I did I'd end up forgetting something important. I grumbled, completely disgusted and bent over to retrieve it. I had only gotten half way down when a pale white hand snaked out and snatched it. I jerked upright, my body moved stiffly, almost unwillingly to turn around. Sean was leaning against the car grinning, seeming to be amused.

Are you serious!? This could not be happening!

"It looks like someone's having a rough afternoon," he snickered. He held the paper out to me.

For a fraction of a second I considered snatching it out of his hand. The top was wet and I knew if I did it would tear in half.

"I'm having a great day," I said, icily. I pulled the paper free of his hand, careful not to tear it. "So much for not coming near me or talking to me."

His lips curved up at the corners. "You looked like you could use some help and I clearly remember someone saying she needed time to adjust to my presence, times up. Besides, the day we had that conversation I was still undecided on a few things myself."

I wasn't sure if I should have been grateful or irritated. "Undecided, right."

I turned to walk away and his hand suddenly snaked out, catching my elbow. My heart instantly flew into a frenzy.

"I don't like being grabbed," I hissed. I fought to free my arm of his grasp.

"In general or just by me?" he asked.

He held onto me until I stopped fighting. His eyes had a speculative look in them, it seemed irritation was winning out over amusement.

"Both." His expressions made sounding hateful difficult.

"That's too bad," he grinned, recovering his good humor. "I have a strong feeling I'm going to be doing more of it."

I glared at him while trying to think of something awful to say. His eyes began to darken in color and I lost my train of thought. I turned away from him and walked towards the building. I expected him to instantly appear beside me like all the times before; he didn't. Then suddenly I heard him laugh.

"What would you say if I were to tell you that *I* want you, Angel?" he called out to me.

I kept walking, ignoring his twisted sense of humor. Now he appeared at my side, easily keeping pace.

"I will credit you for listening to me when I said you should stay away from me. I guess I'm the one who can't simply do it so I'm not disappearing out of your sight anymore."

I stopped walking, scowling up at him. "Do you want me to say I'm flattered by your change of decisions?" I growled.

His eyes narrowed. "No."

"Good!" I snapped. "Because I'm not." With how hard my heart was pounding while I continued to stare at his face that wasn't entirely true. That was something he didn't need to know. "Honestly, Sean, I'm still waiting for you to tell me what it is you want. If you're not then leave me alone."

His expression was stunned, his blue eyes were more liquid than solid. I instantly felt guilty for my outburst. The longer he stood staring at me my heart skipped a few beats. I hated the feeling of weakness his eyes could somehow pulse through me and took advantage of his speechlessness by walking away.

"I want your friendship," he suddenly called out.

I kept walking, though I was unable to maintain the same level of irritation. It amused him every time I stopped to give him attention, there was no way I was giving him the satisfaction. Not this time.

"Angel, wait," he pleaded.

Try as I might to keep walking I couldn't stop my legs from slowing, giving into his plead. I shook my head, sadly and turned to face him.

"Do you take medication for your personality disorder?" I asked, irked.

He pressed his lips together, fighting a smile as he walked to me. "No, why?"

"Maybe you should." I tried again for hatefulness and failed ... miserably. "What happened to we can't be friends?" I threw his words back at him.

"I said we *shouldn't* be friends," he corrected. "not that we can't."

I tossed my hands in the air, angrily. "Boy, am I glad you finally cleared up that misunderstanding. Maybe now I'll be able to sleep at night." Heavy sarcasm.

Anger flashed in his eyes, his lips pressed together in a line, all signs of humor gone. "How is it you can agree to go on dates with that spineless *Wilkins*," ----- he sneered on his name ----- "but you won't agree to simply being friends with me?"

My response came out in a rush.

"First of all, I didn't agree to that date, he pushed it on me. Secondly, when I told you I wouldn't cancel ..." His blue eyes scorched from under his lashes, hypnotic and deadly causing me to run out of steam. I shook my head a few times, needing to regain control of my now tangled thoughts.

"Oh, my God," I sputtered. "I am not having this conversation with you."

I turned to walk away.

"What do you mean he *pushed* it on you?" His voice was dark.

The sound creeped me out, but I kept walking. "You know, Callenger, you're kind of cute when you're jealous," I said over my shoulder. "And, I'll think about it."

He caught up with me when I reached the shelter of the store's overhang. I looked up at him, intending to make a witty remark, but something in his expressions stopped me.

"So you think I'm just going to let you walk away this time?" he asked, a slow, cocky grin spreading across his lips.

Sean slowly backed me against the wall, casually setting both hands on it, caging me between.

My eyes narrowed. "*If* you were a gentlemen, you would."

"It's funny how you don't believe I am," he laughed. "Most of the people around here think I'm an amiable guy."

My heart was pounding erratically, making it difficult to speak rationally.

"I certainly don't see that from where I'm standing."

"Maybe you should stand closer," he suggested.

At that I had to laugh, though the sound was shaky and breathless. "I do believe this is close enough. What I don't believe is amiable; more like cocky, annoying, egoistical or even tenacious."

"I like tenacious," he grinned, amused. He leaned down towards me, his face stopping inches away and let his icy cold breath graze the skin on my face. It smelled of a sweet citrus and was almost intoxicating. "A person don't get too far if they cave in every time they run into a wall. After a while you learn how to climb over it or just simply knock the *damn* thing down."

He moved closer to me and I quickly placed my hand on his cold, hard chest, stopping him. I was already struggling to breathe.

"Or he keeps beating his head against it till he gets a concussion," I offered.

"That's sure to be a great risk," he laughed. "though it would definitely be worth it if the person behind it looked at them the way you're looking at me right now."

"I am not looking at you in any kind of way," I hissed.

"When you forget to hide your attraction to me you do. Those big green eyes get all admirable and soft."

There's only one solution here, Angel, I said to myself. Escape.

"Well ..." I paused to clear a lump out of my throat. " ... this has certainly been fun, but I need to be on my way."

His eyes became gloriously intense, his voice smoldering. "Are we friends?"

The look in his eyes clouded my mind. My voice evaded me.

"Angel?" He was beginning to grow impatient with my silence. I couldn't recover fast enough to

answer so I nodded.

"Good." He stepped backwards, smiling in triumphant. "I'll get out of your way so you can do your shopping. I'll see you later, bright eyes." He turned on his heels, walking back the way we came. "Enjoy your shopping," he called over his shoulder.

I walked in the store, dazed. I immediately felt eyes on me and looked over at the check-out stands. The cashier was staring at me, her eyes were full of concern. I didn't want her to question me so I forced myself to pull it together and grabbed a cart then went in search of the things on my list.

When I got home I unlocked the door, entering as quietly as possible. I placed the keys in the bowl and walked to the kitchen, placing the bag in my arm on the table. I heard the sound of faint footsteps on the porch and continued to ignore it, pulling the strap of my purse down my arm.

"The last of the bags are on the porch," came a soft, musical voice.

I instantly whirled to the sound. Sean was passing me, carrying an arm load of bags to the counter and gently set them down.

"What are you doing here?" I asked. I was stunned.

"What's it look like?" he answered, sarcastically. "I'm helping unload the car. It's raining again so I thought you might like to stay dry."

"I don't know if I'm lucky or cursed today," I moaned.

Sean laughed, the sound bitter. "I'd say both. Are you going to get the others or just stand there looking at me with suspicion?"

"Do I have a reason to be suspicious?" I asked, inadvertently.

"Is it really so hard for you to believe the kindness someone shows you doesn't mean they want

something in return?" His voice was frustrated.

I felt irritation begin to surface and bit down on my bottom lip to keep from snapping at him. Because now I needed the space from him I turned and walked out to retrieve the bags he placed on the porch.

Sean was sitting at the table when I walked back in the kitchen. I stalked past him, keeping my eyes straight ahead. I set the bags on the counter and began unloading them.

After a while the silence began to weigh on me and since Sean wasn't offering a conversation I racked my brain for something that would get him talking. He irritated me beyond a doubt, but there was something about the way he talked that also fascinated me.

"You're following me again, aren't you?" I asked, casually.

"I really wasn't today. I got tired of sitting at home and went for a drive. I was passing the store when I saw you pull in the parking lot." He was unrepentant.

"What would you be doing if I had to work so you couldn't sit here and watch me put groceries away?"

I could hear the shrug in his voice when he answered. "I knew you didn't ... is there a reason everything you touch has to be neat?"

I gave him a dirty look. "No, why?"

He rolled his eyes at me and pointed his index finger towards the cabinet. "Take a close look at how you stacked those boxes."

I looked back at the cabinet, not understanding the reason for his question. "Old habit, I guess."

The conversation ended again. I finished putting things in the bag away, and then folded it up and tossed it in the trash can.

"Since we've cleared up the confusion over your freedom for today," Sean said, breaking the long silence. "could I interest you in going for a drive with me?"

His question was unexpected and I nearly dropped the jar of tomato sauce now in my hand. I walked a little faster to place it in the cabinet next to the stove before my shaking hand dropped it, anyway.

"Why would I want to do that?" I asked, horrified.

As quickly and soundlessly (well, soundlessly for someone normal, obviously not me) as a bird taking off in flight Sean was out of the chair and turning me to face him.

"I'm going to get you over this fear of me, one way or another."

"I'm not afraid," I lied. "I'm just asking why you want me to go anywhere with you."

He reached out, catching a stray lock of hair and wound it back in place. The expression on his face wasn't angry, though it wasn't amused, either. The sudden proximity of his closeness, his cold, stone hands lightly pressing against my shoulders had my heart pounding, wildly.

"Calm down, bright eyes," he grumbled. "I only wanted to show you something other than this house or the diner."

"I've already seen other places," I breathed.

"Going with that little weasel to Toledo doesn't count," he growled. He dropped his head, leveling his eyes with mine. "Just give me the chance to prove I won't hurt you. To be truthful, I couldn't if I wanted to."

So he was following us. And, what does he mean, he couldn't *if* he wanted to?

"Sean," I barely whispered.

"Oh," Bobbie's voice suddenly gasped. "Angel, I'm sorry. I didn't know you had company."

I was so lost in the depths of Sean's blue eyes I never heard her come down the stairs. If Sean had heard her he never showed it. He kept his eyes on me for a second longer, and then stood upright, carefully turning to face Bobbie.

"Hello, Bobbie," he said, his voice soft as velvet.

"Er, hi, Sean," she replied in a faint voice. She looked at me, her eyes wide with shock. "If you need another minute I'll go back upstairs."

I released a deep sigh, grateful for the distance from Sean. I opened my mouth to answer when Sean answered for me.

"That won't be necessary, Bobbie. I need to be on my way."

She answered him without taking her eyes off me. "Are you sure?"

Sean laughed. "Yes." He waited till she moved from the doorway to pass her. "You ladies have a good evening. Angel, I'll see you later."

I couldn't do anything but nod my head. He winked at me and a second later he was gone.

"Wow," Bobbie said, seeming to get her bearings back. "this is twice now that he's been in my kitchen. Did the two of you get something worked out?"

I returned to the counter to unload another bag. "I don't know that we worked anything out. I bumped into him while I was shopping and he said he'd like to try being friends after all."

There was no way I could even begin to tell her what really happened. I thought over how he had caged me against the wall. That was definitely something I didn't want to tell her. She was already getting the wrong ideas and I clearly wasn't going to give her the fuel for her imagination to run wild.

"So ... does this mean he's going to be around a lot?"

"What do you mean by *a lot*, exactly?"

She slowly shook her head back and forth. "Angel, you have gotten yourself in quite a mess."

"Tell me something I don't already know," I grumbled.

I finished putting away the groceries, cleaned up all the bags, and tossed them in the trash can. I could feel her watchful eyes on me and knew there was something more she wanted to say. I was now desperate for an escape.

"I'm going to change," I announced to her. "I'll be back down to start dinner shortly."

I turned, disappearing into the foyer before she could say anything and nearly ran up the stairs.

When I entered my room I closed the door, and then walked to the bed, flopping down on it. My mind swirled around images of Sean from the first time my eyes ever looked at him to the last second before he slipped out the door. There were things I didn't understand, like how he feels so different from me. My skin is soft and warm; his is ice cold and smooth as marble stone. The other thing I struggled to understand was the way my heart reacts to him.

As I thought about everything I knew there was one thing I was absolutely sure of. I *was* erratically and mindlessly falling in love with him. The only question that remained was; could he even love back?

A New Shade Of Blue

As the days continued to pass a deeper depression than I've ever felt began to surface. I took more hours at the diner so I could keep my mind off of it and keep it from alerting anyone. The constant surrounding of green and the rain only worsen the depression. Because I was still stuck here I was beginning to miss colors like brown, blue and even red. Even with all the rain that fell here there was hardly ever a rainbow, giving the gray sky other color options. Everything in Oregon was green.

I came home Thursday afternoon and lying on the table was a Fed Ex envelope addressed to me. I tore it open and reached in, pulling out a hand written letter along with another envelope. I immediately recognized the penmanship as Jennifer's. It wasn't a long letter, yet her words had my breath stuck in my throat as I read what she had wrote:

Angel,
I've been keeping an eye out for the mail at your dad's house. This letter came and I had to get it to you. Hope it's good news. Jen

I laid her letter aside and looked over the envelope she'd sent. It was from Juilliard. My knees must have started to shake because the walls were suddenly wobbling. I could hear the blood pounding faster than normal behind my ears. I gripped the table, slowly easing myself into the chair behind me. The envelope fell out of my hand and I just couldn't bring myself to pick it up and open it.

The next morning I woke to an unusual sight. A clear yellow cast of light was streaming across my bedroom floor. Unable to believe it, I hurried to the window for a better look. I could see the clouds on the horizon and knew the sun wouldn't be out long. I suddenly felt a desperate need to be in it; I needed to stand in it while turning my face up at that beautiful shade of yellow and feel the warm rays on my skin. I dashed away from the window to get dressed.

I wasn't sure what I wanted to do as I drove around town. I still had a few hours before I had to work and I wasn't feeling the need to be in the company of people. The closet thing Newport had to home besides Walmart was a Good Will store. I hadn't been able to stop in and decided I may as well do it now. Maybe I'd find something that would help bring me up, if only for a little while.

I threw a glance toward the library as I pulled in the parking lot of the Good Will store. I briefly thought back to the one night I'd met Sean's sister. Kelsey was strikingly beautiful like Sean and Jonah, though her personality had been much different. I had thought it was crazy when she came up with the idea her and I could become friends. Then again, I *did* agree to being friends with Sean. That was probably crazier.

I parked as far from the building as the parking lot allowed. It wouldn't be long and the warm air and the blue sky would give way to the green-gray cast and the rain. This gave me the opportunity to enjoy the sun while it was still here.

Despite the size of the store there wasn't a big selection of anything but clothes. Several long racks lined the center of the floor and full with shirts of every size and color. There was one rack that only jeans and pants hung from. Some of them looked as though they were left over from decades ago. Each rack ranged in sizes from men's all the way down to children and infants. I wasn't interested in the clothes and passed them to look at the items on the shelves lining the walls.

They were covered in a wide range of knick-knacks, board games, dishes and an endless variety of books. None of which held any interest for me. I was never a fan of the Silhouette romance novels.

When I reached the back wall that was lined with only shoes I started to give up on finding anything. And then there is was, the answer to helping to resolve some of my depression. An electric keyboard was sitting on a stand in the corner all by itself. Unable to believe what I saw I raced to it. An organ or a piano is better for playing Gospel music by far because these weren't made for such things, but I could still manage to play something.

It was hard not to tell it had been there for some time. The keys were covered in a thick, heavy dust. I blew what I could off, and then looked to see if it was plugged in, it was. I turned it on, pushed on one key and a wide smile crossed my lips from the sound.

"You're the first person I've seen bother to play that old thing," came a soft, friendly voice.

My head instantly snapped up at the sound. A slightly large, older woman was standing a distance from me. Her hair was nearly covered in gray, her lips were formed in a warm smile.

"I'm sorry, ma'am," I apologized. "I saw it and couldn't resist."

"It's all right, dear," she chuckled. "it's nice to hear a sound other than the chime on the door. That poor thing has been sitting back here for months. I had given up all hope someone would take it home."

I took a quick scan over the keyboard, looking for a price tag. I was sure one hung somewhere.

"How much are you asking for it?" I asked when I didn't find one.

"The stand is the only thing that comes with it," she informed me.

"That's fine," I said with a shrug. "I don't really need anything else."

"Well then," she answered with a smile. "twenty dollars young lady and it's yours."

I bent over to unplug the keyboard and she walked away.

I carried the keyboard and the stand to the front counter, and then went to see what else I could find. I thought of Bobbie as I browsed the rest of the store. She had been so nice to me and helped me when I didn't have anyone else. Nothing I found in here would cover even half of that, but it would still show her the appreciation I felt. And again, I started to give up when a pair of cow salt and pepper shakers caught my attention. I couldn't resist their cheesy smiles and knew Bobbie would love them. I eventually paid for everything then left the store.

In the short time I was inside the store the clouds had moved back in, taking away the sun and the blue sky. I was disappointed the sun was gone, but it didn't change my mood. I was still happy. My eyes flashed to the library while I placed the keyboard and the stand in the trunk. I didn't have anymore flashbacks after the one night in Walmart's parking lot so I was now able to use the trunk without fear.

The one and only conversation I had with Kelsey entered my mind. I had acted poorly with her when she was only trying to be friendly. And, I did give Jonah my word I would *try* being friendlier and more relaxed with his family.

I closed the trunk lid and headed across the street to the library. My pulse raced, wildly, my palms were so sweaty I had to wipe them over my jeans many times and I wasn't even inside yet. I stopped at the door, making sure I still had my breathing under control, and then opened it. I walked ever so slowly inside.

My eyes instantly began to look around as I walked. The inside wasn't as large as the outside had made it look. Now I understood why I never saw too many cars in the parking lot whenever I drove past. Then again, the librarian wasn't someone of the usual kind, either.

I listened for footsteps while I searched for Kelsey. As silly as I knew it was, I couldn't help feeling like one of those girls you see in horror films, looking for a way out and runs into a serial killer. I secretly shivered and banished the thoughts from my mind. I was nervous enough without scaring myself to death. I passed a row of shelves and looked down the long aisle for Kelsey.

"It's about time you decide to show up," came a scornful voice.

I whirled around and Kelsey was standing inches behind me, her arms crossed over her chest. It took another few seconds for me to respond, I had to get my heart out of my throat. We stood there for a moment, staring at each other in silence, both listening to my heart rate slow.

"Kelsey, you scared me," I croaked. "I'm sorry I haven't been here, I've been busy."

"I don't consider going on dates with someone I wouldn't pass off on my worst enemy, being busy." She sounded so much like Sean it made me wonder how I missed that before.

"Why does everyone keep mentioning that?" I mumbled.

"We wouldn't *if* you bothered to spend time with someone who actually cares about you."

I opened my mouth to defend my actions when the meaning of her words sank in. I closed it and just stared at her.

"I heard you turned down my brother's offer to spend time with him."

"I did," I verified, confused.

"Why?" she asked. Her voice was disapproving.

"He hasn't exactly made my life easy, not to mention one time he tells me to stay away from him and the next he wants to be demanding."

She laughed, the sound was dark. "That's my brother. He never can make up his mind what he wants and he complains about me. Then again, he hasn't been quite the same since you showed up."

In that instant her last statement brought back something close to that she'd said before.

"What does that even mean?"

She rolled her eyes and sighed as though I should have already known the answer. "Sean has always been Jonah's lookout. He would keep watch on things Jonah and Mike couldn't. After finding you Sean can't seem to keep his focus on anything but *you*. That's why I think the whole "let's just be friends" idea is bogus."

Kelsey dropped her arms and turned to head for the counter. This time I was the one to follow.

"What do you want me to do?" I asked, annoyed.

She picked up a stack of books then turned to face me.

"You have the power to make him do anything you want. Take things in a different direction," she suggested.

"Kelsey," I groaned. "I'm not looking for relationships or commitments."

She frowned impatiently at me. "I know you're anxious to get out of here, although I don't understand why. You clearly don't have any family anywhere or anything better to go to."

The letter from Juilliard that I carried unopened in my purse suddenly felt heavy. I almost told her she was wrong, and then I realized that since I've never bothered to open it she may not have been so wrong.

"I have things in my past -----."

"Jonah's watching Troy, Angel. *If* he even thinks you're in danger ... well, let's just say he won't make it anywhere near you or make any more trouble for you."

Her tone wasn't harsh, but the meaning of her words had me shivering with fear. I thought about asking her what she was going to say, but then her butterscotch eyes became intense.

"Just give Sean a chance, Angel," she continued. "I can assure you it's a decision you won't regret."

I doubt that, I said to myself. I've had nothing but bad decisions, starting from the night I left home.

"I've agreed to being friends with him. In no way am I going to push beyond that."

Kelsey tilted her head to one side and stuck out her lower lip. She softly blinked her long lashes, her amber colored eyes began to glow. I stared at her, instantly becoming defenseless as my breathing and heart rate slowed down. My heart beat was barely above a faint pulse.

"All I'm asking you to do is try," she said, her voice smooth as velvet. "You may just find what you never realized you actually wanted."

I knew she was waiting for a response and I wondered how she could expect one when I couldn't breathe. The longer I went without being able to draw even a single breath I could feel my lungs slowly begin to collapse. All I could do to save myself was nod my head at her.

"Good," she said, smugly. I felt her sudden release.

My heart pounded faster, hammering so hard against my chest I thought it might explode. My breathing came hard and quick causing me to feel very dizzy. I leaned forward, placing my hands on my thighs for support and closed my eyes.

"It's such a shame that you don't trust people, Angel," Kelsey's voice stated, her tone thoughtful. "Sean will never hurt you. I'm still clearly confused myself over why they are denying the rescue, but even still truth or not Sean did save your life."

"Are you suggesting I hand it over to him as payment for his kindness?" I asked, weakly.

Kelsey laughed. "It's not quite the punishment you're making it out to be. Besides, Sean will only accept it *if* you're willing to be with him. You have to make the choice all on your own."

"Lucky me," I said under my breath.

The dizziness finally passed and I slowly stood upright. Kelsey's eyes were watching me, though they were no longer glowing.

"Now that we've had the chance to hash out that issue, do you want to sign up for a card?"

I barely shook my head. "I didn't actually come in here for one and from the looks of this place there isn't much of a selection, anyway."

She shifted her weight to one foot and placed a hand on her hip. Judging from the expression on her face I braced myself for another one of her pouts.

"I'm sure you have to be on your way so I suppose I'll let it go. This time."

I had no idea how much time I'd lost, but I was suddenly desperate enough to want out of there.

"I actually do," I confirmed. "I just stopped in here for a minute to talk with you."

Her eyes narrowed, suspicion twisting her features. "I think there was something in particular you wanted to know."

I pressed my lips together, staring at in her in awe.

"You're good," I finally complimented her. "There are a few things I'd like to know that your brother won't tell, but I'm pressed for time."

"We'll have plenty of time to talk again soon."

I briefly nodded my head at her, and then turned on my heels to walk away.

"Oh and, Angel?" she called out.

"Yeah?" I said over my shoulder.

"Don't forget what we discussed." Her tone wasn't bitter, but I clearly heard the meaning behind the words.

"I won't," I promised.

I quickened my pace to the door.

The air outside had gotten cooler and instantly burned my lungs when I exited the door. I leaned against it, giving my organs a chance to catch up before I passed out. That was the last thing I needed. After a few minutes I took several slow, deep breaths, and then walked down the stairs and crossed the street.

Bobbie was picking the paper up from the porch when I pulled in front of the house. I didn't notice she was waiting for me till I opened the trunk and pulled out the keyboard.

"You play those kinds of things?" she asked, her voice louder than usual.

"Yes," I nearly yelled back.

When she saw me pull the stand out she came to the car to help.

"I can't wait to hear you play," she said when she reached my side.

"I haven't played anything like this in quite a while so I'm probably rusty."

She shrugged. "I could never play anything but Hot Cross Buns. Anything you play, even if it is rusty will still be better than that."

I laughed.

After we got inside Bobbie practically begged me to set up the keyboard in the living room. I was in the middle of plugging it up when her voice suddenly filled the room.

"Angel, I want to warn you of something. John called just before you got home. He's in town and is anxious to talk to you."

I stopped messing with the cord and looked up. "What did he say?"

"When he asked if you were home I told him no. He proceeded to tell me it was important he spoke with you and wanted to know if you were at work. I told him I had no idea where you had gone and I didn't know what time you had to be at work."

She never lied to anyone so it surprised me when she admitted to lying to John.

"I'm shocked you lied," I said, my voice stunned.

"Me, too," she laughed. "I was hoping to buy you some time before you had to deal with him."

"I appreciate that." I went back to hooking up the cords and plugging them in. "Oh, before I forget, there's a bag on the table for you."

"You didn't have to buy me anything," she said, sounding embarrassed.

"I know, I just thought it would be nice to do so."

She flashed me a grin then turned, nearly running into the kitchen.

I looked up at the clock when I was finished with the keyboard and nearly panicked. I'd lost more time than I thought. I left everything sitting where it was and ran into the foyer.

"Thank you for the cows, Angel," Bobbie called as I flew up the stairs. "And, don't forget I have that class this evening so it may be late when I get in."

I barely heard her last statement as I closed my bedroom door.

A few of my regulars greeted me in the parking lot. I chatted with them a few moments before walking away. It was then I heard a voice call out my name. I tried not to cringe at the awful, yet very familiar sound as I turned around. John was jogging towards me.

"Could I talk with you a minute?" he asked, nearly breathless.

I fought to keep my voice warm when I responded. "I really have to be getting inside."

He slowed to a walk, and then stopped at my side. "I know, it'll only take a minute, please," he pleaded.

"What is so important it can't wait till I'm not busy?" I was beginning to get impatient.

"I was hoping to have the opportunity to ask you if you'd like to go to the movies tonight."

"I'm afraid I can't. I'm on the closing shift tonight."

I usually hated it whenever I had to work the night shift, especially on the weekends, however I was secretly praising Kloe for it now.

"Yeah, I get that now." John's tone was disappointed. "I'm in town until Sunday, could we plan something for tomorrow?"

"John," I said, trying not to sound disgusted. "it's flattering that you're willing to go through this much trouble for a date. I just can't do it, I'm not interested as I've told you and I have to work all weekend."

"I saw you walking so could I at least offer you a ride home tonight?" I could hear the desperation in his voice.

I opened my mouth to answer, never to get the chance. My name was called out again, this time in panic.

"Angel, we really need you in here!"

I turned to look behind me and Brandi was standing in the door, waving frantically for me to come inside. I looked back at John.

"I have to go." I turned and ran to the building.

"I'll pick you up," was all I heard before the door closed.

When I entered the diner I was immediately horrified. The dining room was pack full with customers, nearly every table occupied. The one's that weren't was still stack with dirty dishes. There was still a line of people at the door, waiting patiently to be seated. Brandi, Anna and the new girl Kloe had just hired were the only ones running the dining room. They were taking orders and delivering them while trying to clean off the dirty tables so they could get other customers seated. I rushed in the back to clock in, and then gave then a hand with dinner rush.

Kloe had twisted the entire staff around for this shift. Mark usually worked the night time and most weekends, tonight it was Kyle. Mark needed the night off. Anna was supposed to be there in the morning, but Marisa begged her to change shifts. Even I was happy about that, it meant I wouldn't be listening to her complaints all night.

Sydney Harper was the new waitress Kloe hired. She had just moved here from Portland and needed a job. Catlyn wasn't working much now that she was preparing for her last year of school and Marisa was starting to spend a lot of time in California. Kloe needed the replacement just as badly as Sydney needed the job.

We stayed busy clear up to close, which meant it would be at least another hour before we could leave. Brandi had a lot of paperwork to do so Anna helped Kyle clean the cook area while I showed Sydney how to stock the pie cooler and roll the silverware. When all she had left to do was to wipe down the tables and sweep and mop the floor I took the tub of dirty dishes to the dish room.

I pulled out the clean dishes and set them aside so I'd have room for the dirty ones.

"Do you need a ride tonight?" Kyle asked. He walked in, carrying an arm load of his own dishes.

"I don't hear the rain beating against the roof so I'll be fine. Thank you."

He shrugged. "All right." He set his dishes on the table beside the dishwasher, waiting for me to finish. "Angel, since we're friends could I ask you something?"

"Sure," I agreed, and then bit down on my bottom lip.

Kyle hadn't asked me out in a long time nor has he flirted with me, yet his tone alerted me we were once again heading in that direction.

"Are you dating John Wilkins?" he asked, bluntly.

How does being forced into one night of dinner turn to dating? I finished putting the last of the plates in the dishwasher then turned to face him.

"No, I am not," I stated, harshly. My quota of patience had been used up for the day. "I'm not dating *anyone*. And, as I've told you before I don't want anything more than being friends."

Kyle leaned against the wall and crossed his arms over his chest. "I know what you've told *me*," he said sourly. "but I've heard conversations between Brandi and Catlyn. They can't seem to shut up about it."

The mentioning of that night and the reminder of him catching me in the parking lot tonight caused my lips to press together in irritation.

"For the love of all that is holy," I glowered. "It was one date and clearly you didn't listen to their entire conversation."

"How do you know that?"

"Because *if* you had you would already know I'm not dating him, as well as the reason why. And, we certainly wouldn't be having this conversation."

"That's not the point," he said, his tone defiant.

I rolled my eyes and turned to pick up the tub of clean dishes. "Kyle, you're sounding extremely jealous right now."

I heard the resentment in his tone when he responded. "I did ask first."

I was completely mystified and turned back around. Kyle was already walking out of the room.

Everyone but Brandi was done and standing by the door when I finally entered the dining room. Kyle waited till I reached them to walk behind me and turn off all the lights. He joined us moments later and we walked out the door. He stopped long enough to lock it then headed to the side of the building. Even though Brandi was still inside Kloe was adamant that the door be locked so no one would enter the restaurant.

I nearly stepped in the parking lot and became infuriated with myself for being a coward. I turned around to face where Kyle was walking; I wanted to demand him to listen to me and knock it off with the attitudes.

"Angel," a voice called out.

I watched Kyle's back disappear around the corner of the building before slowly turning to face the parking lot. John was walking to me, a huge smile on his lips.

"Hi," he said when he reached me. "Are you ready for that ride home?"

I never allowed him to hold my hand, I didn't allow him to kiss me goodnight and I've never taken any of his phone calls, not to mention all the times I've made it perfectly clear I'm not interested. Why hasn't he gotten the point that I'm *not* going to be his next one night stand?

"John, we have been over this too many times already. Please, understand that I'm not interested in having any one night stands or any romances."

"How can you stand here and tell me that when I hear you're spending a lot of time with Sean Callenger?"

I opened my mouth to answer when Anna suddenly walked up, stopping beside me.

"Aren't you up for a little healthy competition?" Her voice was sarcastic.

John leveled a dark look at her. "There's no competition, as I don't have them. I get what I want, that simple."

No one seemed to notice anyone else had joined our party till the smooth voice appeared from the darkness.

"You are absolutely right, there is no competition. However, I'm afraid you're quite wrong where Angel is concerned." Sean's voice was very friendly, though only on the surface. I knew his tones well enough by now to catch the slightest edge of menace.

I heard Sydney and Anna gasp long before Sean stepped into the light in the parking lot.

John's eyes narrowed at Sean. "I don't see how this is any of your business, Callenger," he snarled.

Sean stepped closer to him, a wicked glint in his eyes. "It is when there seems to be some kind of miscommunication. I'll settle the confusion while we're discussing matters concerning Angel. From this moment on she will be unavailable every night, to anyone besides myself. I'm sorry if you find this to be offensive." He didn't sound sorry at all.

"You have pushed the last boundary with me," John stated, shoving an index finger against Sean's chest. "I will have your mother fired."

Sean stared down at John and grinned. "Give it your best shot, *if* you truly believe your grandfather will listen to your ridiculousness."

John lowered his hand, mumbling unintelligently and took a step back still staring at Sean. He called out to the other girls while keeping his eyes on Sean.

"Sydney ... Anna, would either of you like a ride home?"

Sydney laughed. "No thank you. I have my own car and I'm definitely not interested in becoming your next obsession."

Her response had me wondering since she was from Portland if she too knew John well. She walked up next to me and turned to look at me.

"It was nice meeting you, Angel. I'll see you on Monday." She walked away.

Anna held up her keys as she walked away. "I have my own car, as well."

John wasn't thrilled that he'd been turned down by any of us. I expected him to say something to me or Sean, but instead he turned on his heels and stalked off to his car.

"He shouldn't be a bother to you anymore," Sean said as he turned to look at me. "His pride is wounded and he'll drive back to Portland tonight so he can lick his wounds in private." His eyes danced, he was enjoying the idea more than he should. "Do you want to wait here or walk with me to the truck?"

"I'll walk."

As we walked to Sean's truck I thought of something he said to John. I didn't argue it at the time because his voice had frightened me a bit, but also because he was getting through to him when I wasn't. Now it was bothering me to know that Sydney and Anna heard it and soon it would get to Kyle. After the conversation we had in the dish room I didn't need or want any more of his guilt trips.

"Sean, why did you tell John I'm unavailable to everyone but you?" I asked.

We were at the truck now. He opened the passenger door and waited for me to get in.

"You wanted him out of your life, right?" His voice was unemotional.

I looked up at him, his face was expressionless. "Of course I do, but do you realize you just complicated my life?"

Now he grinned. "You mean with Hesner?"

I ignored him and got in the truck. When he moved his hand to close the door I grabbed the handle, slamming it with more force then was needed.

It was dark inside so when Sean got in I couldn't see his face well.

"Would you mind explaining to me why you don't have Bobbie's car in the first place?" he asked.

He started the truck and pulled out of the parking lot.

"What are you, my *daddy*?" I asked, my voice almost a growl. "I don't understand why it's any of your business, but Bobbie had a seminar and needed her car."

"No," he stated firmly. His voice sounded frustrated. "No, I am not your father. I just don't feel it's safe enough for you to walk alone after dark. Wilkins is real buoyant to give you rides and I don't want to have to end that badly. He is the mayor's grandson, you know. Couldn't you have at least taken a ride from Hesner?"

"Kyle?" I croaked. "Are you serious?" I shook my head, angrily. "Need I remind you that I was walking everywhere the first month I lived here?"

"As true as that may be," he fumed. "you didn't have Wilkins waiting in the dark for you. I don't like Hesner, but I'd much more prefer you got a ride from him. I know you wouldn't be in any kind of trouble there."

"Under what rule do I have to concern myself with your preferences?" I griped.

"None, I suppose." I could hear the shrug in his voice. "If we're going to talk preferences then you should just be waiting for me."

"I can't do that when you're not always around," I said, dismissively.

"How do you know that?" he asked, skeptically.

He didn't sound as confident as he usually did. Something in his tone had my head turning to face him despite the fact I couldn't see his expressions well.

"I have noticed when the sun comes out I don't see you or Jonah anywhere."

He pressed his lips together and kept his eyes straight ahead. I couldn't understand why, but I got an eerie feeling I shouldn't have voiced my observation out loud.

"Perceptive," he finally answered. Then he turned his eyes on me. "That still has nothing to do with you being out alone at night."

I bit down on my tongue to keep from snarling and turned my head to look out the window. When I was sure I wouldn't lose control of myself I released it, inhaling deeply through my nose. It was then I noticed for the first time the scent inside the truck. It smelled real sweet, like citrus. It was similar to what Sean's breath had been, just not as intoxicating.

"Could I ask you something?" Sean asked after a few long minutes of silence.

"What?" I asked, icily.

"Why does it seem like you're always working with Hesner?"

I looked at him then, in utter disbelief. His tone had the same edge in it as Kyle's did when he asked me about John. My lips formed into a frown, disgusted.

"Did the two of you happen to walk through a testosterone spill somewhere today?"

Sean laughed, carelessly, shaking the entire truck. I continued to stare at him, bewildered. Despite the number of times I've been with him he's never laughed so freely.

"From your question I'm going to assume you mean Hesner and myself." He turned his eyes on me. They were now glowing, nearly taking my breath away. "The answer is no. Our only common ground is your work place."

"Then I believe you have gone around the bend," I breathed.

He completely ignored my observation.

"Why would you ask such a question?"

I released the breath I hadn't been aware I was holding when the truck slowed and Bobbie's red Ford Escort appeared in his headlights.

"It's not important," I sighed, weakly. I squeezed the handle and pushed open the door. I couldn't have felt more grateful for the freedom from the enclosed space and the cool night air as it grazed the skin on my face. "Thanks again for the ride."

"Angelia," Sean groaned in exasperation. "right now I've got about as much sense as any man can have after spending time with you. Now please, just answer the *damn* question."

Oh, now my statement irritated him!

I turned in the seat to face him. I opened my mouth to answer calmly, instead my words came out in a rush.

"I was just pointing out that you and Kyle have jealously issues tonight."

Sean's face lost all emotions while he stared at me. I feared for a second that I'd made him angry again, but then he suddenly laughed, the sound was close to a roar and I cringed.

"Hesner is jealous of Wilkins." He seemed to enjoy the idea.

I rolled my eyes. "Good night, Sean." I jumped out of the truck and slammed the door.

The only light burning in the house was in the kitchen. I trudged up the stairs and into the house thankful this night was finally over. Bobbie was sitting at the table with a stack of papers in front of her.

"Hey," I said, warily.

She finished reading the paper in her hand then lowered it to look at me.

"Hey," she smiled. "Did you have a good night?"

"Oh, sure," I said with sarcasm. "testosterone issues always adds fun to any situation."

Bobbie laughed. "Problems with Kyle again?"

"And a couple of others," I added, dryly. I leaned over the chair in front of me for a better look at what she'd been reading. "That looks like an awful lot to have to read."

"Yeah." She wrinkled her nose in disgust. "I have enough here to keep me reading for a month."

"Enjoy," I laughed. "I'm going to shower then call it a night."

I turned and headed up the stairs.

After my shower I laid on the bed, staring mindlessly at the window. My body was exhausted, but my eyes wouldn't close. For the first time in a handful of weeks it wasn't raining and the moonlight was casting a glow inside my room. Figuring I wasn't going to fall asleep anytime soon I got up and left the room.

I considered watching TV, but when I walked in the living room my eyes instantly flashed to the keyboard in the corner. Everyone's asleep, I thought to myself. If you take it outside then you can play around with it and not disturb anyone. I weighed out the pro's and con's a moment longer then walked over and unplugged it. I could easily just place the keyboard over my lap so I wouldn't actually need the stand. I picked it up and stopped in the kitchen for a glass of tea, and then slipped quietly out the back door.

The moonlight was unusually bright, allowing me to see in nearly every shadow in the enormous yard. It nearly reminded me of a horror movie I'd once seen. A helpless kid trying to escape a lunatic inside his house and runs into him in the yard. I sat down on the stairs, scolding myself for thinking of such things. I banished the thoughts from my mind before I made myself paranoid.

I turned the keyboard on and began experimenting with the keys. I was rusty just as I knew I would be, but it wasn't long and my fingers were gliding across them. I eventually began playing the number I had planned to play at the audition for Juilliard. It didn't sound quite the same, yet it still gave me satisfaction. I was so deep in concentrating on the Gospel piece I didn't know anyone had entered the yard till I suddenly caught movement from the corner of my eyes. My head instantly snapped up and I watched in confusion as Sean walked casually to me.

"I had no idea you played instruments," he said as he sat down next to me. "Are you trying to make sure you have a spot reserved at Heaven's gate?"

"No," I answered, sourly. "What are you even doing here?"

I lost interest in the song and laid my fingers still over the keys.

"Don't stop on my account, I was actually enjoying the sound. It was a Gospel piece, right?"

"Yes," I confirmed.

"That is really amazing. I didn't think anyone still listens to that kind of music anymore."

"I only do if it's a piece I like."

He stared at me with an unfathomable expression. "Is being stuck here depressing you so badly that you need to play these kind of heartbreaking songs?"

I stared back at him, flabbergasted. "What makes you think I'm depressed?"

He may have been right, but in no way was I going to own up to it.

He shrugged his shoulders halfheartedly. "Why else would you be out here in the middle of the night with a talent none of us were even aware you have?"

"Maybe I was just trying to enjoy this beautiful night," I answered, sarcastically.

I've never had anyone pay such close attention to me before and wasn't liking it. I had already forced myself to admit he bothers me on some deep, elemental level. I couldn't be sure if it was because of the effect his sky-colored eyes had on me or if it was the drawl of his slow and lazy, yet every bit as cocky grin. What more did he want from me ----- admit to him? Not in this life!

Sean laughed softly. "That could certainly be possible, though I doubt it. I think something is weighing on you causing you to have a heavy heart and it's clearly keeping you awake at night."

"And?" I challenged.

He reached out, lightly brushing my hair back over my shoulder. My heart began to pound, wildly.

"I have to say, you put on a good show, Angel," he said, his voice thoughtful. "You even had me fooled for a bit, at some point you're going to have to realize you need to talk to someone."

I frowned at him, unhappily. "Such as who, *you*?"

His blue eyes began to smolder, his accent thick, rich. "It doesn't have to be me, although I wouldn't mind. I do believe it would help your friends have a much better insight of you, as well as help you solve your problem."

The proper punctual of his words brought back the curiosity I'd had these past few months about the century in which he clearly had to come from.

"Sean, how old are you?" I suddenly blurted.

My question seemed to confuse him.

"I'm nineteen," he answered, hesitantly. "Why do you ask?"

"The way you talk … it's like you speak a different language than everyone else."

"I suppose I do," he agreed with a short, hard laugh.

I waited for him to say something else. The seconds ticked by.

"You never did answer my question," I stated, changing the subject when he said nothing.

His brows knit in confusion. "What question was that?"

"Why are you here?" I asked again.

"Oh," he laughed. "I brought you something, but you sidetracked me with your musical abilities."

I never noticed the whole time he was sitting beside me that he had a book. It was now in his left hand and he was holding it out at me.

"I got curious about a habit you have and read up on it," he continued. "I thought maybe if you got a better understanding of it yourself it might help you."

"What habit would that be?" I was confused.

Instead of answering he thrust the book at me. I tore my eyes away from his face and looked down. I instantly became infuriated, my eyes flashed back to his face.

"You think I have an obsessive-compulsive disorder?" I asked, irked.

He slowly shook his head back and forth. "I don't think, I know you do."

When I made no effort to take the book he carefully laid it on the keyboard. I continued to stare at him, intending to tell him what he could do with it. But then, he lifted his arm, slowly reaching out to me and very lightly ran the back of his fingers down my cheek. Despite the warmness in the air his skin was cold as ice, yet they left behind a warm sensation where he touched. My anger instantly dissolved.

"Angel, it is best that you go inside now." Sean's voice was husky. His eyes were cautious, conflict raging in them.

"Okay," was all I could manage.

He pulled the keyboard off my lap and waited for me to stand up. My legs were weak and shook uncontrollably as I fought to get to my feet. Sean handed me the keyboard and the book then reached across where I had been sitting to pick up the glass I'd long since forgotten about.

"Don't leave this out here," he said as he held it out to me.

"Good night, Sean." I took the glass from his waiting hand, and then turned to walk to the house. I entered and closed the door without even looking to see if he was still there.

I set the glass in the sink then took the keyboard in the living room, placing it back on the stand. I didn't bother plugging it in, heading up the stairs, instead.

The weekend was uneventful as I stayed home. I had told John I was scheduled to work all weekend and simply because I'd hoped to avoid Sean. Jennifer called several times and despite my bogus cheerfulness and my outright lies she was alerted to my depression. She asked if it had anything to do with the letter she'd sent me. I tried being diplomatic about it, but I mostly just lied, a lot.

I was barely out the door Monday morning when Brandi stopped in front of the house. Bobbie had an appointment that morning so it left me to walk. The air was warm and it wasn't raining, even as the sky was its usual gray, yet I had my jacket lying over my arm. It may not have been raining, but why temptfate?

"Hey, Angel," Brandi called out cheerfully. "I came by to ask if you could help me out."

"With what?" I asked, confused.

"I have to run to Walmart and pick up a few things for Mom. I could use the extra hands."

"Okay, sure." I walked to her car and climbed in. "Did she run out of something over the weekend?"

"No," she said as she pulled away from the house. "Mom ordered some kind of plant and they're ready to be picked up."

"I see," I mused. "How much greener does she want her garden to be?"

Brandi laughed at my tone. "They're not for the garden, they're for the dining room."

"Isn't it green enough?" I made a face of mock horror.

"Apparently not."

The conversation ended and I looked out the window, watching people as Brandi passed them. I wasn't the only one who was enjoying a moment without the rain.

"Can you believe it's August, already?" Brandi's voice suddenly asked.

My answer was automatic. "No."

She looked over at me then, an odd expression on her face. "Why the need to sound like that?"

"I'm sorry," I said, apologetically. "I didn't mean for it to come out harsh. I had hoped that by this time the nightmare with Jeremy would have been over."

"Have you heard anymore from Mike?"

I sighed. "Not a word."

She did more of that chattering after that, completely changing the subject. I'd only *mmm* and *ah ah ah* in all the right places so she wouldn't think I wasn't paying attention. Brandi was often difficult to stay up with during conversations, as she liked to switch topics easily. Most of the time I never bothered to try keeping up.

Kloe had ordered three tall plants that looked like small palm trees. She spent most of the morning moving them around the dining room trying to find the perfect place for them. Many of our customers complimented on them and that added more enthusiasm to Kloe's jubilant mood.

I walked out the door with Brandi shortly after Anna, Mark and Marisa came in around five. For once I was grateful to be free of the night shift. I was already feeling low about myself, I didn't need Marisa pointing out any of my flaws.

I nearly had a heart attack when I finally noticed a figure leaning against Brandi's car. If she was shocked she never showed any signs of it or voiced it. As we got closer to it I could see it was Sean. A wide grin spread across his lips as we approached him.

"Hello, Brandi," he said in a polite tone.

"H … hi, Sean," she stuttered.

The expression on her face was sheer shock, like she couldn't believe he had spoken to her. I had to press my lips together to keep from laughing.

"Do you mind if Angel goes with me, instead?" he asked, his voice soft as velvet.

"Um … no problem." She shifted her wide eyes to me, trying to read my expressions to be sure it was what I wanted.

"It's fine, Brandi," I said, assuredly. "I'll see you tomorrow."

I knew from the expression now on her face there would be no getting out of talking about this.

"Okay," she breathed. "bye."

When she was in her car and driving away I turned to Sean.

"What's this about?"

"Humor me." He turned and walked towards the truck. I waited a few more seconds before following him. He had the passenger door open by the time I reached his side.

He read the hesitation on my face and sighed. "I just thought you could spend more time with me than simply the few minutes it takes to drive you home."

I eyed him, suspiciously. "Couldn't I have at least gone home and changed first?"

He leaned in the truck and a second later was pulling out a bag. "Since I know you have O.C.D., did you really think I would make you stay like this?"

I ignored his sarcasm and looked in the bag after he handed it to me. The clothes were mine; he had gotten my long-sleeved misty blue shirt and a pair of jeans.

"Did Bobbie give these to you?" I asked, mystified.

A slow, wicked grin crossed his lips. "Are you going to go inside and change or should we just go?"

I stared at him a moment while I thought about demanding an answer then decided it was probably better that I didn't know. I turned away from him and walked to the building.

Anna gave me a strange look when I walked in the door. I held the bag up at her as I continued to walk to the bathroom. I stood looking at my profile in the mirror, trying desperately to calm my racing pulse as I thought about being completely alone with Sean. *Why is it so important I spend time with him, anyway? You promised Jonah and Kelsey, remember?* I reminded myself. I tossed my uniform in the bag, sucked in the deepest breath I could manage and walked out of the bathroom.

Sean had moved the truck and was now parked in front of the building with the passenger door open. I ran out and climbed in, hoping he would speed away before anyone saw us.

"This is a first," Sean said, sounding surprised.

I tossed my bag on the backseat and reached for the seat belt.

"What is?" I pulled it across my body and snapped it in place.

"You have never been interested in being with me for any reason, let alone acting in a hurry to do so."

I rolled my eyes. "I'm already going to be explaining this tomorrow. I don't need any other ears in the conversation."

He raised one eyebrow, a faint smile crossed his lips. "You're friends haven't told *Hesner*" ----- he sneered on his name ----- "about the other night so you don't want him knowing you're with me now."

"Could we just go?" I grumbled.

Sean laughed darkly, and then pulled out of the parking lot.

"Where are we going, anyway?" I asked after a few eerie minutes of silence.

He leaned forward a bit and looked up at the sky through the windshield. "Los Angeles. It'll be dark when we get there, but that will only stimulate what I want to show you."

"*Los Angeles*?" I gasped in horror. "Sean, you can't be serious!"

He sat back in the seat and turned to look at me, with a grin, suddenly amused. "I've been told you have no desire to see the Eiffel Tower so I was thinking maybe you would the Hollywood sign."

I folded my arms over my chest, fully aware of the stubborn set of my chin. "I don't believe I've *ever* mentioned it."

He broke into a roar of laughter, the sound echoed in the truck. I slightly cringed away from it.

I looked away from his face, trying to focus on enjoying the passing scenery. We were outside of town now and the trees were passing by much quicker than the normal fifty-five mile an hour speed. I started to feel like I was in a NASCAR race when my eyes glanced at his speedometer.

"I never realized I was riding with Richard Petty!" I shouted. "Could you slow down!?"

I grabbed onto the bar above the window while my stomach began to twist with every turn of the highway.

"What's wrong with you?" He was startled by my sudden outburst. But the truck never decelerated.

"You're going a hundred and twenty miles an hour!" I was still shouting.

"Don't worry, songbird," Sean spoke softly.

"Don't worry!? Are you trying to get us killed?" I demanded.

"I always drive like this. We're not going to crash so just trust me."

My eyes narrowed. I'd heard that before; *I have secrets I'll never tell you.*

"Well ... I don't," I hissed through my teeth. "If you're wanting me to have no fear when I'm with you then a good place to start would be to follow the speed laws."

He was astonished. He stared at me in disbelief. When he finally spoke, he almost sounded disgusted. "Whether you believe it or not I want you comfortable with me as you are with your friends."

"So how comfortable do you think I'm going to be when you wrap us around a tree?"

Despite himself he chuckled, letting the needle slow to ninety. "Is this better?"

I mumbled, unintelligently and turned my eyes back to the window. My fingers tightened around the bar so tight the skin stretched taunt over the bones and was turning pale white.

Sean reached out and very lightly stroked my hair. "Angelia, you worry too much."

I hated whenever my name was used in a patronizing form. Instead of giving him any more attention I shut my eyes briefly on a prayer for patience and survival.

It was dark, just like Sean had predicted when we arrived on Hollywood Blvd. I could see the huge letters on the hill as the lights surrounding it casted on them. Sean must have been delighted by my reaction, he drove down the boulevard longer than what was called for. I hated to admit it, even to myself, but I was fascinated by the crowds of people lining the sidewalk, snapping pictures of the stars on the walk of fame.

I don't know how much time passed before the lights and eventually the houses began to disappear until it was nothing but a steep road. Twenty minutes maybe and he came to a stop in an empty parking lot at the bottom.

"I'm sorry, Angel, but we have to go the rest of the way on foot."

I looked around, suddenly horrified. "We're hiking?"

He turned his head slightly in my direction, frowning. "How else did you think you would see it?"

"The same way I saw it before, at a distance."

He groaned in irritation. "It is only a three mile hike up the side. Surely, you can make that."

"Three miles?" I shrieked. "Do you have any idea how long it's going to take me to climb that?"

He opened his door and less than a second later was opening mine. He took my face securely in between his hands.

"It's going to be all right, bright eyes," he promised. "I'll be beside you the entire way."

"How in the ..." I trailed off, trying to clear my head, get my bearings. "How did you get over here so fast?"

He didn't answer, continuing to stare into my eyes. I stared back at his concerned, innocent expression and was disoriented again by the force of his crystal blue-colored eyes. What was I asking?

A triumphant smile slowly lit his face. "I solemnly swear I won't let anything hurt you."

"O-okay," I stammered.

Sean carefully released my face and took a step back so I could get out of the truck. I was still dazed, but managed to slide out of the seat and stand on my own two feet. As soon as I was clear of the door Sean closed it. We walked around the front of the truck, and then he lead the way up the very steep hill.

It took me longer to hike the three miles then it did Sean to drive the distance. He was patient with my slowness, keeping the pace next to me. He mostly kept his hands shoved in his pockets and didn't say much. I would peek over at him sometimes to be sure I wasn't alone. I could hear my footsteps as they crunched the rocks, Sean's only sounded like a breeze passing over them. When the incline became steeper Sean would grab my elbow and help me keep my balance.

When we reached the top Sean lead me around a fence then held the gate open for me to pass. Once I was inside he closed it, and then strode down the small hill towards the letters. His strides were so long I nearly had to run to keep up.

"Are we even supposed to be here?" I asked, breathless.

As soon as we were in front of the letters he spun around to face me.

"I called in a favor and had the cameras altered. We've got a few hours before anyone discovers they've been tampered with."

"Well isn't this just great, Angel," I grumbled to myself. "now you're breaking all the rules."

I walked to the letters and lightly brushed my fingers across them before making my way to the edge. I felt so tiny next to them I couldn't help giggling at myself. The view of Los Angeles was breathtaking.

"Magnificent view, isn't it?" Sean asked.

I turned to look at him. He was leaning against the 'w', watching me.

"I have to say, I've never seen anything like this."

"And to think you didn't want to come here," he laughed.

I rolled my eyes at him and turned back to look at the lights spilling around the city.

We lapsed in silence for a long time. Neither of us moved, both seeming to enjoy the quietness and the beauty that was surrounding us. I don't know how much time passed ----- maybe an hour when a voice from behind me finally broke the silence.

"There was a purpose for me bringing you here," Sean stated, his tone serious.

Even as badly as he irritated me I never grew tired of hearing the slow drawl of his accent. He reminded me of a cowboy, just without the boots and the hat. I sighed, and then turned to face him.

"I already had that figured out," I smirked. I crossed my arms over my chest and shifted my weight to one foot.

He ignored my remark. "I want you to tell me what has you so unhappy."

I scowled. "Why are you so convinced that I am?"

"We're not around your friends, Angel. So you can stop with the pretenses."

I had never heard his voice sound so stern before and it took me by surprise.

"Fine then," I sighed. I dropped my arms and walked to his side. "If it means that much to you then I'll show you." I reached in my purse and pulled out the unopened letter from Juilliard then handed it to him.

He looked at the envelope then flashed his eyes back to my face.

"I can't say I understand." He was confused.

"Jennifer sent that to me a few weeks ago. It's something I'd been waiting months for."

He turned the letter over in his hand a few times before he spoke. "You've never even opened it."

"I know, I couldn't," I admitted, shamefaced. "I couldn't handle it if it's a rejection, but I also couldn't handle it if it's an audition date because I'm still stuck here."

"Haven't you spoken with Mike about it?"

I barely shook my head. "Each time I bring up leaving he reminds me I'm not eighteen and there's still the matter over Jeremy."

Sean handed the letter back to me.

"The matter concerning him is close to being over. Jonah didn't want me to say anything to you just yet, but Louisiana is calling their clam on him. The part that is troubling is figuring out when and where he killed Amanda. They can't be sure if she was already dead when he took you or if he'd killed her after he brought both of you to the cabin."

I cringed away from his words and turned around. Sometimes when I was alone I would still see Amanda's face in my mind. Even though I knew I shouldn't have still been thinking about her I couldn't help it. It was painful for me to face the fact that I'd been spared when she wasn't. It was silent for a moment then I felt Sean's hand land softly on my shoulder.

"I'm sorry, I didn't mean for that to sound harsh." His voice was quiet, velvet, muted.

"It's all right," I nearly whispered. "it's still hard for me when I think about her."

"Jonah had learned a lot about your father and his connections with a few of the officers he passes his time with," he stated, changing the subject. "What I'm curious about is your mother."

I felt a tremor flow through me and stepped away from his hand. Talking of my mother wasn't any easier then talks of Amanda. "What do you want to know?"

"For starters," he said, his voice full of concern. "What is she like?"

"She doesn't look anything like me, but she's pretty. I have too much Scott in me ... aside from the temper. She's braver than me, as she clearly found a way to get free of him long before I could figure it out. She's responsible, though slightly eccentric and she's an amazing cook." I stopped. Talking about her was beginning to stir up too many emotions I wouldn't be able to hold back.

"My next question; where is she?" His voice sounded frustrated for a reason I couldn't imagine.

I shrugged, sluggishly. "I don't know."

"Is she deceased, perhaps?" I could hear the confusion burning in his voice.

"I presume she's still alive."

I walked to the edge again, fighting the tears I could feel swelling up. Sean's voice appeared right behind me.

"How did she leave without you?"

I took a deep breath, releasing it slowly. "She didn't just wake up one day and decide to leave."

Now he was really confused. "So then tell me how you ended up in this kind of situation."

"I don't remember her reasons," I said, slowly. "but one day she took me to Scott's, promising to come back for me soon. I never saw or heard from her again."

"I could talk to Jonah and see if we couldn't track her down," he offered, genuinely.

I shook my head. "I appreciate your generosity, Sean. I truly believe that if Samantha wanted her daughter she wouldn't have chosen to stay gone for seven years."

Despite all the effort I had put into holding back the tears, one fell down my cheek. I wiped it away and turned to walk back to the letters. Sean watched me for a few seconds, and then appeared at my side, casually taking my right hand in his. We walked behind the sign, looking at the steel ladders holding the letters up.

"Why haven't you told any of your friends about your upcoming birthday?" he suddenly asked.

I shrugged weakly. "They have always been a disaster so why bother with anymore?"

"How about we change this one?" he suggested. "I could talk to Mike about at least letting you to go New York for your audition."

"I don't even know if I got one."

I looked down at our twined hands then up at him. He was frowning at me.

"You should probably try opening it."

I shook my head and looked away from his face.

"Why are you so interested in my misery, anyway?" I asked.

We reached the end of the sign and Sean stopped, turning to face me.

"I've never seen anyone this shade of blue before."

I'd never heard that expression and opened my mouth to ask what that even meant, but the look on his face stopped me. His face was unusually soft, his blue eyes were full of conflict.

"You may not believe me when I say we have been here for hours, but we have and now it's getting late," he murmured. "I should get you home."

The way we came up suddenly entered my mind and I was on the verge of panic.

"It's going to be much later than you probably had planned," I warned.

His expression turned puzzled and I started talking before he could ask anything.

"You're expecting me to hike down a hill I can't clearly see."

His crystal blue eyes began to shine as excitement lit up his face. "Not a problem."

I pulled my hand free of his and took a step backwards.

"I don't know what you're planning, but you can forget it," I said, sternly.

He slowly stepped toward me. "I promise, it'll only take a minute."

I opened my mouth to protest, never to get the chance. Sean grabbed my wrist and pulled me to him. He slid his hand down my arm, catching it at the elbow and lifted me off the ground. He slung me on his back, as if I weighed twenty pounds, instead of a hundred and twenty and took off in the direction of the fence, moving the speed of a bullet. I couldn't feel his movement, but I could feel the wind hitting me sharply in the face and held onto his shoulders for dear life, eventually burying my face in his back.

It was only seconds later when I heard the passenger door on the truck open. I carefully lifted my head to look and he had me hanging over the seat. I released my death grip on his shoulders and fell on to the seat. Sean waited till I was settled to close the door and walk around the truck. I laid my head back and closed my eyes, trying to control the nausea when I heard the sound of his door open then close.

"I'm sorry, Angel," he apologized, his voice burned with regret. "I didn't think about how my actions were going to affect you."

I waited a second to answer to be sure I wouldn't still vomit. "It's okay, Sean."

"I've just never been able to be myself around anyone other than my family. I often forget my movements are too quick for *human* eyes."

Human eyes? My eyes instantly flew open and my head sharply turned in his direction. It was then I knew he had already turned the truck around and was driving back toward the city. I tried to say something, but somehow my voice had evaded me. This was the first time we were silent in each other's company.

First Dance

Bobbie was already gone when Sean dropped me off. She had left the kitchen light and the porch light on for me. My body was worn out from working all day and from the three mile hike up a very steep hill. I just wanted to take a hot shower and crawl into bed, yet I knew if I didn't call the hospital first to let Bobbie know I was home she would have been sick with worry. I spent a few minutes on the phone with her then drug my tired body up the stairs.

The next morning I took my time getting out of bed and dressing in my awful uniform. The muscles in my legs ached and were throbbing, but that wasn't really the reason for my slowness. I was on the morning shift with Brandi and Kyle. I knew Brandi was at the diner right now, waiting for details about last night. I didn't have a single idea what to tell her or even where to begin. Still, there was something much worse than that; Kyle. He had just started talking to me again and this was clearly going to send him over the edge and create a hostile work environment.

Somehow Sydney nor Anna had spoken a word about the night John showed up and had a dispute with Sean. For that I was thankful because it helped smooth things over between us, but he was surely going to hear my conversation with Brandi, and then here we go again.

I finally forced myself to walk down the stairs and into the kitchen. Bobbie was carrying the gallon of milk back to the refrigerator.

"You look awfully nervous this morning," she noted. "Is everything all right?"

"Not really," I sighed, heavily. I *hated* the fact that my face was so easy to read. "It's just going to be a long day."

I tossed my purse and jacket on the table and headed to the counter for a cup of coffee. I needed the caffeine boost to survive this day. Bobbie picked up her bowl of cereal and walked to the table.

"Does your long day have anything to do with Sean and last night?" she asked.

When we spoke on the phone the night before she had made me aware that Brandi stopped by and told her I was with Sean.

"I know without even a single doubt that Brandi is going to pounce on me the second she sees me, though that really isn't so much the problem."

I finished with my cup and crossed the room, joining her at the table.

"Kyle will just have to except things for how they are," she said, her tone nearly harsh. "and John, too. Which by the way, he's still calling at least three times a day. How are you planning to end that?"

"I don't know," I said with a shrug. "I honestly thought after his altercation with Sean he would have finally given up."

"Any smart person would," Bobbie agreed. "Sean is a friendly, soft spoken person, but even I wouldn't want to see him angry. John is a very determined person and when he's passionate about someone he doesn't give up until he's accomplished his goal of getting her. I've seen him do it."

She finished eating her cereal then set the bowl aside. "Could I ask you a question?"

I immediately got the feeling from her tone it wasn't going to be one I'd like. Why not get it over with? I thought, sourly.

"Sure," I agreed, grudgingly. Very grudgingly.

"Are you ..." Her voice slowly trailed off. There must have been something in my expressions warning her to ask carefully. "... in love with Sean?"

I felt the shock on my face before I heard it in my voice. "Why would you ask me something like that?"

She frowned unhappily at me. "Angel, I've seen the dreamy look on your face after you've been with him. Not to mention the fact you turn down nearly every offer you get for a ride, except from Sean."

"Okay, you're right," I admitted, reluctantly. She has learned my facial expressions a little too well so there was no point in continuing to hide it. "I do feel something when I'm around him. I'm not sure I'd call it *love*."

Bobbie shook her head at me, and then stood from her chair. She picked up her bowl and carried it to the sink. I didn't quite understand her reaction.

"What?" I asked, confused.

She responded without looking at me. "You get a certain look in your eyes whenever anyone mentions Sean. It's definitely love, sweetie."

"Well ... whatever it is, I haven't got a clue what to do about it."

My feelings had become stronger in the sense that my heart pounded erratically just from someone saying his name or if I just simply thought about him. I couldn't stop myself from thinking about how natural it felt when he took my hand while we walked around the Hollywood sign. I couldn't wrap my head around how any of this had even happened.

"Sometimes when you love someone you have to take it by leaps and bounds."

I didn't understand what she meant and snapped out of my reverie to look at her. She was now rinsing off her dishes.

"Meaning, what exactly?"

"Tell Sean," she said, encouragingly. "I bet he feels the same way. In fact after Brandi telling me how he got John to leave the restaurant the other night and the way he acted yesterday I'm sure of it."

How is it Brandi had heard about that conversation, but Kyle didn't?

I viciously shook my head. "No way! I'm only weeks from ..." I instantly trailed off. She was still unaware about my birthday and I was suited to keep it that way. "I mean," I began again, this time slowly. "I don't want or need the hostility while I'm trying to work."

"You mean Kyle?" she asked. Her voice was disgusted. She laid her dishes on the towel and shut off the water.

"And John," I murmured. "I know this all sounds crazy to you." I stood from the chair and pushed it in. "I don't feel anything for them with the exception of irritation. And, even *if*-----" that was a very big *if*----- "I did feel something for Kyle I know what it would mean to Catlyn. I could never do that to her."

Bobbie dried off her hands, and then turned to lean against the sink. I walked up next to her, placing my empty cup on the counter.

"Maybe it's time you told Kyle the truth," she suggested. "He might then understand why you keep turning him down."

She could see that I was about to argue and held up a hand, stopping me.

"Angel, you can't just ignore how you feel simply because you don't want to hurt someone else's or because they choose to make you feel guilty for not having any kind of feelings for them."

"I know that," I grumbled. "I've got to go before I'm late."

I picked up my stuff from the table and walked in the foyer, donning in my jacket.

"Oh, Angel," Bobbie suddenly called out. She appeared in the doorway less than a second later. "I almost forgot to tell you something. When you get home we will probably have company."

Now I was confused. "Who?"

"Ryan and Kelly are coming in town today. They should be here sometime this afternoon. Ryan is planning to stay here until after the weekend."

"That's great," I said with enthusiasm. "What about Kelly?"

Bobbie puckered her lips. "She's either going to stay with Brandi or Kloe."

"Why?" I sputtered. Then felt bad for the way my tone sounded. "I mean, I could stay with Brandi and let Kelly have my room."

Bobbie walked to me and wrapped her arms around my shoulders, pulling me in for a hug.

"It's really sweet of you, Angel, but they have already made their plans."

I hugged her back then nearly ran out the door.

There wasn't a single person keeping the dining room from being empty. It wasn't raining heavily, yet it looked as though they hadn't had even one customer. It usually took the bottom falling out of the sky to make the diner look like this.

I walked in the back, expecting Brandi to suddenly appear and start questioning me. I never saw her till I passed by the cooler. She was arranging trays on the shelf.

"Good morning, Angel," she called out to me. She stepped out a few seconds later.

I fought to keep from groaning. "Good morning, Brandi."

I hung my jacket and purse on a hook, clocked in, and then headed for the prep table. Brandi was already there and was separating cups for the dressings. I grabbed a stack and began doing the same thing.

"So," she said, edging carefully into the conversation. "how is Sean?"

I shrugged. "He's good, I suppose."

She was quiet much longer than usual and I looked up at her. She had a scowl on her face.

"What?" I asked, suddenly feeling very self-conscious.

"Really, Angel," she growled. "you suppose?"

Now it was my turn to scowl. "What more did you want me to say?"

"I don't know," she sputtered. "How about something like he's perfect, great or better still ... fabulous."

"Jeez, Brandi, you're in a crabbie mood this morning."

I looked down at the table and picked up a bottle of Ranch dressing and began filling the first line of cups.

"Well I want details. You had to know I'd be waiting to hear them."

"Believe me, I knew," I said sourly.

She completely ignored my tone while she continued to fill her own cups.

"Where did he take you?"

If I hadn't been dreading this conversation all morning I would have been more prepared for her question. Now I had to think quickly for an answer. I could have been honest, but I doubt she would have believed we made the trip to Los Angeles and back in one day. It was hard for me to believe it.

"We went for a ride along the coast." There, that was simple and kind of true.

"Sounds romantic," she sighed in awe. "Did he kiss you before he left last night?"

I felt my cheeks instantly turn warm with embarrassment and was thankful I wasn't looking at her.

"It's not like that." My voice sounded real close to being disappointed.

"Maybe next time," she said, her tone sounding hopeful.

I looked up at her then, my eyes wide with shock. I opened my mouth to remind her I wasn't interested in things like that when Kyle called out her name. He walked over to stand next to the table and kept his back towards me the entire time he spoke to her. This was exactly what I had hoped to avoid.

That was that last of our conversations. The diner became very busy, not allowing time for standing around and chitchatting. Kyle stayed as far away from me as the building allowed, ignoring me every chance he got. Whenever he had to call my name for an order his tone was resentful. Shortly after lunch rush I saw him in the back. I considered for a moment of blowing up at him and taking Bobbie's advice to confront him. I'm a coward when it comes to confrontations so I turned and headed back up front where I spent the rest of the day keeping to myself.

It was a relief, as it always was, to finally get to leave. I had to fight the urge to run to the car, seeming how I had people I hoped to avoid. I had parked next to Kyle's gold Mustang and was now avoiding even taking a glance at it as I got in Bobbie's car. I speed out of the parking as fast as I could.

I had long since forgotten Bobbie had said anything about having company until I saw the white Chrysler sitting in front of the house. This is just great, I said to myself. I was in a foul mood and was going to have to force myself to be friendly. I got out and took my time walking up the sidewalk and up the stairs on the porch.

I heard voices the instant I opened the door.

"Hey, Angel," Bobbie called out to me.

"Hey," I said as I entered the kitchen.

She nearly jumped out her chair. "I'd like you to meet my brother." Then she turned to him. "Ryan, this is my friend and roommate I was telling you about, Angel."

Ryan stood from his chair and leaned across the table extending his arm out at me. He looked a little like Bobbie, though his skin was pale like mine. He was extremely tall, his light brown hair was cut short, he had a small patch of facial hair on his chin with a trimmed mustache over his lip. His eyes were blue and unlike Bobbie he didn't wear glasses.

"Hello, Angel," he said, politely. "it's nice to finally meet you."

I crossed the short distance (though I didn't need to as his arms were long) and shook his waiting hand.

"Nice meeting you, too." My tone sound flat, even to me. A wave of guilt came over me as I released his hand.

He sat back down in the chair, not seeming to notice my sourness. I walked to the cabinet and took out a glass.

"Ryan is going to sleep on the couch," Bobbie informed me.

How? I asked myself. It's only a loveseat, his legs alone would take it up.

"Okay." I poured tea in my glass, replaced the pitcher back on the shelf then closed the refrigerator door. Because I didn't want to ruin their visit with my sulky mood I excused myself and went upstairs to my room.

Brandi didn't come back to work after that one morning. Derek was planning to end the season for the dance hall with an forty-eight hour music and lights extravaganza that would be starting on Friday evening. Derek was in Nashville for the next few days, leaving Brandi to get things cleaned up and ready. This is what had brought Kelly and Ryan into town. They never missed the yearly tradition.

Kelly took Brandi's place, keeping Kloe from having a heart attack about being shorthanded again. Kelly didn't look much like Bobbie the way Ryan did. She had almost the same face as Bobbie's, though her eyes were hazel instead of brown. Her hair had freshly been dyed burgundy so it was impossible to know what the actual color was. She was friendly like her sister so I felt at ease around her. The best part of working with Kelly was knowing she didn't like Marisa's attitude, either.

Kloe began noticing the hostility between Kyle and I. She questioned me a couple of times and when I didn't give her the reasons she took Kyle off my shifts and asked Ryan to step in. I heard the small dispute coming from her office when she told Kyle. Ryan apparently didn't like the idea much, either.

We got an unusual break with the rain and the sun came out for two days. It seemed to put everyone in a better mood; me included. I was off on Thursday and had spent most of the morning pondering over something I could do that would keep me in the sunlight. Bobbie had left early so whatever I decided to do I would have to walk.

I was still considering my options while I showered. The thought of having the golden opportunity to see Yaquina Bay sparkle in the sun's rays entered my mind. I felt my myself start to fill with excitement, and then the possibility of bumping into John, as I was sure he was here, passed through my mind. I hadn't had any messages from him the past couple of weeks and didn't want to chance anything.

A solution finally came to me while I was dressing. I could just go to the hall and offer to help Brandi. I was almost positive she could use an extra set of hands. It wasn't anything in the sunlight, but it would certainly keep me out of everyone's eye sight. And, *if* John did show up looking for me I would have plenty of places to hide. I quickly finished brushing my teeth and hair and ran to my room, yanking my purse of the hook inside my closet, and then ran down the stairs and out the door.

It was much more complicated helping Brandi then I would have thought. I had no idea how to order snacks, hook up fresh lines to the soda machines or replace any of the lights. I was starting to feel frustrated when Brandi handed me a list of things that needed to be cleaned. I thought about the book Sean had brought to me that I still hadn't read while I cleaned. Stupid book. I don't have O.C.D.!

The sun was long gone and the sky was black when I left. The air was still warm and much to my surprise I could see a few stars when I looked up at it. There had never been a time in the months I was here that I've ever seen such a clear night. I was tired from all the cleaning, but I still took my time walking home. I didn't know when I would see another night like this and was just simply going to enjoy it.

I very nearly had a stroke when I entered the yard and saw a dark figure sitting on the porch steps. Bobbie nor Ryan were home and one of them had left the porch light on, though it didn't help illuminate much. The figure stood up, and then I realized it was Kelsey. I took a deep breath and started walking again.

"Hi, Kelsey," I called.

"Hi, Angel." Her greeting didn't sound like she was too happy to even be here.

"What's up?" I said as I was unlocking the door.

I wasn't paying close attention to her while I opened the door and walked inside, so her next words caught me by surprise.

"I owe you an apology." Her tone still hadn't changed and she certainly didn't sound like she was sorry for anything.

"For?" I prompted.

Kelsey sat down at the table as I walked on to the fridge, taking out a couple pieces of chicken from last night's dinner, placing them on a plate, heating them in the microwave. I poured myself a glass of tea while they heated.

"It seems I wasn't very fair to you the last time we spoke. Don't get me wrong," she paused, pointing her index finger at me. "I meant every word I said. Still, it wasn't fair for me to put you on the spot like that."

Now I understood, someone has forced her into apologizing. The memory of how she'd acted while we spoke had my body slightly trembling in fear, as I thought she may do it again. To be sure she wouldn't see anything on my face I stood in front of the microwave, watching it count down to the last seconds.

"I accept the apology, Kelsey, though I have to admit I'm not sure one is actually needed."

The microwave dinged and I opened the door, pulling out the plate. Instead of joining her at the table, I leaned against the counter and began eating.

"Maybe not to you," she disagreed. "but if asked you can say I did. Did you have a nice time with Sean the other night?"

"I did," I confirmed. "I still can't say I was thrilled to go all the way to Los Angeles, but it was nice."

I took the last bite of the chicken and set the bone on the plate.

"Would you mind if I ask a question?" Kelsey asked.

"Sure," I agreed. I picked up the second piece, taking a bite from it.

"Have you fallen in love with him, yet?"

I choked on the chicken and whirled around to grab a drink from the glass. I drank deeply, then set the glass back on the counter, slowly turning to look at Kelsey.

"*Love?*" I fought to keep my voice from sounding like a shriek.

She shook her head, sadly. "What is it with the two of you?" she grumbled. "The look on your face right now, Angel, is as if I'd just caught you in a criminal act."

"The two of us?" I was confused.

I quickly finished of the last bit of chicken, tossed the bones in the trash, and then set my plate in the sink before my now trembling hands dropped it.

"Sean doesn't give a straight answer, either," she answered sourly.

"Why would you ask that, anyway?" My voice cracked, giving away the horror I felt at the thought of someone knowing. The last thing I needed was Kelsey to know, there was no doubt in my mind she'd have no problem telling him.

Her eyes suddenly darkened in color and I really began to fear her actions. She surprised me by rolling them, instead. "Oh, please, Angel," she glowered. "it's written all over your face. And, there's the way you acted when I asked you about it."

Oy, she knows! *Dammit.*

"How did you expect me to act?" I challenged. "I didn't exactly see your question coming."

Her eyes narrowed into slits. "I sincerely hope you're not actually expecting me to buy that line of crap. I figure people out very easily and I'm sure you knew I would eventually ask."

I did sort of expect something like this after the way she acted at the library, however her statement didn't ease the horror I felt now that she knew.

"I guess this is the part where you go home and tell Sean," I said warily.

"Relax, Angel," she laughed. It almost sounded like a black crow when they're fending off other animals from their prey and echoed off the walls. I tried not to cringe. "I'll leave it up to you to tell him."

"In that case it will remain a secret," I mumbled.

"I doubt that," she countered. "even if you don't tell him he'll figure it out. *If* he hasn't already."

I felt my eyes widen with shock and snapped my head up to look at her. "My life is complicated enough," I croaked.

"Then I'd say it's about to get worse. The only thing Sean knows well about his own emotions is that he's crazy about you and wants to be with you every minute he can. Just embrace it, Angel, as I've said before you will find the very thing you never realized you wanted or needed."

She stood from the chair and pushed it in. "It is time I go," she announced. "I'm expected soon and you look exhausted."

"Can I expect to see you at the hall tomorrow night?"

"Probably." She winked at me, turned for the door and less than a second later I was alone.

I continued to stand there, astonished as my eyes blinked, wildly. It was then the magazine I had read months ago flashed through my mind. *They are believed to have extreme speeds*, the article said. Are the Callengers vampires? No, clearly what I saw was just some sort of trick. Then how do you explain what happened at the library? I asked myself.

I walked up the stairs, dazed. As I entered my room thoughts of a hot shower and maybe some sedatives would be the only options that would help me sleep now. My arms were beginning to ache from all the lifting and cleaning, but that wasn't the reason I needed help to sleep. I knew I wouldn't get Kelsey out of my head. I took some clothes from the dresser and headed to the bathroom.

The sound of the rain falling on the roof the next morning had my eyes opening before the alarm did. I laid there, listening to it for a long while, and then slowly got up. I didn't feel the aches in my arms till I pulled my uniform from the hanger inside my closet. Thankfully, rain like this keeps things at the diner slow. That would be my only way to survive without feeling like my arms would fall off.

Ryan was still sleeping and I tried keeping my noise in the kitchen to a minimum. I got the coffee pot to start brewing then took a bowl and a box of cereal from the cabinet. It was still too early to leave so I sat down at the table and ate the cereal slowly. Ryan never noticed I was even downstairs.

Bobbie didn't come home and it was time for me to leave. I donned in my jacket and carefully opened the door. The rain was still heavy, I stood on the porch a moment longer and scowled up at the sky. If I had any hopes to get to the diner without being soaked they were shot. I wasn't going to have a single dry spot when I got there. I pulled up my hood and walked down the stairs.

I walked close to the edge of the street so if a car were to pass I could lessen my chances of being splattered with the water flooding the street. I hadn't been walking long when the sound of a horn appeared behind me. I got as close to the curb as I could, getting out of its way. Then suddenly the gold Mustang was beside me, moving slowly.

"Would you like a ride, Angel?" Kyle asked through the open passenger window.

I stopped walking and turned my whole body his direction. "Really, Kyle?" I glowered. "You act like a jerk all week and now you want me to forget about it? I don't think so."

I started walking again. I knew it was childish to act like that when it was raining badly, I couldn't help it. Kyle had spent the entire week treating me worse than Marisa did and it bothered me. Especially since Kyle was a friend. I expected him to drive away angry, he didn't. He kept the car moving beside me.

"C'mon, Angel, it's pouring out here."

I ignored him.

"Please?" he pleaded. "If you get in you can yell at me the rest of the way and I won't say anything because I know I deserve it."

I stopped walking again and turned to face the car. I was hesitant for a second, and then walked to his car. He had the door open by the time I got to it and I climbed in.

"Thank you," I said, sourly.

"You're welcome." He flashed me a grin and despite the fact I was unhappy with him I couldn't help smiling.

"Angel, I want to apologize to you. I've been a real *ass* and I'm sorry."

Here we go again.

"Kyle," I pronounced his name carefully. "I want you to *really* listen to me. You and I are friends and there will never be anything more. I know you think I'm being rude about everything, but I'm not."

"But you've become sweet on Sean." His voice sounded disappointed.

I pressed my lips together for a second in hopes of controlling my voice. "I'm not sweet on anyone," I finally stated.

"Then why is he suddenly always around?"

Because he enjoys irritating me, I thought bitterly.

"I don't know, Kyle," I said, frustration coloring my tone.

He was quiet for a long while so I thought the worst was over and relaxed in the seat. I turned my head to look out the window.

"This roll of the dice sucks," Kyle suddenly stated out loud.

"What are you talking about?"

He didn't answer right away and I looked at him.

"I met you first." His voice sounded like a sulky child.

"And?" I challenged.

"I'm just pointing out that you've never taken any rides from me or have gone out even one night with me, but you've gone to dinner in Toledo with Wilkins and you get in Sean's truck almost every time he shows up."

"Kyle, we've been over this," I exasperated. "I didn't go to dinner with John because I wanted to and yes, I did get in Sean's truck the other night. John wasn't taking leave me alone for an answer, what else did you want me to do?"

"You could have said yes when I asked that night. Why did you go with him after work last week?"

So he does know. I inhaled deeply through my nose and released the breath slowly between my lips.

"He wanted to talk so I gave him a chance to say whatever it was he needed to."

"If that's true then why would Brandi think he'd kiss you?" His tone had a hint of bitterness to it.

"I don't know," I growled. "try asking her." I turned my face back to the window.

He completely ignored my suggestion.

"*If* you were to choose one of us to date, who would it be?"

I couldn't believe what he'd ask and turned my head sharply in his direction. "What!?" I snapped.

"C'mon, Angel," he moaned. "there has to be one of us you like more than the others."

We were at the diner now, Kyle carefully pulled in next to Kloe's jeep and parked. I yanked on the door handle and pushed it open.

"You're impossible!" I snarled.

"Angel, wait," he pleaded. His hand snaked out, catching my wrist. "I'm sorry," he continued. "I promise from now on I won't bring it up anymore. I'm not going to lie and say I'm okay with just being friends because I'm not. But, I would still rather have the friendship then nothing at all."

He released my wrist and curled his hand in a fist, resting it against his leg. I tried to hang on to my irritation, but the sadness in his brown eyes softened my will.

"All right," I grumbled. "I'll forgive you this time, but ..." I pointed my index finger at him. "... if you give me another attitude about anything I swear, I *will* stop talking to you."

"Deal," he agreed with a short laugh.

I looked at him a second longer then got out and ran to the building.

I expected to see Anna when I entered, instead it was Kelly. She was setting coffee cups upside down on the tables and placing the rolled silverware next to them.

"Good morning, Angel," she said in a weary tone.

"Good morning, where's Anna?" I walked behind the counter to grab a cup of coffee before heading in the back.

Kelly shrugged. "It's her day off."

"Oh." I knew the word seemed inadequate, but I lacked a better response.

I finished with the cup then trudged to the back.

The morning passed in a blur as we were busier than expected. Derek's show for tonight had brought many people in town. I tried not to dwell on how packed the hall was going to be, it was still too early in the day for hyperventilation. I made myself think of good things, like being able to hide from anyone I didn't want to run into. That worked to calm my fears and put a smile on my face.

Bobbie was still sleeping when I got home and I crept quietly up the stairs. Kyle had given me a ride home so I wasn't wet, still my skin felt cold. I crossed my room to the dresser and took out a pair of sweats, and then went in the closet for my Dolphin jersey. They weren't my best looking clothes, but they were warm and dry.

On the kitchen counter, a small pad of paper was propped up against the wall under the phone. John called again, Bobbie had written. He said sorry he's missed getting with you, he's been in court a lot and just got back. He wants you to call him. If he doesn't hear from you then he'll see you tonight.

I grimaced. I hadn't seen him since that awful night in the parking lot and had hoped not to. I tore the paper from the pad, crumpled it up and tossed it in the trash can. I poured myself a glass of tea, and then walked in the living room and flopped down on the couch. I picked up the remote and turned on the TV, feeling determined not to think about the message before it could convince me not to go tonight.

When Bobbie finally came down Law & Order was in the middle of its second hour.

"Anything good on?" she asked as she walked to the couch.

"Law & Order reruns," I said with a shrug.

She sat down next to me, pulling one of the throw pillows on her lap then wrapped her arms around it, pressing it against her chest.

"Ooh," she said delighted. "I like this show."

I sent her an odd expression and she laughed.

"Did you get the message I left in the kitchen?"

"Yes," I answered, my tone sour. I expected her to laugh or say something, she did neither.

She slightly shrugged her shoulders. "Okay."

When the show ended I got up and went in the kitchen to refill my cup. Two hard brisk knocks came on the door as I entered the foyer. I opened it and there stood Brandi. She was dressed in a black dress and stiletto heels. Her hair was full of curls and was hanging down passed her shoulders. It wasn't until she entered and closed the door I saw the gray garment bag.

"You're not planning to wear that, are you?" she asked, eyeing my clothes.

I glanced down at them then looked back at her. "What's so wrong with them?"

"This is going to be worse than the first time," she groaned.

"What's that supposed to mean?" I asked, irked.

She glared at me. "The first time Bobbie took you to the hall you wore jeans."

"Okay, so?"

She rolled her eyes and sighed as though I should have known that wasn't dress code. "Angel, when going out to places like that you're supposed to dress up. It's all part of being a girl."

"Here we go with that again," I moaned. I shook my head and turned to walk away. Brandi grabbed my wrist before I could even take a step.

"I know it's still kind of early, but since you are in need of rescuing from yourself and I've been through this with you before we are going to get to work."

She went up the stairs dragging me behind her.

"You clearly know I don't have fancy clothes," I reminded her.

"I know, that's why I brought something for you to wear." She stopped at the top of the stairs and yelled down them. "Bobbie, could you give me a hand up here with setting up the bathroom?"

She released my wrist and walked into my room.

"Close the door," she commanded me.

I obeyed silently.

She laid the bag on the bed and was unzipping it when I finally walked up next to her. I was instantly shell shocked as she lifted the dress from the bag. It was mint green, low cut in the front, with only two little straps and an open back. The bottom would be mid-thigh.

"Brandi," I whined. "I can't wear that."

"Yes you can," she growled. "It isn't much different than the last one you wore."

"Yes it is," I countered. "The red one you made me wear wasn't short and it didn't show any of the front." I paused, picking up the dress and turning it to face her. "I wear this and there won't be a single person in the room that will be looking at my face."

A faint smile crossed her lips. "Hopefully after tonight there's only going to be one set of eyes that will matter. Now, I'm going to step out, you get changed and when you're finished open the door."

I watched in awe as she walked to the door and closed it behind her. I don't need any pairs of eyes to notice me, let alone one in particular. I turned towards the bed and tossed the dress on it. I couldn't believe the horror she was going to make me face.

I took off my comfy clothes and put on the dress. It was worse than I thought. I might as well have worn nothing for all it was covering. I walked to the door and opened it. Brandi's back was facing me while she stood in the doorway of Bobbie's bedroom. At the sound of my door opening she slowly turned to look at me. My expression must have been one she didn't like, she scowled at me.

"What?" she asked, sarcastically.

"It's kind of short," I complained. "and, I'm not comfortable with having the top half of my body exposed."

"It's fine, Angel," she grumbled. "I don't know why you give such a fuss over showing off the figure you have. You look fabulous."

I groaned.

She walked to me and reached out, grabbing my hand, and then towed me into the bathroom. And, just like before there was make-up and hair product galore spilled out all over the counter. This was definitely going to be much worse then I feared. She pushed me down on the toilet lid and picked up a can of hair mousse.

Bobbie played cosmetician while Brandi was the hairdresser. She fussed with it till my natural curls had more bounce than usual then pulled the front back, slipping a barrette in it. The more I moaned and complained at her the more torture she made me sit through. I knew if I ever wanted to be free again I was just going to have to sit through it quietly.

Finally, they were done.

"You should really take a look at yourself in the mirror," Brandi told me. "You look just … amazing."

I was shaking my head before she finally said the word she was struggling to say.

"Fine then," she sighed. "Have it your way."

"I'm going to get dressed, now," Bobbie announced. "I'll meet the two of you downstairs shortly." She walked out of the bathroom and in to her room.

I sat in the backseat of Brandi's car compensating the upcoming horror I would soon face. She put me in another pair of heels and was expecting me to walk around and eventually dance in them. She clearly didn't understand my balance problems and this was going to be humiliating. At least now it wasn't raining.

We were at the hall now and Brandi pulled into the parking lot on the side of the building. I guess that was the great thing about being in a relationship with the owner, she had her own place to park. Once we were all out of the car Brandi and Bobbie looped their arms through mine, carefully walking me inside so I wouldn't land on my face. I may not have been able to fall, but I would still be able to sprain an ankle.

I expected to see Derek's band on the stage playing a solo as everyone was showing up. That's what they did the last time I came here, anyway. Instead, the DJ in the corner beside the stage was playing through a list of the current hits. Derek was a stickler about him playing both country and pop music.

The colored lights overhead was flashing, frantically causing much of the floor to look like it had disappeared. Not really a good idea for a clumsy person like me. Even as I tried being diplomatic about all this, I knew it was going to end very badly. I could almost guarantee I'd have a broken neck by the time this night was through.

The girls walked me to the closet soda station then released my arms. Brandi was needed somewhere and had to get going. Bobbie ordered each of us a drink while I stared at the stool behind me, trying to decide if

I should sit down or even if I *could* sit. Since I was so deep in thought I wasn't aware that I was even being approached.

"Wow, Angel," came a shocked voice. "I almost didn't recognize you."

I looked up and Catlyn was standing a few inches away with Kyle by her side. She was dressed in a silver dress, flowing down her legs, a slit in the right side, stopping just before the hip. Kyle wore a pale blue, shirt and faded blue jeans.

Kyle waved a hand up and down in front of me. "You look incredible."

I felt my face start to heat from embarrassment. "Thanks. You two look good yourselves."

Catyln grinned at me. "I had to borrow this from Brandi."

How could she be so excited to wear a dress that belong to her sister?

"Well, we're going to make our rounds," Catlyn announced cheerfully. "Have fun and we'll see you later."

"Okay," Bobbie laughed. "bye."

After they walked away I turned back to the bar and picked up the glass of soda Bobbie had ordered for me. She scanned the crowd then a second later was whispering in my ear before she walked away.

"Just when I thought you couldn't get any more beautiful," a soft voice said. "you prove me wrong."

I didn't have to turn around to know who the voice belonged to. I cursed Bobbie under my breath for leaving me alone and slowly turned to face John. He was barely a few inches from me, he was dressed in a white button up shirt and black slacks.

"Hello, John," I said politely.

A slow song began to spill out from the speakers overhead. John extended his right arm out to me.

"Would you like to dance?" he asked.

I stared at his hand for a minute then looked up at him. The expression on his face was pleasant, but I wasn't going to put myself in a position to keep this nonsense going.

"John, I don't ..." My voice trailed off. I wasn't sure what I could say that I'd hadn't already.

"It's all right, Angel," Kelsey stated as she suddenly appeared behind John.

The sound of her voice caught him off guard and he whirled around to face her. She smiled wickedly.

"I'm sorry, John," she continued, though she didn't sound a bit sorry. "I'm afraid Angel has already been spoken for."

"What is with you Callengers," John snarled. "You come to this town and try to act like you run it."

"Not quite," she laughed. "but maybe someday. Besides, there's still plenty of girls in here you haven't lied to yet. Go disrupt one of their lives and let Angel get where she needs to be ... where she *should* be," she corrected.

"You and your brother are the reason she doesn't return my calls," he accused. "or agrees to go out with me."

"I can assure you we had no part in her decisions. You should probably take a closer look at the trail of broken hearts you have left behind. Don't you think her friends would have warned her about you?"

John stared at her a another long moment before turning to me.

"Angel, I will catch up with you a little later," he said, condescendingly. "Be sure to at least save *me* the last dance."

I opened my mouth, never to get the chance to say anything.

"If things work out as they should," Kelsey said, her voice dark. "She'll be long gone before the last song plays."

John glared at her, and then stalked off.

"Maybe now he'll understand get lost," she grumbled as she turned back to me.

"That wasn't really very nice," I scolded her.

She rolled her eyes and laughed. "I'm sorry, was I wrong about you wanting to dance with him?"

"Well ... no," I admitted. "I've been trying to get away from him for weeks. I'm starting to think

maybe I'm going to have to leave town for a while. If he can't find me then surely he'd get the point."

Kelsey's eyes began to glow. "Should you decide to exercise that plan be sure to let me know. I have the perfect place you can go."

I suddenly became nervous and decided it was time to find out what she wanted then escape.

"Do you really need something or were you just trying to get rid of John?"

She laughed and grabbed my hand and began pulling me towards the door. For reasons I couldn't fathom I was very near the verge of a heart attack.

"Where are we going?" I nearly croaked.

The toe of my deadly shoe got caught on the trim where the carpet met the wood and I stumbled. Kelsey whirled around, catching me before I fell.

"Not *we*," she corrected. "you. You have someone patiently waiting for you."

When it finally sank in who she meant I groaned and tried to pull free of her iron grasp. We were already at the door and she opened it, pushing me out.

The weather seemed to want to comply with everyone's wish for a clear night. The clouds had disappeared, letting the stars come out and the moon was casting its light off the water. I carefully walked down the sidewalk and looked around. There wasn't one single person, anywhere. I was annoyed now and turned to go back inside to look for Kelsey, and then tell her what I thought of her ideas. Then suddenly the sound of a soft whistle caught my attention.

I followed it around to the side of the building and there in the shadows was a dark figure. Normally this would have scared the breath out of me, but now I didn't have any doubts who the figure was.

"Do you always convince your sister to do your dirty work?" I asked, icily.

He laughed, the sound was as dark as the shadows around him. "I usually do my own, but I wasn't sure I could contain myself if I ran into your boyfriends. And, I don't much like crowded places."

"I don't know exactly *who* you're pertaining to," I said frostily. "But you clearly have the wrong idea."

"I can assure you I don't. You seem to forget I've known them longer than you."

He stepped away from the wall and in to the light. I felt my breath catch in my throat as the moonlight illuminated his skin. It even seemed to have an unusual effect on his crystal blue eyes. I had never seen anything or anyone look so beautiful.

"So, what do you want?" I whispered, not giving my voice a chance to break.

"You come here to dance, don't you?" he asked, his voice sounding confused.

"Not in these shoes or caught up in a pair of arms. Sean, what is this *really* about?"

He smiled and walked to me, stopping inches in front of me. My heart began to beat rabbit jumps against my ribs. His eyes slowly looked me over as he examined my Barbie dress.

"Angel, my love, you are beyond beautiful tonight."

I shut my eyes briefly on a prayer for patience. "Sean, are you trying to irritate me?"

He laughed again. "It seems I don't have to try, it appears to come naturally. But no, I'm only asking a lady for a dance."

He held his arm out, offering me his hand. I stared at it for a long second then looked back up at his face. His hair looked windblown, a small strand curled over his brow. The skin under his eyes wasn't the deep purple they usually were. He grew impatient with my hesitation, grabbing my hand and pulled me to him. My heart nearly jumped out of my chest as he possessively wrapped his arms around my waist.

"What's the matter with you, Callenger?" I demanded. "I've made it absolutely plain I'm not interested in dancing with you."

Now irritation showed on his face. "You and I both know that just isn't true."

He saw I was about to argue and lightly placed a hand over my lips to silence me.

"If it was," he continued. "you wouldn't have come out here and you certainly wouldn't look like this."

He dropped his hand and I opened my mouth to correct his notions that the dress wasn't my idea, yet the words wouldn't come out. His breath grazed my skin, dazzling me momentarily and I closed my mouth, focusing on trying to remember how to breathe. Sean took full advantage of my hesitation and began swaying us around.

My mind was slow but I was still determined to find a way out of this. "I honestly can't dance and you're so much taller than me," I complained, nearly breathless.

He looked down at me and rolled his eyes. "The secret to dancing is all in the leading and I'm six-three, Angel. There's only a foot difference. Here -----."

He stopped moving us and tightened his arm around me, lifting me up and sat me gently on his feet.

"Now you're not so short," he teased.

"Hey," I hissed.

Sean laughed.

A song began to play and since I clearly wasn't getting free of his arms I concentrated on *it*. It was a country song, though not one I had heard. It appeared to be perfect for two people who were falling in love in the moonlight. It mentioned kissing in this light and taking things slow. Well, that was where the similarity had ended. I may be in love with Sean, but in no way was I planning to kiss him goodnight while we stood in this beautiful light tonight ----- or ever.

After a while I finally gave up trying to fight what was clearly happening and rested my head against his cold, hard chest, forcing myself to admit this really wasn't as bad as I'd made it out to be. Sean swirled us in perfect time with the song. I would have never been able to dance like this on my own or even at all.

The song ended and Sean kept us moving. It wasn't but a second later and another one started.

"Was your mother at every dance practice?" I asked.

Sean shook us with his quiet laughter. "Not many, though she was adequate that I learned how to show a lady around a dance floor."

"She must be proud," I mused.

"One could certainly suppose she is." His voice was unemotional.

I wasn't sure if I had misread his tone while he spoke of his mother or if maybe he was like me and didn't enjoy talking about his mom. Either way I changed the subject.

"I feel like a three-year-old dancing on an adults shoes," I laughed.

He laughed while nestling his face in my hair. "You certainly don't look three."

His tone reminded me of just how my Barbie dress looked and I scowled.

"This sort of feels like déjà vu," I snorted. "Only this time I *can* remember exactly what I see because there's no drugs to trick me." I was expecting the usual line of denial so I was caught by surprise at his response.

"Well, there went my fantasy." I could hear the smile in his voice.

I carefully pulled back to look at him. "What fantasy?"

"I was hoping you'd tell me I smell like citrus and sunshine again."

His mention of that had my eyes widening with shock. He clearly did smell like citrus, but I would never be brave enough to say that out loud. I felt a tremor run through me and fought against it.

"When did I ever tell you that?" My voice broke anyway.

He tried to hide the smirk on his face when he answered. "The last time you were tucked in my arms."

The song we were dancing to had ended. He kept us moving and I continued to stare at his face, confused. Is he admitting to being in the cabin that night? He read something on my face and suddenly held us still.

"Is something wrong, Angel?"

I wasn't sure why, but I suddenly felt it was time to get away before I sparked his anger. I certainly wasn't in the place to push anything. No matter how unintentional it was.

"No," I said quickly. I struggled to free myself of his arms. "Thank you for the dance, Sean. My friends are probably wondering where I am so I should get back inside."

He didn't budge.

"Sean, please," I pleaded. I placed my hands on his chest, trying to push him to release me. I could have been trying to move a boulder for all the good it was doing me.

"Your friends know where you are," he stated matter-of-factly.

"Therefore, you can just settle down and stay where you are. Now, I'm certain I said something to upset you, what is it?"

I stopped fighting, dropping my arms to my sides. He leaned down and laid his forehead gently against mine, his breath lightly grazing across the skin of my face.

"*Please*, bright eyes, tell me," he whispered.

It took me another moment to remember how to exhale before I could speak.

"Are you," I paused for a second, stabilizing my voice. "admitting to being there that night?"

"Yes," he breathed.

"Why now?" I was confused.

He whirled us once to the song now playing, and then released every part of me but my hand.

"Walk with me." He led me around the building to the dock behind it.

The water was almost crystallized as the moonlight spilled out across it. Sean continued to hang on to my hand while he stared out at it. I wasn't sure I was ready to hear the reasons now, but I knew there would be no way for me to get out of hearing it. I stood at his side, patiently waiting for him to say something. The minutes ticked by.

"Angel," he finally said, pronouncing my name carefully. His voice was unsteady. "It was important for us that you didn't know too much. Like you, we have secrets we have to keep."

"I told you I would never tell anyone anything. I was going crazy for weeks trying to understand what was real and what wasn't."

"I know you did," he agreed. Sitting behind the building, almost against it was a stone bench. Sean walked us to it, and then sat down pulling me into his lap. "I wanted so badly to tell you the truth, but I couldn't."

His legs felt as though I was sitting on the bench myself. I shivered from the coldness and was slightly uncomfortable from the stone feel of his body, yet it felt good to get a break from standing in Brandi's neck breaking shoes.

"Are you going to tell me the truth now?" I asked, carefully.

He looked out at the water then glanced at me with troubling eyes. "Not tonight," he sighed.

"Then I guess our dance is over," I said, allowing acid to leak in my tone. "I'm going back inside with my friends."

He tightened his arms, I couldn't move an inch. "I don't want to fight with you tonight."

"I get it," I said, pressing my lips together in irritation. "the game is only played *your* way."

He glared at me, his eyes instantly turned jet black. "Do you really believe this is a game?" he growled.

My eyes widened and I very slowly back my face away, as I never noticed it was so close to his.

"I don't know what I believe," I breathed.

My mind was racing, my pulse hammering wildly under the skin. I didn't understand how his eyes could change so quickly, but I knew it was time for me to get free.

"Stop making that face," he said firmly. "and just settle down."

"My friends -----."

"As I have said before, they already know where you are. Did you really think Kelsey would bring you out here and not say anything to your friends? They clearly already knew before you even got here that you would be with me."

It was then the statement Brandi had made about one pair of eyes and the way she had acted flashed in my mind. Somehow they had this planned all along. What else did they plan and fail to mention to me?

"You are the most conceited, self-righteous person I have ever met," I growled.

He grinned at me. "That's the nicest thing you've said to me."

"Ugh!" I groaned. "If you're not going to tell me anything then why am I out here?"

He eyed the dress again then looked back at me. "I wanted you to myself a while. I'm starting to consider just simply keeping you for myself the rest of the night."

The statement Kelsey had made earlier about being long gone before the last song plays entered my mind and my eyes widened in horror.

"I *want* free, Sean," I nearly snarled.

"Not a chance," he laughed.

I tried to glare at him, but the look on his face made it impossible. His eyes were somehow still black, yet the humor I was used to seeing in them changed into something else in the space of a heartbeat. And that something else was dark and dangerous. And exciting. My pulse reacted again, thumping wildly.

He tilted his head to the side and slowly moved closer to my face. "Don't move, Angel," he whispered.

I had no problem obliging with his request, I couldn't have moved if I wanted to. His lips were seconds from touching mine when an unexpected voice appeared beside us.

"Ahem." Kelsey cleared her throat.

"Go away, Kelsey," Sean moaned.

"I'm afraid I can't do that," she said, her tone had a hint of sarcasm in it. "I guess you're unaware that the two of you have already been out here most of the night and Bobbie is ready to go home. So unless Angel is spending the night with you then I suggest you let her go."

Sean sighed heavily, and then hesitantly raised his arms. I knew I should have jumped at the chance to be free, yet I couldn't will myself to stand. A strand of hair fell across Sean's brow and I had another urge to reach out and touch it. I reached up very slowly, carefully running my fingers through it, brushing it back. It was soft and thick, as if to have been recently washed. I expected him to push my hand away; he didn't. His breathing became rough and unsteady, his eyes closed. I couldn't quite understand why I felt a strong need in the pit of my stomach to somehow touch his face, but I leaned in slowly, placing a gentle kiss to his cheek. His face felt hard and cold like the rest of his body, yet my lips tingled when I pulled away.

His eyes flashed open as I stood from his lap.

"Good night, Sean." I turned and followed Kelsey around to the front of the building where Bobbie was waiting.

"I'm really sorry for disturbing you, Angel," Bobbie apologized as we walked to Brandi's car.

"It's all right," I sighed. "it is late and I have to work in the morning."

"At least you got away from John," she laughed.

"I guess I did," I agreed with chuckled.

I kept thinking about what would have happened if Kelsey hadn't suddenly appeared. I couldn't fathom the reason, but I felt a deep disappointment that I never got to see that kiss through.

I walked up the stairs to my room in a slow pace, my mind heavily clouded. My body went in automatic mode while I showered then dressed for bed and eventually crawled in it, hazily pulling the quilt over me.

As I laid my head to rest on my pillow my mind still swirled, almost dizzily and full of the images from beside the bay. Even though there had been many times I've been with him, something about tonight had been different. I thought it was comfortable; natural really when he took my hand on that hill the night he drove us to Los Angeles, but the man I saw standing next to the water in the moonlight tonight had been much different than the other personalities I'd had to put up with these past few months. There had been a softness in his face and in his voice that I'd never seen or heard before.

That left me both nervous and excited about the next time I would see him. This also left me to wonder if the next time we were completely alone if that would be the time he would finally confess the truth. I wanted so badly for him to tell me months ago, but now that I clearly understand there is something about him and his family that is definitely wrong could I even stand to hear it?

As I got closer to unconsciousness one thing became absolutely clear, despite everything else. After all that has happened in this one night I was no longer going to be able to love Sean and continue to keep it to myself.

A Girls' Night

The months of being able to sleep well came to a sudden end. That Sunday Kelly and Ryan left for Washington and the sounds I had long since forgotten that had kept me awake most of the night had returned. Only now the pacing sounds were outside my bedroom, as well as throughout the house. I turned the light on a few times and got up to look.

Nothing.

Figuring I was once again losing my mind I went back to bed and turned up the volume on the clock radio and eventually pulled the quilt over my head. And still, the sounds would return.

The week after Derek's two day party returned to normal. Well ----- almost. Sean was now stopping by nearly every morning to drive me to work. I tried turning him down the first couple of times, in fear he would try that conversation I was now content to avoid or finish were we left off when Kelsey had suddenly interrupted. Either way, both were unwelcomed situations.

I dreaded the first few times Sean gave me a ride to work. I would brace myself as I walked in for one of Kyle's sullen moods. Even as he'd made the deal with me there would be no more attitudes over Sean I knew he wouldn't be able to help himself. He surprised me by not showing any interest in my being picked up or dropped off nearly every day and acted like each one was an ordinary day. I was leery of it, but as long as he was keeping his word I maintained my good attitude towards him.

Bobbie became depressed after Ryan and Kelly returned to Washington. As bad as I felt for her, knowing all too well myself what it was like to have someone walk out and never really know when you would see them again, I had no idea how to comfort her. I was still trying to comfort myself every time I hung up from a conversation with Jen. Some evenings to escape the thoughts and feelings I would sit in the living room and play random music on the keyboard. Bobbie would sit on the couch to watch me and listen. It appeared to cheer her up. Sometimes she would even request something in particular.

I cringed every day when I came home that week as I feared there would be messages waiting for me from John. I was prepared for him to be angry with me for not going back inside. By the next week when none had shown up I began to relax. It was then Brandi informed me he had in fact gotten angry when I didn't go back inside the hall that night. He returned to Portland and vowed he wouldn't return to Newport until the following summer. He had gotten the point, finally.

Despite the fact I was once again becoming sleep deprived from all the sounds in the house at night I woke earlier than usual Wednesday morning. It was time to pay the electric bill and this time it was my turn to pay it.

I donned in my jacket as I went down the stairs, grabbed the keys from the bowl and went out the door without even stopping in the kitchen for coffee. I wanted to get to the pay center before the lines started to form. I knew Sean would be unhappy I didn't wait for him, but that would just be something he'd have to get over.

When I entered the diner Brandi, Sydney and Kyle were standing in front of the kitchen doorway engaged in a conversation. Apparently something exciting had happened and Brandi couldn't wait to share it. It was now the tiredness started to set in and I walked behind them for that cup of coffee I didn't get.

"Angel!" Brandi squealed, turning to face me. "I'm so glad you're here."

I knew that tone and fought a groan. Today wasn't one I would easily be able to put up the phony front these kinds of moods called for.

"And why is that?" I asked.

"Between you being here or with Mr. Dreamy I don't know if Bobbie has had the chance to fill you in about our plans."

I sincerely *hated* when she called Sean that. I would peek a look at Kyle every time she brought Sean up to see what his expressions were so I knew what I'd be in for the rest of the day. His face showed no emotions and his tone would still be pleasant. I finished stirring the spoon around in the cup, thinking back over the last few conversations Bobbie and I had. Brandi's name nor any plans with her ever came up.

"No. I do believe this is the first I've heard about it."

She quickly skidded to my side. "Okay, well we are planning to go to Portland once I'm off and I was thinking you should come with us."

The thought of getting out of Newport, even if only for a little while was tempting. Especially since I've been stuck here for three months.

Then the thought of bumping into John entered my mind. I surely didn't want to go through that experience again.

"I don't know, Brandi," I said carefully. "Mike is pretty -----."

"He won't care if he knows you're with us," she stated, cutting me off.

I tried to be crafty as I hid my horror caused by my own thoughts when I responded.

"The plan was clearly made for family time. I don't want to intrude on that, I've already intruded enough."

Brandi puckered her lips in disappointment. "You *are* family," she fussed. "therefore it's only fitting that you go with us."

What would be fitting is for me to sleep, I said to myself. I wasn't convinced my joining them was a good idea, but I knew she would never be out of my way the rest of the day or even shut up about it until I agreed.

"Fine then," I sighed, heavily. "I'll go."

Brandi bounced up and down, clapping her hands like a little kid. "Yay!" she squealed in delight.

I shook my head back and forth, though I couldn't help laughing at her and picked up my cup. I knew something somewhere was waiting for me to finally get to it.

The sky had chosen today to drop its buckets full of water and slow everything down. Kloe had been in and out all day, running bank deposits, helping Kyle unload her inventory when the delivery truck arrived and lining the schedules for the following week. Before she left the last time she asked me if I would mind pulling everything that had been shoved under the front counter out, clean it, and then straighten it up. I wasn't sure why she picked me for the job, but I didn't complain. At least now I'd have more to do then just stand around.

Bobbie came in with Catlyn as I pulled the last bit of stuff out.

"Ew, gross," Catlyn said as she came around the counter. "Angel, why in the world are you touching that stuff?"

"Your mother asked me to."

"Why didn't she have Brandi do it?"

"Because she didn't ask me," Brandi growled.

I tuned out their dispute and looked at Bobbie. She was sitting on a stool with a distressed expression on her face.

"Is everything all right, Bobbie?" I asked. I had never seen that look before and was deeply concerned.

"No," she sighed, heavily. "Apparently Mom had some sort of accident at work. That's why I had Catlyn bring me down here. I wanted to tell you so when I wasn't home you wouldn't worry and I need the car."

The bickering stopped as Brandi was now paying attention.

"Is Aunt Melinda okay?" she asked, worry martyred her tone.

"Kelly says she's not hurt bad, but you know my sister. She never sees any situation bad so I'm going to go see for myself."

While they continued to discuss the matter over Bobbie's mom I walked away and headed to the back. I took the keys out of my purse, removing the house key as I walked back to the dining room. I slipped it in the pocket of my apron as I entered the room. It had gone quiet and it was then I noticed Catlyn had left. I went behind the counter and stood in front of Bobbie.

"Here, Bobbie," I said as I handed the rest of the keys to her.

"Thank you, Angel," she answered, hesitantly. "I know I should get these made off for you. Then we wouldn't have to do things quite this way."

"When would you have time to do that? We're hardly ever home at the same time."

She laughed, though the sound was more sad than happy. "Good point." She wrapped her hand around the keys then stood from the stool. "I'm really sorry this ruins our plans, Brandi."

"Don't worry about it," she said, dismissively. "Aunt Melinda is more important right now. And, just so you know, I invited Angel."

"Oh good," Bobbie answered, her tone sounding relieved. Then she looked at me. "I've been meaning to mention it to you, but you've been working so many early shifts I never have time to say anything."

"I know and it's fine," I said with a shrug.

She gave me an apologetic look then turned her eyes on Brandi.

"I'm only going to gone for a couple of days. Is it all right if we plan the trip for Sunday?"

"Yes, that would actually work out better because I'm off Sunday."

"Great, Sunday then. Bye everybody."

She turned and walked to the door.

I hadn't realized how much the day had finally passed till Catlyn and Marisa walked in the door. It was only then I looked up at the clock. It was a relief to know I could now take my tired body home, even as I was going to have to walk. There weren't any customers, but I finished filling up the sugar jars, and then headed to the back.

I wasn't out the door even a second when movement caught my attention. I looked over and Sean was leaning against the wall, the slow, cocky grin crossing his lips. I fought a groan.

"It isn't raining now and it's not that dark so why are you here?" I asked.

"I know Bobbie is gone and you look like you're too exhausted to walk."

"I've walked exhausted before and survived," I grumbled.

"Angel, don't be absurd," he scoffed. "I'm just trying to be sure you get home safely."

I gave him a dirty look. "I'm not so fragile that *if* I were to trip over the pavement and fall I'd break something."

"Aren't you?" His expression was amused, like I was missing some sort of joke. "Besides, you blew me off this morning so you owe it to me to let me take you home."

"Oh for crying out loud!" I growled.

I hadn't noticed while we were having our debate that Mark or Anna had pulled into the parking lot till they passed us. Anna flashed me a smile before she entered the building. I glared at Sean, trying to think of something sarcastic to say when suddenly Brandi walked out the door.

"Oh, hey guys," she said cheerfully.

"Hello, Brandi," Sean said in a silky voice.

"Well, I guess this means you won't be needing a ride," Brandi said as she turned her eyes on me. "so I'll see you tomorrow ... Sean."

"See you tomorrow," I agreed, sourly.

Brandi laughed as she headed into the parking lot. Her reaction and Anna's had me turning back to Sean. It was now I noticed he'd moved and was standing beside me. I narrowed my eyes at him.

"What?" he asked innocently.

"You're going to have everyone thinking we're dating," I griped.

A wicked glint flickered in his eyes. "Do you *really* care what they think?"

"Yes I do, actually," I said, suddenly feeling a little uneasy. "I don't want to be the subject of their gossip."

It's been months since I've walked by a group of people and heard them whispering my name. I was quite content with keeping it that way.

His lips formed a frown, he didn't much like my answer.

"Are you ready to go?"

"I've been ready since I got here," I nearly mumbled.

Sean walked out in the parking lot and I followed, much too tired to continue refusing his offer.

The sky was a green-gray cast, as it usually was, but it was strange how the air was so cool for an August night. I shivered and began rubbing my hands up and down my arms. Sean's eyes instantly flashed to my face.

"Are you cold?" he asked.

"A little," I admitted.

"Didn't you have a jacket with you?" His voice was disapproving.

"Yes, but it went to Washington with Bobbie."

We were at the truck now. Sean groaned, the sound almost disgusted and opened the passenger door. He leaned over the seat, and then a second later was handing me a jacket.

"Thank you," I said. I slid my arms into the sleeves.

I climbed in the truck and Sean closed the door. While he was walking around to get in I pressed the sleeves against my face, indulging in the sent. It smelled of citrus, I had come to enjoy the fragrance. When Sean's door opened I dropped my arms. The sleeves were much too long; I shoved them back so I could free my hands.

We drove the short distance slower than usual and in silence. I was nearly a hundred percent sure he had something he wanted to say and cringed in the seat, waiting. Normally he would have some sort of music playing, though it always sounded like background noise. I don't think his stereo was even on. When the silence was beginning to become nerve racking he was pulling in front of the house.

"Thanks for the ride." I reached out to grab the door handle.

"Can't I come in?" He was puzzled.

"Sure," I said, agreeably. "if you would like to."

He didn't answer, leaning over me instead and grabbed the door handle. I hadn't been this close to him since the night I spent with him at the hall and my heart instantly flew into a frenzy.

"What are you doing?" My voice was a shrill higher than I wanted.

He frowned impatiently at me. "I know you're not going to wait for me to get around the truck and open your door for you so I'm doing it now."

He stared at me a second longer then I heard the latch click and he pushed open the door. He sat back up and less than a second later was out of the truck. I took my time jumping out and closing the door. Sean walked closer than usual to me as we made our way to the porch.

We were barely in the door and the phone rang. I slipped out of Sean's coat and handed it to him on my way to answer it. He hesitantly took it, giving me an odd expression.

"Hello?" I asked, warily.

"Hey, Angel," Brandi answered. Her tone enthusiastic.

"What's up?"

My body was feeling too exhausted to stand, I crossed the room and sat down at the table. Sean was already sitting there with his legs stretched out in front of him.

"I talked to Kelly myself and she assures me Aunt Melinda is okay," Brandi was saying. "I told her to tell Bobbie to call me when she gets there."

The last part of her statement confused me, I tore my eyes away from Sean so I could concentrate on the conversation.

"Why did you do that?" My voice was stunned.

I could almost hear Brandi roll her eyes. "Kelly said Aunt Melinda cut her hand, but it wasn't bad, though she will be off work for a few days. I'm going to try talking Bobbie into coming back tomorrow then we can go to Portland Friday."

"I have to work on Friday." I tried to sound disappointed.

"Actually, you don't," she countered, her tone sounding smug.

"When did that change?" Now she had my full attention.

"Mom changed it yesterday. She was supposed to tell you before she left, but I guess she forgot."

I was still confused. "Why did she change it?"

"Sydney is supposed to have the weekend off, but she needs Monday and Tuesday. Since you're the only one scheduled to work all weekend Mom traded out the shifts."

Saturday was the one day I was really looking forward to working. It was my birthday and I didn't want to spend it sitting around the house. I knew no matter what I said there wasn't going to be any way out of it. And, Mike wouldn't be able to stop me as I would be a legal adult the next day.

"Fine," I sputtered. "What time are you planning to go Friday?"

"I don't know yet. I have to talk to Bobbie and find out what works for her."

"Okay."

"Oh, and hey," she suddenly blurted. "before you go I've been meaning to ask you something."

The tenor now in her tone suddenly had me nervous.

"What?" I asked, carefully.

"I notice Sean's been around a lot lately, are you two dating now?"

I let out a hiss of breath. "No."

Sean hadn't paid any attention to our conversation till now. He looked at me with one eyebrow raised. My reaction to Brandi's question seemed to make her aware I wasn't alone.

"He's still there, isn't he?" she asked.

"Yep." My lips made a pop sound.

"I guess I'll let you go then and I'll just see you at work tomorrow."

"Okay, bye."

"Bye." She hung up.

I laid the phone on the table then rubbed my hands over my face.

"Is everything all right?" Sean asked. His voice was alluring.

"Not now," I murmured. "It seems I'm too late on keeping the gossip down."

The muscle on the side of my neck began to throb and I pulled one hand away from my face to rub over it. I heard Sean get out of his chair, and then less than a second later he was pushing my hand out of the way and started massaging it. Just the few short seconds his hands touched the skin on my neck they were already beginning to numb the pain.

"I take it you have a date on Friday?" His tone was casual, I heard something else in it.

"*If* Brandi can talk Bobbie into coming back tomorrow," I verified. "She wants a girls night out."

"Where will you be going?" He was unrepentant.

"Portland."

His hands stopped moving and silence was all that came out of him. I wasn't sure why, but I felt, as if I'd said something wrong. I waited, almost impatiently for him to say something or to start moving his hands. The seconds ticked by.

"Sean, are you all right?" I finally asked. I tried to lay my head back to look at him; he quickly held it in place.

"I'm fine, Angel." His voice had a hint of frustration in it.

He placed his hand back on my shoulder, rubbing it in a circular motion. "How do you feel?"

"Much better," I stiffed a yawn. "Thank you."

Sean's hands quickly disappeared from my shoulders and he walked back to his chair.

"I suppose since you're going to be busy over the weekend it won't bother you if I'm gone myself."

His face didn't show any kind of distress, but his voice was still martyred with frustration.

"Doing lookout for Jonah, again?"

His expression turned shocked at my words. "You know about that?"

"Of course, I do." I was slightly irritated that he thought I was an idiot. "You're clearly not the only member of your family I know," I reminded him.

"Kelsey," he grumbled, the sound almost a growl.

I rolled my eyes. "If you're leaving then why did you act so mysteriously when I told you she wants me to go with them to Portland?"

He sighed in exasperation. "Angel, I have a hard enough time being away from you as it is. The idea of you being so far away from me makes me *very* anxious."

"Then why are you leaving?" I was struggling to understand the concept of his words. It didn't help that I was sleep deprived causing my mind to work slower than usual.

He smiled, widely, showing off a pair of ultra-white teeth. "It is prudent for us to leave from time to time."

I looked carefully at his face. His irises were close to black, the skin under them was a deep purple.

"I see," I mused. I dropped my head and looked at my hands for a distraction and to clear my suddenly clouded mind.

"Angelia." He pronounced my name with care, his accent rich.

I looked back up at him, instantly trying to understand the expression on his face.

"What are you thinking so hard about?" His eyes became gloriously intense, nearly scrambling my thoughts.

"You don't really want to know," I whispered.

His face turned hard, with a hint of anger. "After all this time of being with me, you still don't trust me?"

The accusation of his words burned me.

"I didn't say that!" I snapped.

He leaned across the table, his eyes beginning to smolder. "Then tell me ... *please*?" he asked, seductively.

I stared at him, feeling helpless and blurted out the truth. "I'm trying to understand what you are."

"What makes you think I'm any different than you?" His voice was almost a purr.

I suddenly had a difficult time trying to swallow. "I-I-I don't know," I stuttered.

A smile slowly crossed his lips as he sat upright. "I'd love to stay longer, but I've got to be on my way."

"Okay," I said, weakly. "Thank you again for the ride."

He stood from the chair and flashed me a gleaming smile. "Anytime."

He turned on his heels and less than a second later was slipping out the door.

I was still dazed when I got up to put the phone back on the wall then walk up the stairs. As I went up them I decided to take a shower. I smelled of the cleaning solutions it took to clean the counter and I needed the steam from the hot water to help clear my clouded mind.

The next afternoon I took advantage of having the house to myself and put a CD of Bobbie's in the DVD player and turned the volume on the TV as loud as it would go. I cleaned up the entire downstairs and picked up my bedroom. I stripped my bed, and then went in Bobbie's room, stripping the sheets off hers and carried them down the stairs. The buzzer on the dryer buzzed at me as I walked in the kitchen.

I tossed the bedding on the floor next to the washer and bent down to open the dryer door.

"You really shouldn't leave the door unlocked when you're here alone," came a soft voice.

I lost my balance when the unexpected voice startled me, hitting my head on the dryer door.

"Ow, shoot," I nearly howled. I absently rubbed a hand over my head.

My eyes instantly flashed to the kitchen, Sean was standing in the middle of the room. He was staring at me with an unusual expression.

"What are you even doing here?" I stood upright and leaned against the dryer.

He frowned in disgust. "It's nice to see you, too."

"I'm sorry, I know that was rude," I said, apologetically.

He shook his head, waved his hand at me, and then turned to walk to the table.

I watched him, feeling a horrible guilt for my harshness. It was then I noticed for the first time how he was dressed. That bothered me a little bit. Any time I'd been with him I never paid attention to what he wore. I couldn't ever keep my eyes off his face.

He was dressed in a pair of faded jeans and a soft blue sweater. He had the sleeves pushed up to mid-forearm, showing off the smooth, pale skin. The material of the sweater clung to him, showing the counters of a perfectly, broad, muscled chest. My heart began to race and I could feel my cheeks turn warm. I tore my eyes away from his body before I embarrassed myself and looked back at his face.

"I truly am sorry, Sean," I apologized again. "With the music loud I didn't hear you come in so you startled me."

He didn't answer.

I knew I deserved this treatment and I should take it without rebuttal, but I couldn't stop the irritation I felt from surfacing. I turned away from looking at him and leaned over to pull the clothes out of the dryer.

"How's your head?" he suddenly asked.

I thought for a second about giving *him* the same silent treatment he had given me. I knew if I wanted him to believe I really was sorry then that clearly wasn't an option. I mumbled incoherently under my breath while I closed the door, picked up the basket, and then stood upright.

"I didn't feel a goose egg so I suppose it's all right."

I felt too embarrassed to fold my clothes in front of Sean and set the basket on top of the dryer. I headed in the living room to turn down the music then returned to the kitchen. I stopped at the table to pick up my glass.

"Would you like something to drink?" I asked before walking away.

Sean shook his head. "No. Thank you."

I felt his eyes on me while I walked to the refrigerator. "What brings you here?"

His voice was thoughtful when he responded. "I figured since I won't see you over the weekend I would take advantage of having you to myself this afternoon."

I wasn't ready to look at him and kept my back to him while I refilled my glass with tea.

"I'm really a boring person, Sean. I'm going to be real honest here, I just can't understand why you waste your time on *me*."

"On the contrary," he disagreed. "You fascinate me with the things you do."

"I'm fascinating," I grumbled. "right." I closed the door, slowly turning around.

"Everything in here still looks neat," he noted with a laugh. "Have you read the book I brought you?"

I cringed. I hadn't even bothered to pick it up.

I suddenly needed a distraction and walked to the counter, setting my glass on it then headed to the back porch.

"I haven't had much time to read it," I lied.

"Or you're simply avoiding the fact you have a problem," he stated, sarcastically.

I ignored him while I stuffed the bedding in the wash machine.

"Would you like to get out of here for a while?" he asked.

I instantly remembered the speed he likes to drive and shivered.

"And go where, Los Angeles again?" I asked.

Sean laughed.

I poured soap over the clothes and closed the lid, I turned the dial to start the washing machine.

"I was thinking maybe I could leave the truck here and we can see how long it takes to run to Mexico and back."

His statement didn't set in right away. I walked in the kitchen, trying to think of some clever way to say no and picked up my glass. His words began to slowly sink in while I was taking a long drink. I nearly dropped the glass and sprayed the wall with what I hadn't yet swallowed.

"Run to Mexico?" I shrieked.

In a flash Sean was standing in front of me and lifting me up, gently setting me on the counter.

"Calm down, songbird," he said, his voice soothing. "I was just checking to see if you were even paying attention."

He rubbed his ice cold hands up and down my arms, trying desperately to calm me down. I closed my eyes so I could concentrate on breathing normally.

"I'm fine," I breathed. I carefully opened my eyes.

Sean glared at me and opened his mouth to argue with me, never to get the chance. The phone rang. He reached behind me, grabbed it, and then handed it to me. He placed a kiss to my forehead then turned his body and leaned against the counter. His action stunned me and I stared at him in awe. His lips were hard, but the skin felt like satin.

"Hello?" I asked. My voice was shaky.

"Hey, Angel," Brandi answered. Her voice was full of excitement.

"What's up?" I said. My eyes were still focused on Sean.

"I talked to Bobbie," she said, eagerly. "She has agreed to come back tonight and I wanted to let you know before you made plans with that gorgeous guy you have hanging around."

Her implications of my relationship with Sean had me looking away from him and scowling at the room.

"I don't have any plans," I nearly growled.

"Okay," her tone sounded disappointed. "I'll see you tomorrow."

"Okay," was all I could say.

It wasn't even a second later and the line went dead.

I set the phone on the counter beside me.

"I take it your trip to Portland is still on?" Sean asked.

I took a deep breath then looked at him. He had a strange mix of emotions on his face.

"Yes, Bobbie will be back sometime tonight."

"I *really* wish you would stay near me." His tone was almost a plead.

This still confused me just as it had the night before. "How could I if you're leaving, too?"

Sean sighed, the sound uneasy. "I could easily change my plans for another time."

I was shaking my head before he finished.

"Sean, I don't want to suddenly be the reason you don't go do whatever it is you're supposed to do. Jonah is clearly counting on you and I think I've already been more than enough of a distraction for you."

Sean slowly shook his head back and forth. "You're wrong," he disagreed, his voice almost a growl. "and besides, I decided weeks ago to just simply let the chips fall where they may. We're not actually going far, Jonah heard about an accident in Otter Rock and wants to look in to it."

I waited for him to explain just exactly where that was and why it would be important to Jonah. The minutes ticked by.

"Now you're speaking Greek," I finally said. "I have no idea where you're talking about."

It was now he seemed to relax. He laughed and turned his body in front of me, casually setting both hands on the counter, caging me. And, as usual my heart reacted.

"If I could be certain no harm would come to you I'd steal you away right now and drag you with us. I'd no longer have any reason to be anxious and you would know exactly what you're getting yourself into. It's sort of why I came here, I wanted to show you something, but I suppose it can wait a few more days. Could I ask for just one small favor?"

"Anything," I blurted.

The flicker in his eyes made me regret the unconditional agreement. He leaned in closer to my face.

"Enjoy yourself this weekend" ----- he grinned, widely ----- "and don't take any cab offers."

The feeling of his ice cold breath in my face dazed me momentarily.

"I'll be sure to pass the message to the girls." My voice didn't sound as bitter as I wanted it to.

He shook with laughter, kissed my forehead then straightened himself. "I'll see you on Sunday."

He turned on his heels and walked to the door.

I awoke the next morning to the most beautiful thing in the world I had missed more than anything. There cascading across my bedroom floor was streaks of sunlight. I went to the window and pushed it out of my way. I leaned out it, breathing in the soft sent of the evergreens while I turned my face up toward the sky. It had been weeks since the sun had been out. This time there weren't any clouds threatening to take it away.

I left the window open, letting the warm breeze fill the room and walked to the dresser. Though I knew the sun would still be out when we left for Portland I pulled out a long-sleeved shirt. I knew it was silly to start feeling self-conscious now, I couldn't help it. No one had ever stared at my arm nor had they ever said anything about my nasty scar, but I didn't know how anyone in Portland would act. And, that was just something I couldn't risk. I walked out of my room and into the bathroom.

I hadn't ever been aware Catlyn was going with us till she walked in the door with Brandi. I was quite surprised when they walked in and Brandi was dressed in a pair of shorts, with a red tank top. Aside from the uniforms we had to wear at work I didn't think she wore anything but dresses. Catlyn, too was dressed in shorts. Her shirt looked like something she'd borrowed from Derek. It was tattered and black, with words on the front that were faded.

Since Brandi's car had more than two doors we piled in it, Catlyn and I took the back. The drive felt longer than the hundred and thirty six miles the signs indicated. I didn't complain because I was free of Newport and was getting to see the part of Salem the highway went through. That was the only town I'd learned about in school, though what we did learn wasn't much. That was the longest road trip I'd ever taken.

Conscious, anyway.

Brandi pulled into the parking lot of the local mall. We left later then they had planned and because it was Friday the parking lot was full. While they complained about the distance they had to walk caused by where she had to park I welcomed the chance to stretch my legs.

The first store Brandi made us stop in was filled with all sort of fancy clothes and dresses. It was no surprise to me she wanted to go in. As they went to the racks advertising sales I walked to the wall to look at the shoes.

"Angel, wait," Brandi called out, running behind me. "I want to talk something over with you."

"You always want to talk about something," I grumbled.

The only topic she ever wanted to discuss any more was Sean.

"I know," she giggled. "you're hardly ever alone anymore so we don't get to talk much."

"What is so important that I need to be alone?" I was sure I already knew the answer.

She stopped beside me and a pair of shoes caught her attention. She spoke without looking at me.

"Are you sure you're not dating Sean?"

I knew it! *Dang it.*

I looked at her in utter disbelief. "No," I stated, firmly. "I am not."

Bobbie and Catlyn joined us now, each of them had clothes lying over their arms.

"I used to believe that," Bobbie said. "until he began to come to the house nearly every day. She hasn't said whether or not they kissed a few weeks ago, but the way Sean looks at her, he clearly doesn't see anyone but *her.*"

"W-o-w," Brandi exaggerated the word into three syllables. "Did you kiss him?"

"No!" My cheeks instantly began to burn with embarrassment.

"I'm sorry, Brandi," Bobbie said. "but I've got to tell her the truth."

I turned my whole body to face her. "What truth?" I asked, slowly.

Bobbie took a deep breath and turned away from me. I knew then what she had to say was bad.

"A couple of nights before we went to the hall Kelsey approached me as I was entering the hospital and asked if I could help her put you and Sean together that night."

I felt my mouth fall open as she admitted this. I simply couldn't believe what I was hearing.

"She approached me, too," Brandi admitted. "She told me Sean's favorite color on you is green. That's why I called that morning to talk to Bobbie. When she said she didn't have a dress that would fit you I looked through my closet and took out the only one I have in that color."

"You two are unbelievable," I scoffed. "You know how I feel about dating so why would you do that to me?"

"Angel," Brandi grumbled. "you make this all sound worse than it is. We know you're in love with him and if you're not going to do anything about it then you leave us no choice. This is the first time Kelsey has found a reason to talk to any of us and when she confirmed what everyone had thought about Sean I had to help. And, anyways we got you free of John."

She took a pair of silver strapped stilettos down from the wall and walked to a stool, and then sat down, trying them on. I watched her, trying to get my bearings so I could yell at her. It may have finally gotten a point to John ... but still.

"Have you ever had a boyfriend, Angel?" Catlyn suddenly asked.

I shook my head. "No."

She looked at me with stiff skepticism.

"Really." I tried to sound convincing and even as what I said was true I wasn't convincing myself.

"Why not?" she asked.

"I wasn't planning to stay in Kansas," I sighed. "so I didn't see the point in dragging out a relationship." I felt guilty for lying to them when they were my friends, but I couldn't tell them what my life was really like. I just couldn't.

"Well ..." Brandi cut in. "... you may not be dating Sean, but he's definitely dating you. If you decide to leave after the thing with Jeremy is over you will completely devastate him."

There was truth in her words and I knew it, though it didn't mean I liked it. Truthfully, it would have been devastating for me, too.

"Have you been thinking about leaving, Angel?" Bobbie asked. Her tone was confused.

"I have thought about it," I admitted, shamefaced.

"You can't leave now, Angel," Catlyn blurted out quickly. "You have become part of our family whether you realize it or not."

I stared at her, speechless.

They dropped the subject and walked to the counter to pay for their things, and then we left the store.

We walked around the mall, entering most of the stores. Nearly every one of them had a sale on summer clothes and they had to carefully scan each rack. I surprised myself by buying a few of the clothes for me. When they stopped in front of JC Penny's I saw a music store next door. I whispered where I was going in Catlyn's ear and walked away.

I was looking over music books for the keyboard when they finally caught up with me.

"I didn't know you had an interest in playing instruments, Angel," Brandi said after she reached my side.

"Only a few," I answered.

"Don't let her fool you," Bobbie laughed. "She has an electric keyboard at home she's plays. She's really good."

"Where did you learn to play something like that?" Catlyn asked.

"I took music and choir in school," I said, sounding a little smug.

I found a couple of books that looked promising and tucked them in my arm then turned to walk away from the shelves. While Brandi continued to talk Bobbie seemed to lose interest in our conversation and walked away.

"Derek's going to totally flip when I tell him!" Brandi squealed in delight.

I quickly whirled to face her. "Oh, Brandi, please don't," I pleaded.

"Why not?" she demanded.

"I only play for the hobby," I lied. The letter from Juilliard felt like it was shaking my purse.

"Fine," she scoffed. She turned on her heels and walked away.

We looked around the store and when nothing caught our attention I paid for the books and we left.

Everyone began to complain about being hungry. We walked through the food court and when none of us could decide on the same thing Catlyn suggested going to a buffet. We piled in the car and drove to a place they seemed to favor. I didn't complain for there was a variety of things I could have that was different from everything I'd eaten the last three months. There's only so much seafood a person could stand to eat.

It was late when we finished eating and someone mentioned going to the movies. Bobbie turned down the idea, as she was worn out from her long drive last night and wanted to go home to bed. Since I didn't get much sleep the night before exhaustion was starting to weigh heavily on me and I agreed with her. Brandi and Catlyn were disappointed, but they knew it was best and they had to work in the morning so we drove the hundred and thirty six miles back to Newport.

I nearly had a heart attack when Brandi pulled in front of Bobbie's house and Mike was sitting on the porch waiting for us. I tried to relax as I got out of the car as he was now walking towards us, yet the expression on his face had me worried. I couldn't help wondering if his visit had something to do with me leaving town. He wasn't smiling, as he usually did and when he spoke his tone was flat.

"I know this isn't the best night to bring this up, Angel. However, it's important I talk to you."

"Have I done something wrong?" I asked, nervously.

"Of course not," he grumbled. "Angel, I think you're probably the easiest teenager I've ever had around here."

"Hey," Brandi said. Her voice sounded offended.

"Besides, you, Brandi." He smiled at her.

"That's better," she approved. Then she turned to me. "Well, since Mike needs to talk with you we're going to go."

"Thank you for dragging me out today," I smirked.

"Anytime," she laughed. "and just so you know we *will* do this again."

She gave me a hug then she walked back to her car with Catlyn beside her.

"I'll just see you inside, Angel," Bobbie told me. She walked away.

I watched my friends disappear and shook my head, sadly.

"Nothing breaks up a party better than a cop," I said as I turned my attention to Mike.

"I wish I didn't have to do this to you." His voice burned with regret.

"So what is this about?"

Mike sighed, heavily. "Jeremy is being extradited to Louisiana tomorrow morning. I don't have much I can hold him on besides kidnapping and they have found more victims scattered around their state. I'm sorry, Angel."

"What about Amanda's family?" I fumed. "How will they get their closure if he's convicted in Louisiana?"

"I'm sure he will be sent to Santa Fe to stand trial for her. Though they may run into the same issues I've had. It's hard to know just exactly where he took her life. And, without that information we have to let the state with the most bodies have jurisdiction. This is why you haven't heard anything from Kansas. You weren't taken from there and you're clearly not dead so they never bothered to even contact me."

I cringed away from his words just as I had Sean's. I didn't care about

Pittsburg turning their back on me, as they always had, but it didn't seem right to me that he was going to get away with what he'd done to her. She was a person just the same as the others. Her life should matter, too.

"I really wish there was something more I could have done for you girls," Mike continued.

"You have done the best you can," I whispered, nearly inaudible. "Thank you for at least telling me."

"Okay, well ..." His voice trailed off. It was full of emotions and I don't think he knew how to express them. He took a few steps from me then suddenly stopped and turned around. "In case I don't see you tomorrow, happy birthday." He walked away.

Some birthday, I thought bitterly as I watched him walk to his car and eventually drive away. Even as I knew this nightmare was finally over for me it didn't do anything for my heavy heart. Amanda Raines will soon be forgotten to everyone but me and her family and that just didn't seem fair. I didn't care if I lived a hundred years she would never be out of my mind. The hardest thing for me to accept was knowing I was going to turn eighteen tomorrow and she never would be.

Surprise!

And again I didn't sleep well. This time it wasn't just the pacing throughout the house that kept me awake. It was Amanda Raines. Her picture flashed in my mind as I went over and over the conversation I had with Mike. It had been months since the news had said anything about us, yet I could still see her face as clearly as the day I saw her picture on Bobbie's TV screen.

The usual green-gray cast of light shined through my bedroom window letting me know it was now daylight. I stayed in bed, fighting against myself for sleep till the thought of seeing the sunlight again filled my mind. Unable to believe it would back for another day I rolled out of bed. Because it was still early I walked to the window, pushed it open, and then leaned on the windowsill. Even though there wasn't really a thing to see, the air was warm and the sky was still gray, but promised the sunlight would soon appear. I continued to stand there, welcoming the feel of the soft breeze on my skin. I hoped when the sun did finally cast its yellow rays it would help to relieve the ache in my heart.

After a while my stomach began to growl and my throat reminded me I hadn't had anything to drink. I forced myself away from the window, once again leaving it open and walked to the dresser. I took out a pale green, long-sleeved shirt, though this time instead of the usual jeans I pulled out a pair of jean shorts. I pondered over what I could do that would keep me in the sunlight till it faded as I crossed my room to go into the bathroom. Maybe after I eat I can take a walk to Yaquina bay.

I briefly saw a reflection of my face in the mirror as I passed in front of it. It took a moment before I realized something didn't look quite right. I laid my clothes down on the counter beside the toilet and walked back to stand in front of the mirror. Now I knew what was wrong; my eyes were red and swollen. I had no memory of crying myself to sleep, yet the proof was on my face. I was suddenly thankful I didn't have to work, no one would have a chance to see it. I turned away from the mirror and walked to the shower.

I stood under the hot, steamy water, hoping it would unknot the muscles in my body, as well as take out the swelling around my eyes. I tried not to let myself ----- okay, so *let* is the wrong word, it's more like *keep* ----- think about last night. If I did then I would start to cry and had to repeat the whole calming process all over again. When I began to realize I wasn't going to be as calm as I wanted I shut off the water and got out.

Once I was dressed I used the towel to wipe the steam off the mirror. I knew I shouldn't feel a need to look at my reflection and see the sadness raging in my own eyes, I couldn't help it. I needed to be sure my eyes were normal in case Bobbie got up and came downstairs. If she saw even a hint of unhappiness on my face I'd be in for a long conversation. They were still a little red, but were no longer swollen. Satisfied with that I turned my attention to the chaos, known as my hair.

I brushed through it and instead of running the straightener over it or bothering to braid it, I pulled it back into a ponytail. I brushed my teeth then left the bathroom.

I was barely down the stairs and the phone rang. I wasn't in the mood to talk to anyone, but I hurried to it so it wouldn't wake up Bobbie.

"Hello?" My voice was flat and completely unemotional.

"Happy birthday, Angel!" Jen shouted.

"Thank you," I grumbled.

"You're the big *eighteen*," she said, her voice becoming enthusiastic with every word. "What kind of special plans do you have to celebrate?"

"It looks like sitting around home."

My tone alerted her there was something wrong, I heard the deep concern in her voice when she responded.

"You don't have any plans with Bobbie or Brandi?"

"Bobbie is asleep because she has to work tonight and Derek is coming home today so Brandi will be spending time with him."

"Have you done anything for yourself, lately?" Her voice had a hint of frustration in it.

"Yes," I nearly growled. "I went with them to Portland last night."

"It's about time," she said, disgusted. "I have to get to work, I just wanted to call before I left in case you got busy and I couldn't catch you. I'll call you again after I get home tonight."

"Okay," I sighed. "bye."

"Bye." She hung up.

I placed the phone the wall, and then got a bowl and a box of cereal out of the cabinet.

I sat at table, taking my time eating. I kept watching the sky, impatiently waiting for the sun to come out. It was growing lighter in color and the clouds were slowly thinning out and disappearing. Any time now. If I started walking now the sun should be out about the time I got to the bridge. I quickly finished off the cereal and stood from the chair.

Three faint knocks came on the door.

I set the bowl in the sink and headed for the door. I was taken by surprise when I opened it and Sean was standing there. A slow smile crossed his lips as he took in my reaction.

"Hi." His voice was amused.

"Um ... hi," I answered, my voice stunned.

He eyed my clothes then flashed his eyes back to my face.

"Were you going somewhere?" he asked, sounding confused.

"Not yet, but soon."

He stepped inside and I backed up, giving him the room to enter without our bodies touching. He closed the door as I walked back in the kitchen.

"I don't mean to intrude on any plans you have," Sean said as he was entering.

I shrugged. "They're not anything of importance so there's really nothing to apologize about."

I picked up my bowl from the sink and poured dish soap in it, and then turned on the water.

"May I ask where you are off to?" Sean's voice was very compelling.

I kept my eyes on the bowl while I ran the brush over it. "I've been considering going down to the bay."

"Are we feeling the need to jump again?" he laughed.

I gave him a dirty look. "*Ha ha*," I snorted. "It just so happens the sun is coming out again today and I don't want to spend it sitting in here." I looked away from him to keep my attention on what I was doing. I finished washing everything I used, rinsed them off, and then laid them on the towel.

"How about when you're finished you go up and get some shoes on? I'd hate to see you clean the entire

house before we get to go anywhere."

"Did you come here so you could make fun of me?" I growled.

"No," he said with a laugh. "I came here to talk you into spending time with me."

I scowled. "Why?"

He rolled his eyes and sighed. "It's your birthday," he reminded me. "I know your friends are busy since you haven't bothered to tell them and I don't want you to spend it by yourself."

"This isn't the first one I've spent alone -----."

"That was before me," he said, cutting me off. "So are you going to go get those shoes?"

I glared at him, trying to think of something sarcastic to say. He knew I was planning to be in the sunlight and whether I wanted him to or not he would still end up at my side. I huffed a breath and stalked out of the room.

I stood inside the closet, staring at the options I had for footwear. If I was still going to walk then I'd wear my tennis shoes, but Sean clearly wasn't going to want to walk from Bobbie's to the bay. So I don't need the tennis shoes. My eyes flashed to the flip-flops I bought in Portland last night. I knew it was silly when I bought them, knowing I'd probably never get to wear them with the rain, yet I missed having my feet bare. Well, almost bare.

Then I thought if I went ahead and wore them I could take them off while we walked on the sand beside the bay. I was going next to the water this time and didn't care if I had to pass the tourist area to get there. The flip-flops it is. I quickly pulled them out, slid my feet in them and walked out of my room.

Sean was still sitting at the table. I passed him, making my way to the fridge for a bottle of water.

"I was beginning to wonder if you were coming back anytime soon."

His velvety voice was soft, but full of sarcasm.

"I was having a hard time on deciding what shoes to wear." I pulled out the bottle then closed the door.

"Why am I not surprised," he smirked.

I turned to face him and it was then I noticed his clothes. He wore a white button-up shirt, with the sleeves rolled up and a pair of khaki cargo shorts. Even as his skin was paler than mine the color set well with him.

"Should I leave a note so Bobbie knows you're with me?"

"I'm a big girl," I informed him. "and anyways, if I'm not here when she gets up she'll figure it out."

I thought about what they had admitted to last night and shook my head. I still couldn't believe they would dress me up, and then send me out to him, like he had won a contest and I was the prize. Why didn't they just throw me under a bus?

"Are you ready to get out of here?" Sean asked.

"I suppose so," I breathed.

He stood from the chair when I crossed the room and I followed him out the door.

He left me to lock the door and walked to the truck. He had the passenger door open and was waiting for me as I walked down the stairs. I looked up at the sky as I walked, it wasn't clear, but it was changing colors. Sean waited till I was settled in the seat to close the door and walk around the truck.

When he pulled away from the house I dropped my head, nervously tearing at the label on the bottle. It was quiet in the truck, allowing me to hear the sound of my own thoughts. Then something suddenly sank in. I turned my head a fraction to the left to look at Sean. He seemed to be concentrating on where he was going.

"Sean, may I ask a question?"

He shrugged, sluggishly. "Sure."

"I thought you wouldn't be back till Sunday?" I knew it should have been a statement, but it came out in the form of a question.

He looked over at me now. "I wasn't, but then you had to go to Portland last night."

I let his statement turn over in my mind for a moment while I continued to stare at his face. Sean turned his eyes back to the windshield.

"So," I said slowly. "you didn't go with Jonah to Otter Rock?"

"Yes," he countered. "I left him there last night and came back here."

"Why?" I was confused.

He looked at me, a scowl on his face. "Do you not remember what I told you the other night? I was anxious so I left early to make sure you got home safely."

Now I was the one who scowled. "You make it sound like you don't trust Brandi or Bobbie."

"I trust them just fine, it's *you* I don't trust. You don't exactly have the best judgment of people," he laughed.

And again, I missed some sort of joke.

His statement triggered irritation in me and I looked out the window. We were already out of city limits. Where is he going?

"I've answered all your questions," Sean stated. His voice pulled me from my abstraction. "How about you answer some of mine?"

"Such as what?" I asked.

I couldn't imagine, even for a second, anything about me that could be interesting to him. He already knows all the personal stuff, what's left?

"What's your favorite color?"

I turned my head, looking at him, strangely.

"I know it's a little late to be asking now," he said, quickly. "I would still like to know."

"Okay," I said, indifferently. "It's blue."

"Any particular shade of blue?" he asked, earnestly.

I shrugged. "I guess it just depends on the day."

"And today?" His face was somber, as if he were asking me about a crime I'd committed.

I was hesitant and turned my head, keeping my eyes away from his face. I could feel mine reddened a bit.

"Tell me," he finally commanded.

"It's powder blue," I sighed in defeat. I carefully turned my eyes back to his face.

He snorted, dropping his serious expression. "Powder blue?" he asked, skeptically.

"It's the color of your eyes today." My face reddened more.

He was quiet a second and I worried he was thinking I was finally becoming obsessed with him. I wasn't, though I knew eventually what I felt for him would show to him whether I wanted it to or not. Apparently I wasn't very good at hiding it from everyone else. And, I honestly was infatuated with the color of his eyes. I had been since the first time I ever saw them. But his pause was short.

"Now that you can't legally be held here anymore, what's the place you want to see more than any other?"

I sighed in relief, thinking about what state held more of an attraction for me than anywhere else.

His interrogations continued the rest of the drive. He questioned me relentlessly about everything. He wanted to know what movies I liked and the most recent one I've seen. He asked if the keyboard was the only instrument I knew how to play and what music I enjoyed listening to. He wanted to know what flower I preferred. What I missed most about Kansas. With the mentioning of that he asked about Jennifer.

The way some of his questions came across I thought I was answering a hospital survey. How was your stay? How would you rate the service? Did everyone offer to help when needed and did they show courtesy?

I answered all of his questions honestly. When he asked about my dating history I became just as embarrassed as I had when Catlyn asked. Anytime my face flashed red or I hesitated only brought on more questions. I don't think I've ever had to talk so much in my life.

"I have one final question," he stated.

What hasn't he asked already? "What?" I groaned.

"What's your favorite gemstone?"

"Sapphire," I answered automatically.

"Of course it is." His voice was so low I couldn't quite be sure of the words. I saw an odd expression cross his face before he quickly composed it.

"Are you done now?" I asked, warily.

"For now," he grinned. "We're here so I'll save the others for another time."

The word *here* confused me and I looked out the window. It was then I saw he was pulling into a parking lot. The only thing I saw besides the line of trees was a small building. A large sign on it indicated it as restrooms. Sean drove towards the far end of the lot, and then parked. Even after he'd shut off the engine he continued to sit there, staring out the windshield.

"Are you curious enough to see what I brought you here for?" he finally asked. "Or should we just sit here?"

"I've never actually been curious about trees." I was still very confused. Sean laughed.

He pulled the keys out of the ignition and turned his eyes on me.

"The purpose of being here is behind the trees."

"Oh." Now I felt like an idiot. "In that case I guess we should probably get out."

I expected him to laugh again; he didn't.

I hesitantly reached for the door handle, half expecting him to lean across me and do it himself. He never moved. I opened the door and heard Sean open his at the same time. The air was an interesting mix of the evergreen trees and salt water. I carefully slid out of the seat and closed the door. Sean was already standing in front of the truck, patiently waiting for me. I took my time walking to his side.

"Lead the way," I said, extending my arm out in front of me.

Again, I expected the cocky humor I'd grown accustom to. He just nodded his head at me and started walking toward the east. I waited a second to follow, looking up at the sky. The sun still hadn't broke through the clouds, but it wouldn't be long. I took a deep breath and starting walking.

I was nearly at Sean's side when suddenly he stopped and whirled around to face me. His quick movement startled me and I took a step backwards. He reached for my hand, I instantly put it behind my back. He read the confusion on my face and dropped his arm.

"You may not like this, but you're going to have to let me carry you," he grumbled.

"Why?" Paranoia immediately began to sweep over me.

"Angel," Sean groaned. "we're going to have to walk through the trees and you're not wearing the required footwear."

"You could have pointed out that little fact before we left Bobbie's," I griped.

He rolled his eyes. "You can't still be afraid to touch me."

"I most certainly am not," I hissed. The truth is I actually was, I was simply afraid of what would become of me if I allowed that kind of contact. I never even had an interest in touching him till he danced with me. I was content to just love him without all the attached strings, and then I could leave and not feel the devastation of a broken heart. One night alone with him had changed everything and before I could leave him that night I had to touch his hair and kissed his face. Even now as we stood here staring at each other my fingers ached to glide over the contours of his face.

He laughed at my hesitation and reached out, grabbing the hand I didn't try to hide. "Prove it."

He lifted me up by the arm, as if I didn't weigh more than an empty backpack and slung me on his back. I instantly shivered from the coldness penetrating through his shirt. His body felt like I was trying to cling to a stone statue, yet I wrapped my arms and legs tightly around his waist and neck, fully afraid he would run again. Once he knew I had secured myself to him he reached up and patted my hands, and then turned back to the east, walking causally to the trees.

I looked around at the green maze, secretly hoping when he was finished showing me whatever it was he wanted me to see he'd know the way out. Since he was walking a normal speed the hike took most of the morning. There wasn't any sounds from the wildlife and that bothered me. Shouldn't there have at least been singing birds? Despite all the mossy overhangs, which Sean moved if he thought they would hit me in the face and the bracken spread out all over the ground Sean's movements and footsteps didn't sound like anything but a gentle breeze blowing over them.

That didn't just bother me, it made me nervous. He hadn't said anything the entire way so to keep from asking questions I distracted myself by watching the sky.

Finally, we entered an open clearing. It was still surrounded by trees, but it looked like it was once part of a trail. A wide path led either direction opposite of where we entered, a smaller path stretched out in front of us, leading the end of the tree line. A few feet from where Sean stood was a tree that had fallen over.

Sean walked to almost the end of the small trail, and then reached back, carefully pulling me from his back. As he set me on the ground in front of him the sun broke through the clouds. When I made no attempts to look at anything but him he pointed behind me. I slowly turned to look, there was the ocean and the sand. I gasped as I took in the glorious view.

"Exhilarating, isn't it?" Sean's unusually soft voice asked.

I couldn't take my eyes off the view to look at him. "This is just ... amazing," I said, flabbergasted.

"I figured you would like this better than the bridge and you wouldn't be tempted to jump."

Now I looked at him, my face twisted in irritation. "I was never planning to jump," I said frostily.

Sean flashed me a cocky grin.

I turned away from him and walked out on the sand. I kicked out of my shoes, leaving them in the shade of the trees and headed for the water's edge. I didn't notice I was walking alone till I stopped to look out across the water. There was nothing in my peripheral vision. Deeply confused I looked around at each side of my body, and then turned to look towards the clearing. Sean was standing motionless in the shade of the trees, watching me. I motioned him with my index finger to join me, he shook his head at me. I'd had never seen this kind of hesitation in him before and instantly became concerned. I started walking to him.

He stepped backwards when I tried to stand next to him.

"Sean, are you all right?" I was profoundly confused by his reaction to my approach.

He sighed deeply, the sound unsteady. "Not yet, I will be soon. Angel, my love, why don't you go on and enjoy the sun? I promise, I'll let you know when I'm ready to join you."

He wasn't as confident as he usually was and his voice had uncertainty in it. That only added to the deep concern I was already feeling.

"Okay." I instinctively reached out for his hand.

He pulled them back, quickly shoving them into the pockets of his shorts. I was suddenly torn between staying there with him or honoring his request for me to walk away. He smiled faintly at my hesitation, slightly nodding his head to encourage me. I took my time as I searched his eyes for the reason to his mysteriousness. His irises were normal in color and the deep bruise-like shadows I've grown accustom to seeing was gone. Since I couldn't find anything and was now completely frustrated, as I was sure something was wrong I turned and walked away.

Thoughts of Amanda and Jeremy crept back in my mind as I walked the shore. I couldn't help wondering if Jeremy was already on his way to Louisiana. I almost wished there was a way I could sit in the court room during his trial, just so I would know if he got the same impending sentence he had given Amanda and all his other victims. In my mind, that was only just a small price for all the pain and grief he had brought to each of the families.

I scolded myself for thinking about such things when I was supposed to be enjoying the trouble Sean had gone through so I could spend this day surrounded by beauty. I caught the sight of porpoise several hundred yards out as I was turning my head to look out across the water. For a long instant I was starstruck and was suddenly wishing Jen was here to see it with me. She would have been delighted.

The reminder that I wasn't alone had me turning to see if Sean had seen them. It was then I saw he'd moved and was now sitting on the fallen tree, watching me. I argued with myself about walking over and joining him. Then I reminded myself he clearly wasn't ready for me to be at his side, seeming as he hadn't come out on the sand or called my name. I didn't want him upset with me for not taking advantage of being in the sunlight. I decided it was probably better to stay where I was till he was ready to join me.

I tore my eyes away from Sean and walked out into the ocean till the water was barely above my calf. The temperatures hadn't reached the high it was supposed to be yet, the water was extremely cold. I continued to stand in it despite the fact I was starting to freeze, for I knew it would be a long time before I got another opportunity like this.

I wasn't out there long when I heard Sean call my name. I took one more long breath, breathing in the smell of the salt water, and then turned to head to Sean's side. I slipped my shoes on before I entered the tree line. Sean patted his hand against the tree, indicating me to sit in the open spot.

"You looked deep in thought out there," he said as I sat down. "Are you all right?"

"I was just thinking about how great it would be if Jennifer could see this."

Sean looked at me, his expression skeptical. "Your face looked more pained then that. So before you go trying to downplay your feelings again I know Mike spoke to you last night."

Dammit. I need to start standing in front of a mirror and practice controlling my facial expressions so I can tell a decent lie.

"Okay," I grumbled. "I was thinking about some things he told me last night. I have this horrible guilt that won't let my mind escape the imagines of Amanda."

"You have nothing to be guilty for." I turned my face away from him, he reached out, grabbing my chin and forced my head to turn back to him. "There wasn't anything you could have done to save her life."

"I know," I breathed. "I just can't help it."

He released my chin and I dropped my head to stare at the ground. Sean stretched his arm out behind me and began playing with my hair.

"Would you mind if I did something?" he asked.

"No," I blurted, then bit down on my bottom lip.

What if he tries to kiss you again? I asked myself. My heart began to pound, wildly.

Sean slid his fingers down strands of my hair before reaching up to pull the rubber band out. Since my hair was completely dry and windblown the band didn't slide down, it broke instead.

"That wasn't what I was aiming for," he stated. I could hear the frown in his voice.

I shrugged. "It's not a big deal. Honestly, I'm surprised I was even able to get the rubber band around my hair in the first place."

He laid the broken pieces in my hand then reached back, gently shaking my hair loose. When it fell over my shoulders and was now hiding my face he seemed satisfied. I kept my face towards the ground, giving my heart a chance to slow down. Sean's fingers stroked through my hair as he carefully pushed it back from my face. I closed my eyes.

"Angel?" His voice was low.

"Yes?" I answered, the word was shaking and nearly breathless.

"Are you still curious to see what I brought you here for?"

Now I was confused. I opened my eyes and carefully lifted my head to look at him. His blue eyes were soft, his face was full of emotions. Some I could name, worry, concern, and fear; others I couldn't. He stared hard at me, seeming to be unsure of himself. For reasons I couldn't quite fathom this made me extremely nervous.

"I'm not sure I understand what you mean," I said, slowly.

"I had something I wanted to show you a few days ago, remember?"

His eyes were closer to liquid then solid and was nearly taking away my ability to simply hold on to a single rational thought.

"I remember," I whispered.

"Well ..." His voice trailed off. That only intensified my nervousness. " ... it's time to show you."

"I thought this place was what you wanted me to see?" I wasn't sure why, but I desperately wanted to change his mind about whatever his intentions were.

"It is," he confirmed. "There's more I need to show you."

"Does it *have* to be now?" As badly as he was acting I wasn't sure I wanted to see anything.

Ever.

"Don't worry, love," he laughed. "when it's over I have something that is even better."

I frowned at him. "What could possibly make up for showing something horrible?"

His eyes widened, his expression turned innocent. "What makes you think what I want to show you is bad?"

"Oh, please," I sputtered. "if it wasn't then you wouldn't be acting so strangely."

"Perceptive," he mused. "You're a beautiful, yet silly girl. If you're still willing to be with me after I've finished showing you something that is important, I'll give you my gift."

"How nice," I said, acidly. "now you're patronizing me."

Sean shook with laughter. "I really wish you would learn to see yourself more clearly, Angel. You are quite charming."

I folded my arms over my chest. "Right," I growled.

He laughed while brushing his fingers through my hair. His eyes met mine for another long moment then he stood up, his fingers slowly unbuttoning his shirt. He had it completely undone before it registered in my mind what he was doing. I felt my face turn to shock then to horror.

"Sean ..." He raised his hand, silencing me.

When he was sure I wouldn't try to say another word he lowered his hand and opened his shirt, slowly sliding it over his shoulders and down his arms. His broad shoulders and chest tapered down to a narrow waist and hips. His white skin was stretched taut over the bones. I tried not to stare, but it was nearly impossible to look away. His chest was more muscular then I had ever imagined ... and perfect. The butterflies in my stomach fluttered, frantically.

He laid the shirt on the tree where he had been sitting and reached for my hand. I was hesitant, but I placed it in his, letting him pull me to my feet. My legs shook, almost uncontrollably and I was thankful he was hanging on to me. It would have been humiliating to faint in front of him. He continued to hold my hand, walking us to the edge of the clearing. When we reached the sand he released my hand, placing his on my back and gently pushed me out into the sunlight.

His actions confused me and I whirled around to face him. Those beautiful eyes were on my face and raged with conflict. He closed them briefly, took a deep breath, and then stepped out in the sunlight.

Sins of a Killer

Sean in the sunlight was both shocking and scary. I felt my mouth fall open as I stared at him and fought to close it. His skin crystallized, becoming as transparent as a blank sheet of paper. The veins in every part of his body was clearly visible. They were a deep blue and completely collapsed as there was no blood pulsing through them. It did surprise me that he never spontaneously burst into smoke or flames as the magazine article from months ago flashed through my mind, the word *vampire* flashing brighter than a neon sign.

Now full of a deeper fear than I had ever felt I finally pulled my bottom jaw up and tried to take a step back. My legs may as well have been trapped in cement for all the good it was doing me to make them move. I fought to control the expressions on my face so he wouldn't read the fear written all over it. He was already scrutinizing my face, it seemed I was much too late.

"Now I have frightened you." His voice was quiet, velvet, muted.

"I'm not frightened," I quickly lied. "just shocked."

He looked skeptical.

"Okay," I sighed, sheepishly. "maybe a little."

"And here you thought all this time I was a hero," he laughed darkly.

I scowled at him. "I don't believe I've ever called *you* a hero."

I waited for one of his sarcastic remarks, but he turned away from me and headed back inside the trees. I shut my eyes briefly on a prayer for the courage to be able to remain by his side, and then slowly followed behind him to the fallen tree. He was already sitting on it, pulling his shirt over his arms.

"I have more to tell you," he said as I approached him.

"How much do you think a person can take in one day?" I grumbled.

He laughed, without humor and patted the spot beside him. I carefully searched his face for anything to alert me something had changed. I didn't see anything different in the contours of his eyes and carefully sat down next to him.

"You can calm down, Angel. The worst is over."

"I'm trying," I said, weakly.

He took a deep breath, closed his eyes and pinched the bridge of his nose with his thumb and forefinger. I was leery to look away from him, I knew if I didn't I would never get my racing heart calm enough to sit through whatever it was he still had to say. I turned my eyes to the end of the clearing, gazing out at the water.

"I'm in love with you," he suddenly blurted.

My eyes widened in shock, my head instantly snapped sharply in his direction. His eyes were now open, as he was watching me closely. I could feel panic start to surface and quickly suppressed it.

"This is why I was fighting so hard to convince you to stay away from me," he continued. "I felt a deeper feeling for you than I've ever thought possible and even though I didn't understand it at the time, I knew if I were to act on them it would be dangerous for both of us."

He paused, staring at me, as he seemed to be waiting for a response. I had absolutely no faith in my voice and remained silent. He finally spoke again, his voice velvet soft.

"It turns out *I'm* the one who couldn't walk away, now you have to spend every minute of your life careful not to make any wrong or sudden moves. I'm sure you have it figured out, since you now know why you have never seen me in the sun, but I'll say it, anyway. I'm a vampire, Angel."

Adrenaline pulsed through me again at his final words. It was bad when I thought he *was*, it was much worse hearing him say it. I sat motionless, more frightened than I had ever been in my life. Even after the things I suffered through with Jeremy, this was much worse than that. Sean's quick eyes saw it on my face before I had time to control myself.

"*Please*, don't be frightened," he pleaded. "I promise, I won't hurt you. Truth is I *can't*. I don't hunt people and even if I did I'm not thirsty today."

At that I had to laugh, though the sound was shaky and nearly breathless. I looked away from his face to calm myself down, as well as convince myself to stay. I also needed a minute to reassemble my now tangled thoughts.

"Are you all right?" he asked, his voice uneasy. His hand snaked out, gently grabbing mine.

Even as I was terrified, his hand in mine reminded me how deep my love was for him. Vampire or not.

"I think so," I whispered, half to myself. I wasn't ready to look at him and continued to stare at the ground. "Why are you telling me this now?"

I heard Sean sigh, deeply. "It is nearly impossible for my kind to be altered, for we can never change. Because I have fallen in love with you I have been altered and it can never be undone. You have become my life now so I could no longer wait. I have just become so *damn* tired of wanting you and not being able to have you."

My head instantly snapped up and I flashed my eyes to his face. "Tired of wanting me?" I repeated, my voice almost a shriek.

His eyes darkened in color. "Listen to me, Angel," he commanded. "When I say I'm tired of wanting you, it simply means I've grown tired of not being allowed to be with you when I want to be. I'm hoping by telling you this it will eliminate all the secrets between us so maybe someday I could earn your love in return."

I wasn't sure why, but I suddenly got the urge to put some space between us. I needed some air that didn't smell of the citrus radiating from his body and a chance to clear my clouded mind. My only hope was that my legs wouldn't tremble causing me to stumble. The last thing I wanted ... or needed was a reason to be in Sean's arms. I pulled on my arm and he willingly released my hand. I kept my eyes away from his face while I got to my feet.

My legs were steady, yet I still struggled to put one foot in front of the other. I felt Sean's stare boring into my back as I slowly made my way from the tree. I hadn't gotten far when I could no longer put forth the effort it took to walk.

"Are you still worried?" he suddenly asked.

"No," I lied. My voice broke. "More surprised actually ... I'm trying to understand all of this and figure out why you waited till today to do this."

I heard the breeze move the bracken and knew Sean was behind me before his hands were on my shoulders, turning me to face him.

"I told you, I want you for myself. As for today, well I guess it was fate. I've been trying to tell you for months. I even tried telling you when I left the magazine on the table."

My eyes widened in horror. "You ... left ... it ... for ... me?" I tried out the words, confused by the way they sounded.

"Yes," he stated, matter-of-factly. "I thought if you read the description it gave you would draw the connections. That's why I waited for you on the porch the next morning. I needed to see if you had read it and how you would react to seeing me."

I stared at his eyes, my mind was beginning to cloud and I fought against it, trying to think back over the last three months I've known him. It was now everything started to make sense; the color changes in his eyes, the quick movements, the feel of his body and his skin. And, how he naturally smelled of citrus.

I opened my mouth carefully to speak calmly. "This is more like a twist of fate."

He pulled his hands away from my shoulders and laughed softly. "It does seem like that for you, doesn't it? I never believed in such things until I found you."

"Literally," I mumbled.

He chuckled blackly. "I wasn't meaning in quite that sense, but never the less, it's true."

Something he'd said earlier entered my mind, I was just as confused as I'd been when he said it.

"If being with me is really what you want ..." I had to give myself a second to keep my voice stable. "... then why do you always leave so quickly?"

He sighed deeply. "I knew you were trying to figure things out about me, as you did read the magazine and you acted just as I'd suspected you would when you walked out the door and I feared *if* you did know the truth I would lose you all together, but it was what I had to do. Then that day on the bridge you treated me just the same as you did anyone else, in which I didn't expect. So after that I decided I couldn't let anyone else have you. I thought if I only spent a few minutes with you then I was getting what *I* wantedand the short time would prevent me from having the urge to touch you."

"Why did you and Jonah deny rescuing me?" This was the one thing that had always bothered me the most.

"We weren't supposed to be in town so it would have looked bad if anyone knew we were in the woods. Jonah had me place you in forest ranger's truck then we could get out without being seen. By the time it was called in Jeremy had already been contained, giving us a chance to escape before the rangers could get there."

My legs began to feel like mush, I knew if I didn't try to make the short walk back to the tree I would end up on the ground. I took a step back from Sean and walked away.

"You have clearly overcome the fear of touching me," I said as I sat down. "yet, you still pull away or demand me to move. Why?"

He stared at me, his eyes penetrating before finally relaxing enough to walk toward me and speak, again.

"I see your reaction to our temperature difference and I wouldn't have handled it well if you found my touch repulsive. I also wasn't sure if I could even hold your hand without hurting you."

He sat down next to me, taking my left hand, and twined our fingers. I took a minute to focus on them, giving myself time to remain calm and think about my next question. Sean didn't seem to mind, he absently rubbed his thumb over the skin on my hand.

"Then why did you force me to dance with you?" The memory of that night both infuriated me since I now knew what my own friends had done, but it delighted me at the same time. I meant to scowl and puckered my lips, instead.

Sean laughed. "By then I was no longer undecided about what *I* wanted. I spend hours alone, practicing handling a glass vase and holding bubbles."

"Bubbles?" I asked, skeptically.

He rolled his eyes. "Yes, bubbles," he said sarcastically. "If I'm paying close enough attention to what I'm doing I can catch a bubble while it's in the air and roll it across my fingers without ever popping it. The next time we're out remind me about it and I'll show you."

I opened my mouth to make a witty remark, then something he said sank in.

"Why would you be practicing anything with glass?" I asked.

My hair shifted when I moved my head, shielding my face from Sean's eyes. He reached out and brushed it back.

"Compared to me, Angel, you're as fragile as glass. I thought if I could control myself while I held on to it then I can do it when I'm with you."

All the jokes he'd made about my being in a fragile state finally made sense.

"How did you even know I was attracted to you?"

"At first I couldn't be sure," he said, his voice thoughtful. "your heart rate would change so frequently it was difficult to tell if it was caused by attraction or fear. When you told me you needed time to adjust to me I decided then to test my theories. When I finally figured out it was attraction I was having feelings of my own. I was torn then; part of me wanted to steal you from your bed and ask my father for the biggest favor. The other part couldn't live with knowing what I was willing to do so that's when I began trying to stay away from you."

The same look he had the night he caught me playing the keyboard crossed his face; his eyes were cautious, conflict raging in them. The urge I had to touch his face became so strong my free hand lifted without a conscious decision to do so, my fingers softly stroking the side of his face. It wasn't even a second later and Sean's white hand caught my hand, pressing my fingers to rest against his skin. His eyes closed, his breath unsteady.

"You simply can't imagine how warm your skin feels," he whispered. "or how it feels to finally have you touch me on your own."

He opened his eyes and confusion burned in them.

"I've touched you before," I fumed.

"Not without force," he disagreed.

"I wasn't forced when I kissed your cheek," I said, smugly.

A faint smile slowly lit his face. "Yes, well … I must say you certainly surprised me when you did."

"That's makes two of us," I mumbled.

Sean shook with laughter then removed his hand. Now that I was freed I pulled mine away, lying it in my lap.

"We will always have time to talk, for now I can tell you anything you want to know," he said, softly. "There isn't much time of the sun left and I'd hate to think I brought you all this way for nothing."

I glared at him and he laughed.

He slowly lifted his arm and softly traced my bottom lip with his index finger. He allowed it to linger there a second before finally deciding it was too much and dropped his hand. I hadn't expected my body to react, as it filled with an ache I'd never felt, my skin heated up. I had to fight to control myself to speak calmly.

"What about you?" I asked, nearly breathless.

He grinned, a playful smirk on his face. "I think I'll wait here, at least until the sun shifts."

I considered demanding to make my own choice to stay or walk away, but my heart was racing wildly and I did need some air that wasn't full of his scent. He stared at my lips again causing my skin to feel like it would soon burst into flames. I turned my head sharply from him and carefully got to my feet. I wasn't sure I could remember how to make them move, as it was an extremely slow process, but I managed to move them forward.

I could feel the blaze of the heat, as now the temperature had changed, the breeze from the water felt so good I walked to the edge, and then into the water. I stared mindlessly out at the horizon, trying to make sense of everything that had happened and think about how this was going to affect the plans I'd been making for this day.

I haven't admitted I'm irrevocably in love with him when he was clearly giving me the opportunity, though with what he had said I couldn't. I had always thought my feelings for him were a problem, now I had an even bigger one; he isn't *human*. Maybe it's time I made an appointment to speak with a psychiatrist. I knew I would be considered crazy, possibly even thrown in an asylum so they could be sure I couldn't do anything to harm myself. I would no longer be seen as a normal person.

What normal person falls in love with an immortal? I asked myself. The hardest thing for me to figure out was; do I give into the love I feel and risk my own life every day to be with him or do I open the letter I've been carrying for months and still leave for Juilliard at first light?

I sighed, heavily then turned to look at Sean. He was still sitting on the tree, statute still, his eyes watching me cautiously. Then I thought I had to be fair. I owed it to him and to myself to give him the chance to tell me everything he had brought me here to say. I took a long, slow breath while I built up the courage to sit beside him again. I started walking back to him.

"Okay," I said, warily. I sat down next to him, rubbing my suddenly sweating palms against the sides of my shorts. "Tell me how you plan to make this work."

He was puzzled. "Make what work?"

I rolled my eyes. "I know enough about *vampires*" ----- the word felt like it would burn my tongue ----- "to know you need blood."

"That's very perceptive," he complimented me with a grin. "You're more observant than I've ever given you credit for."

I gave him a dirty look.

"And yes," he continued, ignoring my expressions. "blood is an essential we must have."

"You mentioned earlier you don't feed from people." I paused, fighting to hold back the shiver trying to course through my body.

"I said I don't *hunt* people," he corrected. "My eyes are blue, not red."

"Oh, right," I sputtered sarcastically. "I clearly know what that means."

Sean laughed darkly. "It lets humans know we don't hunt them."

My brows creased in mystification and I tilted my head. "Then *what* do you hunt?"

He eyed me carefully before answering. "We feed from the humans that are already deceased."

That didn't sink in right away. I was preoccupied with figuring out if I could even do this. Then what he said about his eye color confused me.

"What does feeding from humans have to do ..." It sank in. "Wait, what? You feed from people who have died?"

"Yes," he sighed, the sound uneasy.

I felt the horror on my face before I heard it in my voice.

"Amanda!"

"Give it rest, Angel," Sean growled. "We would never feed from a helpless victim!"

My eyes narrowed in confusion. "Then just how do you get fed?"

His beautiful, but troubled blue eyes watched my expressions. "Once we became newborns, Jonah taught us to only feed from the humans who were being prepared to be laid to rest."

"Why?" I was still deeply confused.

The mention of Jonah had my heart racing in panic. I looked away from Sean's face to keep him from seeing it in my expressions. I could tell from his tone this was difficult for him to share, I didn't want my poor reactions keep him from talking.

"The mortuaries have to drain the body of blood before they can put in embalm fluid or cremate them. Since the blood is already unneeded we can get our essentials without taking an innocent life."

Then something else scrambled my mind. "Jonah did this to you?" I whispered, not giving my voice a chance to break.

He didn't answer right away and I peeked over at him. He was staring at the ground, his face was somber. I looked away, again, letting him take his time. The minutes passed.

"Yes," he finally admitted.

"What made him do such a thing?"

"I will let him answer that himself."

The conversation ended again, this time I allowed it. I needed time to process everything, as well as figure out how to get to the answers that defined *our* situation.

"Okay," I said slowly. "Since you don't consume the blood of live people." I paused, this was by far the hardest concept for me to grasp. "Are you ever tempted to?"

"I can't speak for the others," Sean answered. His voice was very alluring. "but, I have been a few times."

"Does mine ...?" I swallowed a lump, unable to finish the question.

Sean reached out, placing a long finger under my chin and lifted my face so I was looking at him. His face was hard and expressionless.

"No," he stated firmly. "I will admit you smell good, like a meadow of lilacs. I am not drawn to that flavor, you've got nothing to worry about."

Nothing to worry about!? Is he serious? His answer made me nervous and I tried to turn my head. He wasn't having that, he cupped his hand around my chin, holding my face in place. We both waited for my hammering heart to slow.

"Why do you stop yourself?" I asked. The words were on the verge of being slurred.

"Jonah has built a life based on the beliefs he was taught. His parents were deeply religious and believed thou shall not kill. Jonah still believes in that today," he explained. "He says even though we have been given a dishonorable situation doesn't mean we have to give into the temptations."

"Isn't it difficult for you not to?"

Sean stared in my eyes for a long second then finally released my face. I breathe a sigh of relief.

"Yes," he admitted. "Some human scents are stronger than others. I have found a few that were so powerful they nearly consumed me."

"How do you control the need?"

"I don't want to be a monster," he said, firmly. "I keep the monster in control because *if* I took an innocent life I wouldn't just destroy myself, but my family as well."

I didn't know what my expressions were, but something in them made Sean grow somber. We sat staring at each other in a long silence. The more the minutes began to pass it was becoming eerie.

"Is something wrong, Sean?" I asked, carefully.

His eyes narrowed into slits. "I guess I'm just waiting."

I waited, almost impatiently for him to say more. He let the seconds pass.

"For?" I prompted.

"I'm waiting for the realization of this to set in your mind. That moment when it finally grasps the concept you're surrounded by monsters and worse still, one of them has admitted *he* loves you. I will completely understand when it finally does if you feel the need to run from me."

I scowled at his choice of words. "I guess you're going to be deeply disappointed. I may need a psychiatrist after this, for I have always known something about you wasn't normal. Granted, I can't say I've ever believed in mythical creatures, but it doesn't change the fact I'm still here."

His face turned teasingly outraged. "You'll only need that psychiatrist if you agree to having a *monster* for a boyfriend."

I rolled my eyes and shook my head. "You're not a monster, Sean."

He gave me a disbelieving look.

"Fine," I breathed. "maybe the exterior is, there's clearly a compassionate soul underneath."

"What makes you so sure?" he asked, sounding skeptical.

"Why else would you have saved my life? Which, by the way" ----- I lifted my hand, holding my index finger in the air. ----- "brings us back to my most important question."

"What are you going to make me admit to, now?" Sean grumbled.

I lowered my hand, Sean's snaked out in flash, catching it before I even knew what was happening. I sat bewildered, watching as he lifted it to his face. He very lightly grazed his lips over the skin. They were hard and ice cold, yet the skin felt smooth like satin. My heart beat rabbit jumps against my chest, threatening to just leap out of the skin.

He flashed his eyes to my face. "You had an important question," he reminded me, condescendingly.

What was I even going to ask? I finally tore my eyes away from his face, trying desperately to remember. When the clouds vanished from my mind I looked back at him.

"You can smell blood ..." I had to swallow a large lump I never noticed had formed. " ... even if it's not exposed, right?"

"Yes." As if to prove a point he kept his eyes on me, lifting my hand to his nose. He skimmed it over the skin, inhaling deeply. My heart stopped for a second, picking up in double time once it restarted.

"Isn't it amazing how my actions cause your heart to misbehave?" he grinned.

"Um ... yeah." I fought to regain control of my voice. "I'm sure you've noticed since I'm *human*, I'm also clumsy." I pulled up the sleeve of the shirt, exposing the scar. "Translation ----- I tend to bleed often. How are you planning to handle that?"

A confused expression appeared on his face as he lowered my arm. "I never noticed that," he grumbled. Then looked back at me. "If and when the moment comes to your blood being exposed I'll do what I did the night we found you."

"Right," I said frostily. "I can clearly remember that!"

Sean laughed, the sound was close to sounding like the roar of a large cat. It echoed through the trees and I cringed.

"I wasn't sure if there were any open wounds on you and Amanda's blood was spilled throughout the cabin so I held my breath."

"There were many things wrong and somehow I didn't have any open ..." Something suddenly sank in. "Wait, what? Did you just say Amanda's blood was spilled in the cabin?"

"Yes," he sighed. "She was already gone, there wasn't anything we could have done for her."

"And you held your breath?"

He rolled his eyes and sighed as if I should have known that. "It helps with the temptation, preventing us from not being able to resist and end up revealing ourselves."

"How long can you hold it?"

He shrugged. "Indefinitely I suppose. It's uncomfortable whenever I have to so I've never tried it."

I frowned at him. "For someone who doesn't allow himself to be exposed to blood, you're taking this casually."

"Angelia," he scolded me. "*if* I thought for a second I couldn't handle it I'd never allow myself to be alone with you, such as this."

His tone instantly irritated me and I pulled on my arm. Sean kissed my hand once more, and then reluctantly released it. I looked out at the water, contemplating getting up and walking away.

"You were supposed to be feeding this weekend, weren't you?" I wasn't sure I wanted him to admit it, yet I couldn't help wondering.

"Yes," he snorted. "We went to Otter Rock, I told you this already."

"I know," I agreed. I turned my eyes back to his face. "I didn't know then what I do now."

"I wanted so badly to drag you out of the house and tell you everything. And then, Brandi called and all I could think about was you going to Portland. I went home and talked Jonah into leaving then."

"Then what were you doing while I was in Portland?"

He looked away from me and began rubbing a long pale finger over a small branch still attached to the tree.

"I was in Portland." His voice was so low I couldn't be sure I heard him correctly.

"You seriously followed me while I was with my friends?" I asked, astonished.

He flashed his eyes back to me. "It's not as bad as it sounds, Angel. I just needed to know you were safe. That's how I know Mike was waiting for you. I saw his car parked in front of the house and hid in the shadows of the neighbors."

"If separation is such a hassle for you," I said acidly. "then why didn't you drag me away from

Bobbie's?"

It was clear he didn't like my tone, his eyes narrowed into slits.

"It was for two reasons," he growled. "Reason one: I couldn't be sure you wouldn't get hurt while we feed. Whenever we feed we give ourselves over to the monster inside. I am unable to consciously control it at those times. Reason two: and this is only a second reason, I have to protect myself and the others."

Now I was confused. "How so?"

"We are supposed to stay unnoticed so when we enter the mortuaries we have to be careful not to touch anything or trigger any alarms. Your human reactions to seeing us feed would not only cause us to harm you, but it would certainly alert someone to us. It's very dangerous for both of us should your kind learn we exist."

"By that, you're saying there's more like you somewhere?"

It was scary knowing there were more traveling the world.

Sean nodded his head. "We haven't crossed any nomads since we've been here, but yes."

This was yet another concept I couldn't quite wrap my head around.

"How is it dangerous for you if we know your *people* exist?" I waved a hand up and down in front of him. "It clearly isn't possible to get free of your grasps, (this I knew first hand) let alone destroy you." I made a face as I thought of all the times I tried to get out of his iron grip. "I know, I've tried," I said under my breath.

"No it isn't," he confirmed, pretending not to have heard my tone. "We certainly can each other and like the humans, we have rules we must follow."

Now I wasn't just confused, I was worried, too.

"If it's dangerous for me to know the truth about you, where does this leave me now?"

He looked at me earnestly before answering. "Jonah isn't just law enforcement for your kind, he's also a member of our law makers. Therefore, if something were to happen that would put you in any danger he would protect you."

"What would happen if another *vampire* passes through and discovers I know your secret?"

He flashed me a grin. "I just told you we haven't seen more than us here, however should one pass through we'll know and Jonah will handle it."

"If you're supposed to live in the shadows, why do you walk so freely here?" I asked, my tone almost a groan.

His lips curved up at the corners. "I'm sure you never have, but I'll ask anyway. Have you ever had to live in one light?"

What an odd question; I'm human, so of course not. "No."

"I didn't think so," he stated smugly. "Out here we have more freedom as there's never many days of the sun keeping us from being trapped."

"Aren't you at all concerned everyone will eventually notice you're not ageing?"

He shrugged, seeming to be unconcerned. "We will leave before they do."

I stared at him, stunned while I let his answer turn over in my mind. He looked extremely young like me, though his language and articulation was clearly that of another century. I figured that out almost from my first days here. How have they been here this long and no one else notice?

"If you're not wanting to be so conspicuous how are you convincing everyone you're still nineteen?"

"When we arrived here eight years ago your friends were still in school. Becca pretended to home school us to prevent talk and scandal. It didn't just keep our secret, it also gave us a longer amount of time we could stay."

"Genius," I mused.

I looked out at the opening in the clearing and noticed the sun had shifted. I had spent the entire afternoon trying to understand something I never believed was real. Sean answered everything I asked, yet I was still no closer to my resolve. There was one topic we hadn't discussed. I kept my eyes safely away from Sean's face.

"You were hunting the night you found me?" I said it more as a question then a statement.

"Yes," he answered, his voice soft.

"If you don't hunt people then how did you know I was in that cabin?" I still couldn't quite look at him.

"Angel, for the last time," he growled. "we don't hunt people. We were passing through the woods on our way to Eugene when we caught the smell of blood. We knew the cabins were supposed to be empty and went to investigate. We picked up the sound of your very faint heartbeat before it was in sight and moved faster."

My head snapped in his direction. "You heard my heartbeat?" I asked in disbelief.

Sean sighed and rolled his eyes. I guess my brain doesn't work quickly enough to process his words. A small gust of wind blew through the trees causing my hair to flow out from my head. Sean's hand snaked out, catching strands of it and twisted them around his fingers.

"I have excellent hearing, as well as perfect eyesight," he informed me.

I continued to stare at him, bewildered.

"Anyway," he continued. "we followed the sound to the cabin. Jonah looked through the front window while I went in search of another. I peered in it and seen you weren't moving, your heart was beating way too fast and was unsteady. Jonah told me to enter the cabin while he dealt with *Jeremy*" ----- he sneered on his name, his upper lip curling back over his teeth.

His sudden reaction startled me and I instinctively jumped to my feet. My movement caused Sean's body to turn to stone, his eyes were black, wild and fierce and watched me closely. He looked like a true vampire. My body was rigid as a plank, my hands balled into fist at my sides, my breathing erratic. I knew if I made even the slightest movement the vampire would attack.

A few minutes passed and his eyes changed back to blue as his body began to relax. I waited till his eyes were completely blue and soft to thaw out and turn away from him. I started walking away.

"Don't you want to hear the rest?" His voice still had a hint of darkness in it.

I shook my head. "I've heard enough, if you continue this I may never sleep again." After what I've seen and heard today I may not anyway ----- I thought.

I stepped out on the sand, moving quickly to the water's edge. I didn't bother stopping to kick out of my shoes.

"I'm sorry for frightening you," Sean softly apologized.

The sand muted the sound of his footsteps causing the sudden closeness of his voice to startle me. I slowly turned around, in fear any sudden movements from me would trigger him again. The sun was low so he still looked slightly normal. His skin had a small glow, I couldn't see through it.

"It seems to be the story of my life," I stated. My voice gave away the stress I was beginning to feel. "Aren't you the least bit concerned about someone coming through and seeing you?"

His shirt was still unbuttoned, exposing his chest. I felt my skin start to heat again as my eyes traced over the contours of it and I quickly forced myself to look at his face.

He laughed. "Humans very rarely come this far. You were paying attention to how long it took us to get here, weren't you? People don't generally like to hike quite so long." He looked away from me, gazing out at the water. "I used to spend much of my time here."

"Used to?" I asked, confused.

He flashed his eyes back to me, a gleaming smile crossing his lips. "I have things that keep me in town now. Would you be interested in taking a walk with me?"

"Okay."

Sean walked to me, took my hand in his, and we strolled the shore. We were silent until a tide would roll up to the shore. Sean would gently push me into it until I was completely drenched. I had never been able to laugh so freely. Whenever the breeze would blow my hair across my face Sean would reach out and brush it back.

"Angel, I need you to tell me something," he finally said after a while.

"What?"

Sean stopped walking, his sudden holt tugged on my arm, sharply bringing me to a standstill. He causally stepped in front of me, his blue eyes grew soft.

"After everything you have learned about me," he said, his voice velvet soft. "Do you think it could ever be possible for me to earn your love?"

"You already have," I admitted, sheepishly.

Excitement suddenly flared in his eyes. "I have?"

He waited for a response, I couldn't answer. I wasn't sure I trusted him, the last time I'd seen that look in his eyes I went for a very scary ride. My lack of response made him anxious.

"I know I have frightened you many times today and for that I am truly sorry. I did promise if you were still willing to stay I have something to give you."

His eyes flickered when he released my hand and reached in a pocket of his shorts. I stared at him, wildly, worrying what that might have meant. He flashed his eyes to my face as he slowly lowered himself to one knee. He smiled at me and opened his hand. There, resting in his palm was a small velvet box. My heart pounded so badly I couldn't will myself to move.

He raised one eyebrow, his voice ominous. "Aren't you curious enough to open it?"

My hand shook uncontrollably as I reached for it. I briefly curled my fingers into my palm, trying to gain control of it. I carefully lifted the box up and opened it. It suddenly became difficult to breathe.

The ring inside was gorgeous. A heart shaped, crystal blue stone sat on a gold band, surrounded by small diamonds. It wasn't difficult to figure out it had come from another decade.

"I am simply courting you, not asking you for marriage," Sean stated, softly. "If you decide to accept my gift, it is not only being given as a birthday gift, but also as a token of a promise. I promise to love you unconditionally for the rest of my existence. Will you allow me to have your hand in this condition?"

A million different things swirled through my mind. I could say the gooey things I was sure he wanted to hear, though it was sure to surprise him I was capable of such things. Yet, I had no experience with relationships and feared I would do nothing more than deeply embarrass myself.

A wave of a deeper emotion then I had ever felt pulsed through me, I could feel tears swell up in the corner of my eyes. I stared at the ring a second longer, giving my voice a chance to be strong.

"Yes," I whispered. My voice failed me. "Yes."

Here's the answer to your resolve, Angel, I instantly said to myself. You really should make an appointment with that therapist.

He smiled that cocky grin I hated but loved at the same time and pulled the ring from the box. He carefully lifted my left hand, sliding it gently on my third finger. He stood up and the box disappeared out of my hand.

"I know it's a bit old fashioned and the stone isn't Sapphire. I thought you would like something to remind you of me every time you look at it."

The wetness in my eyes intensified, a single tear fell before I could recover my emotions. I quickly turned my head away from Sean and wiped it off my cheek.

"It's beautiful, Sean." My voice was barely above a whisper. "And, there's nothing wrong with old fashioned."

Sean placed a long cold finger under my chin, turning my face to look at him. His eyes blazed under his long lashes. His voice was silky when he spoke.

"The ring was my mother's. My father gave it to her for a gift shortly after my birth. I was born in December which is why the stone is blue. It's also the reason I asked about your preference of gemstones."

"Your father had taste," I teased.

Sean laughed and released my face. "I wanted you to have it as a symbol of my cold, silent heart, which is now yours." He grabbed my left wrist, lifting it up at the sunlight. "If the sun catches it just right it'll crystallize the same way I do."

The image of him in the sunlight this afternoon flashed in my mind and I shivered. Sean completely misunderstood my response. He released my wrist.

"If you don't like it we can go to any jewelry store of your choice and buy one you do like."

"No," I blurted quickly. "I love this one."

He sighed, the sound relieved. The breeze blew my hair across my face and he reached out, brushing it away.

"I have an idea," he grinned, suddenly amused.

I may have now understood how his moods could change so suddenly, that certainly didn't mean I liked it any better.

I narrowed my eyes, suspicious. "What?"

"How about we have a race down the beach?"

"Right," I snorted. "like I could even keep up with you."

He grinned, wickedly. "I would be more than happy to oblige you."

I took a slow step backwards, shaking my head at him. "No thanks, I still haven't fully recovered from the night in Los Angeles."

"If you close your eyes this time it might not be so bad," he teased.

I shook my head again and he crouched down, like a cat waiting to pounce. There was a wicked glint in his eyes.

"You do realize I could easily make you, right?" he purred, playfully.

"You wouldn't dare," I contradicted. I backed further away from him.

He raised one eyebrow. "Wouldn't I?"

He growled, a low sound coming from his throat and pulled his lips back over his teeth. My heart raced, wildly as I took another step backwards. My eyes never strayed from his face, yet still I never saw him leap at me. But suddenly I was airborne, I didn't ever feel the jolt of his body hitting mine, and then we crashed in the water. Sean had me wrapped in his arms, like they were an iron cage. I wasn't sure how, but when we landed Sean was on his back, holding me securely against his chest. I stared at him in alarm, his eyes were still light and his jaw was completely relaxed when he grinned.

"Wouldn't it just been easier to agree to run with me?" he laughed.

I glared at him.

I began trying to struggle free of his hold, he wasn't having that. He rolled us, gently pressing me into the sand. The water crashed over us and the expression on his face changed. The humor in his eyes changed into something else in the space of a heartbeat. My mind was too perplexed to let me panic.

"I want to try something, Angel," he whispered. "Don't move."

He lowered his face closer to mine, stopping to linger just before they touched. He didn't linger to judge my reaction, he was testing himself, to see if this was safe. He needed to be sure he was still in control of himself. And then, his cold, satin lips pressed ever so gently against mine. What neither of us could have been prepared for was my reaction.

My blood boiled under my skin, burning nearly every part of me. My breath came out a moan while I wrapped my arms around his back, clutching him closer to me. My lips parted, his ice cold breath touched the back of my throat and I became very dizzy.

He broke the kiss when I struggled to breathe, moving his lips to the hollow beneath my ear. The first breath I sucked in that wasn't his burned my throat and lungs.

"Where did that lack of self-control come from?" he whispered. His cold breath lightly blew across my ear and I shivered. He softly kissed my neck then rolled to his back.

"I don't know." The words were nearly breathless.

He laid still a moment then rolled to his side and propped up on his left arm. He reached out, carefully rubbing a long finger over my bottom lip.

"Have you ever …?" His voice trailed off. He seemed to struggle for the words to finish his question. Until today I had never seen him struggle with anything.

It took a few seconds for it to sink in what he was trying to ask.

"No!" I said, quickly. "I've never even experienced the whole lust thing."

He looked skeptical. "I can't be the only one besides *Hesner and Wilkins*" ----- he sneered on their names ----- "that finds you attractive."

I rolled my eyes and looked away from him. "No one has ever approached me the way the three of you have. But it was mostly because

I had a dark secret. It was shameful enough to me that Jennifer and her mom knew what was happening. I couldn't bear the idea of anyone else knowing."

Sean reached out and turned my face back to him. His eyes had grown very soft, he grazed his fingers along my cheek.

"You are completely safe now," he informed me. "No harm will ever come to you again."

I said nothing.

He leaned in towards me, stopping inches from my face. "You smell incredible in water."

I stared at him in horror, my heart now pounding frantically. Sean found amusement in my horror, his body shook with a loud laughter, the sound almost a roar.

"Angel, my love, you are too funny." He pressed his lips to mine then a second later was on his feet. "The sun has faded and the sky will be dark soon." He held his right hand out at me. "How about we get you home so you can change into dry clothes?"

I hadn't noticed the sun was nearly gone till he mentioned it. I looked up at the sky, instantly becoming disappointed. I hated knowing a perfect day would soon end. I held my hand up for Sean to grab, he carefully twined his fingers with mine then slowly pulled me to my feet. He released my hand long enough to allow me to wring out my hair.

We reached the trees and he dropped my hand, turning his back to me and squatted down in front of me. I climbed on his back, securing my strangle hold on him. He waited till I was no longer moving to get to his feet.

He turned his head to look back at me. "May I?" he snickered.

I started to say no. He is at least asking ----- I told myself. Even if you say no he could choose to do it anyway.

"Fine," I breathed.

He gave me just enough time to shut my eyes.

Forbidden Secrets

Sean surprised me by showing me he was capable of driving the speed limit. It made me think that for once he wasn't in a hurry to take me home. He drove one-handed, holding my hand on the seat. It appeared to please him he could now touch me anytime he wanted. His hand felt, as if I had mine wrapped around a marble stone, it was cold, but not really uncomfortable and even I was content with having our hands twined together.

He had the stereo turned on, the music wasn't loud, nor was it anything I knew. Since he was quiet I used the rare opportunity to let my hair blow in the open window, allowing it to dry while I admired scenery I had never before seen.

"Tell me something," Sean suddenly said, shaking our twined hands.

I kept my eyes towards the open window. "What?"

"You mentioned a few weeks ago you weren't planning to stay after today. Does that still stand?"

I shrugged halfheartedly. "I don't know. I'm almost certain Salt Lake City has more to offer then people like Tony … I mean, Jeremy," I teased.

Sean growled, a deep, menacing sound. "I'm serious, Angel!"

I turned my head sharply in his direction. "Oh, lighten up!" I growled back. Mine didn't sound as fierce as his. "I was only kidding."

Sean stared out the windshield, breathing deeply. I turned my head back to the window, letting him have time to get control of himself. I couldn't help smiling while I thought about our afternoon. For the first time in years I had a birthday I wouldn't work so hard to forget.

"Why were you in Salt Lake City in the first place?" His tone was now calm.

So much for happy memories ----- I thought sourly.

"When I was younger my mother talked a lot about a brother she had there," I grimaced. "I thought maybe I could find him, as well as get a fresh start."

"Starting over isn't as easy as it sounds," he reflected to himself.

I looked over at him, waiting for him to say more. The seconds passed, nothing. I nearly turned back to the window when suddenly he released my hand. I watched him as he removed the CD, changing it for another. I picked up my hand and laid it in my lap.

"I guess you would know better than me," I stated, grimly.

He snorted, dropping his serious expression. "I have seen more places in this life then I ever did as a human."

I pondered for a fraction of a second to ask about his human life. I didn't want to upset his buoyant humor and decided against it. The music spilling out of the speakers caught my attention and I raised my eyebrows at him.

"Something wrong?" he asked, skeptically.

"Is this even anything *you* really listen to?"

Sean shook with a quiet laughter. "I cannot say I listened to country much before you, but yes, I do like some of it. I have listened to every kind of music from every decade. I actually like the sixties, as I believed the sound was better. I cannot stand the disco of the seventies, opera bored the *hell* out of me. The eighties and nineties weren't bad, though they didn't have much soul."

I rolled my eyes and shook my head. Sean seemed to enjoy the humor, he reached over to the stereo, turning up the volume and sang along with Blake Shelton as he bellowed out Nobody But Me. I chuckled at how human he looked and went to look out the window.

I was instantly startled when suddenly he was grabbing for my hand. I watched in awe while he readjusted my ring, and then kiss my fingers before laying our twined hands to rest against the seat. My heart pounded, wildly and I cringed. It was embarrassing, especially since I now *knew* he could hear it.

The sky had grown dark and I silently watched for the lights of Newport to come into view. Sean lifted our hands, readjusted our fingers, and then brushed my cheek with the back of his hand.

"What are you thinking so hard about?" he asked, earnestly.

I sighed deeply. "Just trying to piece together a mental puzzle."

He pulled on my arm causing me to look at him. He inclined his head, indicating me to move closer to him. I carefully slid next to him, stopping just before our legs touched. Sean waited till I was no longer moving then laid our twined hands on my left leg.

"I meant what I said about secrets," his soft voice began. "If there's anything I can say to help with that puzzle, please allow me."

I snorted. "There's one of the missing pieces."

He was now puzzled. "You're going to have to be more specific than that."

I peeked at him from the corner of my eyes, taking in his expression. I had already learned talking about his life brought out disturbing expressions. There were no signs of indecision on his face.

"Your accent and articulation," I said carefully. "Where are you *really* from?"

He didn't answer, the seconds passed, and still ... nothing.

He let go of my hand, leaning forward to turn down the music. I waited patiently for him to respond. He leaned back against the seat and sighed.

"West Virginia," he finally sputtered.

The way he set his lips I thought the conversation was ending. It was now I felt guilty for even asking.

"I'm sorry, Sean," I apologized. "I don't mean to upset you."

"You haven't upset me," he murmured. "It's just somethings I don't remember well. Human memories begin to fade as the decades pass."

He threw a pointed glance in my direction and I smiled.

"I was born in Elkins, West Virginia in 1915," he spoke slowly. "Jonah found me in 1934 when I was nineteen."

"That's one piece in place," I reflected to myself. "Now the properness makes sense." Then I looked at him. "Where were your parents?"

"They died as a result of a car accident." His voice sounded distant, like he had gone back in time.

"You're not actually *related* to any of your family, right?"

"Most of us are not in the biological sense."

The way he stated that made it sound like there was more to their story than I had thought. I considered for a fraction of a second of having him elaborate, I'll come back to it.

"Is that how you have convinced the town Jonah had adopted you and Kelsey?"

His brows creased for a moment, then smoothed as his eyes began to darken in color.

"Yes. If we want to remain in the human world we have to put up the pretenses."

"Were you an only child?" I asked, curiosity thick in my voice.

He laughed blackly. "Ha! How I wish, but no. I had a younger sister ... have a younger sister," he quickly corrected.

Now I was truly fascinated. "Really? Is she still alive?"

We were in town now. The sky had gone completely dark, the moonlight was brightly casting its light.

It almost made everything it touched look magical. Sean turned off a few streets before Bobbie's and drove to the park. He let the truck slowly roll to the end of the parking lot, put it in park, and then shut off the engine. He waited a few seconds then turned his beautiful eyes on me.

"Yes," he said, breathing deeply. "though not in the *human* form."

"I'm not following you," I said confused.

"You have already met my sister." His voice sounded frustrated.

"Kelsey?" I gasped.

Sean pressed his lips together and nodded.

"So if you were nineteen," I said, my voice calculating. "How old was Kelsey?"

"Sixteen," he stated grimly. "Jonah actually met her first."

And again, the mentioning of Jonah caused my heart rate to speed up. I let the silence fill the truck for a moment while I tried deciding if I still wanted to continue this. Sean allowed me to take my time, picking up my left hand and mindlessly playing with my ring.

"How?" I finally asked.

Sean lifted his face and looked at me, a flicker flashed in his eyes.

"Before I answer that," he suddenly grinned. "there's something I would like you to do for me."

Oh, crap! *Please*, let it be reasonable.

"What?" I wasn't a hundred percent sure I wanted to know.

Sean laughed at my reluctance. He kept his hold on my hand and switched Blake Shelton for another CD. "Dance with me again."

"Sean, be serious," I growled.

"I am."

He turned the key over so the stereo would come on and began pressing the skip button. When the number he was looking for appeared on the stereo face he paused the CD. I tried to pull my hand free of his iron grip.

"If you didn't want to discuss your life you could have just said so," I griped.

"I never said I didn't want to," he countered. "When I tell you I'll give you anything you want, it's never a lie. All I'm simply asking for is one more uninterrupted moment."

I didn't budge.

"Aren't we passed all the evasiveness yet?" he snickered. "You have already kissed me so you can't still be afraid to touch me."

"No," I snapped icily. "I am not afraid of you or of touching you."

He raised one eyebrow in utter disbelief. Then he flashed a wide, wicked smile.

"You shouldn't have said that," he purred.

I opened my mouth, never to get the chance to say anything. Sean growled, a low sound in the back of his throat. I didn't see his door open ----- his movements way too fast. I only just found myself suddenly being yanked out of the truck, though barely jostled. All the while he caged me in the iron contours of his arms. I was nearly gasping as I tried to right myself.

"What's the matter with you, Sean Callenger?" I demanded. "You pushy jerk!"

His eyes danced, he was enjoying my sudden discomfort more than he should. "Instead of telling me you're not afraid of me, all you had to do was say yes."

I was still struggling to get free. He kept his arms wrapped tightly around me, carefully sliding them to my waist, as he carried me to the front of the truck then very gently set me on his feet. When I finally gave up the fight to get free, as I knew I wouldn't no matter how hard I fought he removed one arm from around my waist and reached in his pocket, pulling out a small remote. A second later the song filled the silence.

"You bought a CD for this one song?" I asked, astonished.

I would never have admitted it to him, but it flattered me to know that night meant as much to him as it did me.

Sean looked down at me while shoving the remote back in his pocket. "I do if the song is special. How would I not want the song I danced to with the woman I love?"

I stared at him, mystified and my mind went blank. I had no idea how to even begin to respond. Satisfied with my silence Sean began moving us to the music.

"Now," his soft voice said. Then looked down at me. "I will answer all your questions to help with that puzzle."

"Okay," was all I could say.

His beautiful eyes shinned as bright as the stars above us, taking my breath and my thoughts away.

"There is one last thing I would like to have before I let you ruin a perfectly good moment."

"What?" I croaked.

He laughed, leaning down towards my face, his citrus breath grazing the skin. I was already struggling to breath, this wasn't helping.

"What I was not able to have the first time we danced. A kiss in the moonlight."

My eyes widened, but I couldn't answer.

Sean lightly pressed his stain lips to mine. All the stress in my body simply dissolved. He slightly parted my lips, letting his ice cold breath fill both the back of my throat and my head. I became so dizzy I felt my knees collapse. He finally pulled away, leaving us both breathless.

"All right," he said, his voice unsteady. He placed a soft kiss to my forehead then straightened himself. "You still want to know how Kelsey met Jonah?"

Since he hasn't been human for decades he seemed to have forgotten our brains don't function as quickly as his. My mind was deeply clouded, preventing me from collecting myself to answer. I could only nod my head.

Sean was quiet again, as he swirled us around, seeming to need a minute to recall his memories. I gladly gave him the time, for I needed it to clear my own mind.

"I didn't know it at the time," Sean's velvety voice suddenly began. "but she was in the car with my parents. I was preparing to leave for college the following week and my parents were planning a surprise party. They had sent Kelsey off to boarding school so that night they went to pick her up from the airport. It had been raining, making it difficult to see the roads or other vehicles visibly. My father had been driving and hit head on into another car causing them both to slide of the road and into an embankment. The driver in the other car and my parents all died on impact.

"Jonah and Becca were on their way home from their feed when they heard the sounds from the crash. They rushed to the scene to try administering aid, but were too late. Kelsey was the only one barely alive. Jonah tried to use CPR to keep her heart beating until Becca could call for help, but she was losing blood too quickly. It was because she had been so young he couldn't let her die. That's when he decided to change her."

I watched him set his jaw and close his eyes. I stayed quiet, resting my head against his chest, allowing him to have all the time he needed. The song ended, and then restarted.

Sean took a deep breath. "I missed my time to start Yale because I had to bury my parents. A week later Kelsey showed up with Jonah by her side. I had seen him around town many times, it puzzled me how he knew my sister. Kelsey had been gone two years before he and Becca arrived in town. She proceeded with explaining to me about the accident and what Jonah had done to her.

"There was a noticeable difference in her voice and her eyes were the wrong color, but I thought she had gone completely crazy and threatened to call the school to send for someone to come for her. I picked up the phone and she flew across the room in an unbelievable speed, grabbing my arm to stop me. It was then I began to realize she wasn't crazy. What she had claimed to become was indeed true."

He stopped talking again and I pulled back to look at him. His eyes were closed, but a second later he was opening them, staring into mine. He seemed to forget the whole conversation for a moment. I kept all emotions off my face, hoping he would continue.

"When I questioned why she had waited so long to tell me, she claimed Jonah told her it wouldn't be safe for me if she came home right away. I demanded her to tell me the reason she had come then. She said she didn't want to be alone and begged me to go with them." He paused, taking a breath, the sound uneven. "Right there in the family room of our childhood home I willingly surrendered my humanity to Jonah so my sister would never have to be in this world alone."

He heard the sudden intake of my breath and looked at me. I quickly pressed my lips together a second to control my reactions.

"What was that like?" I finally asked.

He waited a few seconds to answer, watching my expressions closely.

"It is the most excruciating thing I have ever lived through. And just so we're clear, I have no intentions of ever doing this to *you*."

His tone wasn't harsh, but I heard the tenor behind his words.

"You do understand that, don't you?" he asked.

I simply nodded my head.

The conversation ended and I used the quiet time to let everything he'd said turn over in my mind, slowly processing it all. The mention he made about Kelsey's eyes reminded me of something he had said earlier about his own.

"I am a little confused about something."

Sean lowered his head to look at me. "What?"

His eyes blazed, the blue in them darker than I had ever seen. It took a minute for me to find my voice and reassemble my now tangled thoughts.

"You have mentioned eye color changes twice now. How does feeding from human blood have anything to do with them changing?"

"The elements and cells the human blood is made from are what changes them."

I don't know what my expressions were, but they must have still been confused. Sean sighed and stopped moving us.

"The more elements in the blood the more it causes the affects. Such as, if I were to taste your blood it would change my eyes because the elements and the cells are strong from your heart pulsing it through your body. But because we choose to feed from blood outside the body the elements are no longer strong, therefore it doesn't affect anything, allowing us to keep our natural color."

"But you said Kelsey's were the wrong color," I stated. His explanation made a little more sense than before, yet it still sort of contradicted it at the same time.

"I know, it has never made much sense to me, either. Jonah has a theory that maybe the effects the blood has are somehow different in genders."

The song started to play again, this time Sean pulled the remote from his pocket and stopped it. He lifted me up by the arms and set me gently on the ground in front of him. He stared at me for a long second, and then raised one arm, gliding his long cold fingers along the contours over my cheek. My heart leaped, erratically.

He dropped his arm then turned away and walked to the truck. I hadn't notice till he walked away the night had grown cool. Despite the long-sleeve shirt I still shivered. I absently wrapped my arms around my torso and followed Sean. I wasn't aware he was watching me till his soft voice called out to me.

"Angel, are you cold?" he asked, concern coloring his tone.

"A little," I admitted. My jaw instantly began to chatter, as if he needed the proof.

It wasn't even a second later and he was wrapping his jacket around my body. I didn't hesitate to slide my arms through the sleeves.

"Why don't you get in the truck?" Suddenly afraid he was going to take me home before we finished his story I flashed my eyes to his face. He read the hesitation on my face and sighed. "I'm not taking you home just yet. It will be warmer for you inside and we can talk some more."

"Okay." I let him lead me to the driver door, and then I climbed in the truck.

Sean closed his door then started the truck and turned the vents towards me before adjusting the knobs.

"It should start getting warm soon."

We sat listening to my teeth chatter. Sean reached for my left hand and slid the sleeve of his jacket and my shirt up my arm. I tried to fight the horror I felt as he stared at the ugly scar while his long, white finger traced lightly over it.

"You brought this to my attention, yet never told me how it happened," he said, his tone thoughtful.

I tried to be crafty as I fought to hide my horror and control my facial expressions.

"Yes, I did," I lied. "I'm clumsy."

He looked at me with both eyebrows raised in disbelief. "I admit you seem to have a problem with simply walking across a flat surface, but you're not this clumsy."

"How do you know that?" I asked, skeptically.

"That day on the bridge is probably the angriest you have ever been at me. I knew while you were cutting up those poor vegetables," he suddenly pressed his lips together to try hiding his amusement. "it was my face you were seeing in your head. Never once did that knife so much as slip in your hand. Now, tell me what he did to you."

"You were spying on me?" I nearly yelled.

He flashed me a dark look. "I followed you home determined you were going to listen to me. After you went in the house I considered breaking down the *damn* door and dragging you to me, even if you were kicking and screaming and show you everything I was feeling. I talked myself out of it, I knew I would have broken you with just the force of kissing you. So instead, I stood by the window and watched you."

"What else have you spied on me for?" I asked, allowing acid to enter my tone.

He refused to be distracted. "What did he do to you?" He enunciated each word slowly.

His tone irritated me as he made it sound like I was moron. I was sure telling him the truth was a bad idea, but ...

"Fine," I sighed in defeat. "Troy lied to my father and told him he had seen me with a boy while I was watching Jennifer's game. Scott flew into a rage, screaming at me about how I was boring and no one would ever find me attractive. He broke the bottom off of his whiskey bottle then sliced my arm as he told me it was for my own good."

Sean's jaw clenched, his eyes disturbed, as a deep, menacing growl rumbled from his chest. The sound frightened me and I tried to shy away from it. I pulled on my arm to get free from his grasp, he complied, instantly releasing it. He spoke from between clenched teeth.

"You are so boring that it drives me crazy when I have to wait until the next time I can see you so I can hear what the first thing you say to me is. And, surely there's nothing sexy about you, I just have nothing better to do than fight against myself to keep my hands off you!"

I sat in silence, watching his face while his blazing eyes stared out the windshield. I waited till the murderously angry expression faded from his face to speak.

"Are you okay?" I asked. My voice was hoarse.

"No," he said curtly. He closed his eyes and pinched the bridge of his nose with his thumb and forefinger.

"Okay," I said weakly. "just remember *you* forced me to tell you."

"I know." His breathing slowed down and he dropped his hand, carefully opening his eyes. They were almost normal when he looked at me. "Are you finished with finding your missing pieces?"

"Not yet, I was waiting for you to calm down again."

"I'm sorry for frightening you again, Angel," he apologized. "I have a bad temper and in certain situations it takes me a minute to rein it in."

"Okay."

It was quiet in the truck with the exception of the heater and Sean's rough breathing. I began playing with the end of the jacket sleeve, waiting patiently for Sean to collect himself.

"What else do you need to put your puzzle together?" His voice was still harsh, but it was calm.

I couldn't look at him, I didn't want to see what was in his eyes. I kept my head down and continued picking at the jacket.

"Aside from you and Kelsey, do each of you come from the same place?"

"No, Jonah came from Memphis, Tennessee. He met Becca somewhere in Kentucky and we were in Atlanta, Georgia when me met ..." His voice suddenly trailed off. His reaction wasn't what I had expected and I raised my head to look at him. He took a deep breath while running a hand over his face. Then he looked at me. "I have an even bigger secret I have to tell you."

Now I was nervous. "Do I dare ask?" I said, carefully.

"You already know that there are four members of my family. The truth is... there's seven of us."

He spoke the last part so slowly, his voice so low I couldn't quite be sure I'd heard him correctly.

"Did you just say seven?" I asked, cautiously.

"Yes," he exasperated. "They are my siblings."

"How does no one here know of them?"

"A coven this size raises too many questions and can bring in a number of bad situations. Whenever we start over somewhere there's always three of us that remains in the shadows, so to speak. I'm usually one of those three," he paused, flashing his eyes to my face. "though this time I'm glad I didn't."

"So, then where did the others come from?"

"As I said, we were in Atlanta, Georgia when we met Luke Bradford and Cameron Lewis. Luke found Mariah Maraschino while we were in Maine."

"Now it makes sense why everyone thinks you came from there," I reflected to myself. "And, each of them are actual couples?"

He half smiled. "Yes, I'm the loner of the group ... or at least was," he laughed. "You do realize you can no longer have late night rendezvous with Hesner, right?"

"I don't know what rendezvous you're talking about," I said frostily. "but I'll see what I can do."

Sean laughed and reached out for my hand. He had to push up the sleeve to free my fingers before he could twine our hands together.

"Are you warming up?" he asked, serious now.

I slightly nodded my head. "You could turn the heat down."

He lifted our hands to his face, kissing mine as he leaned forward to turn the heater to low. My heart missed several beats.

"So we can clear up a misunderstanding before it gets started," Sean said, his tone sounded like he was deep in thought. "The town is aware of Luke, they just don't tie him to our family."

"I've never heard anyone mention him," I said, confused.

Sean sighed, heavily. "Luke is one of the forest rangers."

I gasped in horror. Sean's eyes flashed to my face, concern flickered in his eyes.

"Just calm down, songbird," he instructed me. "He clearly didn't do you any harm."

We waited silently for my rapidly beating heart to slow. I took small, deep breaths while trying to decide if I had enough for one night or too curious for my own good.

"Were Luke and Cameron already ... what was the words you used earlier? *Nomads* ----- when you met them?" I asked, trying to get things back on track.

"No, they were human." Sean's voice was unemotional.

I waited for him to say more, he didn't seem interested in elaborating.

"How did fate change the direction of their lives?"

Sean looked down at our hands and began playing with my ring while he spoke.

"We had gone to Atlanta so Jonah could get help from his family. He needed to have papers drawn up to make it look as though he and Becca had adopted us from our parents. Everywhere we had gone before then people were whispering about Kelsey and Jonah's relationship because she looked so young. Luke and Cameron were a couple of construction workers Kelsey had met in a gas station."

"Kelsey went in a gas station?" I asked in disbelief.

I didn't know her well, but from the couple of times I'd spoken with her she didn't seem like someone you would run into in those places.

Sean rolled his eyes and laughed. "We do clearly drive, Angel. Anyway, she became so hooked to Cameron she would often sit near whatever site he would be at and watch him for hours. She did that every day for nearly a month. After that time people began to notice things about us and the gossip started to spread. They weren't very imaginative and often got it wrong, but Jonah felt it was time we moved on to spare his family.

"The day we were leaving it had started to rain. Kelsey begged Jonah to let her say goodbye to

Cameron. He was reluctant, but we knew she had fallen in love so he agreed. Cameron and Luke were busy lying pipes for the new general store when we arrived. It had begun to rain harder by this time and Kelsey got out to make her way to Cameron. She hadn't gotten far when suddenly a bolt of lightning struck the light pole causing it to crash to the ground.

"Cameron nor Luke had seen it coming so they couldn't get out the way before a power line snapped loose and wrapped around the pipeline they were carrying. They were instantly electrocuted."

The sudden intake of my breath was so loud Sean snapped out his reverie to look at me. His eyes narrowed as they watched me struggle to compose myself.

"How horrible," I said softly.

Sean watched my facial expressions a second longer before he spoke again.

"Jonah informed me that if we wanted a chance to save them we had to act fast. Becca tried to sooth a panic stricken Kelsey while he and I ran across the road to the dying men. It took a few long seconds for us to get them free of both the power line and the pipe. Once they were free Jonah immediately bit them. It was daring for him to do so in the open like that, but they wouldn't have survived long enough for us to pull them out of sight. Cameron made his commitments to my sister and Luke just decided to stay with his creator."

"Wasn't it extremely painful for you to touch the live wires and their bodies while electricity was coursing through them?"

Sean made a face. "I won't say it felt pleasant, but it didn't hurt, either. It was mostly just uncomfortable."

"Jonah's family knows neither he nor the rest of you are human?" I wanted to ask when he had said it, but decided to wait till he finished the story.

I had gotten overheated and began slipping out of Sean's jacket. His quick eyes caught my discomfort and he stretched out his arm and turned off the truck.

"Yes." He laid his head against the seat. "Though now all the ones who did are deceased."

"Well ..." My voice trailed off. I wasn't sure how to respond to that. I then decided to change the direction of the conversation. "All the accents make more sense to me now."

Sean turned his head towards me, a confused expression twisting his features.

"I know I may not have met all of your family... though I didn't know they existed," I mumbled. "but it was one of the first things I noticed about Jonah, aside from the unusual coloring under his eyes."

His face lost all expressions and emotions as he continued to stare at me. I instantly felt self-conscious.

"Is something wrong, Sean?" I asked slowly.

"No," he breathed. "I guess I'm just a little surprised at myself."

"Why?"

"I don't know what I expected to feel once I was finally able to share my forbidden secrets with you, but I feel extremely relived. Maybe even a little ... happy."

I laughed. "You make it sound like you've never been happy."

"Angel," he sighed, the sound almost a growl. "I have walked this planet ninety some years and until finding you I didn't really know what being happy was about."

"Didn't you have a happy childhood?" I asked, skeptical.

"Mine wasn't as bad as yours, though it wasn't the best of times, either."

I fought to keep from cringing at his words. But then, as his eyes dissected my expression his became somber.

"You're still waiting for the need to run?" I guessed.

Sean pressed his lips together and nodded his head.

"As I said before, you're going to be deeply disappointed."

Sean chuckled and turned his head, staring mindlessly out the windshield at the now completely dark sky.

"Did we get that puzzle of yours pieced together?"

"I believe so." There were still a few missing pieces, with his tone I figured it was time to let the conversation go. I could fill the rest in later.

"I should get you home," he said, sounding more like he was talking to himself than me. "You've been with me much longer than I expected and I'm sure Bobbie is waiting for you."

I opened my mouth to protest, as Bobbie would have already left for work and I wasn't ready to let a perfect night end. My stomach suddenly growled, reminding me I hadn't eaten since this morning and I closed it. Sean looked at me and frowned.

"And, it appears I've kept you from eating as well." He released my hand and started the truck. He turned it in a complete circle, and then headed to Bobbie's.

The ride had gone quiet. I played with my fingers while racking my brain for something to get him talking. I still hadn't come up with anything when he pulled in front of the house. Sean's headlights reflected off Bobbie's car and I was instantly stunned, forgetting about wanting him to talk. I threw a glance at the house, the kitchen light was burning. Sean shut off the truck, opened his door, and almost simultaneously was opening mine.

I hadn't collected myself as I slid out. Sean's hand snaked out and caught mine then he walked me to the porch. When he opened the door for me I slid his jacket down my arms, and then decided to keep it. The smell of hamburgers filled the air causing my stomach to grumble. I hadn't noticed Sean didn't enter the house till I turned to close the door. He was standing on the porch, leaning against the door jam.

"Would you like to come in?" I asked.

He reached up and softly brushed the back of his hand across my cheek. My heart skipped a beat then raced frantically against my ribs. A faint smile appeared on Sean's face causing mine to flush with embarrassment.

"Not tonight, I'm going to let you spend time with Bobbie. I'll be back in the morning."

"Okay," I said, feeling slightly disappointed. "thank you for an amazing day."

A slow, cocky grin crossed his lips. "This is only the beginning."

I nearly groaned when he suddenly leaned in the door and placed his cold, satin lips on mine. This kiss was softer than the others and left behind a tingling sensation after he pulled away. He dazzled me so badly I had to remember how to breathe. I hadn't fully recovered when he rested his forehead gently against mine, the tantalizing, richness of his citrus breath lightly graze across my face. My breath … gone.

"Happy birthday, songbird," he whispered.

I opened my mouth, but nothing would come out. Sean laughed and reached up, closing it for me.

"Good night, Bobbie," he called out more loudly. He kissed my forehead then straightened himself.

She appeared in the doorway a minute later. "Would you like to join us for dinner?" she asked, her tone thoughtful.

"Not tonight," he answered. He turned his eyes on her. "I've had Angel longer than I planned. I'm going to go on home and let the two of you finish out the evening."

"Okay." She sounded deeply disappointed. "Good night, Sean."

Sean looked at me, grinned and winked, and then turned to walk off the porch.

Bobbie was already back in the kitchen by the time I closed the door and entered the room. It was then I saw two plates on the table filled with a hamburger and fries. She was now carrying two glasses of tea to the table.

"I know it's not the gourmet stuff you usually make," she chuckled. "but I hope you like it."

"You did all this for me?" I was shell shocked.

"Of course I did, silly," she laughed. "Sean told me about your birthdays so I wanted to make this one you could remember without the sadness and the heartache."

Normally that would result in him getting a good growl from me, but now I couldn't even be mad. He had managed to make this the best birthday I'd had in years. I slipped out of his jacket and laid it over the back of the chair.

"I don't know what to say ... thank you." An unnoticed tear slid effortlessly down my cheek and I wiped it away.

She smiled widely at me. "You are very welcome."

I pulled out the chair and sat down. She stared at me for a long second then leaned over, picking a box up from the floor.

"I was going to wait until we had cake to surprise you," she said as she was sitting upright. "I just can't hold back the anticipation any longer."

She set the silver wrapped box on the table and pushed it to me. I hadn't noticed my hands were trembling until I tried tearing at the wrapping. I curled my fingers around it while mentally calming myself. The box she had wrapped was plain, with the lid on top instead of on the side. Bobbie waited, seeming to be almost impatient as I lifted the flap.

She had placed a portable CD player and a Luke Bryan CD inside.

"I hope you like them," she said, her tone uncertain. "I wasn't sure if you would like that particular artist, but he really is good."

I lifted out the CD player, thinking about that day on the bridge with Sean. I had been so mad at him, now it all seemed so silly. Despite myself I couldn't help laughing.

"Bobbie, these are just perfect. Thank you."

"You're welcome," she beamed at me.

I laughed and placed the CD player back in the box. My stomach was beginning to get impatient with my slowness. I picked up the hamburger, taking the biggest bite I possibly could.

"Did you have a nice time with Sean?" Bobbie asked carefully.

I nodded my head, swallowing the bite. "Yes I did actually. We spent the entire afternoon at a little spot by the ocean."

"That at least explains the sand all over your clothes," she noted.

I had forgotten I had even been wet and looked down at myself. Sure enough, there was still sand stuck to my shirt and all around my legs.

"Oh!" Bobbie suddenly gasped. "Angel, that is just gorgeous."

My head instantly snapped, my expression confused. "What is?"

She pointed her index finger at my left hand. "Your ring," she clarified. "Did Sean give it to you?"

I looked at it, my lips instantly formed a smile. "He surprised me with it," I giggled.

"So, does this mean you're dating him?" she asked with caution.

"I suppose it does," I sighed.

"Good," she said with a extra wide grin. "then you have to stay." She picked up her glass. "And so does Sean," she added before setting the glass against her lips.

I took another bite of the hamburger and her words sank in. I finished it, looking at her with an odd expression.

"What do you mean?"

"Sean left town last year and had only been back a couple of months when the rangers found you in the woods."

Another piece of the puzzle.

"Why did he leave?" I tried to sound curious, though I believe I failed.

She puckered her lips and shrugged. "I'm not really sure."

I laughed at her expressions then we lapsed in silence.

This was one of the many things I enjoyed about living with her. She never hovered, invaded anyone's privacy and she didn't like to gossip. When I stood to take my dishes to the sink her eyes flashed to my face.

"I'm sure you're tired and want to shower, but could I talk you into having a slice of cake?"

I couldn't remember the last time I'd had any cake. "Sure."

She jumped up from her chair, nearly running to the back porch. She reentered a second later, carrying a small cake, with a powder blue frosting. I felt my face heat from embarrassment.

"My gosh, Bobbie," I blushed.

"Happy birthday, Angel," she laughed.

She took the cake to the table while I got a couple of small plates from the cabinet and a knife out of the drawer.

"Did Sean finally kiss you?" she suddenly asked.

I nearly missed a cut in the cake when she uttered her question. My cheeks were now on fire.

"Yes," I said, barely a whisper.

"Wow," she mouthed. "What was that like?"

"I don't think I could really describe it," I said with a sigh. "I only know amazing doesn't even come close."

I handed her a slice of the cake then served myself. The direction of the conversation changed as she began to tell me about Derek's trip to Florida.

It took three times of washing my hair to get out all the sand. I couldn't help laughing when the bottom of the shower was covered in it. By the time I was finished it had enough that it could have been its own little beach. After I finished cleaning the sand out of the shower I crawled into bed. My body was completely exhausted, yet my mind still raced. I turned on the clock radio, adjusted the quilt over my body and almost instantly fell asleep.

I hadn't dreamed in years ----- not one I could ever remember anyway. But I wasn't sure if maybe I was or if I was still slightly conscious when I felt something cold and smooth gently brushing the side of my face. I very slowly opened my eyes and Sean was sitting on the bed beside me. The room was dark, all I could really see of his face was where the red glare from the alarm clock shinned on him.

"Hi," he whispered.

"Hi," I yawned. "I thought you went home."

"I did, but then I remembered something else I have for you. You distracted me and I forgot it," he chuckled.

"It couldn't have waited until tomorrow?" I grumbled and rolled over.

Sean's quiet laughter shook the entire bed. "I suppose it could have, though it wouldn't have been a birthday gift."

I pulled a pillow over my head, determined to go back to sleep. It wasn't even a second later when the light came on and the pillow disappeared. So much for the dream theory ----- I thought sourly. I rolled back over with a resigned sigh, frowning at Sean.

"What?" he asked innocently.

"I would like to sleep before daylight," I said, grimly. "so what else do you have?"

Sean laughed again, leaning over to place a soft kiss on my lips. When he pulled away he rested the pedals of a beautiful red and white rose against my nose.

"I'm assuming you have something to put this in."

"I think so." I wasn't a hundred percent sure. I took the rose from his hand and sat up. "I'll go look."

Sean carefully pulled it free from my hand, and then stood from the bed. "I'll do it."

"Bobbie," I hissed.

"Is asleep," he nearly growled. "I can have this in a vase and be back in here before your door closes."

I gave him a dirty look seconds before he disappeared in the hall.

I listened as he walked through the house. His footsteps weren't heavy, they sounded faint, like an animal walking across the hardwood. Sean was back in the room when it finally sank in that I'd heard those same sounds before.

"This isn't the first time you've been in here, is it?"

Sean set the vase on my dresser then walked to the bed. He was hesitant to answer, confirming my suspicion. He sat down on the bed, his eyes assessing my expression.

"No," he finally answered. "I have been in here many times."

I pulled my knees to my chest and wrapped my arms around them. "Why?"

He sighed, heavily. "The first time I came I was trying to be sure you wouldn't speak of the rescue to Bobbie. Then when you didn't, I wanted to know why. I came in the window, wanting to see if you talk during your sleep so then maybe I could figure you out. But then you stirred and I knew you had somehow heard me. I was barely out when you appeared at the window."

I scowled at the room, remembering how terrified I had been as I knew someone was in my room.

"Why didn't you just bother to ask questions like a normal person?"

"Every time I talk to you I always end up saying too much. I was trying to deter you from the truth, had I asked you would have known then something wasn't right. I couldn't take that chance."

I snorted. "Little did you know, I had already figured out something wasn't quite right."

"I know," he mumbled. "We weren't counting on you to be so observant."

He reached over the side of the bed and less than a second later was handing me an envelope. I hesitantly took it then watched him lay on the bed, crossing his long legs at the ankles and fold his left arm under his head.

"What is this?" I was confused.

He narrowed his eyes at me. "Something you have had for far too long that you never bothered to open."

I looked down, it was the letter from Juilliard.

"Sean," I barely whispered. "I can't open this."

He reached up to play with the strands of my nearly dry hair. "Yes, you can. It is time to allow yourself some pleasure. You deserve to know their answer."

I stared at his face for several long minutes then tore open the envelope. My hands shook, almost uncontrollably as I pulled the letter out and opened it.

I was in. They had the date for my second audition set for January 20th.

"Congratulations," Sean said, his tone pleased.

I looked at him, stunned. "How ----- how did you know?" I stammered.

"I saw their answer shine in your eyes."

I looked back down at the paper, it was already gone. Sean laid it on the table beside the bed then balled his hand in a fist in my hair and pulled me backwards.

"We can worry about how this affects us tomorrow. It is time for the human to sleep."

As soon as my head was resting against his chest he turned off the light.

"What if I can't sleep with you here?" I hedged.

"You do it nearly every night," he reminded me.

I scowled at the darkness, trying to think of something witty to say. It wasn't long and Sean was humming the melody of the song playing from the radio. The sound was so soothing my eyes drooped and soon the night washed over me.

What a Strange Family

The sound of the rain falling against the roof had me becoming alert long before I was ready. I groaned and grabbed a pillow, pulling it over my head. It didn't seem to help, I still tossed restlessly around the bed. My hand flopped against the open spot of the bed where another body would lay and very slowly began to realize it should have hit something … or someone. I knocked the pillow off my head and sat up.

My eyes scanned the room then flashed to the window. It was closed and I was alone. Had I been dreaming after all? I nearly flopped back on the bed when my eyes caught sight of the rose sitting on top of the dresser. I smiled widely as the disappointment I felt seconds ago faded. I fell back against the bed and looked at the clock. It was only six-thirty in the morning and I was already awake. I rolled over to face the door and pulled the quilt over my head. Maybe if it makes the room look dark enough I could fall back to sleep. Sean will be here before long, I reminded myself. I sighed, pushed back the quilt and got up.

I took the rose from the vase and pressed it to my nose, my lips forming a huge smile as I thought about my afternoon with Sean. After a few minutes I set it back in the vase and turned to leave the room when the idea of taking it downstairs where it would have more light crossed my mind. I looked back at the rose, still undecided and stared at it. It probably would last longer in a window downstairs, I told myself. I sighed then picked up the vase and walked out of the room.

It never occurred to me the kitchen light was on or that there was anyone moving around the room. I mindlessly hummed the melody from the song I danced to with Sean while looking around for the perfect place for the rose. I wanted it to get plenty of light, but also be right in view. The kitchen only had two windows; one was right next to the table, it would have been in view, yet there was also the chance it would be knocked over. The other was across the room next to the fridge. It was bigger and the vase would have set perfectly on the lip, but it was kind of out of view.

"Put it in the living room," Bobbie suggested. "The windowsill is wider and there's no chance of the vase being knocked over."

I snapped out of my daydreaming to stare at her. It was now I noticed she was standing in front of the stove frying bacon. An expression of amusement twisted her features as she took in my reaction.

"Hi," she laughed. "That's a mighty pretty rose."

"Thanks," I beamed. "Sean brought it to me before I went to bed."

"I figured, as you appeared to be lost in daydreams about him to never notice me."

My face reddened a bit. "Sorry, I was just thinking about yesterday." She laughed.

I walked in the living room and set the vase in the front window. There, I thought dreamlessly, it'll be seen from the porch. I lingered a second longer to stare at it then went back to the kitchen.

"I forgot to mention last night, but Jennifer called," Bobbie informed me.

It had slipped my mind that she said she would call once she was home from work.

I cringed. "Oh, crap!"

Bobbie finished stacking her plate with bacon strips and went to sit at the table.

"Did you tell her ...?" My voice trailed off. I just remembered I hadn't told her about Sean.

"No," Bobbie stated. The tone in her voice called my attention back to her. "I told her I wasn't sure where you had gone."

Now I was confused. "Then how did you know I was with Sean?" I walked to the cabinet and pulled out a box of cereal and a bowl, and then went to the fridge, taking out the milk.

"I didn't at first. When it got to be dark and you hadn't come in then I figured you were."

I poured milk in the bowl, put it back in the fridge, and then took my bowl to the table and sat down.

"What are you even doing up this early?" she suddenly asked.

I puckered my lips and pointed to the window. "Do you hear that?"

"The season is getting ready to change," she laughed. "It's why I'm up early myself, I'm going over to help Aunt Kloe get her garden ready for fall."

"Oh," was all I could say.

The conversation ended while we focused on eating our breakfast. I hoped to be finished and have the dishes washed before Sean got here.

I didn't want to hear his crude remarks about my cleanliness. Bobbie finished off her bacon then stood from the chair.

"What time is Prince Charming going to be here?" she asked.

I wasn't expecting her question nor for her to have a particular name for him other than his own and nearly choked on the bite I hadn't swallowed. "I'm not sure," I said as I gasped for air. "and he's no *prince*," I added after I got my throat cleared.

She laughed then disappeared up the stairs.

I finished off the cereal and took the bowl to the sink. I turned on the water to wash the dishes and the phone rang. I grumbled at the empty room while I turned it off then reached for the phone.

"Hello?" I asked somberly.

"I called last night and you weren't home," Jen complained.

"I know," I sighed. "It was too nice of a day to stay inside."

"And you couldn't have called when you got back?" she asked, her tone doubtful.

"I wasn't aware you had called," I sputtered ruefully. "and it was late when I got in."

"What did you do that kept you out so late?" Her voice was frustrated.

I took a deep breath, preparing myself for the reaction I was sure I'd get for telling her the truth. It might not be so bad had you told her about him sooner, I told myself.

"I was with Sean," I stated carefully.

I slightly cringed, waiting for a scream or the sound of something from her side hitting a wall. She did neither.

"Who's Sean?" she probed. Even though her tone was calm I didn't relax. She would yell soon.

"A guy I met shortly after I moved here." She was still unaware of my situation as somehow the story never made it there and I never offered the information. When Mike told me no one had contacted him about me I stopped keeping an eye on Troy.

"And?" she urged.

I was trying to think of a crafty way to explain it to her when three faint knocks came on the door. It wasn't even a second later and Bobbie was running down the stairs.

"Prince Charming is here, Angel," she yelled.

"Angel, tell me!" Jennifer's voice suddenly commanded.

"He's my ... boyfriend," I answered, hesitantly.

Too much was happening at once, preventing me from being able to think clearly. I wasn't sure what to call Sean, as he and the word *boy* couldn't have been further from one another.

"Boyfriend!" she exclaimed. "When did this happen?"

I opened my mouth to answer, Bobbie entered the room less than a second later with Sean right behind her. He flashed me a gleaming smile as he casually walked to me, causing me to completely forget the conversation for a moment. He leaned down and softly kissed my open lips.

"Good morning, beautiful," he whispered.

He straightened himself and turned to walk to the table. I watched him while trying to remember how to close my mouth, seeming how I was unaware it was even still open. He sat down in the chair and looked at me, an amused smile twisting his lips.

"Angel," Jen growled.

"Ummm ... what?" My mind was deeply clouded, it took me a minute to remember what she had asked. "Yesterday," I said slowly. Sean's eyes were somehow softer than usual in color, keeping me focused on him, instead of what I was doing. I closed my eyes and turned around so I could concentrate on the conversation. "I really have to go, Jen. I'll call you later."

"Please, Angel," she begged. "You promised I'd be the first to know if something like this happened."

"You are," I sputtered defensively. "Other than Bobbie," I quickly added when her voice answered a question I never heard.

Jen seemed to catch on. "He's there now, isn't he?" she asked.

"Yes," I sighed. "I promise, I will call, okay?"

"You better, bye!" I could hear the impatience in her voice.

"Bye, Jen." I knew it was pointless to utter the words when she was already gone.

"Okay, I'm going," Bobbie suddenly announced.

I hung up the phone, slowly turning to face her. Her eyes flashed to mine, and then narrowed.

"I should be back some time this afternoon."

"There's no need to rush," I stated dryly. "I'll most likely have everything done, anyways."

"Okay," she shrugged. "have fun. I'll see the two of you later."

She eyed me a second longer than disappeared in the foyer.

I turned back to the sink and turned on the water, catching the faint sound of Sean moving his chair.

"It's nice to know Bobbie is all right with my being here," he said as his arms slipped around my waist.

"Yeah," I agreed. "it makes my life a little easier."

His nose grazed the skin on the side of my neck and I shivered.

"I don't know about that," he laughed. "she did call me *Prince Charming*."

I rolled my eyes. "Yes, well ... don't let that go to your head."

I felt his lips form a smile against my skin. "Too late."

I ignored his humor, fighting to keep my focus on washing the dishes used for breakfast. Sean moved his lips carefully around my neck, deeply breathing in my scent.

"I have waited for hours to get my hands on you," he mumbled.

His icy cold breath sent shivers through my body. I reached for the skillet and Sean kissed my neck, released me, and then stepped back, allowing me to move more freely. He leaned against the counter and crossed his legs at the ankles.

"You're the one who left at whatever time it was," I reminded him. "but I'm sorry you had to wait so long."

"You don't sound sorry," he complained. "and I left so Bobbie wouldn't have too many questions for you. How would it have looked if I came down the stairs with you and my truck wasn't here? But it's still hardly fair I have to wait so long for you to awaken when you never have to wait for me."

I looked at him, instantly regretting it. His crystal blue eyes were scorched and clouded my mind. I had to look away to recover my now tangled thoughts.

"That's not exactly true," I disagreed. "Every time you leave I have to wait for days before you come back."

I heard the smirk in his voice when he responded. "So, you don't like it when I leave?"

I didn't answer.

I finished washing the skillet, rinsed it off, and then laid it on the towel. Sean slid his arms back around my waist while I was pulling the plug out of the sink.

"I suppose since I did leave this morning this little situation does makes us even," he grinned. "though, you still owe me for the wait seeming how I let you sleep in." His nose grazed my ear before he skimmed it along my neck. My heart pounded so hard I feared it would finally jump free of the skin.

I rinsed out the sink then stepped backwards, trying to push Sean back so I could be free from the entrapment between him and the sink. I may as well have tried to push a boulder loose for all the good it did me; he never budged. He kissed from the hollow beneath my ear to my collarbone. He made the circuit numerous times before I could gain enough control of myself to speak.

"And just how would I make it up to you?" The words were nearly breathless.

I felt his lips pucker as he seemed to think about it. "I don't think you can," he finally answered.

His arms loosened, giving me room to move. I very slowly turned to face him, as not to startle him. His eyes were light, his expression amused.

"How about if I did ...?" I raised up on my tiptoes, watching his face closely and gently pressed my lips to his.

I wasn't prepared for his reaction. His eyes widened for a fraction of a second, and then he caught my face in between his iron hands, pressing his hard, cold lips to mine. My heart raced wildly, as I froze and stared at him in alarm.

"Kiss me back, Angel," he murmured. His lips parted mine, my fear instantly resolved as his breath touched the back of my throat and my mind was dazzled.

I was struggling to breathe and shook my head. Sean complied, slowing the urgency in his lips and eventually pulled away.

"I'm sorry," he said apologetically. "I haven't quite gotten used to you being willing to do this on your own. When you did it caught me off guard before I could control my own needs." He paused, calming himself. Then flashed his eyes to mine. "That is definitely a step in the right direction, but I'm afraid it isn't quite enough." He dropped his hands from my face.

His eyes were smoldering causing every thought I had to instantly disappear and I blurted out a truth I'd been holding back from him.

"I love you."

He raised one eyebrow, his voice ominous. "You may have just found success after all." He lifted up an arm, softly brushing his fingers along my cheek. "I love you, too."

Now I was the confused one. "Sean, you already know I love you."

"Yes," he agreed. He let his fingers skim over my lips before dropping his arm. "It is nice to hear and this is the first time you have actually said it."

"I told you yesterday," I challenged.

Sean was shaking his head before I finished.

"When I asked if it would ever be possible for me to earn your love, you said I already had. That certainly is not saying the same thing."

I stared at him while I thought over that conversation. Then remembered I didn't tell him the words directly. I nearly opened my mouth when he causally leaned down toward me, softly placing his cold, satin lips against mine. I forgot what witty remark I was going to make as his lips parted mine. His kiss was so gentle it caused my head to spin and my legs to weaken. Sean's arm caught me around the waist before I collapsed. It wasn't even a second later he pulled away, leaving us both breathless.

"Why don't you get dressed?" he nearly whispered.

"Why?" The word was shaky as I was still light headed.

He suddenly grinned. "I have a few more things I would like to show you."

I instantly became leery. "Such as, what?"

"My house," he enunciated carefully while closely watching my face. "and the rest of my family," he added when I didn't react or respond.

I felt my breath catch in my throat when his words finally sank in. Sean lifted his right arm, using his thumb to smooth out the crease on my forehead.

"Why do you suddenly look so stressed?" His eyes darkened in color and were now filled with concern.

I fought to keep my voice from shaking. "You want to take *me* ... to your house?" I failed in my attempt, miserably.

He scowled and dropped his arm, slipping it back around my waist.

"You already know Jonah and Kelsey, so clearly there's nothing for you to get excited about. I just think it's time you met the others."

"You want me to meet all of them?" I croaked. "What if they don't like me or that I know all of your secrets?"

That slow, cocky grin appeared on his lips. "They are very much aware you do and I can promise you, it is all right. They're all excited to finally get to officially meet you."

"Why are you doing this to me?" I whined.

Sean laughed his quiet, musical laugh. "As I told you yesterday, I love you and you are my life now. I want to share every part of it with you, including my family."

I opened my mouth to say something and Sean instantly pressed his lips to mine, silencing me. He continued to kiss me until he was sure I wouldn't try to argue. I struggled to breathe and became light headed, I shook my head and he carefully pulled away. While I sank against the sink to collect myself he stepped away from me and leaned against the counter beside me. When I was sure I could walk without falling on my face I stepped away from the sink. I not only had to remember how to walk, but concentrate on getting one foot to move in front of the other, too.

I searched through my closet and the dresser relentlessly, trying to figure what to wear. I had no idea what you're supposed to wear when you meet your boyfriend's family, let alone what to wear to the home of a *vampire* family. They'd had already seen me at my worst, via the night in the woods ... but still.

I finally settled on a long-sleeved dark blue shirt, as I didn't want the ugly scar exposed and a pair of jeans. After I was finished dressing I went in the bathroom to brush the tangled mop that was my hair and my teeth. My hair was so mangled I had to use the straightener on it before I could even get the brush through it. Because it was now flat and straight I tied it back in a ponytail. While brushing my teeth I remembered I still had Sean's jacket. I quickly finished then rushed in my room to grab it.

Sean was standing in front of the door watching the rain when I tromped down the stairs. A smile instantly crossed his lip when he turned to look at me.

"That color of blue looks good against your skin," he complimented me. "Your hair looks ..."

"I know," I grumbled. "I couldn't do anything with it."

He shrugged. "Maybe now I can pull it down without breaking anything."

At that I laughed. The thought of seeing his family flashed in my head causing my heart to race, again.

"Sean, I don't think I can do this."

"Angel," he moaned and in a flash he was pulling me the rest of the way down the stairs. "Yes you can. There isn't anything for you to fear."

Sure there is, I thought dryly. I'm the only *human* invited to a vampire party.

"You may not think so," I disagreed. I tried (and failed) to pull away from him. "Please, don't ..."

He groaned , the sound almost a growl and kissed me, silencing my plead. It didn't even take a second and my knees were weak. Sean effortlessly slipped his arms around my waist and lifted me up from the stairs. When he was sure I wouldn't try to plead with him again he pulled away. My breath and my thoughts had evaded me.

"Now," he said, his breathing rough. "let's get out of here. You have family waiting for you."

"Okay," was all I could manage.

He walked out the door then set me down in front of it so I could lock it. My hands shook so badly I couldn't put the key in the lock. Sean took it from me, locked the door himself, and then pulled his jacket free of my hands and wrapped it around me. He waited till I slipped my arms in the sleeves to walk me to the truck.

I was so nervous I kept my head down and played with the sleeves of Sean's jacket. I would occasionally look out the window, I was then reminded of how he drives and looked back to my hands to ward off panic. It was silly to act like that and I knew that, yet I was unable to stop it. I still wasn't sure of Jonah, especially after the things Sean had told me and now I was going to meet ones I never knew even existed.

Sean took one-oh-one south to Bay Blvd, driving along the side of

Yaquina Bay for miles. The water was as dark as the sky, white-caped and heaving to the gray, rocky shore. I watched in awe, taking in all its beauty despite the rain. After several miles he finally turned off on a road with no marker or any kind of sign. He drove down the long stretch, passing houses till they were getting further and further apart before finally coming to the one at the end of the road.

I expected it to look like the others, as they were clearly farm houses. This one didn't. It sat in the middle of the large lawn, elegant, and graceful. It was a mix of the past and present brought together in perfect harmony. It was the classic white, two stories tall, the structure looked original, a perfect restoration with an added preference. A set of stairs twisted around one side leading to the second floor gallery where a small table and two chairs sat overlooking the horizon. A deep porch wrapped around the first story. Sean drove all the way to nearly the base of it.

"Listen to your heart fly," Sean said, breaking the now awkward silence. "It is going to be all right."

"I know," I sighed, weakly. "I can't help that I'm nervous."

Sean opened his door and less than a second later opened mine. He gently grabbed my hand and pulled me out of the truck. Once I was standing he placed a long, cold finger under my chin, lifting my face up to look at him. His face was hard, yet his eyes were soft.

"I would *never* take you anywhere that isn't safe."

"I know," I said, shamefaced.

He leaned down, placed a soft kiss to my forehead, and then released every part of me, but my hand.

I briefly saw a massive, three door garage sitting off to the north of the house, a deep forest stretched for miles behind it and the house. A dark sedan was the only car parked in front of the doors and I immediately recognized it as Jonah's. My heart pounded harder as I thought about the one night I had rode in it. Sean sensed my distress and rubbed his thumb in circular motions over my hand.

The door was a double, with carvings and long arched panels of glass on either side and a half-moon glass topper. I couldn't help tracing my fingers over the smoothness of the glass and the wood before Sean opened it. I had never seen anything so … amazing. It appeared to be Old World with a touch of *southern*.

When we stepped inside my breath instantly caught in my throat at the sight of the wide loblolly pine floor. The living room was large, one side a high rise platform. The lower side was covered by a light beige carpet, the only window was massive in size and covered with a curtain of the same color. It had been tied back, allowing the room to look open.

The staircase was the focal point. It was in the far wall rising up, wide to the second floor and curved off to the right.

The furniture was all white; a couch sat in the middle of the lower side facing a big TV, with a wide stand holding a variety of game consoles. A large cushion chair sat next to the window, with a small table containing a lamp beside it. There were pictures and various paintings hanging all around the room. I wasn't sure what I expected to see, but it certainly wasn't this. It looked so ... human.

Sean gently tugged on the back of his jacket. I looked at him and he gestured for me to take it off. I slowly slid it down my arms, and then handed it to him. I watched him walk to the door, hanging the jacket on a hook beside it.

"Are you disappointed, yet?" he teased.

"I don't know," I said warily. "Is the basement lined with caskets and old bones crumpled in the corners covered in spider webs? Or bats hanging from the ceilings?"

Sean shook with laughter. "This old place never had a basement and I don't believe there's even one web lurking in any of the corners, as Becca doesn't like spiders. As for the bats, our kind turning into one is nothing more than a myth."

"Then yes," I said with a hint of sarcasm. "I am deeply disappointed."

Sean laughed again, taking my hand and pulling me further into the room. I expected his family to enter when the sound of our voices filled the room. No one ever did. It was now Sean called for them, his voice barley above a whisper. Deputy Callenger and a small woman, I presumed was Becca, entered less than a second later. Though I had seen him a number of times his appearance was still striking. He wasn't dressed in his usual uniform, he wore a plan t-shirt, with a pair of jeans. The woman at his side was dressed in jeans, with a faint pink sweater. She was extremely beautiful, she had a soft-looking oval shaped face, light golden brown hair, with almost gray eyes. I couldn't help wondering what color they had been when she was human.

They were careful about how close they approached us, staying on the lower side of the room. I tried not to stare, but was unable to help looking over their faces. I looked for any signs of the blackness in the irises, as well any purpling on the skin under them. Their eyes were light in color, the purple was gone. I relaxed, a little.

"Jonah, Becca," Sean finally said, breaking the now awkward silence. "This is Angel."

"It is good to see you again, Angel," Jonah stated as he stepped up on the high rise.

He extended out his arm to me and I carefully made the extra step to shake his waiting hand.

"It's nice to see you, too, Deputy Callenger."

"Now, Angel," he scolded me as he released my hand. "We have spoken many times before. Please, call me Jonah."

"Jonah," I breathed. "got it."

Becca swatted his arm as she made her way to me. "Leave the poor girl be, she's nervous."

The sound of her octave voice instantly sent my mind back to the woods. She had been the voice I heard as she stroked my hair. I waited for her to hold out her hand, instead she wrapped her cold, stone arms around my shoulders and pulled me into a vice-tight hug.

"It is nice to finally get to officially meet the girl who has captured my son's heart," she said softly.

Sean groaned as she pulled away from me, she raised her eyebrows, as if to silently scold him.

"I'm glad to finally have the chance to meet you as well," I blushed. I surprised myself with my own admissions and that I truly was.

"It is nice of you to come here," she smiled. "Jonah wasn't quite convinced you would."

"Thank you for allowing me," I said, extremely embarrassed. "You have a very beautiful home."

And before she could respond another couple entered the room from the stairs. Becca returned to Jonah's side, giving them room to reach me. The male intimidated me with his size and I fought to stand still. He immediately reminded me of Paul Bunyan; his chest and arms were muscular and tapered down to almost a narrow waist. He was dressed in his uniform, his short black hair combed neatly in place. It wasn't till he was nearly in front of me that I began to recognize his piercing blue eyes and the name badge on his shirt. I had seen them in a few flashbacks, though I wasn't sure they were real memories. Now I knew they *were*.

His mate was very different. She was taller than Becca and Kelsey, extremely thin, her silvery blond hair hung loosely to the bottom of her waist. She was dressed in jeans, boots, and a white blouse that was tucked inside her jeans. Her skin had just a hint of olive under the silvery, chalk pale gray, but it was the color of her eyes that was the most unusual, yet stunning; they were violet.

"Angel," Sean's wind chimed voice said. "This is Luke and Mariah."

Luke stopped inches from the platform and flashed a grin at me. "Those eyes are much greener than I remember," he noted. "Welcome to the family."

"Thank you." My face flushed a deep red, I struggled to say the words coherently.

Luke laughed, a deep sound, almost a bear growl. "Now I get why Sean couldn't leave her alone."

I faintly heard Sean mumble something to his brother, the words were much too fast for me to catch.

"Oh, knock it off," Mariah interjected. The sound of her high octave pitch voice and the color of her eyes now made sense to why she was always one to stay out of sight. She would definitely be the one to make the town become suspicious.

Just as she stepped close to me she suddenly went rigid and she stopped moving. She stared at me with the strangest expression on her face. It wasn't hostile, yet her violet eyes turned black ----- coal black. Sean carefully squeezed my hand, a low growl rumbling from his chest while he pulled me behind him. Mariah flashed her dark eyes at him then turned and in a flash disappeared from the room. I stared at the now empty doorway, stunned, wondering if my presence had somehow offended her. Luke sent me an apologetic look then vanished in the same direction as his mate.

"Kelsey?" Sean suddenly called out.

She appeared a fraction of a second later with a deep blond male at her side. I expected her to be dressed in the usual biker look I'd grown accustom to seeing. Instead, she wore a dark brown sweater, the sleeves pushed up to mid-forearm, with a pair of jeans.

"There's no need for the yelling," she grumbled. "I'm right here."

She causally walked to Becca and handed her some sort of package, seeming to be unaware I was standing there. I had to press my lips together to keep from laughing.

"Did you get done what I asked?" Sean asked, ignoring her sourness.

"Yes," she growled. Then turned to look at him. "Angel!" It wasn't even a second later and she was to me, pulling me in for a vice-tight hug.

I saw Jonah and Becca cringe, seeming to fear something. After a few minutes when they didn't hear any of my bones crack they relaxed.

"I'm so glad you came. Why haven't you been by to see me?"

I couldn't help laughing while hugging her back. "I've been working a lot of hours and spending time with your brother."

She pulled away and slipped one arm effortlessly around my waist. "You do realize since yesterday was your birthday and my brother chose to be greedy, keeping you to himself that you and I are going to have to take a day and go shopping, right?"

"Kelsey," I groaned.

"No is not an option," she warned. Then pointed her long white finger at the male she entered the room with. "That is Cameron."

He too, was tall. His dark blond hair looked windblown, his eyes the color of cornflower. His gaunt build was gangly compared to the other three men. Cameron wore a black t-shirt, with dark blue, almost black colored pants, the legs were tucked neatly inside his boots. He never made the effort to approach me.

"Hello, Angel," he said politely.

"It's nice to meet you, Cameron," I answered shyly.

Kelsey tightened her arm around me, turning her eyes back to my face. "I'd love to stay and play like everyone else, but I've got a ton of things at the library I need to get done."

Sean growled beside me at the choice of her words. She completely ignored him.

"I'll see you soon," she promised. She lightly kissed my cheek and less than a second later her and Cameron were gone.

I stared at the empty doorway, astonished, vaguely hearing Sean's voice.

"I'm going to show Angel the rest of the house," he announced to Becca and Jonah. Then he looked down at me. "Are you ready?"

"No spiders or bats hanging upside down anywhere?" I verified. I tried to sound sarcastic to mask the anxiety I felt but genuinely failed.

"No spiders or bats," he promised.

He led me to the massive staircase and I looked back to where Jonah and Becca had been standing. They had disappeared. I turned my attention back to the staircase, my hand gliding along the satin-smooth rail. The long hall at the top looked the same as the walls downstairs. They were white, with paintings and pictures hanging all around.

"Kelsey and Cameron's room … Luke and Mariah's room … Jonah's private room …" Sean gestured as we passed the open doors. They were all open, exposing the neatly made up bedrooms except Jonah's. The door to his room was closed.

"Where is your room?" I asked when he never pointed out his.

"I don't stay here," he answered. His tone sounded flat and unemotional.

His response left me to wonder why he wouldn't want to live here.

"Then where do you stay?" I asked carefully.

"We will get to that." He went silent again, I waited for him to say more. Time only passed without another word.

We reached the end of the hall, stopping in front of a door built in an odd shaped wall. Sean opened it and all I saw was a steep, yet very narrow staircase. I looked up at him, nervously. He read the hesitation on my face and sighed.

"Yes, it was once an attic. Becca has turned it into her own personal space."

"Then why should we enter?" I asked earnestly.

He leaned down towards me, stopping just mere inches before his lips brushed mine. "Her room will tell you the kind of person she is and help you understand her." He gently placed his lips against my forehead for a long second before straightening himself.

He let go of my hand and stepped away from the door. Great, I thought sourly. I get to go first. I drew a huge breath and carefully stepped up on the first stair. I took my time walking up the rest, unsure of how steady they were.

The room looked like an old tower. The floor was paneled with the same floorboards as the living room. A high curving window was in the far wall, allowing me to clearly see the silvery glistening of the rain drops atop the trees. There weren't any pictures hanging on the walls, as rows of paintings rested against a wall, in the center of the room was an easel holding an empty canvas.

I walked to the window and pressed my hand to the glass, and then slid my fingers over the smoothness. I smiled a little at the distant rumble of the thunder and thought of Becca and Jonah standing here watching a storm build, waiting for it to crash over the house as the rain slid effortlessly down the glass.

"Are you sorry you came?" Sean suddenly asked.

I let my fingers slide over the glass one last time then dropped my arm as I turned to face him.

"No. I admit I was nervous, honestly I still am and I do clearly find Luke a bit scary. But it's nice to finally know the truth and to put real faces with images."

His brow creased in confusion. "You had images of the others?"

"Not all of them," I corrected. "just Luke. I only remembered seeing a name on his shirt and his mirrored blue eyes. I had no idea he was so ... huge." I fought to hold in a shiver as I thought about his size.

Sean laughed darkly. "I suppose to a little human Luke would be quite scary."

I frowned at what he was implying. "It is normal for humans to be intimidated by something bigger and a thousand times stronger than us."

Sean grinned. "My beautiful, yet deeply insecure little human isn't a coward, is she?"

I glared at him. "At many things, yes. Others, such as you and your family have me trying to convince myself that it may be time for me to check myself into an asylum."

I watched as he fought to hide the smirk on his face. "Should you decide to do so, I don't want you to worry about being alone. I promise to visit regularly," he snickered.

"How thoughtful of you," I said icily.

Sean pressed his lips together, all signs of humor gone. "I do have to be honest about something."

"What?"

I wasn't sure what my expression was, but something in it made him grow somber. The silence lengthened as his features became immobile as stone. He sighed then spoke, voice velvet soft.

"There is a part of me that hopes what you see here will cause you to grasp the concept of the danger you're truly in and makes you turn to run as far away from me as you can get. At the same time there is an even greater part that hopes you never do."

I continued to stare at him while I crossed my arms over my chest and shifted my weight to one foot.

"Sean," I pronounced his name slowly. "I'm not going to tell you that part of me isn't frightened because it is. You have convinced me I am safe so I take comfort in believing you. Other than Luke's size, I don't find any of you scary or dangerous."

His jaw flexed as a growl rumbled from the back of his throat. "Every minute you're too close to me is dangerous!"

I narrowed my eyes. "You don't harm people, Sean, so how am I in danger?"

"Angelia," he groaned. He walked to me and reached out, brushing the back of his hand along my cheek. My heart rate accelerated with his touch. "You simply allowing me to touch you is a danger. If I'm not careful enough, or paying enough attention to what I'm doing I could only mean to touch your face, yet crush your skull, instead. Do you have any idea how hard it would be for me, having to live with that? To know I'm the reason you no longer exist?"

I took a minute to answer, giving my mind a chance to think and to keep my voice stable. "I still trust your judgment. You have gone through a lot of trouble to carry around glass and play with bubbles, clearly I'll always be around."

His pretty blue eyes shimmered as he smiled crookedly and dropped his arm. "Humans change as they age," he informed me. "You never know, Angel, you may just outgrow me someday."

"*Ha ha*," I snorted. "Don't hold your breath on that."

Sean broke into a roar of laughter. "Good one!"

I cringed as the sound echoed off the walls and walked to the paintings lined along the walls.

"Are these ones Becca isn't very fond of?" I asked tentatively.

Sean looked at me, his forehead creased in confusion. "Meaning what, exactly?"

I bent down to take a closer look at one. It looked like some sort of meadow, a luscious spread of colorful flowers all about.

"I noticed there are a number of paintings and pictures hanging throughout the house, yet there isn't anything hanging in here and these are simply stacked together on the floor."

"Oh." Sean's forehead smoothed back to marble stone as his eyes took on a knowing look. "The one's downstairs are personal favorites created by Leonardo da Vinci. Becca is a very big fan of the Renaissance art."

I carefully looked through the canvases, mesmerized by the beauty Becca had created in each one. I felt my breath catch in my throat when I saw a woman she had painted. The woman was as beautiful as a dream ----- the fine-featured oval face, the alabaster skin. Rich red-gold hair was swept up off her neck, full, soft lips were curved, though just a little. But it was the eyes that drew me; they were green, the expression in them, such quiet sadness. Such inner pain. It took several long minutes for me to realize I was staring at my own reflection.

"Becca had always been drawn by your innocence and the emotions that display in your eyes," Sean's soft voice stated.

"When did she paint this?" My voice was shaky, the words nearly breathless.

"About a week after we found you."

I pushed the canvases back in front of it then rose, turning to look at Sean.

"Would you like to look at the others, as well as the photographs?" he asked.

I slightly shook my head. "I think I've seen more than enough already and I don't want to pry into anyone's personal life."

Sean rolled his eyes at me and groaned. "Angel, they would be more than happy to let you hear stories of their past. I don't know if you have ever bothered to notice, but they really like you. Jonah, especially."

I gave him a doubtful look.

"What?" he asked innocently.

"I think you may just be wrong about *all* of them liking me."

He frowned at me, unhappily. "I can assure you I'm not. In fact when I came here this morning to get the truck Becca asked when I was planning to bring you here. I hadn't gotten a chance to answer when the others cast their pleas for me to do it today. They couldn't seem to wait any longer to meet you."

"Mariah and Cameron didn't appear to be thrilled I'm here," I contradicted.

"Cameron has always been standoffish ----- shy if you will. As for Mariah I am not certain as to why she acted so poorly, but I assure you they were not offended by your presence."

I still wasn't convinced. "If that is so true then why did Becca tell me Jonah didn't believe I would come here?"

"He knows his presence makes you uncomfortable, therefore he couldn't see you agreeing to enter his home."

He had me there. It was true I couldn't control the emotions that pulsed through me anytime I was near him. I did somehow manage to control it when Sean introduced me, though I think it was mostly because I saw someone a bit scarier than Jonah. Luke made him seem harmless.

"Though I don't understand why you wouldn't be," Sean continued when I said nothing. "Jonah is the less likely one to ever slip."

I narrowed my eyes at him. "Isn't *he* the reason you and the others are no longer human?"

"Moot point," he growled. "Do you want to look at the photographs or not?"

I kept my eyes on him, stepping backwards towards the window. "Isn't the old saying *'the less you know, the better'* safer for all of us in this situation?"

He didn't answer, glaring at me, instead.

I felt my back press against the window and for once, thought I was doing good at holding my own. Then, in a movement much too fast for my eyes to catch Sean was to me, grabbing my arm and pulling me to him. He wrapped one arm around my waist, lifting me up and carried me across the room, and then down the stairs.

Memoirs of a Painful Past

Sean set me down next to the first door at the top of the stairs. The wall beside it was where the first line of framed pictures and the paintings began. He didn't speak a word, walking down the long hall to the closed door then leaned against the wall opposite of it. I watched him, feeling a sense of guilt for what he was clearly forcing me to do. I looked away from him, turning my gaze to the staircase mentally calculating my chances of getting to the bottom before he could catch me. I had to admit they were slim. Because I was no longer paying attention to Sean I was unaware he was still watching me and guessing my plan.

"I'll just drag you back," his voice warned. "and if that don't work I'll just simply have Jonah come up here and hold your hand."

His tone wasn't harsh or bitter but his threat had me banishing the plan quickly and looking back at him.

"But I suppose the choice is yours." His face was expressionless, his eyes watching me intensely.

I pulled in a long, ragged breath, and then turned my body to face the wall.

It wasn't the paintings that eventually captured my attention. It was the photographs in the frames. Many of them were of Jonah and an older man, with a withered face. It wasn't hard to figure out the man with him had been his father. The similarities were the same though Jonah appeared to be taller and slimmer. They were all in black and white, but they didn't hide the emotions on their faces or how handsome Jonah had been as a human. One picture in particular held my interest, it was clear it had been taken on a hot day. Jonah and his father stood next to a horse, Jonah had his hat in one hand and was wiping sweat off his forehead with the other while his father's back faced the camera.

I carefully slid my eyes to the photo beside it, instantly becoming fascinated and heartbroken at the same time. Two little girls stood on the rickety porch of their home wearing eighteenth century dresses. Their little faces wore the saddest expression I had ever seen. I lightly brushed my fingers over the glass inside the frame.

"Who are the girls?" I asked in a mere whisper.

"Jonah's younger sisters," Sean answered, his voice sounding unemotional. "They were twins."

"Why do they seem so sad?"

"That particular picture was taken sometime after Jonah had left."

His tone sounded bored and uninterested, I threw a glance his direction.

"Just looking at it breaks your heart."

Sean simply shrugged his shoulders. I felt my face fall a tiny bit as I frowned at his lack of emotion. I glared at him a second longer then turned my eyes back to the picture now in front of me. It looked to be a very young, school-age Jonah. I leaned in for a closer look when I heard a door open.

"Come here," Sean commanded me. "I want to show you something."

I eyed him for a long minute while trying to think of something witty to say. There was something in his expression that kept me silent and obeying his demand.

Sean had the door open and the light in the room turned on before I reached his side. When I made no effort to look away from him he pointed an index finger in the direction of the room. I slowly turned my head, the intake of my sudden breath was so loud it caused Sean to look at me with one eyebrow raised. A large canvas hung on the far wall containing the faces of Jonah and his family. The colors were pastel, bringing out the beauty in each of their faces. There were framed photographs hanging on nearly every wall, yet it was the canvas that pulled me in the room.

"They are all so beautiful," I said, half to myself. "Are the girls still alive?"

Truthfully, I wondered about all of them, but since learning Jonah had been a vampire for a number of decades I didn't figure his parents would be. I never noticed Sean didn't enter the room till his voice came from the open doorway.

"No. Gretchen, Jonah's mother died the night he disappeared. The girls, Jenna and Jamma lost their battle to scarlet fever five years later and William, Jonah's father passed days after the tenth anniversary of the girls."

I wasn't sure why, but something in his response bothered me. I couldn't take my eyes off the canvas to look at him.

"What does that mean, the night Jonah disappeared?"

I may have been uneasy around him for obvious reasons, with the way

I've heard him speak of this family I couldn't see him willfully walking away from his human one.

"I was on my way to town when I was attacked by what was called creatures of the night," came a soft, yet firm voice.

Jonah's unexpected voice startled me and I quickly whirled to the sound. It was then I noticed how far I had entered the room. Jonah stood beside Sean, struggling to conceal the tension behind his serene expression.

"I'm sorry, Jonah," I apologized uneasy. "I don't mean to invade your private life."

He smiled timidly at me. "I am not offended, Angel. It is time you know where our stories begin."

Jonah entered the room, causally walking to my side, and then stopped, staring up at the canvas. I flashed my eyes nervously to Sean's face. He remained at the doorway, the expression on his face assured me it would soon be all right. I carefully turned my eyes on Jonah, he was still staring at the canvas, seeming to be lost in his memories.

"The year was 1886, it was barely a week past my twenty-fourth birthday," his thoughtful voice began. "when my mother fell ill with the fever. That was the year gasoline fueled cars were available for the first time and we were the only cotton farmers who couldn't afford to purchase even one. Money was nearly scarce, all we owned was a small number of horses. It was almost the middle of the night when mother took a turn for the worst. My father pulled me from my bed requesting I retrieve one of the horses from the barn and ride into town. He needed me to make our request to the local doctor for his help. We lived only a few miles from town, yet somehow I knew it would be the longest ride of my life." He paused for a moment, walking away from me to stand in front of a framed photograph opposite of the canvas. I continued to stand motionless, watching him and waiting for his soft voice to begin again.

"My family were one of many that was part of the Catholic congregation," he finally said. "and though for years I thought the priest had a wild imagination, he was quite the vigilante. He believed vampires, or creatures of the night as we were called then roamed our sewers late in the night. He had many innocent people burned because he claimed they had been infected by these creatures. Many believed and carried lit torches behind him to burn such creatures while he preached to the open wind and many did not. My family was among the non-believers.

"It was a Saturday night and I expected to see the shadows of the torches reflecting off of buildings and quiet houses as the congregation walked the dark streets. For reasons unknown to me, there wasn't a single person out, the only light I could see as I neared town was the few natural ones, providing just enough light to reflect off the streets. I had only barely entered town when my horse began to become nervous. He shook his head, ferociously, stomping his hooves against the ground.

"I was unable to understand why he was acting so strangely. I held tight on the rein while I leaned over, trying desperately to calm the animal. In my distraction I was completely unaware I was being approached, and then suddenly I was knocked off the horse with one powerful blow to the chest. While I lay on the ground, fighting to catch the breath that had been knocked out of me the horse ran away."

Jonah had made a complete circle around the room and was now walking back to stand beside me. He was silent, staring into the eyes of his family, seeming to be lost in his memories. I waited patiently, careful not to make any sudden moves for him to speak. The minutes passed.

"I never got the chance to scream or fight," he said, his voice was full of emotions. "I had already been bitten before I could even understand what was happening. I could feel my body burn as the creature sucked the blood from the base of my neck. As more blood was drained from my body I was sure I would soon die. I must have passed out, the next thing I remember is my body feeling like it had been set on fire. I opened my eyes and saw the sky had grown to light and I could hear voices of the townsfolk wandering close by. I was in a deeper pain then I have ever felt, but used what strength I still had to get up from the ground and run away."

Jonah stopped talking again, this time turning his eyes on me. All I could see in them was sorrow and a deep sadness. He seemed to be searching my face for something to alert him to my fears. I kept all emotions off my face, faintly smiling in encouragement for him to continue. He let the seconds pass before looking back at his family.

"The towns people got word of my disappearance and searched twenty-fours for me before finally giving up all hope I could still be alive. They had gotten close to me a few times and as hard as it was not to cry out in pain and agony I remained quiet. It was almost impossible, the burning so excruciating, yet I knew what would become of me should they find me. A couple of days passed and the burning finally stopped, leaving behind the stone skin, unbelievable strength, and a deep, nearly uncontrollable thirst. I didn't understand the need of it at first, but as I headed home I caught the scent of some nearby humans.

"I was drawn to them before I realized what was happening. My rational side kicked in, preventing me from attacking them as I held my breath and turned to run in the opposite direction. Even as I knew now how dangerous it was for me to be near people I couldn't stop myself from going back to my childhood home. I waited for night fall then crept closer so I could look in on the girls.

"I could hear them cry for mother while they asked our father why I hadn't come home. Once hearing that mother had passed that same night because I didn't return I couldn't bear to hear anymore and since the girls were fine I left."

My heart felt heavy with despair as I listened to his story and watched the sorrow cross Jonah's face. I couldn't imagine having to live through something so painful. The silence lengthen this time as Jonah was much quieter than he'd been when he began his story. He set his lips and I suddenly got the feeling it was all coming to an end.

"How did you come to know your sisters had died?" I suddenly blurted.

My sudden curiosity had him looking at me. I wasn't sure why, especially since his facial expressions weren't hostile or the least bit angry, but I fought to keep from cringing away from him, anyway. Jonah's brows creased for a moment, then smoothed as his eyes took on a knowing look.

"I eventually felt a deep guilt for leaving so I went back, learning how to control the monster while keeping an eye on them. It was then I learned the girls had caught the scarlet fever. I knew my father was struggling to tend to the land and care for the girls so I would wait in the shadows for night fall, and then once my father had gone to sleep I worked the fields and plowed the ground to plant more seed. I was there the night they finally passed."

I tore my eyes away from Jonah and looked at the faces of his family. "That must have been unbearable," I nearly whispered.

Jonah sighed, the sound unsteady. "I take comfort in it as I believe they knew what I had become."

His statement confused me and I turned my head to look at him. "How?"

"After I heard the doctor tell my father there was nothing more he could do for them I slipped in the house. I knew it was a daring move for me to get so close, yet I had to try something. Jenna was weaker than Jamma, I picked her up from her bed and placed her carefully on Jamma's. I laid between them, holding them tightly against my body. I thought the coldness of my stone skin would break the fever."

I was still confused. "That doesn't explain why you think they knew."

Jonah looked down at the floor, and then glanced up at me from under his long lashes, with troubled eyes.

"They begged me until they took their last breath to save them as I had been saved. At the time I didn't know the rules our kind have about children, they were only ten years old, nor could I be sure I could even do it without killing them, anyway. Becca was with me then, her heart was seconds from stopping completely when I bit her. The blood in her body was weak so I wasn't tempted to saturate the thirst. The blood in the girls was full of the scarlet fever, yet it was still very strong."

"There's rules about children?" I asked, artlessly.

Jonah slightly nodded his head. "I have seen what a three-year-old can do to an entire village when they throw a fit. They can wipe it out completely in under two minutes. Our lawmakers not only have to kill the child, but also his creator to keep other humans from being alerted. Our actions will not only cause a war in your kind, it would have the same effect in ours, as well."

The mentioning of his law makers reminded me of something Sean had said about Jonah the day before.

"How did you became a part of your lawmakers?"

"After a number of people in my village had been attacked members of our lawmakers, with a few of their talents who protect them came to assert the situation. Most of the newborns were wild and reckless, causing more mayhem with leaving half unfinished bodies lying all over, creating more wild newborns and they were killed. Because I was civilized and showed no potential signs of being a threat they spared me. They watched me for days to see how I was managing so well. My civilization intrigued them, as they had never seen such wonder. They believed peace could be kept between our world and yours with me so close, they granted me a member then left."

"Wait, did you say talents?" I was astonished.

"Yes," he verified.

"What kind of talents?" I half expected Jonah to get annoyed with my questions the way Sean sometimes did; he didn't. He seemed comfortable with my interest.

"Sometimes we find vampires with the power of magic."

I don't know what my expressions were, but they must have been confused. Jonah sighed, seeming to think of a way to explain it so I could understand.

"Have you ever heard of people who came make things disappear or move things without touching them?"

"Like David Copperfield?" I asked. His name was out before I realized how idiotic it sounded.

Jonah laughed. "Yes, like David Copperfield. It is rare, but sometimes members of our kind can have some of those same powers. With just simply a wave of their hand they can change the scene you're looking at or they can lift you up and toss you across the room without ever touching you."

"Wow," I mouthed. "If there wasn't to be any more of your kind made how did you get away with creating this family?"

"Because I feed much differently than those of the usual kind I knew I wouldn't be caught. Of course, I sincerely didn't want to do this to someone else. But once time began to pass I became depressed from the loneliness. I found myself searching faces for companionship as I walked by young women. Each of them had husbands, children and lives I couldn't bring myself to willfully take from them. And, I couldn't be sure that *if* I did they would even stay."

"Then how did you meet Becca?"

For the first time since he entered the room his green eyes began to shine.

"When I ran away from Tennessee I spent a lot of time in Kentucky experimenting with a number of things to figure out how to control the monster side. Most of the folks in those parts were drunk on moonshine so they never made the difference in me, allowing me to walk as freely as I wanted.

"One night I was on my way to a neighboring town when I caught the scent of a burning fire. I followed the smell to the home Becca shared with her husband David. The entire house had been engulfed in flames, knowing I could burn if I got too close to them I ran inside, anyway. I could only hope I hadn't been too late.

"David and Becca were asleep in their bed when the fire started. David had already died as a result of smoke inhalation. Becca was alive, though she was barely breathing and her heart was beating less than two beats a minute. I knew if I got her out she would still have a chance, I snatched her from the bed and ran outside. When I laid her on the cool ground she opened her eyes for a brief moment. It was in those short seconds I looked into her faint green eyes something in me changed.

"I begged her to hold on as I was there to save her. She smiled kindly, called me her hero, and then closed her eyes. Her heart beat three more times then stopped. I knew I had to do something then or I would be too late. I leaned down close to her ear, whispering for her forgiveness, and then sank my teeth in the skin just beneath her ear."

He looked away from me and back to the canvas, seeming to forget the conversation for a moment. I let the silence linger while I processed everything he had shared. The explanation he gave about kids made sense to why he didn't save his sisters, yet it didn't explain Kelsey, who had been sixteen.

"If kids are not allowed ..." My voice trailed off as I tried to think about how I wanted to ask. Jonah looked down at me with an unfathomable expression. "... Kelsey was still a kid when you changed her fate." I knew it wasn't a question, but the way Jonah was looking at me made me nervous and I blurted out the obvious.

"Yes," he sighed. "she was. However, she wasn't a young child. You see, Becca was happy with me, yet there was still something missing for her. When she was human she had made plans for children, her life was altered and changed directions before ever getting to see those plans through. The night of Kelsey's accident I saw that look in my wife's eyes when she looked at Kelsey. I knew then I had to save her.

"Angel, I sincerely hope now that you have heard my story you can understand why I had to make my decisions. It has been brought to my attention that you fault me for being so willing to take Sean's humanity. I assure you I did not take that decision lightly, I did not steal his life, Angel. I only simply found a way to keep a family together."

Even though his explanation sounded crazy, for the first time I *did* understand. Somehow in that moment the man standing beside me didn't seem to be quite the monster I feared. I wasn't sure why, but I suddenly thought about Mariah.

"I understand why you saved Luke and Cameron, for they nearly died right in front of you. If Mariah wasn't in any kind of trouble then why is *she* one of you?"

Jonah eyed me for a long second before answering. "I'm guessing Sean hasn't told you?"

I only shook my head.

Jonah flashed his eyes to his son for a fraction of a second then looked back at me.

"It is almost impossible for us to change, Angel. When we do it is permanent, we can never be altered again and we mate just once. Luke experienced the same things Sean had when he met Mariah and like Sean he had to make a very difficult decision ..."

"Ahem." Sean loudly cleared his voice, cutting Jonah off. I hadn't been aware he had even moved till his voice appeared behind me and his hands rested lightly on my shoulders. "I have not gotten to that, Jonah. Angel, why don't we go downstairs and look at the paintings Becca has hanging on the walls?"

There's something he doesn't want me to know, I said to myself. I tried to look up at Sean, but he quickly held my head in place. Right then my suspicion was confirmed, as he'd done this very same thing before. I saw Jonah's lips moving, but the movement was too fast for me to catch any words, his voice much too low for even hearing like mine to hear.

Sean turned my body towards the door then dropped his hands from my shoulders. He took my right hand and pulled me from the room, closing the door behind us.

While we walked down the long hall my mind began trying to add more pieces to the puzzle. It was

frustrating when some of them didn't connect. We were at the stairs before the silence seemed to weigh on Sean.

"You really shouldn't twist your face like that. What are you thinking so hard about?"

"My puzzle," I mumbled almost incoherently. Then I looked at him. "I understand how he became a member of his own law, but how did he get into *our* law enforcement? Wouldn't that require him to have six weeks of the academy?"

Sean laughed, the sound nearly a roar. "No. Remember yesterday when I told you about his family helping to forge papers?"

I bit down on my bottom lip while I thought back to the conversation. "Yes," I finally answered.

"That's how he became a deputy in the Newport sheriff's department," he stated. I don't know what my facial expression was, but it made him sigh, and elaborate. "Angel, sometimes even in this life you can stumble across crooked humans, such as lawyers, doctors, and even some politicians. For the right price they will not only keep their secrets, but *ours*, too. Especially, if their lives can end more abruptly."

He flashed a wide grin, showing off the ultra-white teeth he carefully keeps concealed. I secretly shivered at the meaning of his words and the thought of what his teeth could do.

We were now down the stairs and Sean all but drug me to the far wall in front of the front door. I pretended to look at the framed photos while I placed a few more pieces in the puzzle.

"So," I said, slowly. "you're saying Jonah found some lawyer to fake papers so he could take a job at the sheriff's station?" I lost interest in the photos and turned to face him.

Sean nodded his head. "The papers also help with getting passports and a driver's license, as well."

His statement had my brows knitting in confusion. "How do you take pictures when you're supposed to be invisible to cameras and mirrors?"

Sean's face twisted into a scowl, disgusted. "Those are myths," he growled.

"Really?" I wasn't convinced.

Sean snarled something unintelligible and grabbed my arm, pulling me in front of a particular photograph. He pointed directly to it and snarled "there". I gave him a dirty look before turning my eyes to follow where he was pointing. I was instantly shocked. The photograph was of Jonah and Mike standing side by side outside the door of the sheriff's station. They each wore a big cheesy grin.

"Are any of the legends true?" I asked, astonished.

"No," Sean stated firmly.

He finally released his grip on my arm and I moved along the wall, looking over the other pictures.

"Jonah did say you can be burned by fire." I didn't intend for that to be said out loud, Sean never seemed to be bothered by my observation.

"Yes, though I hope you don't believe we will stand and let your kind do it," he laughed.

I ignored his twisted sense of humor and continued browsing the wall. I had forgotten about Bobbie mentioning Sean's departure from town till I saw a picture of his family and he wasn't in it. I didn't study it long, as Mariah's eyes were stunning, but creepy, too.

"Why did you leave last year?" I suddenly blurted.

I reached one of Becca's paintings and because I wasn't ready to see the expressions on Sean's face I pretended to study it. I heard him take a deep breath.

"I've already told you about this," he stated, his voice unsteady. "but I guess you may as well hear it all. The Johnson family had a visitor last year and though that's not unusual for the humans around here, this particular one created a bad situation for my family. He was a young kid, he was in the library when I stopped in to give Kelsey a message. I was almost to the front counter when he walked past me. His scent was so strong it made me delirious, my mouth watered uncontrollably. I followed him to the back of the library before I realized what I was doing. I instantly held my breath and ran out of there, and then came here long enough to tell Jonah I was leaving."

He wasn't his usual cocky self and like the day before when he was hesitant I became concerned. I

turned my body slowly to face him. He stared at the floor for a long moment before finally lifting his glorious, agonized eyes to mine.

"Why did it take a year for you to come back?"

He stared at my face, seeming to be undecided about answering. I continued to look back at him, waiting patiently for his response. The seconds ticked by.

"We have a very long memory," he finally spoke, with a deep sigh. "and I wanted to be sure I let enough time pass, as well as give myself complete control before I came back."

"Did it work?" I asked, carefully.

"He was gone when I got here, so I suppose all is well."

I hadn't been prepared for the relief I would feel from his answer till it pulsed through me. He hadn't killed, I thought gratefully. "That's good," I mused. I hoped he wouldn't notice my answer was for both of us.

"Since you're not running out of here screaming from everything you've seen and heard," he suddenly laughed. "do you really want to listen to any more depressing stories or would you like to see something else?"

Even after all this time I still hadn't gotten used to how quickly his emotions could change. The tenor now in his tone caused me to eye him suspiciously.

"Such as?" I said.

He laughed. "I was under the impression you wanted to see where I stay."

His eyes shimmered and I suddenly didn't trust him. "Maybe we'll just save it for next time."

"I promise you will like it better than this," he said, his voice smoldering. "Trust me."

I didn't budge an inch.

Sean broke into a roar of laughter at my hesitation and in less than a second he was to me, grabbing my arm and dragging me from the room.

"C'mon, you little coward," he said, darkly.

He moved so quickly I nearly had to run to keep from getting my arm ripped off. He pulled me through the kitchen, and then out the back door. The sky was black, but it was no longer raining. It took a second of looking around for it to sink in what he had in mind. He released my arm the same instant panic began to swirl through me and I took a step backwards.

"Oh, Sean," I whined. "I can't run with you, again."

He looked at me, his lips twisted in a wicked smile. He pointed to the trees without ever looking at them.

"Where I stay is a few miles that way."

My stomach was so nauseous I shook my head, not giving myself a chance to be sick.

"Give it a rest, Angel," he growled. "You have ran with me before and you were fine."

He never gave me a chance to react or respond. His hand snaked out, grabbing my arm and he tossed me on his back. I only had a second to hide my face before he ran, the speed of a bullet to the trees.

Alone at Last

I knew the ride was over when Sean reached back and ruffled my hair. Because he had ran into the forest I was nervous over where he had taken me and slowly lifted my head. Sean was standing at the edge of a luxurious lawn, trees spread about seeming to have been built around it. The house in front of us rose up toward the sky like a calling beacon, it was a deep shade of brown, blending in with its surroundings. It was Victorian style, three stories tall, a deep wrap around porch on the bottom and the second floor. A set of twin stairs twined on both sides of the house to the gallery on the third story. The house was timeless, graceful and looked like it had been built during the Old World, though I doubted it had been here that long, unnoticed.

The forest encroached around it, seeming to protect it from all invasions. There were two rocking chairs sitting next to the door and were side by side. It wasn't hard to figure out they had been placed there for Jonah and Becca; I couldn't see Luke being so willing to be romantic with Mariah like that. Sean walked to the porch then reached around and pulled me from his back, and then gently set me down on the steps. It was then I noticed it had same style doors as the other house and walked to them for a better look.

"Well, what do you think?" Sean finally asked.

"It's ... charming."

I stepped away from the door when he reached my side and he opened it for me.

The inside was even more stunning. It was bright, more open than the other house and very large. It was one large room, all the walls inside with the exception of the north and east, even the back, south-facing wall had been entirely made of glass. They gave a clear view of the cedars and the lawn, as they stretched beyond the back of the house for miles. A massive staircase dominated the west side of the room, rising up in nearly the same fashion as the one in Jonah's house. The ceiling was soaring, with a ballroom setting painted across it. The detail was fascinating, gentlemen dancing with their maidens, the dresses they wore had been detailed, perfectly. The hardwood floor was covered with carpet in various shades of beige.

The furniture consisted of just one long white couch and a big TV, in the far corner of the east wall was a cabinet that had been built into it and was full of movies. The focal point that really drew my attention was the fireplace taking up most of the north wall. It was odd to me, especially since fire is the one *true* enemy they have. An unusual smell lingered through the house and confused me; it was a bit out of place with nearly all the walls being nothing more than sheets of glass. And, the floors clearly hadn't been repaired.

"Why does it smell like something has been varnished recently?"

"When Jonah and I built this house fifteen years ago we never put in a bathroom or a kitchen," Sean explained. Then he turned his eyes to me. "Since we now have a human in the family those have clearly become essential."

Fifteen years ago? I thought they have only been here eight?

"How did you build this that long ago if you have only been here for the last eight years?" I asked, mystified.

Sean walked away from me to the fireplace and picked up a box of matches from the mantel. He bent down in front of it, seeming to need to take his time answering my question. I waited patiently for his response while watching him strike the match and toss it on the wood. A few seconds later a fire started and Sean slowly stood up, replaced the box of matches, and then turned to face me.

"We came here for a few years before going to Maine," he said with a heavy sigh. "Jonah wanted solitude and freedom from the humans. He chose Newport for its size, as well as its climate. If we were seen by a human we would still be safe, as they wouldn't see us for what we are."

For a brief second I remembered what he had looked like the day before as he stood on the sand in the sunlight. I shivered at the memory then quickly banished it from my mind, not giving any time for him to read something on my face and misinterpret its meaning.

"If you were getting what you were looking for here, then why make the move to Maine?"

"After a couple of years Becca began to get depressed from the isolation. Jonah came up with the idea of going back near our birthrights, but not quite the same states. He wanted to test a theory to see if we could walk amongst your kind for an extended period of time without anyone being alerted to us. Your natural instincts tell you something is wrong about us so you keep your distance, but we were never rejected, either. That was also when we figured out by keeping only a small number of us in the public view gave us more advantages. It wasn't until we came back eight years ago that anyone ever knew we were here. It had worked out for us to walk freely with the humans, that is when Jonah decided to take a job with Mike. Becca charmed the mayor with her wit and her talent and he decided she would make the best choice for his secretary."

"I see," I mused. "So I guess it's safe to say you can keep a permanent residence here?"

"Yes," he confirmed. "though we will still have to leave every so often to give the humans a chance to forget us before we can come back."

"Good luck with that," I snorted.

The movie cabinet kept drawing my attention as I wondered what kind of things would interest a group of vampires and walked away from Sean to look. I felt his eyes on me while I walked to the cabinet and open its doors.

"Are you interested in watching a movie?" he asked, doubtful.

"No, just curious what you have."

"Everything from comedy to the traditional horror flicks and there may even be some plays." He walked to me and slipped his arms around my waist.

"Plays?" I asked, skeptical.

I could almost hear him roll his eyes. He reached one long arm out in front of me and pulled a sealed case from the shelf.

"As in Romeo and Juliet," he muttered as he held it in front of my face. "There's also Phantom of the Opera and so on ---- I do sincerely hope you're not a fan of the operas, that would just be the final nail in my coffin," he laughed.

His choice of words had me muttering in disgust. Sean shook us with his quiet laughter.

"Do you want to stand here longer and look over movies you're not interested in or are you brave enough to see my room?" He placed the movie back on the shelf and I closed the doors.

His bedroom? "Sure," I agreed, reluctantly.

He removed his arms from my waist and stepped backwards. I turned my body carefully and wound my fingers in his. He must have been eager for me to see it because he wasn't satisfied with my hand or human velocity. He released my hand, scooped me up in his arms and nearly flew up the stairs. We made it up two flights of stairs before he set me down at the door and darted to the double doors at the end of the room, and then opened them.

The room was massive in size, double glass doors led out to a gallery. The walls, the high-beamed ceiling were various shades of white. The floor was covered with a light gray carpet, his furniture consisted of a small leather couch that brought to mind of one in a psychiatrist office, a black leather recliner sat in front of the doors, with a large bookshelf against the wall beside it. A large stereo sat inside a hole built in the far wall, with shelves hanging around it and was lined with CD cases.

He was back before I'd taken a step, but I ignored him and went to the doors he had opened. The air was cool, I instinctively wrapped my arms around my torso as I looked out at the view.

"I know the view isn't as magnificent as Los Angeles," Sean's soft voice stated. "but it is still a beautiful sight."

"You're right," I chuckled. "I can certainly understand why you took the highest room in the house, though I am quite surprised this room has actual walls." I turned and walked away from the doors, my teeth were close to chattering. My eyes scanned the room again while I walked to the shelves on the wall. "If this is your bedroom then where is your bed?"

Sean shrugged his shoulders, sluggishly. "I don't have one."

I stopped in front of the first shelf and looked carefully at the cases. "Why not?"

"I don't sleep."

I wasn't sure what alerted my attention the most ----- his statement or the tenor in his voice. Either way I lost interest in his music and turned to face him.

"Ever?" I was shell shocked.

Sean only shook his head.

"Is your family more fond of their memories than you?" I asked tentatively.

His forehead creased in confusion. "Meaning, what?"

"I saw a few of Becca's paintings hanging on the walls that are not made of glass downstairs and there's lots of frames all over at the other place, but I don't see a single thing hanging around in here."

"Oh." Sean's forehead smoothed back to marble stone and he pointed to the bookshelf. "Any memories I have that are well worth remembering are written in books."

When I first saw it I thought the books were probably his favorites. Now that he had directed my attention to the bookshelf I saw a various variety of psychiatry.

"Oh." I felt like an idiot. I walked to the chair and sat down, examining the books. "Would you mind my asking why you have these kinds of books?"

"Remember yesterday when I told you I had been accepted to Yale?"

I pulled a book from the shelf, carefully opening it . "Yes."

"I was planning to major in psychology."

My eyes widened as his words sank in. It was now everything made sense; the way he had acted when I mentioned the possibility of needing a therapist, the couch in this room and why he went through the trouble of reading about obsessive-compulsive disorder. And, now that I was thinking about it, the comment he had made while we were in Becca's room.

"Great," I grumbled sourly. "I now have my very own shrink."

He barked a laugh, more loudly than usual. "I guess now you know the sessions won't cost you much, as all I will require for payment is a night spent with me and a kiss from time to time."

I ignored his twisted sense of humor and replaced the book back on the shelf.

"Where did your interest in becoming a psychiatrist come from?"

And before he could answer the rain suddenly fell heavily from the trees, the slight breeze that had filled the room now became intense. Sean walked to the doors and closed them. It was then I noticed night fall had taken its claim on the day.

"It's getting late," I said standing from the chair. "Bobbie ..."

"Knows you're a big girl," Sean interrupted.

Thunder boomed, echoing through the trees before he walked away from the doors and I jumped.

"I think -----"

"Way too much," he growled. I looked up at him, he had a scowl on his face. "You're not going anywhere tonight, Angel."

He's had a motive all along! I shut my eyes briefly on a prayer for patience and that I could keep my voice calm when I responded. Sean was staring down at me when I opened my eyes.

"You've had this planned the entire time," I accused.

"Yes I did," he admitted. "I wanted you for myself tonight. Didn't you find it the least bit consequential that I asked Kelsey if she'd done everything I asked? How else would there be wood in the fireplace and food in the refrigerator?"

I crossed my arms over my chest while I glared at him. "Isn't it illegal to hold someone here without their permission?"

"In most cases, yes," he agreed. "I knew you would turn me down if I had told you to pack a bag. You hear what it is beginning to do outside and I'm not taking you out there."

I looked at the doorway, mentally calculating my chances of getting out before Sean could catch me. There were about three things I was sure of; first, I didn't *actually* see the way up here, as Sean's movements were too fast for my eyes to catch anything as it passed. Therefore, I'd be lost trying to find my way to the bottom floor. Secondly, he would have me caged against his stone body before I even got to the doorway. And third, *if* I was even lucky enough to break free I would never find my way through the maze of the forest to get back to Jonah's.

Translation ----- I was stuck.

"Are you really going to force me to make Bobbie worry?" I asked as I slid my eyes back to Sean's face. "I also have to work tomorrow since I had to trade the weekend."

"I have a phone you can use." His voice turned sharp. He reached in his pocket and a second later was pulling out a cell phone. "You can easily call her to let her know you're safe with me. When you are finished I'll take you downstairs so you can fix yourself something to eat."

When I made no effort to take the phone from him he picked up my left hand and shoved it against my palm. Once my hand cupped around it he turned away from me and walked to his closet. I glared at his back a second longer, and then opened the phone, dialing Bobbie's number. While the line rang I walked to the bedroom doorway and leaned against the door.

"Hello?" Bobbie asked.

"Hi, Bobbie," I grumbled.

"Hi, Angel," she answered cheerfully. "Are you having a good time?"

"Sure," I mumbled. "I called to let you know I'm going to hang out with Sean tonight."

"Good," she said, her voice sounding relieved. "We are in the middle of a bad storm."

Sean walked to me, stopping inches in front of me, with a plain white t-shirt in his hand. I ignored his facial expression while I kept my focus on the conversation.

"I know, that's why I'm staying here. I have to work tomorrow so I'll be back in the morning."

"I'm glad you let me know. I would have worried about you all night."

Now I glared at Sean. "I knew you would. Good night, Bobbie."

"Good night, Angel."

I snapped the phone closed and laid it in Sean's waiting hand.

He put it in his pocket then put his hand lightly on my waist and pulled me with him as he walked through the door. Sean didn't say anything as we walked down the long hall. After we walked down the flight of stairs and down another long hall I noticed other rooms. Each were bedrooms, each had beds in the middle of the room and what I could see as Sean continued to push me along, they each had their own gallery's.

We'd come to a stop in front of door just before the top of the last set of stairs and Sean turned me to face it.

"Your bathroom," he informed me. He opened it, reached in and turned on the light, and then lightly pushed me inside.

I half expected the walls to be made of glass like the rest of the house. They were all dark, paneled and gave the room a deep sense of privacy. The over-sized room nearly took my breath away. They had outdone themselves when they built this room. I stared at the long counter, a sink was set in the left side leaving the rest open for the paraphernalia of a beauty salon and was covered with nearly every hair product available, a hair brush, a straightener, a cup sat next to the mirror holding a toothbrush, a tube of toothpaste right next to it. Someone (probably Kelsey) had placed a low, green chair in front of it. The shower had sliding glass doors and offered every option modern technology had. The floor was covered by white tiles with shards of granite sparking from them.

This was nothing more than a princess bathroom.

"This is all a bit unnecessary, don't you think?" I asked, turning to face Sean.

His face twisted into a scowl as he stepped in and laid the shirt on the counter.

"I don't believe so," he grumbled, his tone disgusted. "You deserve to have something more than anything that is ordinary."

"But I am ordinary," I countered.

"Angel," he groaned. "you couldn't be further from it." Then his lips formed a grin. "Ordinary people don't spend the night with monsters."

"*Ha ha,*" I snorted. I walked out the door and went down the hall to the stairs. "I think I can find the kitchen on my own," I said over my shoulder.

The kitchen was another shocking sight. The walls were all glass, the floor was covered in the same tile as the bathroom. There was an island in the center of the room, with a dishwasher built in on one side, a mini cooler on the other. A single bottle of what looked to be champagne was on the top shelf, laid over on its side. A double door refrigerator sat on the east wall, a gas range stove beside it. The cabinets and counter tops had been in white, giving the room a bright look.

I took my time looking over the shelves in the refrigerator. I've never been fond of cooking for one, it's too hard to figure out what to fix for myself. I suddenly missed the leftover options I always had at Bobbie's. I finally decided to make an omelet and pulled out the carton of eggs, the small bag of shredded cheese and a single pack of lunch meat.

Sean entered the same time I found a skillet and was placing it over the fire. He stood next to the island, I could feel his eyes on me as I poured the mixture from the bowl to the skillet then pick up a spatula. He causally walked to me and was gazing at me, studying my every movement. I tried to ignore him, but it made me self-conscious.

"What are you making?" he suddenly asked.

"An omelet," I said, a hint of smugness in my tone.

He eyed my dinner with a teasing look on his face before turning abruptly back to me.

"It doesn't look very appetizing," he noted.

I gave him a sour look. "I realize it's no pouch of blood ..." I felt a tremor flood through me as the words slipped out of my lips and fought to control it.

When the omelet was finished I turned off the burner, picked up the skillet and slid the omelet on a plate. I set in on the counter and went to the cabinet for a glass. Sean already had the gallon of milk out of the fridge by the time I turned around. He poured it in the glass and was replacing it on the shelf as I picked up the plate and walked out of the room. Sean followed seconds later.

I sat my food on their dining room table, and then paused.

"I'm being rude," I amended. "Can I get you anything?"

He rolled his eyes, setting the glass of milk on the table beside the plate. "Just eat, Angel." He pressed his cool lips delicately to my forehead, and then walked out of the room.

I sat down at the table wondering what else he had on his agenda for me.

When I was finished I loaded the dishes into the dishwasher, started it, and then wiped down the counter and the stove. The rain began to fall from the trees again, big drops pinging against the glass walls and I watched it, mindlessly. I don't know how much time had passed ----- ten minutes, maybe when the sound of Sean's breeze-sounding footsteps entered the room. I quickly returned to running the dish rag over the counter then turned around.

I instantly regretted it. He was dressed in only a black pair of shorts, his curly hair was in disarray, a strand hanging over his brow. I could feel my body start to heat up, a foreign feeling, as I stared at the perfect contours of his body. He stood in front of the open cooler on the island, the statue of a perfect Greek God, staring abstractedly at the shelf. Then he pulled something out and closed the door, his eyes now on me and smiled crookedly at me. He walked slowly to me, pausing a few feet away, he reached out to touch his fingertips to my cheek.

"I think the kitchen is as clean as it is going to get," he laughed. "Why don't you go get yourself ready for bed?"

"Okay," was all I could manage.

Sean laughed again, dropped his arm, and then walked out of the kitchen. I waited a few more seconds to follow, giving myself a chance to regain control of everything I was feeling.

I stood staring at my reflection in the mirror even after I'd finished brushing my teeth and took my hair down. My heart thudded audibly against my ribs and my breath got stuck in my throat as I was nervous about going back downstairs wearing nothing but Sean's shirt. It hung past my knees and I knew it was silly to feel so self-conscious, I couldn't help it.

Whenever my thoughts drifted back to Sean wearing only his shorts my breathing would start to accelerate again and my hands trembled ----- so much that I feared I would soon be sick from the dizziness swirling through my body. I closed my eyes and hung my head over the sink, praying Sean wouldn't come looking for me before I got it together.

Don't be such a coward, Angel, I growled at myself.

I took a deep breath, and then slowly opened my eyes. I turned away from the mirror, quickening my steps to the door before I could talk myself out of ever leaving the bathroom.

All the lights in the living room had been turned off, I could see the flickers of the fire reflect off the staircase.

"Okay," I said as I bounced down the stairs. "I'm dressed for bed."

Sean was waiting at the foot of the stairs, closer than I had thought and I bounded into him. He quickly steadied me, holding me carefully by the shoulders for a few seconds before gently crushing me against his body.

"Wrong again," he murmured in my ear, and then skimmed his lips across the skin at the hollow beneath it. "You are too undressed ----- no, that's not right," he corrected. "You are too utterly tempting and it's hardly fair."

"Tempting how?" I asked, the words nearly breathless.

I felt him sigh then he pulled away. He took my face between his hands and slowly inched his face to mine. The smell of his citrus breath caused any rational thoughts I had to instantly disappear.

"Must I really explain how you are tempting me?" he asked.

I knew it was clearly a rhetorical question, yet I couldn't make sense of it. My hands were limp on his bare chest, my breathing erratic and I was lightheaded. Sean tilted my head slowly before touching his cold, satin lips to mine, very carefully parting them.

And then I collapsed.

"That's definitely a first," Sean laughed, encircling his arms around me. He lifted me up from the stairs and carried me to the fireplace.

"I'm sorry, I don't know what happened." I shook my head trying to clear it. "I think I may have forgotten to breathe."

He measured my expression for a long moment then set me carefully down in front of the fireplace. He reached up on the mantel and took down a tall wine glass then handed it to me.

"Maybe a drink of this will help." He eyed me closely as I set the glass on my lips and sipped from it.

"Sparkling grape juice?" I asked in surprise.

"You're not old enough to drink champagne," he grumbled. "I was aiming for a romantic evening done in human traditions, though I wasn't counting on you nearly passing out on me."

"Then where is your glass?" I completely ignored the last part of his statement.

He chuckled despite the weary expression on his face. "What I drink you would certainly find repulsive and I'm not thirsty."

I looked away from him to hide my expression of disgust from the thought of actually seeing him drink *blood*. It was then I noticed he had blankets lying out on the floor in front of where we stood and somewhere in the room music was playing, the sound barely above being considered background noise. That feeling of panic I had earlier started to surface again.

"I hope you are at least enjoying the drink and the soft music," Sean suddenly said.

I carefully turned my head to look at him, hoping I had erased the panic from my expressions.

"Spending the night with me isn't quite as bad as you make it seem, is it?" he smirked. His eyes shimmered for a fraction of a second before turning to smolder.

"Did you get all this from the movies you have in the cabinet?" I meant to sound sarcastic, but the look in his eyes made it impossible.

"Bobbie's romance novels helped as well," he laughed.

"You read Bobbie's books?" I nearly shrieked.

He rolled his eyes and groaned. "What else did you think I was doing nearly every night I sat in the house?"

"I have no idea," I breathed. "I don't understand why you were in the first place."

"As I have tried to explain before, I had this deep need to protect you. And, because we couldn't be sure *who* or what exactly you were running from I had to stay close."

I turned away from him and walked to bedding and sat down. I took several more drinks from the glass before Sean finally joined me. He took the glass from my hand, setting it on the floor beside him, and then positioned his body. My cheeks flushed when I saw the way the muscles in his chest flexed and quickly dropped my head, directing my attention to my hands before his sharp eyes caught anything.

"Are you warm enough?" he asked.

I peeked at him from my peripheral vision, feeling the heat course through my body. He was stretched out, with his legs crossed at the ankles, his left arm tucked under his head. I answered, keeping my face down.

"A little too warm." My embarrassment was in my tone causing my face to redden a little more.

Sean laughed and reached for my hair, balling his hand in a fist and gently pulled me backwards. He locked me in the bend of his arm and laid me over his chest. He didn't put a blanket between us so I fully felt the stone coldness radiate from his marble body. With the heat fusing from both the fireplace and my own body I didn't mind. I never noticed my hands were trembling till I went to lay one on his chest. I balled it in my palm for a brief second then hesitantly traced the contours of his chest.

"Your heart sounds a bit unsteady," he noted. "Am I making you uncomfortable?"

"No," I lied. I slightly cringed, waiting for him to comment as I was sure he heard the tenor in my voice. He lay quiet for a moment and I listened to the steady sound of his even breathing, mystified he could breathe so freely without his chest having to rise and fall.

"I know I'm pushy at times, Angel," his thoughtful voice began. "I do however want you to tell me if I ever hurt you or I cross any lines that you're not comfortable with."

"*At times*?" I snorted. "You're demanding and very often abrupt."

He shook us with his quiet, musical laughter. "I suppose I am. I would still like you to tell me just the same."

I said nothing.

Suddenly, without even the slightest warning he flipped his body, pinning me between him and the floor. My heart instantly flew into a frenzy and I stared at him in alarm. His eyes were light, he wore a dazing smile and seemed to be in complete control of himself. I relaxed, though very little.

"There's something you have yet to tell me," he murmured next to my ear.

He softly kissed my jaw, and then slowly moved his lips down to the base of my throat. I knew he was waiting for a response, my heart had accelerated to the point it was painful, my breathing coming hard and quick. I closed my eyes on a prayer I could even speak.

"What?" I asked breathlessly.

"You're mine," he whispered against the skin on the side of my neck.

I opened my mouth to answer, but shivered at the feel of his icy cold breath.

"Say it," he murmured.

I tried to push the words out, but he was driving my body so crazy I couldn't think of what it was he wanted to hear.

"*Dammit*, Angel," he growled. "say it."

He stopped kissing my skin and I could feel his eyes boring in my face. I sighed with caution and slowly opened my eyes. His eyes had a speculative look in them, irritation was winning out over amusement and he was on the verge of growling again. I thoughtlessly threw my fingers against his lips, indicating I was planning to answer. In that instant I realized my actions weren't my best choice, yet I wasn't in the best position to upset him, either.

"I accepted the ring and your terms," I breathed. "I've even told you I love you. If that doesn't answer whatever theory you have conjured up in your mind then I don't suppose anything will."

He stared at me, his eyes scorched and were dangerously close to being hypnotic. I carefully lowered my hand while trying to shy away from them.

"Just because you accept something or say I love you, it doesn't necessarily mean you belong to someone," he grumbled. He placed a hand to my lips when he could see that I was about to argue. "I could give the same token to Becca or Kelsey and it would mean nothing more than the love of family. The ring on your finger is a token of a promise that *I* belong to you. All I'm asking from you in return is to hear you say you belong to me and only *me*."

"And we're back to Kyle and John," I mumbled against his hand.

He removed his hand, but never said a word. I sighed deeply, slowly reaching up and locked my arms around his neck.

"I'm yours, Sean," I promised. "Now to forever."

A triumphant smile slowly lit his face and he pressed his cold, satin lips to mine, very carefully parting them. I expected him to pull away after a few minutes, he didn't and I could no longer breathe. I shook my head and Sean complied, his lips never left my skin as he brushed them over my face, and then down the side of my neck. His breath sent shivers through my body and I struggled to get any coherent thoughts.

"You seem to be more at ease with physical contact," I noted.

I felt his lips form a smile against my skin.

"It turns out you're crazy about my touch," he laughed. "You may not understand this, but you have helped me to rediscover my human instincts."

"I thought you said after so many decades you no longer remember them," I said, confused.

"I did," he confirmed. "They are always there, Angel, they're just buried under the monster we become. Once I was decided about wanting you, no matter what price I would pay, they slowly began to surface."

"The price you would pay?" I moved my head to try and look at him. My sudden movement caused him to instantly freeze.

"Oops," I breathed carefully.

After a few long minutes when I didn't move his body began to relax. He slowly lifted his head, staring at my eyes.

"That's an understatement! Am I doing something wrong?"

"Not exactly," I said weakly. "you're driving my body insane."

I could almost see the wheels turn in his head as he processed my words. Then he placed a soft, gentle kiss to my lips and rolled to his back with me locked in the bend of his arm. He laid me over his chest, and then readjusted the blanket where it was tucked around me.

"You should sleep now, my love," he whispered.

"I don't know if I can." I yawned involuntarily.

He laughed softly. "Sure you can. You didn't have any trouble last night, not to mention you've been doing it nearly every night these past few months."

I scowled at the darkness. "I also wasn't aware you had made Bobbie's house a home."

He laughed again.

He softly kissed the top of my head and began stroking his fingers through my hair while humming the tune of the song playing. I was quiet, listening then my eyes grew heavy, and eventually closed letting the night close over me.

My eyes slowly opened the next morning to the sound of crackling wood. I was still lying in Sean's arms, he was mindlessly running his fingers up and down my back. They had just made another circuit when the color of the light caught my attention. My sudden movement caused him to react and he pulled my hair. In that instant I realized how dangerous my action had been and I froze, even breathing with caution till I felt his body relax.

"It's morning," I nearly whispered.

"That usually happens when twilight ends," he laughed.

"No, I ----- ouch."

"Sorry," he muttered, reluctantly releasing my hair.

I tried to push myself up, but he held me firmly in place.

"Going somewhere?" he purred.

I looked up at him and scowled. "Yeah, I have to work today."

I tried again to twist under his arm and he wasn't having that. He laughed and rolled us over. He encircled my wrists in his iron grip and dragged them over my head. When his mouth captured mine, I strained under his grip, my pulse jittering in quick, rabbit jumps.

His body somehow felt colder than usual, yet the heat suddenly fusing from mine seemed to create a balance. After a few seconds I was lightheaded and he moved his lips to my neck, lingering them there a moment before finally ranging lower. He released his hold on my wrists, using one hand to carefully push up the bottom of the shirt while his teeth lightly nipped at my rib cage.

Got to stop this ----- I told myself. And I absolutely will.

His icy cold tongue gently slid over my stomach.

"Sean." I tried to whisper but his name came out in a moan.

"No." His voice was stern. "I only want to touch you, let me see what it does to you."

He continued to skim his lips over the skin of my stomach while his hands slid up my ribs, pushing the shirt up toward my head. I began to fight, only to realize I was fighting myself instead of him. I couldn't do anything but writhe under his hands, my breath coming out in sobs. He kissed his way back up my body then captured my lips, again. I locked my arms on his back, pressing him closer to me. And then, without warning his lips turned to an unresponsive stone beneath my lips, his body turned to a stone statue. I immediately opened my eyes and saw his guarded expression.

"I'm sorry I let this get too far," he whispered. "I wasn't thinking and this was purely a selfish act, Angel. Being selfish is still something I am *damn* good at cause I have to be."

His body finally relaxed, he pressed a delicate kiss to my forehead, and then rolled away from me. I stayed motionless, trying to catch my breath and try to make sense of what just happened. I heard Sean sigh, his voice was rough when he spoke.

"I was simply just trying to experiment how close I can be to you and how much I can touch you before it gets to be too much. I didn't expect the way you would react and nearly took you without giving a *hell* of a lot of consideration to what could happen to you if I lost my control."

I felt tears begin to surface and I took a deep breath to hold them back. I couldn't understand why I suddenly felt so uneasy, why I wanted to jump up and run from the room. It took me a minute to realize the moisture in my eyes was an instinctive reaction to rejection. I'd never allowed myself to be so vulnerable before and I had no idea how to recover myself.

"I'm sorry," was all I could manage.

He sighed longingly and rolled to his side, propping up on his arm. "Angel, *please*, do not apologize for my behavior. It will only make me crazy." He reached out, placing a long, white finger under my chin and turned my head so I was facing him. I don't know what my expression was but it made his eyes narrow.

"What?"

I hadn't completely banished the reflex reaction that convinced me I was indeed undesirable and tried to twist away from his gaze.

"Nothing," I mumbled.

His finger moved and now my face was cupped in his hand while he scrutinized my expressions for a long moment. Then his own expression became horrified.

"Did I hurt your feelings?" he asked, his voice burned with regret.

"No," I lied.

I wasn't sure he believed me and waited for his usual growl, but then he released my face.

"Just so you know, I'm still not in full control of myself. If you're wanting to get back to your humans today ----- or any day ----- then you should get up. Should your body lie here this way any longer I'll be tempted to kiss you again and this time I can guarantee I won't be strong enough to stop."

At that I slowly sat up, and then got to my feet. I hung my head as I walked to the stairs, fighting the urge to run into the bathroom and allow myself to fall apart.

I avoided looking at my reflection in the mirror while I changed into my clothes and ran a brush through my hair. The thought of getting in the shower entered my mind, yet I knew it wouldn't be possible since I didn't have fresh clothes. And because I couldn't use the steam from the hot water to hide anything in my eyes all I could hope was that if they were red and cloudy the ride home would change them before Bobbie could see them. I didn't want her thinking something horrible had happened.

Rejection was the only horrible thing I was facing. I knew it was irrational to think of it that way as Sean was just being very clear that his sudden reaction to stop everything was only for my safety. I couldn't help it.

I forced myself to stop thinking about it, not wanting to allow myself to spend any more time in there so I could leave soon. I quickly brushed my teeth while still keeping my eyes safely away from the mirror. I picked up Sean's shirt, tossed on the counter, and then walked out.

Sean had the fireplace extinguished and the bedding picked up from the floor. The room looked just as it had when I saw it the day before. He was dressed in a pair of dark denim jeans, with a white sweater, the sleeves pushed up to mid-forearm. He appeared to be interested in what was on CNN, not seeming to notice I had come down the stairs or even entered the room.

I walked past him, without even a second glance, opened the door and walked out on the porch. It wasn't raining and the air smelled of the cedars. I took in a few deep breaths welcoming the soft scent.

"Do you need to eat?" he suddenly asked from the doorway.

"No," I answered softly. "I should go."

I heard the door close and less than a second later Sean passed me and walked down the stairs. He stood statue still, waiting for me to climb freely on his back and wrap myself around him in a strangle hold.

The Odd Couple

I drove the few short blocks to the diner wishing I had called Kloe and asked for the day off. I still hadn't gotten control of myself, even after spending an half hour in the shower, nor could I get the image of Sean's expression as I climbed out of his truck out of my mind. The anxiety now running through me seemed to intensify the pounding in both my head and my pulse. There was something clearly buried in his eyes I wasn't sure of and that scared me. Will what happened this morning change his mind about us?

The morning passed slowly. And, because Brandi had spotted my ring nearly the second I walked in it made time seem to move even slower. While she talked endlessly about it and calling everyone over to look at it I was still focusing on the questions I should have asked Sean as he drove me home. Did I do something wrong? Could I have done something differently? And more importantly, where was this leading our relationship?

Kyle and Marisa were the only ones who completely ignored me, as well as Brandi's request to look at the ring. I tried to talk to Kyle a couple of times, but he'd turn around, as if I wasn't there and walk away. I felt such a horrible guilt. I had finally gotten him convinced I didn't want any personal relationships with anyone, and then I surrendered myself to the one person who irritates me the most.

Catlyn came in for a few minutes after school and immediately noticed the tension between Kyle and I. When she asked me about it I lied, claiming it was simply because Kyle didn't like Sean. Even though it was partly the truth, everyone in the restaurant knew it was a lie. I expected Catlyn to see through my outright lies as the others had, somehow she believed them.

I intercepted a number of unfriendly glances from Marisa, which I didn't understand until I entered the dining room. I was right behind her, maybe a foot from her and she was evidently unaware of that.

"... don't know why *Angel*" ----- she sneered my name ----- "doesn't just quit. She suckered Sean with the bogus good girl act and from the looks of that ring he clearly has no objections to her spending his money," I heard her muttering to Catlyn.

That really bothered me; a lot. I'd never worked with Marisa very many times and really didn't know her, certainly not well enough for her to dislike me so much. It also bothered me knowing she thought I had "suckered" Sean into having a relationship with me.

"Marisa," Catlyn crowed, her tone disapproving. "Angel is a very nice person and she's my friend."

Right then part of me wanted to confront Marisa and demand to know what her problem with me was. But I didn't quite have the guts no matter how crappie she had made me feel. Since neither of them noticed me I turned and walked away. I had already heard enough and didn't want to hear anymore.

That night I laid in bed staring at the window, wondering if Sean had come in the house. I didn't hear anything moving downstairs, once I threw back the quilt to get up and open the door; I knew he would hear me and disappear before I ever got across the room. I tightened the quilt around me and rolled onto my side, facing away from the door, fighting to keep from crying myself to sleep.

Things at home began to change as the days passed. Bobbie became busy as she was taking extra shifts at the hospital and when she wasn't working she was gone for other reasons. The more things began to change the more I was starting to miss the way everything had been before what was now turning into my dreadful birthday.

Bobbie finally made me aware of the events taking place in her life while we were having dinner Thursday evening. She had been going out on dates with Josh. She asked if I wanted to join her, Josh, Brandi and Derek in a trip to Salem.

"Are you sure you don't want to go?" she persisted when I told her I didn't.

"No, Bobbie, I don't," I assured her. "Thank you for asking."

"It will be really fun." Her attempt to convince me were flattering and almost tempting.

"You have fun with Josh," I encouraged.

I hadn't told her of any problems Sean and I were having ----- now it seemed we had yet another. We were the odd couple, as we would never be able to join my friends for dinner. What would I say when Sean refused food or even drinks? Sorry guys, my boyfriend is a vampire so he doesn't eat. I shivered at the thought of their reaction to my honesty.

It was foggy and dark outside my window Friday morning. As I dressed I hoped the rain would hold off till I got to work. Despite wearing a jacket my legs would be exposed to the wind and eventually the rain. I knew I could have just thrown the dress in my bag and wore a pair of jeans with a long sleeved shirt to work, and then change before I had to start my shift, but I didn't want the bag soaked, ruining my uniform, anyway.

I stopped in the kitchen long enough to eat a blueberry muffin, chase it down with coffee, and then walked to the door. I donned in my jacket, zipped it up and stepped out the door. It was still unusually foggy; the air was a smoky-gray so thick I could have probably cut it with a knife. The mist from the rain was cold enough to make me shiver each time it touched the exposed skin on my legs. These days I didn't much look forward to being at work, however this morning I couldn't wait to get into the warmth of the kitchen.

Because the fog was so thick I was seconds from taking a step off the curb when suddenly I realized there was a vehicle parked there: a white truck. Since this was the first time in a few days I'd seen it my heart thudded, picking up speed in double time. I didn't see him standing there, yet he instantly opened the door for me.

"You look cold," Sean's soft voice stated. "Would you prefer a ride, it's already warm inside."

I opened my mouth to mention his absence the past week, and then changed my mind as I did want the warmth rather than the cold and closed it. He waited patiently, his features were twisted into the same serene mask he wore the last time I saw him. He clearly still hadn't gotten over last Monday. I inhaled deeply through my nose and climbed in the truck. Sean waited till I was settled to close the door, he got in the driver's seat and head toward the direction of the diner.

By the end of the ride the silence was becoming monotonous. I never liked to be the one to break it, but it was starting to look like it was my only option if I ever wanted to get past this. It is what you said you wanted to do when he came back, I reminded myself.

"Will I see you later?" I asked as the truck rolled to a stop in the nearly empty parking lot.

"I suppose so," he said, indifferently. "You're going to need a ride home."

That wasn't what I meant. It was now panic began to surface again. Sean leaned across the seat, softly placing a kiss to my forehead before opening my door. I was able to climb out before I was hyperventilating over how everything seemed to be coming to an end. He just needed time, I told myself. He was probably still upset with himself, he will get over this.

Work dragged.

I felt a surge of relief when I walked out and saw Sean's truck parked in the lot. I waited a second for him to drive up to the doors as he usually did once he saw me. The truck never moved and I walked to it. The relief was short lived after I got in. Sean's mood hadn't changed and neither did the silence.

He stopped in Bobbie's spot, never putting the truck in park. I knew then he wasn't planning to stay. I felt another piece of my heart fall to the pit of my stomach.

"Are you sure you can't stay?" I asked. Even as I wished to talk this out so I knew what I had done wrong I expected his answer.

"I'm sorry, Angel," he apologized. His voice was unemotional. "I'm afraid I can't."

Can't or just simply won't? I dropped my head and took a deep breath, contemplating taking off the ring and handing it back to him, ending it all right here. Another week, I pleaded with myself. Just give it another week. I pulled on the door handle, cracking the door.

"Thanks for the ride," I said weakly.

I pushed the door open and jumped out. He drove away while I stood there waiting, though I wasn't sure what I waited for. Maybe it was because I hoped something would change his mind and he'd turn around, jump out of the truck and scoop me up into his arms again. I hadn't noticed it was raining until I was dripping. I gave up waiting for something that was clearly not going to happen. My legs felt heavy when I turned and trudged to the house.

A large FedEx box was waiting on the table for me with a quick note from Bobbie placed on top. I glanced over it, and then laid it aside, reading the label on the box. It was from Jen. I got a pair of scissors out of the kitchen drawer and used them to cut the tape. After opening it and looking in I immediately recognized the contents inside. She had somehow managed to get a few of my things out of my bedroom. She sent my pictures, a few of my books and all of my notebooks. She had even placed my corkboard in the box, with a note attached to it asking me to call.

That was the longest conversation in my life. It didn't help much when she caught onto my depression almost from the second she answered the phone. I lied a lot, telling her it was because I was working too much, not leaving me a lot of time to spend with Sean. She finally accepted my outright lies and began questioning me endlessly about my relationship with him and why I waited so long to tell her about him. Her last request was for me to send her a picture of us together. I knew it was more about Sean, but I reluctantly agreed.

The sun seemed to have evaded our part of the world, giving us nothing but endless rain. It was usually heavy, turning to downpours in an instant. It only added to the depression. The days passed, becoming weeks and nothing changed.

Sean was in a foul mood when he drove me to work Friday afternoon. It was the first closing shift I'd had with Kyle in over a month. I couldn't understand what he was so bent out of shape about. Kyle hadn't spoken one word to me since I walked in wearing my birthday ring and Sean hasn't spent more than the five minutes it took to drive me home since I had spent the night with him.

We were busy all afternoon and most of the evening, preventing many hostile situations. I watched throughout most of the night, Catlyn stare at Kyle with a dreamy expression. It made me wonder how he never noticed. I considered mentioning it to him, but since I was now his least favorite person I kept it to myself. Whenever an opportunity would arise, putting them in the back at the same time I would stay in the dining room. At one point I thought I had been successful with my silent matchmaking till I saw disappointment in Catlyn's eyes when she left. I moaned in exasperation.

We had slowed way down after she left and Kloe sent everyone home, leaving only Kyle and I to finish closing. This was definitely going to be a long night.

Kyle followed the last customer to the door, and then locked it. I grabbed a rag and a spray bottle from under the counter and was on my way to the table when Kyle's sulky voice filled the room.

"So you and Callenger, huh?"

My earlier feeling of awe for Catlyn's affection toward him disappeared. I began to wonder what it really was she saw in him. I sprayed the table and ran the rag over it to keep from looking at him.

"You haven't said two words to me for a month and this is the way you want to start a conversation?"

I heard him groan. "I don't like it."

"You don't have to," I snapped. "It's clearly none of your business, Kyle."

"Maybe not," he muttered resentfully. "You tell me you're not interested in him, me or John then leave for two days just to come back wearing a ring Callenger bought you."

"I wasn't interested," I glowered. "but sometimes things happen and change."

"It still isn't right that you wouldn't give me the time of day, but you end up with him." Kyle's tone was rebellious.

The tenor in his voice frustrated me. I stopped wiping down the table and looked at him, fighting to keep my voice warm when I responded.

"Even if I hadn't, even if I would have considered yours or John's pleas for my time and attention I still wouldn't have said yes to either of you."

I looked away from Kyle and picked up the empty dishes, and then walked to the counter. Kyle had gone to the doorway to the kitchen and leaned against the door jam. His arms were folded over his chest, his legs crossed at the ankles.

"Why not?" he asked, sounding offended.

I set the dishes on the counter, placed the spray bottle back on the shelf and grabbed the big, gray dish tub.

"Really, Kyle," I said condescendingly. I set the dirty dishes in the tub, picked it up, and then turned to look at him. "We've had this conversation many times, then somehow you always seem to make me repeat the same things. I like you as a *friend* and nothing more. And anyways, are you truly that blind?"

His brows knit in confusion. "What's that supposed to mean?" he snapped.

I rolled my eyes while shaking my head, sadly. I stepped towards him and he stood upright, letting me pass him.

"It means I could never hurt Catlyn like that," I said over my shoulder.

Kyle followed me to the dish room.

"What does any of this have to do with her?" he asked, his tone skeptical.

"I probably shouldn't say anything, since it really isn't my place, but you're irritating the *hell* out of me. It's clear from the expressions on her face she likes you and you're too busy being an idiot to notice."

I set the tub down on top of the dishwasher and began unloading the dishes.

"How do you know that's really what you saw?" he asked.

I stopped what I was doing and turned to face him, a scowl on my face. "Is it really so hard to believe? I realize it must honestly be difficult for you to stop fussing over me to bother looking, but try actually paying attention. Then just maybe you will see for yourself."

I hadn't quite gotten all the dishes loaded in the dishwasher, but in that moment I needed the space. I tried to pass Kyle, he stepped in front of me and lowered his head, locking his eyes on mine.

"Is this really about Catlyn or is there a real reason and you don't want to tell me what it is?"

Now I was annoyed. "What other reason would I possibly have?"

His brown eyes filled with speculation. "If you want the truth, I think this has all been about Callenger all along."

My eyes narrowed. "You couldn't be more wrong," I growled. "and this may not be something you will understand, I believe in fate."

He stared back at me a second longer then straightened himself, shaking his head. "You're right," he breathed. "I don't."

He turned on his heels and walked away. I breathed a sigh of relief and walked back to the dishwasher to finish loading it.

That was the last conversation. Kyle stayed in the back till it was time to leave. For the first time in months I didn't feel any guilt for turning him down, or being rude when he pushed. I just had to hope Catlyn wouldn't be upset with me for telling her secret.

Sean was sitting in the truck waiting for me when I walked out of the diner. I stared at the truck for a fraction of a second, considering walking straight home without even a simple hello. By this time I was beyond fed up with all the attitudes seeming how my quota of patience had already been used up for the day. As I got closer to the truck Sean leaned over the seat and opened the door.

"Hi," I breathed, warily.

"Hello." His answering smile was dazzling. "How was work?"

My face fell in utter disbelief from the sudden change in his moods. "It was to be as expected," I grumbled.

His eyes shifted their focus to the passenger window. "Really?"

I heard the loathing in his tone and glanced behind me. Kyle stood on the sidewalk staring at us before finally walking away. I looked out at the parking lot, not ruling out walking.

"Are you planning to get in any time soon?" Sean suddenly asked.

I carefully turned my head, my eyes slid to his face.

"Yes," I moaned, almost unintelligently. I climbed in the seat and closed the door.

Despite the little bit of conversation in the parking lot the ride home lapsed in the same eerie silence it had been for the past month. Sean drove slowly, slow for him, anyway. His face was smooth, unreadable, there was still something wrong with his eyes ----- they still seemed to be trying hard to hide something. I felt a spasm of uneasiness course through me and fought to control it. He stopped in Bobbie's spot and put the truck in park. I looked out the passenger window and huffed a deep breath.

"Good night, Sean." I squeezed the handle and pushed open the door.

"Can't I come in?" he asked.

"Would you like to?" I couldn't quite hide the shock I felt at his words. I had gotten so used to his shortcomings with me.

"Yes, if it's all right." I heard his door open then close and almost simultaneously he was standing next to mine.

He waited for me to get out then closed my door.

"You haven't been interested in going inside for a month," I noted. I was still stunned by the sudden change in his behavior.

"I know," he sighed heavily. "I thought it was time we talked about it."

He walked beside me to the house then on the porch. He took the keys from my hand, unlocked the door, and then opened it for me. I stepped inside, walking on to the kitchen, leaving him to toss the keys in the bowl and close the door.

"I want to apologize," Sean said as he entered the kitchen.

I turned to look at him with one eyebrow raised. It didn't take even a second for him to see my suspicion.

"I promised you much better than things and have chosen to be an *ass*."

I let that go for the moment and walked to the fridge. Sean sat down in one of Bobbie's shabby kitchen chairs while I concentrated on getting last night's pizza out, placing a couple of pieces on a plate, heating them in the microwave. I didn't take my eyes from the plate turning inside as I spoke.

"Did I do something wrong that morning?" I asked casually.

"Hmmm?" He clearly hadn't been paying attention as he sounded like I had pulled him from some train of thought.

I still didn't turn around. "Had I done something wrong?"

"No, you didn't."

Now I whirled on him. "Then why have you let me spend this past month driving myself crazy?"

"I've never had these kinds of feelings before." He spoke matter-of-factly. "I needed the time to sort through that morning, as well as get control of it all. I couldn't trust myself around you until I was sure I wouldn't lapse, again."

I continued to stare at him while letting his words turn over in my mind. I spent these last few weeks obsessing over something I did, only to learn it hadn't been me all along.

His expression shifted instantly to chagrin. "Are you angry with me?"

"That depends," I answered ruefully.

"On?" he urged.

"If you're planning to explain it all to me now."

Instantly, his movements the sound of a moth's wings, he was in front of me, carefully taking my face in his hands.

"Don't be upset," he pleaded. He dropped his face to the level of my eyes, holding my gaze. I tried to look away.

"You have my word," he whispered. "I will tell you everything. I have not meant for you to take the blame for my actions upon yourself. Nothing that happened that morning shadows any blame to you."

"I was beginning to think we had somehow reached the end before we ever really got started." He released my face and I hung my head.

He pulled me against his chest, softly wrapping his arms around me. "Don't sell us so short," he whispered in my ear. "I may act senseless, as I'm learning how to be what you need, you must never believe in an ending. I vow to you that I am here for as long as you will have me."

Then the phone rang. When I made no effort to move Sean reached behind me and picked up the receiver. He placed it in my hand, and then turned to walk back to the table.

"Hello?" I hoped the person on the other end couldn't hear the stress in my voice. I grabbed my dinner from the microwave and sat down at the table to keep my now shaky legs from causing me to stumble.

"Hey, Angel," Jen greeted me. "I know it's late, I called earlier and Bobbie said you had already left for work."

The sound of her voice reminded me I hadn't called her in a while.

"It's okay, I haven't been home long. I'm sorry I haven't called lately," I apologized.

"It's not a big deal," she said dismissively. "I know you're busy."

Something in her tone wasn't right causing my mind to instantly become unclouded. I tore my eyes away from Sean's face so I could focus on the conversation.

"Has something happened?"

"No," she said, the word come out in a rush. "I found out this morning that Dad is getting remarried. I just wanted someone to complain to about it," she laughed.

"Jason is remarrying?" I couldn't be sure I had heard her correctly.

"Yes." She enunciated the word, as if she were talking to someone incompetent. "I'm not sure how to feel about it."

I was so distracted by Jen's news I never heard Sean get out of the chair or walk to me. Suddenly he was placing a long, white finger under my chin, lifting my face up so I was looking at him.

"I'll be back," he whispered. He pressed his lips gently to mine then pulled away. "I love you."

And I was alone.

"Angel?" Jen's voice sounded muffled and distant.

"Ummm ... what?" My mind was clouded and I shook my head to clear it.

"Did you hear anything I just said?" she asked, annoyed.

"Sorry, but no," I admitted shamefully.

"I said they want me to fly out for the wedding. What should I do?"

"I'm not sure," I sighed. "Maybe you should go," I said only as the thoughts began to come to me. "At least meet your dad's fiancée," I quickly added when I heard her grumble. "I know you haven't heard from him in a long time, but since he called to tell you before he married her then clearly it's important to him for you to be part of it."

Jen let out a long groan and jumped into reminding me of how he left. I tried to be optimistic while pretending to follow the conversation. I knew my focus should have been on Jen, I couldn't help wondering why Sean had left. He'd heard my conversations before and they didn't seem to bother him.

"I have to go," she said abruptly. "Pass my hello to Bobbie and I will talk to you soon."

"I will," I promised. "bye, Jen."

"Bye, Angel." She hung up.

I took my food with me to hang up the phone, scarfing it down as I went. I filled a glass with milk and gulped it down. I was in a hurry to finish and be done with the dishes and a shower before Sean came back. Of course, now I was keyed up over the thought of him coming back after a long month of his absence.

It wasn't till I quickly scrubbed my dishes clean in the sink, I realized my hands were trembling. I took a deep breath, forcing myself to calm down before I broke a plate. I rinsed it and the cup off and placed them upside down on the towel to dry. I turned off the kitchen light as I headed up the stairs.

I stopped in my room long enough to grab my pajamas from the bed and rushed into the bathroom. I brushed my teeth fiercely, making sure I removed all traces of the pizza. The hot water refused to be rushed, leaving me to clean and straighten up the counter while I waited. Once it was hot and I stepped in it immediately unknotted the tense muscles throughout my body and calmed my pulse.

I shut off the water, taking my time toweling and dressed in my pajamas. The shower had relaxed me enough that I would now be able to concentrate on the conversation I needed to have with Sean. I had hoped he was finally over things and we could get back to where our relationship started.

I rubbed the towel through my hair again, and then ran the brush through it. I threw the towel in the hamper, straightened up the counter again then returned to my room.

I sat in the middle of my bed, with my notebooks scattered around me. I flipped through the one in my hand with wary curiosity. It had been months since I felt the deep urge to compose my own music. As ridiculous as I knew it was, I still didn't feel the sense to hum even one note.

Sean still hadn't returned. I didn't want to admit it to myself that he was the reason I was still up, pretending to have an interest in the notebooks, but of course he was the exact reason. I was still hopeful his change of mood before Jen called would allow us to finally talk it all out.

Then after the hours passed, after my hair had completely dried and he still hadn't appeared in the house I turned out the light and laid down. I was able to lay there for a long moment before the panic really hit. What if what he wanted to say tonight is bad? What if he had convinced himself he can't be with me after all?

Again, I didn't sleep well.

The next morning I woke to the sound of music. I thought nothing of it, at first, figuring it was the clock radio. I squeezed my eyes tighter and pulled a pillow over my head. Then I realized it wouldn't have been the radio, as it was my day off. I knocked the pillow off and sat up, listening to the melody. It wasn't coming from anywhere upstairs. I pushed the blanket back, stood from the bed and walked to the door. The music became louder after I opened it.

I had to cover my hears to keep from going deaf before I reached the bottom of the stairs. Bobbie was mindlessly dancing around the kitchen, singing along with the song, not seeming to notice I had entered. In that moment I was reminded of the morning after my birthday when I was looking for the perfect place for my rose. The same memory that brought back that day also brought back the reminder of how my days have been spent since then. I banished the thoughts before they could bring me down and walked to a cabinet. It was now when Bobbie finally saw me.

"Morning, Angel," she said cheerfully. She continued to sway around the room, seeming to be the least bit embarrassed I was there.

"Morning," I laughed. "the music's a little loud, don't you think?"

"Oh, I'm sorry," she gushed.

She dashed past me, disappearing into the foyer. A second later the music stopped and she was entering the kitchen from the opposite doorway.

"I'm really sorry, Angel," she apologized again. "I didn't realize it was that loud. It's just when I hear that song it makes me want to dance."

"I saw that," I chuckled. "don't worry about it, I have a few that does the same for me."

I hadn't noticed she had a basket on the table till I watched her carry a container of potato salad to it, and then place it inside. "Are you working today?" she asked casually.

"No." I finished stirring the spoon around in the cup then rinsed it off.

She whirled to face me. "Do you have any plans?"

I narrowed my eyes at her, suspicious of where she was trying to lead me. "Nothing that involves leaving the house, why?"

"Well ..." she paused, seeming to think about her answer. "Josh's parents invited us out to the farm for an afternoon of horseback riding. If you're not doing anything why don't you come with us?"

Balance wasn't one of those things I had, so horseback riding was glaringly outside my range. I learned that lesson a few years back when I went with Jennifer to her grandfather's farm.

"I'm afraid I don't do well with horses. You go have fun and don't worry about me."

Her expression shifted to indecision as she watched me sit down at the table.

"Has something happened between you and Sean?" she suddenly asked.

I wasn't expecting her question and nearly spit out the coffee I hadn't swallowed. I choked on it, instead.

"No," I coughed. "Why?" I thought my near gagging would cover my lie, but when I looked up at her and saw her lips pressed together in a hard line I knew she saw through the lie.

"It has only just occurred to me that I haven't seen Sean since your birthday," she stated carefully. "I had no idea you've been spending all your time alone until I talked to Jennifer a few days ago. Angel, why haven't you said anything to me?"

My face slightly fell from her statement and I fought to control it.

"Sean's been ... busy," I said the word only as it came to mind. "and anyways, it's not really that big of a deal. With Catlyn back in school, leaving her only able to work on the weekend and Marisa being gone a lot, has left the diner short staffed. Truthfully, I've been working to cover for them so I haven't actually been *alone*."

Marisa had gotten a few modeling offers in California and had been gone the last couple of weeks. Too be completely honest I wasn't the only one at work who had enjoyed her absence.

Bobbie opened her mouth to respond to me, never to get the chance. The sound of a car horn filled the house. A deep disappointment crossed her face.

"I really wish you would at least consider the offer." She held up a hand when she saw I was about to argue. "I'm not going to push, as you clearly have your reasons."

The horn blazed again, she quickly closed the lid on the basket, eyed me for another second, and then hurried out the door.

I looked around the kitchen and noticed it was a mess. The sink was piled with dirty dishes, the table had stacks of newspapers nearly covering it and the floor was streaked with dirt. I released a deep sigh, stood from the chair and headed up the stairs.

I changed into a pair of sweats and a t-shirt. I grabbed the hamper out of the bathroom, tossed all the clothes still laying on my bedroom floor in it, and then stripped the bed, tossing the bedding on top. The hamper overflowed causing me to take my time carrying it down the stairs.

I started the first load of laundry then worked on the dishes. I only had it in my mind to straighten up the room, but before I knew it I had cleaned everything, including washing the windows and sweeping the floor.

I got the mop bucket from the laundry room and three faint knocks came on the door. I set the bucket in the basin, and then went to answer it. Sean was leaning against the door jam, with rain drops glistening in his hair. His eyes were light, the purple shadows under them gone.

"Hi," he smiled. "enjoying your day off?" He leaned in the door, softly kissing my lips before I could respond.

Even after he pulled away it took another long second before I could recover my now tangled thoughts and my breath.

"I don't know if *enjoying* is the right word," I breathed. "but I'm getting caught up on some cleaning."

He shook his head and muttered something unintelligible. I thought I picked out the words "O.C.D."

I scowled at him. "If you're not interested in watching me clean up then why did you bother coming here?"

I walked away from him and headed in the kitchen.

"We have a discussion left unfinished," he called after me. He entered the room less than a second later. "How much are you behind on?" His eyes did a full scan of the room before stopping on my face.

"Besides my laundry, this is it."

He watched as I poured Pine-Sol in the bucket then turn on the water. The aroma filled the room less than a second later causing him to wrinkle his nose in disgust. He causally walked to me and leaned down, whispering in my ear.

"I'll just be in your room." His lips brushed my cheek, and then I was alone.

I mumbled bitterly at the empty room, shut off the water, and yanked the bucket out of the sink.

When I finished with mopping the floor I dumped the dirty water over the front porch, carried the empty bucket back to the laundry room, and then headed up the stairs.

Sean lay across the bed, engrossed in a book I had left open on the table beside my bed, his left hand behind his head, his feet dangling off the end, seeming to be perfectly at ease. My entrance had him laying the book face down against his chest.

"This is the kind of stories you like?" he asked, drumming his index finger against it.

I made a face. "I can see how stories such as Bonnie and Clyde wouldn't be of any interest to you, as you were clearly around at that time, but I find their lives fascinating."

I crossed the room and sat down on the bed, folding myself in half.

"It isn't so much the interest I'm not impressed with. It's the antiquity. How can you honestly read stories where the characters are ghastly people out to ruin their lives along with others around them? Couldn't you find better bitter sweetness in stories such as Romeo and Juliet or even Pride and Prejudice?"

"If you're interested in classics pertaining to women committing suicide over what they believe is life after love," I snapped. "I've never been a fan of those types of stories. And anyways, I find reading about real people beats having your mind filled with fictional romances or with mythical creatures."

His face was thoughtful as he considered my words. After a long moment he smiled a teasing smile. "I still believe their story would have been better if they had one redeeming quality. As for the lack of interest you have for mythical creatures ----- don't I fit that category."

Now I laughed. "Are you implying that you're nothing more than a figment of my imagination?"

He frowned, a low growl rumbling from his throat. "Hysterical, Angel."

He placed my book back on the table. He stood from the bed and walked across the room to stand in front of my corkboard. I kept my eyes on him.

"Is this your mother?" he suddenly asked, pointing to a picture directly in front of him.

"Yes," I sighed deeply. "it's the last one ever taken of us together."

"You're right you don't resemble her," he noted.

"I know," I nearly mumbled. "I don't have any photographs of Scott, but I took more from him."

He leaned closer to the board, and then took down a different picture.

"Who's the girl standing next to you?'

"Her name is Jennifer Collins. She's my best friend."

He turned his whole body so he was facing me. "Is she who called while I was here last night?"

"That was her," I confirmed. "I'm afraid she isn't going to be very happy the next time I talk to her," I laughed.

"Why wouldn't she?"

His sincere curiosity disarmed me. "Because," I said, scrambling for coherency while his gaze unintentionally scattered my thoughts. "you have seen her before she has gotten a look at you."

An expression flickered across his face as he tacked the picture back on the board.

"I can't say I understand her reason," he mumbled, the words so low I barely heard them. "I must say." He paused, turning to scan the room. "I don't remember seeing these things the last time I was here."

"Apparently Jennifer's been sneaking around inside Scott's house when he's gone. She gathered a few of my things from the old bedroom and sent them to me."

"That was a brave move," he said, his voice thoughtful.

"Did you really come up here to see what new things I've consumed in your absence?" I asked.

He rubbed his fingers over his forehead and sighed. "No, I thought this would be a safer place to have our discussion without Bobbie catching anything." He sat down on the bed beside me, putting a cold hand on mine. "Where is Bobbie, anyway?"

"She left with Josh this morning."

We sat there for a moment in silence, both seeming to think of how to start what was sure to be a long conversation. It was now I remembered the laundry in the washing machine.

"Could I have a minute to take care of something?" I asked.

"Certainly." Sean gestured with one hand for me to proceed.

I looked at him for another minute watching, as his body become a statue on the edge of my bed. I hopped up, crossing the room. I slipped out the door and left it open as I headed towards the stairs.

I took my time going down them and entering the laundry room. My stomach twisted into knots as I thought about Sean sitting in my room, waiting, because I was sure so many things had changed over the past month.

I switched the clothes to the dryer, started it, and then refilled the washing machine. My stomach was now beginning to flop as I made my way back to the stairs. I considered prolonging my time downstairs, but quickly changed my mind, reminding myself it had already been more than a month since Sean had been so willing to sit in the same room with me.

Sean hadn't moved an inch, still sitting statue still, staring toward the window. I closed the door behind me and went to his side, sitting cross-legged beside him. I took a deep breath to steady myself as my pulse began to pound. I knew Sean heard my distress when his hand snaked out, catching mine and pulled it over his lap.

"Again, I'd like to start by apologizing for my rudeness and shortcomings." I looked up to see that his eyes were earnest. "I needed time to be sure of my self-control. I've spent these past few weeks thinking about our differences and about how many ways they affect certain areas of our relationship. It is because of those differences intimacy will never be possible for us."

"Tell me if I have done something wrong." I tried to sound detached. "I can handle the truth."

He sighed deeply. "You did nothing more than what your human hormones reacted to. Your body is so soft, so fragile that should I not be in mind of my own actions I could very easily kill you as I've explained before. I can never afford to lose any kind of control when I'm with you."

I looked away from him to stare at the lines in the floor. The hand over mine moved under my chin and he pulled my face up till I was looking at him.

"What now?"

"In your own human instincts …" I began. He waited almost impatiently for me to finish. "Well, do you still have those kinds of desires, at all?"

"I may not be human," he chuckled humorlessly. "but I am still a man. Angel," he sighed heavily, serious now. "in the decades I've walked nearly each state in this country and others, surrounded with both my kind and yours I have never come close to finding anyone who holds even one hundredth of the attraction you hold for me."

I made a face. "You never came across a beautiful being like yourself and found her the least bit attractive?" I was skeptical.

A wide grin flashed across his face as he released my chin and reached out to twirl strands of my hair around his fingers. "It turns out I'm intrigued by redheads with golden locks."

I didn't respond.

The smile faded as Sean scrutinized my face for a long moment, not allowing me to turn away from his gaze. His brows furrowed and he pulled his fingers free of my hair.

"I have hurt your feelings again, didn't I?"

"No," I said icily. "I was just thinking you may not have found anyone to explore lust with, but should I ever have another moment when I'm in desperate need I shouldn't have too much trouble convincing John or Kyle."

Sean's eyes instantly darkened, a deep growl rumbled from his chest. "Are you trying to test my resistance for taking a human life!?"

I used to be frightened by that look, I had since grown immune to it.

"No," I stated ruefully, ignoring his outburst. "If you're always going to have to fight against your own instincts so love and lust never keep the same company then why do you bother with a human?"

His eyes closed and he pinched the bridge of his nose with his thumb and forefinger.

"Angelia," he said, almost a growl. "it is much too late to sit here and discuss what I fall in love with, or with *whom* I devote myself to."

He slowly opened his eyes, staring into mine. I watched as they began to lighten, knowing the storm was over. I'm not sure what expression was on my face, or how it all happened, yet suddenly I was in his arms, cradled against his chest while he rocked us back and forth.

"*Please*, understand why I must say no," he murmured. "You know I want you, I have already proven it."

"Do you?" I asked, my voice full of doubt.

"Of course I do." He stopped rocking us to look down at me. His eyes had darkened in color. "How could you ask such a question after all that has happened?"

I completely ignored his question and the look in his eyes.

"Do you ever think your life might be easier ..." He raised one hand, placing it over my mouth.

"No," he said sternly.

I tried to push his hand away, I may as well had been trying to move a boulder for all the good it was doing me. He waited for me to stop fighting against him before finally dropping his hand and his serious expressions. I glared at him causing him to laugh.

"Let me make sure I have this right." I raised my eyebrows. "You're saying that unless I somehow end up sharing your fate you're never going to sleep with me?"

His eyes widened innocently. "Technically, I can't anyway."

I let out a huff of breath. "What was the word you used earlier ... *hysterical*, Sean."

Sean shook us with his musical laughter. "As previously discussed I will never allow what has happened to me become who you are, too, but yes that is correct."

I continued to stare at him, my lips puckered. He completely ignored my expression and stood from the bed.

"Since we are now past the worst of everything how about we get you downstairs? I don't want your O.C.D. getting the best of you before you have the chance to finish your chores."

"Hey!" I hissed.

He laughed, shifting me ever so slightly to open the door. "What man wouldn't be pleased to have his own version of Cinderella?"

I opened my mouth to snarl something hateful, never to get the chance. His icy arms tightened around me, crushing me closely against his body, his lips pressed against mine; his cool breath sending my mind into a tailspin.

Special Delivery

As I sat waiting for the ever so slow changing traffic light to change to green I could see the faces of the pedestrians standing on the sidewalk staring in my direction. It wasn't hard to figure out their conversation was about Sean's truck (as they pointed to it while they spoke). Before deciding to define his relationship with me Sean never made many appearances throughout the sleepy little town. Each passing second they continued to stare and gossip I silently cursed Sean for forcing me to keep the big beast.

I kept trying to convince myself no one even knew it was me because of the dark tint on all the windows. They think it's Sean, I promised myself. They're not staring at you. I almost had myself convinced till I looked to my right. In her flashy SUV Mrs. Wilkins had her entire torso turned in my direction. The folks on the sidewalk might not have known it wasn't Sean, but she did! She may not have known it was me inside, she definitely knew it wasn't Sean.

His family left Thursday evening after Jonah learned about a hiking accident at Mount Saint Helens. A small group of kids, with little hiking experience made a choice to try climbing a volcano. Sean wasn't comfortable about it, as it was kids they were planning to feed from. His irises were darkening by the day, the bruise-like shadows under his eyes were becoming more define.

Because they had to travel to Washington and scope things out before they could get their blood supply safely they were going to be gone longer than usual. Mrs. Wilkins knew they had left as Becca was her husband's secretary. Even as I knew she couldn't see me I was unable to stop myself from sliding down in the seat.

"Arg!" I groaned in exasperation.

The light finally changed and in my haste to get free of her stares, I stomped on the gas with more force than necessary causing the truck to jolt forward so fast the tires squealed. I felt my face burn with embarrassment as I merely tapped the brake pedal. Any thoughts Mrs. Wilkins may have had about who would be driving Sean's truck were gone now. She got her answer without having to see me with her own eyes. With the toe of my shoe, I gently pushed on the gas pedal to keep the truck moving ----- this time without drawing any more attention to myself.

Though I was now free of everyone's gawking and whispers I still cursed Sean as I drove through town. Normally I only drive from home to work, but I had run out of shampoo this morning, leaving me no choice to run the errand to Walmart. This was just my third time driving the truck, I wasn't accustom to driving big vehicles, still worse than that was *how* I had to drive. The seat was pulled up so I could reach the pedals causing the steering wheel to nearly touch my torso. It was coming up on my turn to buy groceries, but I was continuing to put it off this week just to avoid being in public.

I managed to reach my goal without any more incidents, the diner. As I turned slowly and carefully into the parking lot I made sure to park a ways from the other cars, to ensure I wouldn't back into anyone when I left. I took my time walking to the building. I wanted the few extra minutes of the sunlight; my mind began remembering two nights ago when Sean told me he was leaving me the truck ...

As Bobbie and I were cleaning up the kitchen from dinner I looked out the window in time to watch Sean pull up behind Bobbie's car. Completely confused, as I knew he was preparing to leave with his family I handed Bobbie the dish rag and walked out the door.

Sean was a few, short feet from walking up the stairs when I exited the house.

"What are you doing here? I thought you were supposed to be leaving?"

"I am," he countered. "I just had one small thing to do before I leave."

Sean's cool hand grabbed mine and he turned it over, palm up, and then gently placed his keys in it. I stared at them for a second then turned my gaze up to his face.

"What is this about?" I asked, confusion strong in my voice.

"I'm giving you the keys to the truck." Both the look on his face and the tone in his voice stated I should have already known that.

"Why are you giving them to me?" I was still very confused.

"Aren't they usually essential when you need to drive?"

My eyes widened in horror when his question finally sank in. The keys suddenly weighed a hundred pounds against my palm. I tried turning my hand over so the keys would fall into Sean's, but his fingers formed a grip on mine, closing them over the keys.

"I can't drive your truck!" I shrieked.

"Stop fidgeting, Angel," he commanded me. "And, yes you can. Please try to grasp this concept, it's no different than driving Bobbie's car."

"Easy for you to say. You fit perfectly in it."

Sean quietly laughed, leaning in to kiss my forehead. "You're going to do fine. I'll see you on Friday."

I could only stare at him horrified as he walked off the porch.

I shook my head, clearing it of all the thoughts and opened the door, entering the diner.

My days at work had slowed down after Brandi's endless complaints convinced Kloe to hire another waitress. Sydney, Brandi and I had been switching between opening and closing shifts to cover Catlyn and Marisa. Even then it still left us one waitress short. It really wasn't that noticeable till the weekends. Whether it rained heavily or not the restaurant was always packed on Friday and Saturday nights. Those were usually the nights *I* ended up on the closing shifts.

After what was a long consideration Kloe hired Kerri DaSoto. I found it a bit ironic that she was an old classmate of Bobbie's and Kerri's mother was a close friend of Bobbie's mother. It seemed Kloe was finding ways to keep the diner family oriented. The only outsiders besides myself was Mark and Sydney.

Kerri was the same height as me and I was delighted. I was no longer the shortest person. And, like me she was shy, too ----- I secretly hoped Marisa would soon call Kloe to inform her she wouldn't be coming back. I didn't want Kerri to take any hits on her self-esteem caused by Marisa's endless criticism.

I was thankful for Kloe's decision to hire Kerri ----- because the only closing shifts I had now was

Tuesday and Wednesday, allowing me to have the weekend with Sean. He had already been gone four days and I was anxious to have him home. I couldn't help smiling while I punched my numbers in the time clock.

The week passed more quickly than any ever had before. Despite Kloe hiring Kerri I was still working a lot, and then there was the work load waiting for me at home. Bobbie wasn't home these days, leaving me with the chores. I didn't complain, as they allowed me to have a neat and effortless pattern to follow. And of course, Bobbie got her wish; Sean and I finally talked things out so I wasn't miserable anymore.

Because I wasn't keeping track of the days I was taken by surprise when I got home tonight. Becca was waiting on the porch when I pulled up in front of the house.

"Is it Friday already?" I asked as I scurried up the walk.

"No, it's only Wednesday," she informed me. Since this was only the second time I had seen her, her striking beauty stunned me. My heart began to pound rapidly as I joined her on the porch and I fought to control it.

I don't know what my expressions were, but they had her speaking quickly.

"We returned a few hours ago," she continued. "It isn't safe for the town to see us yet, as the sun is to last one more day. I simply came here to have the chance to speak with you."

I stared at her for a long moment before finally walking to the door and unlocked it. It was then I realized my hands were trembling.

"What can I do for you?" I found my voice was more stable when I didn't look at her while I spoke.

"Sean has told me you are amazingly talented with a piano."

I whirled on her, my eyes wide with horror. It was in that moment I finally saw the colored folder in her hand.

"Why did he do that?" My tone was an octave higher than I was aiming for.

She eyed me carefully before answering. "He knows I'm in need of a piano player. He suggested I speak with you about the matter."

I was shaking my head before she was even finished.

"*Please*, Angel," she pleaded. "I'm really desperate, as there are not many talents around here. I know Derek Woods is great, but he's leaving for New York in the morning and he's very busy with his own career, not leaving much time for my project."

She didn't appear to act the way Kelsey does when she doesn't get her way, yet my will to reject her pleas were still weakening caused by the look in her soft gray eyes. They made resisting harder than it should have been. You do owe her and her family, I reminded myself. Why am I such a pushover?

"What exactly do you need a piano player for?" I asked cautiously.

Her solid gray eyes melted into liquid as an encouraging smile crossed her lips. "Mrs. Wilkins's birthday is a week before the Thanksgiving holiday your kind celebrates. Mayor Wilkins has requested a special party for her."

"How big of a crowd are we talking?"

"The entire town is invited," Becca answered as we walked in the kitchen. Because that wasn't the answer I was expecting I threw her a quick glance. "It will be great practice for Juilliard," she added, as if that somehow justified her answer.

Now that I was made aware she knew about my piano abilities I wasn't surprised she knew about Juilliard, too.

"All right," I sighed in surrender. "Where do I find a piano for practices?"

She smiled widely, showing off her ultra-white teeth and handed me the folder before reaching in her pocket, pulling out a single brass key.

"The banquet hall is a block from City Hall on Main. This key opens all the doors, you must make sure to lock them as you leave." She held out the key as she spoke. As I reached for it, she dropped it into my palm.

I looked at the key for a long second, and then turned my eyes back to Becca's face, my heart was still beating rabbit jumps against my ribs. The sound of it and my lack of self-control had her brows furrowed in frustration.

"Angel," her thick accent caressed around my name. "you must learn not to be so anxious in our company. I assure you we would hurt ourselves before we ever hurt you."

She took slow, unrushed steps to stand next to me, carefully wrapping a cold, marble arm around my shoulders. She lightly pressed her stone, cold lips to my forehead, and then a second later I was alone.

I made myself a Turkey sandwich, filled a glass with tea, and then sat down at the table. As I ate I looked over the music sheets inside the folder. For reasons I couldn't fathom they brought back my choir days from so many months ago. My place in the stage lineup was always in between Jennifer and Kendra Dalton. Kendra had amazing voice and was planning to leave for Nashville after graduation; I wonder ----- did she ever make it? Sigh. I suppose I'll have to ask Jen.

I was looking over the second song in Becca's play list when faint knocks appeared on the back door. Who in the world would that be? ----- I thought. I picked my empty glass up from the table and went to answer it. Sean was there, dressed in a long-sleeved black shirt, with a pair of dark colored jeans. I examined his face, his eyes were light, nearly shimmering, his irises were normal, and there weren't any purple shadows on the skin under them. A slow, yet cocky smile crossed his lips as he took in my reaction.

"Hi," he said, clearly amused.

He didn't give me the chance to respond, his lips were on mine, moving softly, but quickly. Without breaking our kiss he pushed me backwards, entering the laundry room and closed the door. I could no longer breathe and shook my head. Sean complied, pulling away. My head spun while I turned away from him and walked in the kitchen.

Still completely dazed I carried my empty glass to the refrigerator for a refill. Sean went to the table and sat down in one of the shabby kitchen chairs.

"I see Becca has decided to speak to you about Mrs. Wilkins's party."

I finished pouring the tea in my glass, set the pitcher back on the shelf, closed the door, and then turned to face him. He had the page I had been looking over in his hand and was humming the melody. The sound was so soothing I hated to have to cut it off with the sound of my own voice.

"She was waiting on the porch for me when I got home." I crossed the room to join him.

"Jonah wondered where she was off to," he reflected to himself. "Did you agree to do it?"

His question reminded me of something Becca had said causing a sour expression to appear on my face. Sean laid the sheet in front of me then slid his eyes to mine.

"What?" he asked innocently.

"Did you really have to tell her about Juilliard?" I griped.

"I'm not understanding why you're upset about it. Wouldn't it be helpful having the practice playing for an audience before you sit in front of the judges?"

Now I scowled. "I'm not really sure I'm going to the audition."

He frowned, unhappily. "Why wouldn't you?"

I sighed, heavily.

"Sean," I pronounced his name carefully. "I'm barely eighteen and I have a job. I can't just pick up my life, again."

"Angel, you clearly have dreamed of this nearly all of your life. Kloe will understand how important this is, you should know that as Marisa Hadley is in California as we speak. You're purposely trying to complicate this. Tell me why."

"When I first decided to try I was looking for a way out of my life. Now it's just about money," I whispered, half to myself. I looked down at the table to hide my face. "I don't have the money to pay for the ticket or the hotel stay."

Sean reached over the table, placing a long, cold finger under my chin, lifting my face till I was looking at him. When our eyes met, his were soft and shimmering. I forgot how to exhale.

"What's mine is yours," he stated matter-of-factly.

It took a few long seconds, but I pulled away, shaking my head, fighting to gain control of my now tangled thoughts and to answer him.

"I don't want your money, Sean," I said, the words barely audible.

He let his arm drop against the table, his face became hard and expressionless. I rubbed my hands over my face and sighed.

"I wasn't trying to sound ungrateful." A deep sense of guilt pulsed through me. "It's just I've never had anything handed to me and I'm not looking to change that now."

"So then if you don't want me giving you anything, what do you want from me?" His voice was hasty.

"I didn't say I *don't* want anything," I corrected. The memory of how he acted when I simply went to Portland with my friends entered my mind. "Even if I were to take your money and leave what would you do while I was in New York?"

There was a long pause. I peeked at him through my fingers, then he suddenly shrugged.

"I suppose I would be going with you."

I dropped my hands, staring at him dumbfounded. "And do what?" I growled. "Sit inside the hotel for days watching TV?"

"You're not flying alone."

I felt my blood start to boil and thought for a second about making a witty remark, but realized it wasn't worth the fight.

"Since we're discussing flying have you ever thought about asking your friend Jennifer to come out for a visit?"

I glared at him, suspicious, trying to understand where this had suddenly come from. Even more so after he way he had acted when I mentioned her ever seeing him. "No. It has never crossed my mind."

His expression was carefully bright and positive; only adding to my suspicion.

"Well, there is still time before it gets really cold and prevents you from showing her around. Why not have her come? I bet she would enjoy seeing the bridge you have considered jumping from," he laughed.

Again I glared at him. I thought it over for a short minute before deciding it wasn't a bad idea and truthfully I was missing her.

"I'll talk it over with Bobbie first."

"Good," he said smugly.

His cockiness irritated me causing me to consider responding with sarcasm. Then it hit me that I had no idea why he was even here.

"Why are you here, anyway? We have one more day of the sunlight."

He flashed a wide grin, showing off his teeth. "Just because I can't be here during the day doesn't mean I have to sleep alone. I'll be out of your room long before Bobbie even knows I'm here."

I glared at him and stood from the chair, not saying a word. I picked up my dishes, Sean was already leaning against the counter, his arms crossed over his chest, a cocky grin on his face.

"You're not going to make me go another night without you, are you?" he purred when I reached his side.

My eyes narrowed. "What difference does it make, you don't sleep, anyway. Besides, doesn't separation make the heart grow fonder?"

He laughed, leaning in close to me, letting his ice cold breath lightly brush along my cheek.

"My cold, silent heart has belonged to you since the night I carried you out of the cabin so separation is nothing more than an irritation I can live without." He paused, crossing his wrist and offered them to me. "If you would much whether have another night to yourself then I suppose you had better drag me out and chain me to a tree."

Oh right, I thought bitterly. Like I could drag you anywhere. Yep, his head is still as thick as his accent!

"Okay!" I snapped. "The vampire can stay."

He kissed my cheek then quickly disappeared out of the room before I could throw something at him. I had planned to wash up the dishes, instead I continued to growl at the empty room while I walked back to the table, picking up the folder, and then turned off the light and headed up the stairs.

The next afternoon I had everything I could do in the house done. I didn't feel mellow enough to watch TV or play the keyboard. I considered calling Jen to ask if she could visit, but then realized it was two hours later in Kansas and she would be at work. So then reading it is. I headed up the stairs.

I walked in my room wondering if I could even sit for a long period of time, let alone read. Then suddenly the brass key Becca had given me seemed to glisten, capturing my attention. I could play a real piano! I stared at it, biting my lip. I don't know how long I stood there weighing out the pros against the cons ----- giving in to the temptation of gliding my fingers across the smooth ivory, versus staying here so I wouldn't have to drive Sean's truck again. Twenty minutes maybe. The pros were valid while the cons were not.

The sun was still out, keeping Sean trapped, giving me the opportunity to leave the truck here and walk. He wouldn't know anything, as surely I would be back long before it was dark enough for him toget here.

I snatched the key and the folder off the table and ran down the stairs. Because I had been lost in my scheming I wasn't aware Bobbie was home till she appeared in the kitchen doorway.

"Where's the fire?" she laughed.

"Oh." I huffed a breath, as her sudden appearance startled me. "I was just on my way to the banquet hall."

"Is there something going on today?" Confusion colored her tone.

I had no idea if she was supposed to know about the upcoming party, as Becca never told me it was a secret to anyone aside from Mrs. Wilkins.

Besides, could I really keep secrets from my roommate? She doesn't know Sean stays here, I reminded myself.

"Ummm … no. I have been asked to play the piano so I wanted to get some practice in."

"Is Mrs. Callenger planning another fundraiser?" She could see I was in a bit of a hurry. "Never mind, we can talk when you get home."

"Kay, thanks." I quickly yanked open the door and ran out on the porch.

The inside of the banquet hall reminded me of a high school cafeteria only without all the long tables and the chairs. The piano sat near the corner of the back wall.

Anxious to touch the keys I rushed to it and sat down on the bench. I pulled the first sheet of music out of the folder, placed it at the top of the keys and began playing the first few notes. I was a little rusty, as I knew I would be in the country-western and pop influence technique. Because of how long I had been out of practice I was extremely grateful Becca gave me a couple of months before I *really* had to play. I stopped and restarted the song a few times before it finally came out right.

"Well, hello," came an unexpected voice.

My fingers froze the same instant my head snapped up. A tall, older gentleman stood a ways from me, his eyes watching me closely. My heart pounded, wildly as I stared back at him. He wasn't anyone I had met before, yet there was an odd familiarity in his face.

"Um … hello," I answered weakly.

"You must be Angel Johanson."

I was taken by surprise when he didn't use my full name, as most of the people here did when they met me. "Yes I am," I verified.

He relaxed his stance, slowly making his way to the center of the room. "I'm Mayor Dean Wilkins. It's nice to finally have the chance to meet the girl everyone talks so much about," he said with a smile.

Now I understood why his face was oddly familiar. He looked a little like John, he was slightly taller, gray was starting to streak his hair, his face still looked young, aside from the crow's-feet around his eyes.

I tried to respond, but my voice had evaded me.

"I'm sorry for startling you," he continued. "I saw the door open as I was passing by and stopped to check things out."

"It's all right." My voice was shaky as I still hadn't gotten my heart calmed. "I wasn't expecting anyone to come here."

"To be honest, I figured it was you when I heard the music flow through the door. You play beautifully, Angel. I am glad Becca suggested you for this project and that you decided to take the offer. Did she mention you would be paid for your time?"

"Thank you, Mayor Wilkins, and no she didn't."

"Well I certainly can't have talent like yours play for my wife and not compensate you for your time. Since I now know what everyone will hear I may have to pay just a bit more."

"That won't be necessary, as I'm happy to do it," I blushed.

"Now, Angel, nothing around here goes without proper payment."

"Yes sir," I whispered.

He nodded his head at me. "I'm going to run along now so you can carry on. Again, it was nice meeting you." He turned, walking to the door then stopped. "I am deeply sorry for what happened to you and your friend." He said over his shoulder. "You should know Mike did everything he could to get justice for you girls." He never gave me the chance to respond, walking to the door.

I watched in awe as he disappeared through it.

It was nearly dark when I finally decided to quit practicing. I nearly ran home so Sean wouldn't catch me out without the truck. The last thing I wanted was to hear his complaints about my walking. Especially after dark. I hadn't seen or gotten any more calls from John in months, Sean was still somehow convinced my run-ins with him were far from over.

There wasn't anyone home when I got there. I breathed a sigh of relief as I unlocked the door and went inside. Figuring I still had a while before Sean arrived I headed up the stairs for a shower.

It was raining heavily when I woke the next morning. Again, I was anxious to get to the hall for a few hours of practice. Because it was raining so heavily I sat down at the table with a bowl of cereal while I waited for it to slow. Sean had taken the truck when he left this morning and I was thankful Bobbie was at home. I could just drive her car.

Finally, the rain stopped. I quickly shoved my arms through the sleeves of my jacket, grabbed the folder off the table and rushed out the door.

I walked out of the house and less than a second later a black Harley-Davison motorcycle pulled up in front of the house with a blue SUV behind it. The driver of the bike was Kelsey, the driver of the other befuddled me. Which member of her family would drive that and why would they follow her here?

Kelsey was off the bike and was walking to the porch before I even reached the stairs. Sean was just getting out of the SUV by the time I met Kelsey on the sidewalk.

"What do you think, songbird?" he asked, excitement filling his tone.

"What is this?" I asked when I reached the front of the SUV.

"It's yours," he stated, his tone sounding as if I should have known that.

"Mine?" I mouthed. Is he out of his mind?

I stepped closer to him, peeking inside the open driver door. The inside smelled of new interior, the seats were just a shade lighter than the body of the SUV. Sean reached out, taking my hand and pulled me around the door.

"I had the color made in Sapphire with metallic flakes," he informed me.

I looked up at him, intending to make some kind of sarcastic remark, his face was closer than I thought. His pretty blue eyes were smoldering, an angelic smile on his lips. I opened my mouth, but couldn't remember what witty remark I wanted to make.

Sean never gave me a chance to recover, he placed his cold marble lips on mine and wrapped his arms around my waist.

"Ahem." Kelsey cleared her throat loudly behind us.

Sean's lips didn't leave mine though I felt them form a smile. He kissed me one more time, and then pulled away. He started talking before I was coherent.

"Your new car is a Toyota Highlander. It's not as big or as durable as the truck, but I am promised it will keep you safe should you become involved in an accident."

I scowled at him. "I'm *not* that fragile."

He reached inside the vehicle, pulling the key from the ignition and continued on, as if I hadn't said a thing.

"It is fully loaded with driver and front passenger mounted airbags, as well as driver knee airbags. This little box ..." He held it up for me to see. "... has a start button and a panic button."

I frowned, unhappily. "That's kind of lazy, isn't it?"

His eyes widened innocently. "Wouldn't you like it to be warm when you get in?"

I slowly shook my head back and forth. And again, he ignored me.

"Climb in and take a closer look," he suggested.

He turned on his heels and walked around to the passenger side. I watched him for a second in awe then flashed my eyes to Kelsey's face.

"Is he serious?" I asked, completely astonished.

She had an apologetic look on her face. "I warned him he should have talked this over with you, but you know my brother."

Sean was in the passenger seat, waiting almost impatiently for me to join him. I released a slow breath as I climbed inside.

"This has a built-in GPS," Sean began as he pointed a long index finger at the dash. "I have already programmed Bobbie's address." He pushed a button on the built-in monitor, turning it on. "All you have to do is type in where you're going, the computer will map out the route for you."

He put his address in and a second later a map appeared, showing the names of the streets around Bobbie's house.

"What's wrong with reading a map?" I asked, incredulous.

It was now impatience began to show on his face.

"I would much rather you weren't trying to drive and read, too," he growled. "Do you know how many accidents Jonah sees because the roads are slick and drivers are not paying attention?"

"All right," I sputtered.

Kelsey laughed.

Sean glared at me, holding my eyes. "If you need to call someone the SUV has a hands-free phone with voice command. There are also buttons for it on the steering wheel."

His eyes finally released me, I quickly looked down to regain control of my scattered thoughts and my breath.

"I have also programmed all the numbers you will need," he continued.

I closed my eyes, concentrating on taking slow, deep breaths. I heard Sean call out his own name and less than a second later a phone rang.

"You have never said what you think about all of this," he suddenly said.

I slowly wrenched back my eyelids to stare at the steering wheel.

"I think you have finally outdone yourself," I answered softly.

"Would you much more prefer to continue driving the truck?" he growled.

"No." The word came out in an automatic response. I sucked in another deep breath, releasing it slowly and tried again. This time calmly. "No, I wouldn't."

I looked at Kelsey for help, she just rolled her eyes.

"Angel, I have to be getting back. Would you be opposed to taking his demanding self home?"

"No," I breathed. "it'll give me a chance to try out Sean's fancy gadgets."

"Have fun with that ... and *him*," she said sourly. "I will see you later."

She leaned in, wrapping her stone arms around me, giving my body a gentle squeeze, and then turned on her heels, walking to her bike.

"Have you talked to Jennifer about her visit, yet?" Sean asked as Kelsey's taillights disappeared.

"No," I said, shamefaced.

"Why not?" His voiced sounded offended.

"She's busy making plans to see her dad before he gets married." I paused, turning my eyes to his face. "Why are you suddenly so interested in my seeing her?"

He stared back at me, his face showed no trace of anything but morbid curiosity. "I just thought it would be a nice gesture, as I know how much you miss her."

As much as I hated it he had me there. Maybe I still needed that therapist, as I was now seeming to question his motives when he wasn't clearly being anything but thoughtful.

We sat there in silence, both not seeming to know what to say. After a long lapse Sean freed me from the SUV. Since he was here I gave up the idea about playing the piano, watching TV, instead. I offered to drive him home before I ate dinner and showered. He rolled his eyes at me, stating he wasn't planning to leave and if he was he runs faster than I drive. I had to restrain myself from sticking my tongue out at him, like a six-year-old.

My nerves were rattled when I drove to the diner Monday evening. I hadn't had any hostile conversations with Kyle for weeks, but I was sure they would start again. Bobbie had told Brandi about my car and I was sure the gossip had spread throughout the diner.

Kloe's jeep was still in the parking lot when I pulled in. I parked next to her, worried something was wrong. She's never here this late in the day. I got out, nearly running to the building to get out of the rain. Kerri was the only one in the dining room, she was moving chairs and sweeping under a table.

"Good evening, Angel," she greeted me.

"Hi, Kerri. Why is Kloe still here?"

She shrugged. "Something about inventory, I guess."

I shook out of my jacket as I walked in the back. Kloe was mindlessly walking around the room, stopping occasionally to stare at a shelf. She had a clip-board in her hands.

"Are we short on something?" I asked as I walked to the time clock.

"No," she said. She looked down at the board and wrote something on the paper. "I do this once a year to see if I need to order more dishes or cookware."

"Okay," I said, sounding indifferent.

Kloe left an hour later, sending Sydney home because we weren't busy. Since we didn't have any customers we all decided to give the diner a complete wash down. Brandi and Kyle worked on cleaning the grill area while Kerri and I washed down all the tables and swept and mopped the floors before finally moving on to the prep room.

I carried a tub full of dishes in the dish room and began loading the dishwasher. I caught the sound of footsteps long before a voice appeared behind me.

"Angel?" Kyle asked.

His tone was friendly, yet I wasn't ready to face him.

"Yes?"

"I want to apologize to you." I heard the sincerity in his voice and it surprised me.

I turned then, slowly, almost unwillingly. "For?"

"I wasn't fair to you about the whole Sean thing. *If* he really makes you happy then I'm all for it."

So now we have resorted to reverse psychology?

"Why the sudden change of heart?" I asked, suspiciously.

His face fell a tiny bit, his brown eyes full of sorrow. "I don't want our friendship ruined, Angel. And anyways, I took your advice about Catlyn."

"And?" I urged.

He smirked at me. "As usual, you were right."

I couldn't hold back the sudden laughter that consumed me. "Your apology is accepted."

He shook his head at me, a wide grin on his face, and walked away.

I turned back to the dishwasher feeling proud of myself. He didn't say they were dating, but I had a strong feeling they soon would be. Once the dishwasher was loaded I walked back in the prep room to finish helping Kerri.

I drove home with more confidence than I've ever had in my life. Sean and I had gotten our relationship back on track and everyone was finally beginning to accept it. There were no longer questions I couldn't answer nor did I face working in a hostile environment.

I pushed my Luke Bryan CD into the stereo and turned up the volume, singing along loudly. For the first time in my life I was at peace with my fate and deliriously happy.

Suspicion

The sky was so deeply hidden behind the dark, gray wall of clouds that it was hard to believe the sun had been out at all. After the long drive to take Jen back to the airport my heart felt as heavy as a single one of the rain clouds.

"You've been exceptionally quiet," Sean observed. "Are you all right?"

"No, but I will be."

"Are you sad that you didn't go back with her?"

"I couldn't be more relieved to never have to go back there. It's just sad to think that after this we may never have the chance to be together again."

He raised one eyebrow at me. I sighed heavily, turning my face toward the window. It was always nerve racking that his eyes were almost never on the road when he drove, seeing any tears escape my eyes would only cause panic ----- on my part, anyway.

"Jennifer is more ... excepting of her dad's new life than I would have ever thought she would be."

Sean laughed. "That's the thing about the humans. They can adjust to changes pretty quickly. Take everything you have been through, you survived all the changes and you're doing well, all things considered. I saw the way you two were together the last four days and I promise this isn't the end."

I knew he was right, though here and now it certainly felt like the end. She did try to pressure me into agreeing to return to Kansas for Thanksgiving. I tried being crafty in my response, as I reminded her of the surprise party I had been hired to play the piano for.

It really wasn't that part of our conversation I kept playing over in my mind, slowly convincing me our lives have changed so much our paths were no longer parallel, nor would they ever be again.

This morning the sun had come out and we'd gone for a walk along the shore under the bridge. She'd also wanted some time alone with me before she had to leave and that was easily arranged. Bobbie left to spend the day with Josh and Sean fabricated a job he still had to do for Jonah. That was the part Jen appeared to struggle the most with; Sean's dad was a sheriff deputy.

Jen and I ambled along the path, trying to stay out of the way of people riding their bikes. Though it was cool and kind of early everyone was getting those moments of freedom and exercise in before the rain returned. The air was heavy with moisture, but Jen never complained about how our last moments were spent.

"You know, Angel, Sean is really something," Jen said, looking out at the crashing waves as she spoke.

"He's something all right," I agreed.

"Don't be like that," she scolded me. "He really cares a lot about you."

"I take it you like him," I mumbled, keeping my eyes on a couple of joggers as they were heading towards us.

"Very much so," she said, her tone approving. "he looks good on you. I have to say Bobbie wasn't kidding, he's extremely gorgeous. And leave it to you to be the lucky one to have him." She pretended to be offended and I laughed.

The conversation ended, both seeming to enjoy our surroundings. I knew something was weighing on her mind when I saw the corners of her lips tug into a frown. I was content with the silence, giving her the time she needed before telling me what was on her mind. The minutes ticked by.

"I was surprised when you called and asked me to come out here. I'm glad you did."

I was completely oblivious to where she was leading me. "I couldn't be more happier that you did."

Jen sighed, not meeting my gaze. "I have decided on something and this gives me the opportunity to tell you in person."

"What's going on?" I asked, anxious now. "Has something happened?"

"It's not bad." She shook her head. "I've been accepted to the University of Texas and after going to see Dad before he gets married I have decided to take their offer. I not only get to move forward in my life, but I can also use the time to spend with him, as well as get to know Linda."

I felt the shock on my face before I heard it in my voice.

"Really? That's great!" I knew my voice had more enthusiasm then what she was looking for when she gave me a dirty look. "What made you finally decide?" I asked, ignoring her glare.

"It all starts with you." Jen's face was apologetic now.

"How does any of your decisions relate to me?"

She continued to stare at me, her lips pressed together in a hard line. I looked away to focus on where we were going.

"To be perfectly honest here, Angel," Jen finally said. "I was hoping your life was really miserable then I could talk you into leaving with me today."

"What a rotten thing to say!" I yelled. Everyone within a five-foot radius turned to look at me.

"Now hold on a minute," she growled. "there's no need to get all testy. It's not as bad as it sounds."

There was nowhere to look now without meeting curious eyes.

"How is it not!?" I demanded.

"I never said I *didn't* want you happy," she said, defensively. "I can clearly see it's not and you're surrounded by people who care a great deal about you. Therefore, I can leave you behind and go on with my own plans."

"That's nice to know," I stated bitterly. "but I still don't see what any of this has to do with me."

"Because fear has a way of stopping us from doing what we want."

I waited, almost impatiently for her to say something that made sense. The seconds passed.

"I was considering going to PSU (Pittsburg State University) later this year," she finally continued.

"whether than taking the acceptance from Texas. I couldn't have lived with myself if I left and Scott or one of his shadows did something to you."

"How does my leaving help you overcome your fears?" I asked quickly. There was a flutter in my stomach. I'd forgotten how much she didn't know; my abduction, Amanda's death or the reason Scott, nor any of his storm troopers have found me. This had never been a problem before. Until now, there had never been a secret I couldn't tell her.

She laughed, and then gestured toward the open spot in front of us, stretching to the gray caped water.

"You bought a plane ticket to almost nowhere with nothing more than a backpack. Now look, you're surrounded by this beautiful place, even if it does rain a lot. You have a brand new SUV, a much better life and a superrich ----- yet extremely gorgeous boyfriend."

I laughed, though the sound was closer to being bitter than humorous. "I hope you don't honestly believe I have chosen to stay here for the things he can give me."

"You'd be crazy not to," she countered.

Other than her worries about me, she was happy. Her eyes shined when she talked about Texas. Her life was full and satisfying. She wouldn't miss me much, even now …

Sean's icy fingers brushed against my cheek. I looked up, blinking wildly, slowly resurfacing back to the present. He leaned across the seat and kissed my forehead.

"We're home, songbird. I know it's late, but time to awake."

We were stopped in front of Bobbie's house. The porch light was on and the only other vehicle parked there was mine. As I examined the house a deep sense of dread washed over me. Sean took my keys and unlocked the door. Without even a second thought for a shower or food I trudged up the stairs to my room.

I was having a rough week. After Jen left it took a few days for me to get back to myself. I knew essentially nothing had changed, yet nothing was quite the same. I found myself spending more time than usual with Sean's family.

The party for the Mayor's wife was only a few weeks away and I still had a number of songs on Becca's playlist I hadn't gotten to. It was foolish for me to waste this time just sitting around their house when I could have been practicing. I wasn't helpless, nor in any danger so I couldn't understand why I had to be under anyone's watchful eyes.

But no one would listen to me.

Jonah had said, "I know how important playing the piano is to you, Angel. I think it's just as essential that you spend some time here, as it is equally important you have time to see and understand Sean's world."

Becca had said, "Please don't be so anxious. Everything you are working for will turn out." And then she'd given my shoulders a gentle squeeze before kissing my forehead.

I'd hoped Kelsey would at least take my side. She wasn't much help in my defense.

She rolled her eyes and said, "I am deeply offended. You would honestly whether be around your humans than here with us?"

I eventually gave up, tolerating Sean's nonchalant behavior. Mental note to self; *never* allow Sean to see you depressed again.

All in all a very rough week. But today there was finally a break from the nonsense. They were going to be leaving early Friday morning.

Even as the news was better than music to my ears I was still irritated with Sean's behaviors when he drove me to work Thursday afternoon.

"This is ridiculous," I complained.

"I'm staying in town with you tonight, end of discussion," he told me flatly.

"Sean," I nearly snarled. "you're leaving before first light so wouldn't it be easier if you were at home? I'm sure this may be difficult for you to understand, but I am not so fragile that I will fall apart because you're not here."

His lips curved up at the corners. "Are you sure? Humans tend to be supplicate where their feelings are concerned."

"Well thank you for the psychoanalysis, Dr. Callenger." Heavy sarcasm.

He grinned, suddenly amused. "You're welcome. Look, I only want to spend these last few hours with you before I leave." He paused to lay a hand over his heart. "Five days is a long time for one to be away from his love."

I let out a hiss of breath and opened the door. "Bye, Sean." I jumped out of the truck, slamming the door behind me.

Figuring I had several hours I could put into piano practices I awoke just before day break to see Sean out. I had to fight the excitement threatening to consume me and pretended to be sad when I all but kicked him out the door to go fill his needs with his family. I think he saw through my phony pretenses. Though only a little.

Now I had an empty Friday to practice on the piano after my morning shift at the diner. Because I didn't want to be early for work, I ate my breakfast slowly while reading over the newspaper. Then, when I'd washed the dishes I cleaned up the kitchen, grabbed the folder from my room and slipped out of the house.

The weekend passed uneventful. I bounced in almost agitation everyday waiting for my shifts to end so I could get to the banquet hall. I got an unusual sight after I entered the house Sunday evening. Bobbie was standing at the kitchen counter packing her lunch bag.

"I have to go in early tonight," she stated when she saw the confused expression on my face. "If you're hungry there's a box of pizza on the table."

I looked at the box then slid my eyes back to her face. She quickly zipped her bag, picked it up, and then rushed to the door.

"See you in the morning," she called out. Then I heard the door close.

I awoke the next morning, my stomach fluttering with a bad feeling. Unable to ignore it I rolled over and turned off the alarm. It was then I heard the rain pounding on the roof. Sigh. I hadn't been aware anyone besides me was in my room till I sat up. Sean had his back facing me and was standing in front of the table.

"Morning," I yawned. "weren't you supposed to be gone until tomorrow?"

He spoke never turning my direction. "We returned a few hours ago and I didn't want to wait until tonight to see you." He paused, finally turning to look at me. "I hope you don't get difficult with me, but I brought you something."

"Ugh!" I groaned. "Haven't you given me enough? I'm pretty sure it's my turn to buy for you."

"Angel, don't be absurd," he growled. "I'm a vampire, what material items could I possibly need?"

"The same things you seem to think I need," I complained.

His scowl turned into a wide grin. "Then you're in luck. I already have one so we're even."

I wasn't sure I wanted to know what he was going on about, I knew I'd never escape the room until he showed it to me.

"All right," I glowered. "what is it?"

He didn't answer, stepping away from the table instead. There behind where he had been standing was a stereo with the speakers sitting on each side of it.

"I'll put the speakers up later when Bobbie is gone," Sean said, shattering the now awkward silence.

"Nice," I commented, letting acid leak into my tone.

It wasn't even a second later and Sean was hovering over me. He was careful to keep his weight off of me, though I could still feel the coldness of his body through the blanket. I shivered, involuntarily.

"I thought it would be nice for you to have something to listen to your music on and you wouldn't have to use Bobbie's television to play your CD."

"You can't be serious," I mumbled.

"Well ..." He leaned down, kissing just under the bottom of my jaw. "... I guess I'll have to change your mind."

I shivered again at the feel of his ice cold breath on my skin. His iron grip encircled my wrist, dragging them over my head. His lips moved to the hollow at the base of my throat.

I stopped breathing.

"You need to breathe, Angel," he reminded me.

My lungs burned when I sucked in a breath.

"Do you mind telling me what it is about the stereo you object to?" he whispered next to my ear.

"It's unnecessary," I gasped.

He moved back to my face, shaping his lips ever so gently around mine. My heart hammered so loudly I could barely hear him laugh.

"That's debatable," he disagreed. "It is very difficult to enjoy listening to your music in here when you have it playing it downstairs."

I thought about that while his lips slowly moved along my cheek, down my throat and back up. He made the circuit numerous times before I could concentrate well enough to speak.

"I really only have one CD anyway," I said, breathless.

He smelled a victory. "Exactly." I felt his lips form a smile. "Having the stereo allows you to play your favorite radio stations so you would no longer have to use the alarm clock."

I scowled at the ceiling. "Fine, you win."

He shook with laughter. "I got to say I like how that sounds on your lips."

My body was on the verge of reacting to him the way it had in the woods and I began to worry about his reaction. I strained under his grip, fighting to get free. He didn't budge.

"You made your point," I said weakly. "May I get up now? I don't want to end up being late for work."

He laughed again, kissed the tip of my nose as he released my wrist, and then rolled to his back on the bed. I continued to lay there a second longer, catching my breath then stood up. I snatched my uniform off the top of the dresser and walked out of the room.

Work was brutal. The rain was coming down in buckets causing everything in my world to appear to move slower than usual. It had been hours since our last customer and I couldn't take standing in the empty dining room doing nothing any longer. I pulled chairs away from the tables then pulled the tables away from the walls. I swept along the baseboards and all along where the tables sat from the back of the room to the door. Brandi, Anna and Kyle stood behind the counter watching and whispering to each other, not seeming concerned I was close enough to hear them.

"Anyone know why Angel is unstable today?" Brandi asked.

"I don't," Kyle said, with a shrug. "She's been acting strange all week, like she has anxiety or something."

"Maybe it has something to do with Sean," Anna added.

From the expressions now on their faces, none of them noticed I had stopped sweeping to look at them. I felt mine twist into a scowl.

"I don't have anxiety," I nearly growled. "and just to clear up all the misunderstandings none of my actions have anything to do with Sean," I quickly added. "I'm just bored."

Kyle and Anna looked away quickly, shuffling their bodies to make themselves look busy.

Brandi threw her hands in the air, palms towards me. "Okay, there's no need to get snappy about it."

She joined Anna and walked to the kitchen doorway.

"I still say it has something to do with Sean," Anna muttered under her breath.

I glared at their backs, but said nothing.

I was so glad to escape boredom, nearly running to my car. Because I was beginning to suffer with exhaustion and it was late I skipped my night practice and went home. So I was surprised by the silver Ferrari parked behind Bobbie's car when I pulled up in front of the house.

"Still just as beautiful as ever," John said, smiling.

He held out a small bouquet of roses. His smile slowly faded when I made no effort to reach for them.

"I'm sorry I haven't called," he said, shaking his head with mock sadness. "I heard you were seeing Callenger so I had to come see for myself. From what you're driving I guess it's all true."

That awful feeling I had this morning came flooding back, I started to feel uncomfortable.

"I've been dating Sean since my birthday."

"Angel, I was so sure you and I would end up together. It was the only thing that ever made sense to me. This *thing* between you and Callenger is just ... unnatural."

I'd never seen him struggle for words before, under normal circumstances I would have felt bad for him, but the way he spoke of my relationship with Sean unnerved me causing me to fight to keep my voice warm when I responded. I also wasn't aware if Bobbie knew he was here and certainly didn't want this turning into an argument and pull her from inside the house.

"My relationship with Sean isn't just a phase or a crush. I am truly sorry things didn't turn out as you had hoped, as I warned you in the beginning it wouldn't."

"I'm going to be perfectly honest with you, Angel. I don't like it," he said, his tone rebellious.

"You don't have to," I snapped. "and anyways it's none of your business, John."

He glowered at me.

I waved him off and walked past him with a resigned sigh. His hand snaked out, catching my arm. He shoved the flowers against my chest and leaned in close to my face.

"This isn't over," he warned. Then kissed my cheek before walking to his car.

I quickened my steps to the door and entered the house, something stronger than fear battering recklessly against the walls of my stomach. I went straight to the trash can and dropped the flowers in it.

"Is everything all right?"

In my haste to get rid of the flowers while letting my argument with John become a distant memory I never bothered to make sure Bobbie wasn't in the kitchen.

"Yeah," I lied weakly. I turned my body carefully to look at her. She was standing by the table with her lunch bag in her hands. "It's been a long day and though that wasn't enough I just had a run-in with John."

Her brown eyes widened in horror. "Here? Just now?"

So she didn't know he was here. Great, now I have no choice but to tell Sean. Could this night get any better?

"He was waiting for me when I got here. That's where the flowers came from."

She stared at me for a long moment while she mindlessly played with the strap of her bag.

"Do you want to talk about it?' she asked, earnestly.

I hesitantly shook my head. "It's not really that important."

"Angel," Bobbie groaned. "Sean needs ..."

"I'll tell him," I said quickly. "Now, get out of here before your late."

"All right," she grumbled. "if I find out there really was something wrong ..."

"You won't," I blurted, cutting her off.

She eyed me for another long second, and then walked out.

I breathe a sigh of relief when I heard the door close. The last thing I needed was her to make something bigger out of my argument with John and tell Sean about all the problems I'd had with him months ago.

After she was gone I locked the door then headed up the stairs for what I hoped would be a soothing shower. But how long could the soothing last when I tell Sean about tonight? I banished the thoughts from my head, simply focusing on getting things together for that shower.

I was immediately pleased when I arrived at the diner the next morning. The dining room was packed, nearly every table occupied. I was taken by surprise as Marisa entered from the kitchen. She was different, her silver blond hair was cut short, her make-up she usually wore wasn't as visible. Kerri was carrying an arm load of dishes to the tub under the counter.

"Boy, am I glad to see you," Kerri called out to me.

"It looks insane in here," I laughed. I walked to her side, pulling an apron out from under the counter.

"You have no idea," Marisa said, a smirk in her tone.

I ignored her, keeping my attention to Kerri. "How long have you been busy?"

"The last couple of hours."

Now I was annoyed. "Why didn't anyone call me?"

Kerri frowned at me, unhappily. "You're already working a long shift today and after six it's only going to be you and Kyle."

"I still would have come ..." Then something she said sank in. "Wait, what? Mark is on shift tonight and I thought Anna was the other closing waitress?" I knew the last part of my statement shouldn't have been a question, yet suddenly nothing seemed to make sense.

Kerri just slightly shrugged her shoulders. "Mark is sick or something so Kloe called Kyle to cover him. She only just told him a while ago and Anna isn't going to be here tonight, she didn't say why."

"Well, that's just great," I mumbled.

"I'm only here for an hour," Marisa informed me, her tone despiteful. "Kerri leaves at six so it looks like you'll be on your own. Good luck with that."

It was now I turned, glaring at her while trying to think of something awful to say. Kerri saw my expression and reached out, patting my shoulder.

"Don't let her get to you, Angel. She's just mad because the last photographer talked her into cutting her hair and now no one is calling her for photo shoots." Her tone was friendly, but I saw her fight to hold back a laugh.

"I can see why," I grumbled.

Kerri laughed then walked away.

I was near exhaustion when Kyle and I walked out of the diner. He slipped around the corner on the opposite side, leaving me to cross the gravel lot alone. My heart instantly hammered erratically when I caught movement next to the car. The movements were much too fast, pacing? Sean caught me up in his arms before I could make sense of what was happening.

"Angel," he said, relief strong in his voice. His arms tightened around my waist, pressing me against his body, preventing me from being able to respond.

"Hi," I finally managed. "I thought you were going to wait for Bobbie to leave to come over?"

"I was," he said, pulling away. "Something has come up and I need to discuss it with you."

"Aw," I whined. "Couldn't it wait till tomorrow? All I want right now is a nice hot shower and sleep."

Sean chuckled at my reluctance. "You will get them when we're done." He held his hand out at me. "Give me your keys."

My hand instinctively curled tightly around them. I pursed my lips, deliberated, then shook my head.

"Nope. Not going to happen. I can drive the three blocks home just fine."

He raised his eyebrows in disbelief. I took a single step around him, heading for the driver's side. He might have let me pass if I hadn't stumbled over a large rock I couldn't quite see. Then again, he might not have. His arm created an inescapable cage around my waist.

"We're not going to Bobbie's. Angel, I'm not about to let you behind the wheel of a vehicle when you can't even walk without threatening to land on your face." I could smell the unbearably sweet citrus fragrance coming off his chest and began getting woozy.

"What do you mean we're not going to Bobbie's?" I objected.

He didn't answer at first; he simply bent his face to mine, brushing lips softly along my jaw. I trembled from the coldness.

"I'm taking you to my house." He enunciated the words as if he were talking to a small child.

"Sean, please," I begged.

"Give it a rest, Angel," he growled. "What I need to discuss with you is important and I don't want any interruptions."

That only brought on panic; what could be such a big deal he wouldn't want anyone to hear? There was no way around it; I couldn't resist it any longer, nor would he have released me until he got his way. I held the keys high in the air and dropped them, watching his hand flash like lightning to catch them soundlessly.

"Take it easy on my nerves and my car."

"Some trust here would be nice, Angel," he grumbled.

He walked me to the passenger side and opened the door, continuing to stand there till I was settled in the seat. He closed my door then seconds later was climbing in the driver's seat. I wanted so badly to demand him to tell me what this was about, but his eyes dark in the shadows inside the car, his expression unreadable I sat very still. And very quiet.

Sean turned down the radio causing it to barely be above background noise and sped out of the parking lot. The road was only visible in the headlights, the trees looked like a black wall. I wasn't sure what had me worried more, the thought of crashing into the trees or the way he was acting. The more I thought about it all the harder the muscles in my stomach fluttered, becoming painful.

"Sean," I spoke carefully. "would you please tell me what's going on before I panic?"

He didn't answer right away; he reached across the open space, taking my left hand and twined our fingers together.

"Everything's going to be all right," he said, condescendingly. "I've got it all under control."

I scowled at the darkness. "That's not telling me anything."

"I promise, I'll explain everything soon. Right now I just want to get you where it's safe."

I froze.

He had reacted poorly last night when I told him about John's visit, but he didn't have me scared. Had John done something to make Sean think I'm in any kind of danger? I racked my brain, thinking back over the few months when I met John. Nothing seemed out of the ordinary, nor has he ever came across as scary or dangerous. What could have changed? I looked over at Sean, he never took his attention off the road, nor showed any signs of slowing down. I waited for him to say something; he didn't. I had no choice but to let the long silence continue.

"I'm going to park inside the garage when we walk out I want you to stay near me." His voice was quiet, velvet, muted.

He turned his troubled eyes on me, clearly waiting for a response, but I couldn't speak. I sat without moving, more frightened of everything than I had ever been. I finally forced my head to nod. Seeming to be completely satisfied with my response he turned his attention back to the windshield.

Sean parked next to the truck, opened his door, and almost simultaneously was opening mine. He held out his hand to me in his normal gesture, somehow everything suddenly felt strange. I took his icy hand, not yet knowing I needed the support more than I thought. My balance was all but stable. Sean was content walking beside me with our fingers twined together until Luke appeared out of the darkness.

He then proceeded to sling me onto his back, when in place I clamped my legs and arms tightly around him. And then he was running.

He streaked through the dark and the trees like a bullet. I tried to close my eyes, but I was too terrified. Though the night was cool the forest air whipped against my face and it burned.

Then it was over. The house appeared in front of us, welcoming us with its burning lights and promises of warmth. Sean reached around, pulling me from his back and gently set me on my feet. He released every part of me but my hand, walking us up on the porch.

"I'm sure you're hungry," he said, opening the door for me. "go on to the kitchen and make yourself something to eat. I'll be behind you in a minute."

I watched, bewildered, as he disappeared up the staircase. The uneasy feeling I'd had all night suddenly felt as though it would consume me. I planted my feet, balling my hands into fist at my sides. It took a few seconds of breathing deeply for me to force my legs to move.

I was replacing the contents for making a sandwich on the shelf inside the fridge when Sean entered the room. He had my Dolphins jersey and a pair of sweats in one hand, my toiletry bag in the other.

"I had Kelsey retrieve a few of your things from Bobbie's house." He laid my things on the island in front of him.

"Are you ever going to tell me what all this is about?"

He stared at me with an unfathomable expression, sighing deeply. "Jeremy has escaped from prison."

My knees must have started to shake because the walls were suddenly wobbling. I could hear the blood pounding faster than normal behind my ears. Sean's lips were moving, though I couldn't hear his words or simply understand them. I don't think it was even a second and Sean was taking me in his arms, carefully pressing me against his marble body.

"It's going to be all right," he reassured me. "I'm here, you're completely safe."

I suddenly felt foolish for my actions, as I've been taught to never show weakness. I slowly began to try pulling myself free of his arms. Sean reluctantly released me, watching me intensely. I eyed the sandwich I had made, feeling my appetite disappear. I wasn't ready to look at Sean's face and kept my eyes down while I spoke.

"When did he get free?" Try as I might to sound in control of myself my voice broke anyway.

Sean reached around me, pushing the plate holding the sandwich in front of me. "You eat and I'll talk."

It was then I looked up at him, instantly regretting it. His mood shifted; his eyes turned brooding. I quickly looked away, slowly picking up the sandwich. Sean waited till I took a bite from it to speak.

"We received word about it tonight, but it was two days ago."

I let that turn over in my mind while I took another bite of the sandwich.

"And you're convinced he's on his way here?"

"It's a possibility we are considering," he answered, hesitantly.

Sean's sharp eyes noticed I didn't have a glass on the island. He took a glass from the cabinet and walked to the refrigerator. He poured milk in it then handed it to me.

"Why would he risk coming back here?" I asked. I didn't realize I was thirsty till I took the glass. I gulped down nearly half before setting the glass on the island counter.

A low growl rumbled from deep inside Sean's chest. "To tie up his loose ends. You are his only surviving victim."

I thought about that for a second then shook my head. "That doesn't seem right," I disagreed. "He didn't find me here, he *brought* me here. Therefore, he couldn't know I would still be here and I can't see him risking everything to come back. Especially after his encounter with Luke."

The image of Luke entered my mind causing an involuntary shiver to cast down my spine. I couldn't for even a second imagine anyone wanting to cross him; let alone a second time.

"We believe that's the point. He knows you're still here."

Now I was confused. "How?"

Sean's eyes narrowed into slits. "You don't believe John Wilkins's visit last night was simply coincidental, do you?"

John's last words flashed through my mind causing my eyes to widen in horror. "John's a criminal lawyer, he would never participate in any harm coming to me."

"Maybe not," Sean hedged. "He certainly would if he thought it was a way to get back at me."

I couldn't argue with that, especially when I *knew* how much John loathe Sean and the idea of us together. I picked up my glass, drank down the rest of the milk then collected the plate before turning to the sink. I may have no longer been able to see Sean's expressions, but I could feel his blue eyes boring into my back. Figuring I could use washing the dishes as a reason not to turn around I poured soap over them, and then turned on the water.

"Okay," I said, my voice unsteady. "let's say hypothetically that you're right. What do you suggest I do?"

"It's going to take a few days with how your schedule is to get things lined out, but I'm currently arranging everything so that you stay out here with me."

I was shaking my head before he finished. "Jeremy was cleaver enough to navigate undetected for however long he held Amanda and I captive in the cabin and you only caught him because of the blood he spilled in it, therefore he can clearly do it again. If you truly believe he's coming back for me then keeping me out here is a bad idea."

"That's exactly my point, Angel," Sean growled. "if he wants you then he'll have to find his way around. If you stay in town he will have no trouble finding you, as Wilkins knows everywhere you go, except here. Corbin is a smart and brutal man, he's not going to offer you a cab ride this time. I can keep you protected from both of them out here, if you stay in town ..." his words trailed off, ending in a snarl.

I cringed at his statement, continuing to wash and rinse off the dishes. It was quiet while I laid the dishes on the towel. I knew Sean was waiting for me to look at him before he went on. I turned off the water then slowly, almost unwillingly turned around. Sean picked up a hand towel and tossed it to me.

"I am accustomed to smart, brutal men and I've already spent enough of my life being afraid."

"Which is why you need to be here," he countered. "There are seven of us, Angel. He's not going to make it out this far, let alone anywhere near here."

"Sean," I said his name carefully. "I'm not going to let some prison escapee intimidate me or make me afraid to walk out of the house."

His eyes instantly turned black as he rubbed a hand over his forehead. "*Dammit*, Angel! Now is not the time for you to be difficult or become hardheaded."

I let out a quiet breath, slowly walking around the island, putting distance between us.

"Must you really use that language?" I fumed. "And for the record I'm not being difficult or hardheaded. I'm just simply taking back control of my life."

He stared at me, frustration clear on his face. "It's only just possible to take bravery to the point where it becomes insanity."

"What's that supposed to mean?" I asked, irked.

He exhaled angrily and looked away for a moment. "There isn't just one I have to battle here and I can't protect you in town." He looked back at me, the frustration was now in his eyes. "The only option we have is going to be to kill Jeremy."

That didn't sink in right away.

"Sean, I can't just stop my life ... wait, what?"

Sean sighed and rolled his eyes. "I'm sorry, Angel, I truly am. Sometimes there aren't other options."

I waved off that explanation. "We'll get to that problem in a minute. Did you just say you're going to kill Jeremy?"

He slowly nodded his head.

My eyes widened in their sockets. "Sean, you can't!" I yelled. "What happened to your 'thou shall not kill' rule?"

Sean flashed a grin, showing off his perfect teeth. "We're not going to consume his blood, Angel," he said with a chuckle. "We can't take the chance that he may expose us, either."

Now I was confused. "How did you keep that from happening the first time?"

"Since Luke was all he remembered he was considered insane." Sean's voice was unemotional.

"Wouldn't that still hold up? I mean, now he's in extra trouble for the escape."

Sean only shook his head. "This time he stands to face all of us. With Jonah being law enforcement he would not only have to prove Jeremy's accusation false, he would also be subjected to his peers and a Judge. With Wilkins in the mix how well do you think he'd fare?"

I turned my eyes away from his face, my mind picturing the faces of his family. Even though I have wished someone would kick Luke's behind sometimes when he's irritating everyone I couldn't stand the thought of any one of them being forced back into the darkness. The idea they stood a chance of being exposed for what they were because of something that started with me was unbearable.

"There has to be another way of ending this." I flashed my eyes back to Sean's face. "I will not be responsible for the destruction of your family."

In a move too fast for my eyes to catch Sean was in front of me, placing both of his hands on each side of my face.

"Angelia," he said, his accent rich. "this is not your fault. You never asked for any of this."

I opened my mouth to protest, he quickly placed a cold hand over it. I stared at him, helpless. His face was hard, his eyes were jet black and looked, as if they would burst into flames at any second. When he was sure I wouldn't try arguing again he removed his hand then traced his index finger under my eye.

"You look tired," he said softly.

"You're seriously expecting me to sleep after what you told me?" I was appalled.

News flash, I don't think so! My mind screamed.

Sean's hard expression suddenly turned teasingly outraged. "If you're not interested in sleeping yet, then I suppose after your shower I could find ways to entertain myself, as well as help your body relax."

I opened my mouth to make a witty remark, and then the meaning of his words sank in.

"For someone who says physical intimacy isn't possible," I grumbled. "sure likes to tread in dangerous waters."

He laughed loudly, the sound echoing through the house causing me to cringe. "A kitten is nothing to fear."

I scowled at his perfect face. "I'm not a kitten," I hissed. "What I meant is, are you trying to find out if spontaneous combustion is possible?"

Sean rolled his eyes. "You're not going to burst into flames, Angel."

"How do you know?" I hedged. "Have you ever had your body driven to the point it becomes insane?"

He shook us with his laughter, kissed my lips ever so gently, and then released my face.

"How about you get in the shower? I promise there will be a very comfortable place for you to sleep when you're finished."

"Again with the sleep," I growled.

Sean laughed again. "I can argue this all night, it is true. However, my little human cannot."

He could see I was about to argue and he stopped me by placing an icy cold index finger against my lips.

"You can plead your case with me in the morning. Tomorrow is going to be a long, yet very stressful day for you and I need you to be well rested."

"Fine," I surrendered, reluctantly. "Just let me my things."

Sean smiled in triumphant and dropped his hand, stepping backwards to let me pass.

It wasn't till I walked away from him I noticed how truly tired I had become. I made it a few short steps and my legs folded. Sean's arm caught me around the waist seconds before my face met the floor. He stabled me a moment then placed one arm under my body, lifting me up and cradled me against his chest. My head fell against him in exhaustion making him pick up my bag and turn off the light as he walked out of the kitchen.

As much as I hated being carried for any reason I let my body relax in his arms and for the first time in days I felt completely safe.

And I'm the Difficult One

The dull light of another rainy, cloudy day woke me. I stayed horizontal, pulling the quilt over my eyes, still very groggy and dazed. I knew my attempts to remain asleep were pointless while my mind was becoming alert, as something was fighting to be remembered, breaking into my consciousness. I moaned, rolling on my side, hoping it would all just go away. And then the color of the blanket caught my attention, reminding me where I was.

I flopped over on my back and stared up at the bedpost of the colossal, king-sized bed. I had to admit I was surprised to see such a thing in a house where nobody ever slept, as I had become accustom to the family the house protected. Since the room was much larger than the average bedroom none of the other furniture had to be rearranged to fit it.

The coverlet was a soft turquoise, the frame was bronze, made of patterned wrought iron. Sculpted metal lilacs wound up the tall posts, forming a bowery lattice overhead. I had to laugh at the irony, as Sean once described my sent to him as being a meadow of lilacs.

With a contented sigh, I reached out for Sean's arm. And then last night flooded back into my awareness. My eyes widened now, I pushed back my tumbled hair and sat up. I did a quick scan of the room ----- I was alone. I tossed back the blanket and threw my legs over the edge of the bed, and then the door opened.

"Breakfast time," Sean said, a dazzling smile on his face.

He was carrying a tray in his hands, a bowl of cereal sat in the center, with a glass of orange juice and a single rose in a clear vase. I couldn't help smiling at how human he seemed.

"Very human," I teased. "You just think of everything, don't you?"

"Just of you." He grinned as he carefully sat the tray over my legs then leaned down a bit further for a leisurely kiss. "Enjoy your breakfast.

I hope you don't mind my cutting a fresh rose for you." In a flash he was around the bed and stretching out beside me.

I took the first bite, watching him as he gazed back at me, studying my every move. It suddenly made me self-conscious. I looked away, focusing on picking up the glass of juice to wash down the food so I could get him talking.

"What's on the agenda for today?" I asked.

"Hmmm ..." He kept his eyes on my face while he considered his answer. "What would you say to simply spending the day here with me?"

"I would have to say no deal. I need to get back since Bobbie knows nothing of where I am and I'm meeting with Becca and Mayor Wilkins today."

His eyes bulged at the mentioning of Wilkins. He reached in his pocket, pulling out his phone. "There is no way I'm letting you near Wilkins, I don't care which one it is," he said, his tone clipped. He picked up my left hand, shoving the phone against my palm. "You can clearly call Bobbie so she knows you're safe with me."

I was about to respond when suddenly Sean's body became statue stiff, his eyes darkening in color, focused on the doorway. I followed his gaze as my own ears caught the faint sound of a breeze flowing over the carpet. Luke entered the room less than a second later.

"You can tell Jonah Angel is fine." Sean's voice was dark.

Luke ignored him, crossing the room to my side. He leaned down and placed his icy cold, satin lips lightly on my cheek.

"How you doing little sister?" he asked, his southern accent rich.

I could feel the blank incomprehension on my face. "Great."

He laughed, the sound close to thunder then stood upright. Sean was already off the bed and standing a foot away.

"I'm sorry, little brother," Luke apologized. His tone certainly didn't sound the least bit sorry. "I know you want to handle things with Angel on your own, but Jonah thinks it's best all of us discuss this."

Sean glared at Luke, his lips moving so fast I couldn't catch any words. Suddenly feeling awkward I clutched my hand around Sean's phone, moved the tray, and then stood from the bed.

"While you two are hashing whatever this is out I'm just going to take my bowl to the kitchen," I informed them.

Neither of them looked my way or watched me exit the room.

With the exception of Cameron and Mariah Sean's family was now comfortable touching me, acting like I had always been a member of their family. My heart would hammer profoundly, I always had to fight back a cringe. Cameron and Mariah stayed a distance from me, occasionally watching if I walked in the room. Cameron wasn't much of a people person, and Mariah … well, she looked like she was in extreme pain anytime I was too close to her. So I was surprised when I exited the stairs and she was standing in the middle of the living room.

"Hello, Angel," she said in her high octave voice.

"Er … hi."

I couldn't think of anything else to say and she didn't speak. Her amethyst eyes focused on the empty bowl in my hand for a fraction of a second before turning them back to my face.

"I know this may come across as strange to you, but could I speak with you a moment?"

"About?" I urged.

"Why Luke and I are here," she whispered, the strangest expression crossing her face.

I pointed an index finger toward the ceiling. "I'm sure you can hear them better than me, but I got the feeling that is what they are fighting about."

She sighed, the sound was almost aggravated. "Yes, I clearly hear them. They have done this often over the last eight years. I know Sean is not going to allow Luke to tell you anything, that's why I came with him."

"Oh." I knew the word was useless and inadequate but I lacked a better response.

She laughed a high pitch shrill, sounding like a hyena and I cringed.

"Anyway, Jonah is requesting your appearance in the main house."

I was suddenly confused. "Why?"

Sean was suddenly standing beside me, as if he'd been there all along.

"Jeremy," he snarled. His jaw made an audible snap and I flinched.

Mariah glared at him then flashed her deep violet eyes back to me. "At least consider Jonah's request."

I nodded once, and then she turned toward the door with Luke by her side and ghosted out it.

Sean gently placed his hands on my shoulders, turning me to face him. "Angel," he fought back another snarl. "you don't have to do this. We can handle the situation without you having to worry."

"Too late for that," I mumbled under my breath. I shoved my empty bowl and the phone against his stomach. "I'm going to take a shower. Since you fixed me breakfast you get to wash dishes."

"The dishes are not important at this moment." His voice was still angry and bitingly sarcastic.

"I disagree," I glowered. "There isn't going to be anyone here and dishes left unwashed become disgusting and mold."

I stalked past him, heading for the stairs, muttering to the air the entire way.

I finished adjusting the water temperature and stepped in the shower, closing the door behind me. I stood under the steam for a long moment, letting the heat unknot the muscles in my stomach. I poured shampoo over my head and lathered it up, it wasn't even a second later and the bathroom door flew open so fast it hit the wall.

"What the *hell*!" I nearly shrieked. "Sean, have you lost your mind?"

"I could ask you the same thing," he growled. "We're going to discuss this."

"And we're back to the possessive pinhead," I hissed through my teeth. "I'm going to hear what he has to say, Sean. After all your family has done for me I owe him that much."

Since I was now irritated the shower wasn't going to offer me the comfort I was looking for. I rinsed out my hair, quickly washed down my body, and then shut off the water. I reached up, pulling down the towel laying on top of the shower doors and wrapped it tightly around me. It took a little more self-control than usual for me to push the door open carefully.

At six-three, Sean filled the doorway, and was so blatantly male. If I hadn't been irked from his attitude it would have made me smile. His face was incredulous, with a hint of anger.

"I don't see what the big deal is. It's not as though somethings going to happen to make me helpless."

"I know," he growled. "You can take care of yourself. I'm beginning to think I was wrong about you being hardheaded, this is just simply ... stupid."

My blood boiled under my skin. "Now, wait a minute -----."

"No, you wait." To emphasize his point, he pointed a long, pale index finger at me. "I'm not letting you out of my sight as long as John is still in town."

My hands automatically curled into fist at my sides. "You're not going to start taking over my life."

"So, to be stubborn, you'll ignore the obvious reasons to protect yourself because I think you should and take a chance that Wilkins might actually hurt you."

"Don't put words in my mouth," I tossed back. "I can't just hide out here and act like I'm untouchable. If you really believe these men are out to get me then you seriously can't expect me to just leave Bobbie alone."

A stunned expression crossed his face. "Why didn't you simply say this was also about Bobbie?"

"Because you were too busy handing out orders."

"We will figure something out for Bobbie, in the meantime you're still not going to see him."

"Jonah?" I said, stunned. "Well, of course I'm going to see him."

He exhaled angrily. "No, you're not."

"I just told you, you weren't going to take over my life," I reminded him.

"I don't give a *damn* what you told me. There's no way in *hell* I'm going to let you waltz out of the main house and put yourself in danger."

I knew I needed to be patient with Sean. He wasn't unreasonable, he just didn't understand why protecting Bobbie was as important to me as saving me was to him. That's why I needed to talk with Jonah, I had to make them all see the danger ----- if there was any ----- that Bobbie faced if they chose to drag me out of town. I hesitantly uncurled my hands, placing them on Sean's broad chest.

"You don't *let* me do anything. Get that straight. Next, if what you say is true then this isn't just about me. If John and Jeremy are conspiring against us, it clearly affects all of us, including Bobbie. I won't allow anything to happen to her because some overbearing baboon says I should. Now move."

And then I shoved against him, trying to push him out of my way. I knew I could not succeed alone, but he responded as I knew he would.

I stalked down the long hallway to the last set of stairs reminding myself to breathe. I went to the bed, pawing through the small suitcase Sean had open. It took a moment before realizing I didn't recognize even one article of clothing. There was a lot of cashmere sweaters in various colors, white cotton chemise to wear under them and jeans. Not just any jeans. Designer tags. Ralph Lauren; Charter Club. These were Kelsey's clothes.

"I'm guessing you have figured out she didn't pack your favorite sweats," came a soft voice.

"Has she finally gone around the bend?" I dropped the clothes on the suitcase and turned to face Sean. I intended to make a sarcastic remark, but something on his face stopped me. I swallowed a large lump and dropped my head to stare at the floor.

We were both silent for a long moment, as he walked in the room. He stopped in front of me, and then his cool finger was under my chin, coaxing my face up. His glorious eyes were agonized, they nearly took my breath away.

"Sorry. Really."

"I know," I breathed. "I have to see him, Sean." My voice turned pleading.

"Fine," he sighed. He dropped his hand to his side. "I'll go along with this. I'm not doing more than humoring you, you understand that?"

I scowled at him. "I'm not an idiot."

He chuckled, leaning into to place a soft kiss on my forehead. "I'll meet you downstairs."

I watched him walk away feeling a deep guilt for our fight. Truthfully I wasn't that anxious to talk with Jonah, but if I wasn't going to be left a choice then I had to think of Bobbie. I turned back to Kelsey's idea of a look for me, sorting out the color I could live with.

I climbed on Sean's back and buried my face into his shoulder. I never felt the jolt of his run, though I could feel the wind pass over me in a fast speed. Then what only seemed like seconds later Sean's fingers were lightly gliding over my hands.

"It's over, love," he whispered.

I carefully lifted my head and opened my eyes. We were next to the stairs leading up to the back porch. Sean effortlessly uncurled my death grip around his neck, pulled me from his back, and then gently set me on my feet.

He held my hand while we walked up on the porch and through the kitchen, around the corner to the bright dining room. Becca appeared at my side, wrapping her stone, cold arms around me. Sean released my hand, walking on to the table.

"Welcome, Angel," she said in a soft tone. "I'm so glad you agreed to join us. It is always such a pleasure to have your company."

If it weren't for the fact that I knew and loved this family that might have been creepy. Instead of cringing as I usually did I hugged her back.

"Thank you."

In the center of the room, under an turn-of-the-century chandelier, was a large, polished rectangular table surrounded by seven chairs. Jonah was suddenly at my side, holding out a chair for me at the head. I was caught by surprise at his appearance, suddenly looking around the room. The family had filed in, taking their seats, with the exception of Luke. He stood leaning against the wall behind Mariah. Jonah sat down on my left, and Sean on my right.

"Angel," Jonah said in his soft voice. "I'm sure none of this is easy for you or makes any sense to you, but thank you for coming."

I opened my mouth, never to get the chance to respond.

"Why is this even necessary?" Sean snarled. "Especially since we are still unsure of all the details."

A hiss slid between Luke's teeth. "Sean, you're making a bigger issue out of this then it is."

"Easy for you to say," Sean growled, the sound rumbling from deep in his chest. "it has never mattered to you if Mariah was human or not."

Luke's eyes turned black, in a flash he lunged at Sean. In a move much too fast for my eyes to catch Jonah was out of his chair and was placing a hand in the center of Luke's chest.

"We need to just remain clam," he said firmly. "We are not talking about Angel's renovations right now, it is too early to jump to that conclusion." He kept his eyes on Luke till he nodded his head and went back to stand next to the wall.

"It is true we don't have all the details," Jonah continued, returning to his chair. "However, you compromised everything bringing Angel here without anyone knowing of her whereabouts and I do believe she should hear all the options available should the situation become more profound."

"I told her what was safe enough," Sean growled.

I wasn't really following the conversation, as I was still stuck on the part about my "renovations".

"Hold on a minute," I said. My voice sounded half strangled. "What do you mean you're not discussing my renovations right now?"

"No!" Sean roared, loudly.

Jonah stared at him with an unfathomable expression, seeming to wait for him to calm himself before answering my question.

"Sean never wanted you to be informed of a future you face should you choose to remain with us. And, as much as I'd like to honor his wishes for you I'm afraid I simply cannot. Angel, you will eventually have to become one of us."

I felt the rush of shock cross my face, my mouth fell open, as I stared at Jonah face's. Sean let out a earsplitting roar causing me to cover my ears. Becca was suddenly beside me, placing her ice cold hands over mine to help muffle the sound. I don't know if it was seconds or minutes we sat like that. But I knew the storm was over when her hands disappeared. I carefully composed myself, keeping my eyes safely away from Sean's face.

"For the record I have no intentions of renovating my body." I paused to swallow a lump I barely noticed had formed and to keep my voice stable. "Next, could it really be certain Jeremy is coming back here?"

"No. Though I do sincerely believe coming here is the motive for his escape."

His answer confused me just as Sean's had. "If he was declared insane, why would he risk everything to come back here?"

Jonah's expression turned thoughtful when he spoke. "He may just simply want to prove he isn't insane. I'm clearly not worried about this for our protection, it is for yours. He may believe you're tied with us so he will try to use you to call us out."

"Which is exactly why I think Wilkins is in on his plans," Sean countered. "Jeremy wouldn't have any way to know for sure without someone close enough to keep watch."

I bit down on my bottom lip, letting that turn over in my mind for a second. Jonah shook his head in disagreement.

"Sean, he would never -----"

"I'm sorry," I blurted apologetically. "Let's say hypothetically that Sean is right, what can I do to prevent both Bobbie from being in danger and your family being exposed?"

Jonah raised his eyebrows at me. "I must admit the options are limited. Where Bobbie is concerned I cannot see her being hurt, as she clearly has nothing to do with the situation."

"No disrespect here, Jonah, but I disagree. *If* John is partnering with Jeremy Bobbie is very much in danger. John knows I live with her, as well as our place of work and maybe even our routines. Jeremy would use her for another piece in his game. I can't allow that to happen."

His expression turned calculating while I spoke and I instantly became nervous.

"There may be a couple of options available to us. Option one I can say with all honesty I don't like myself. It has been brought to my attention that you have been invited to Kansas for your upcoming holiday. We can get you there safely, but first you must convince Bobbie to leave for Washington."

I glared at Sean. "That is clearly not an option."

"Angel," Sean moaned in frustration. "you wouldn't be going alone. It is a better idea for us to get you out of Oregon, at least until Jeremy is contained."

"So you're fine with throwing me into a tank of sharks?" I snapped.

"Don't be so melodramatic," Sean hissed.

I ignored him, flashing my eyes back to Jonah's face.

"I have no desire to return to Kansas for any reason, more importantly Mrs. Wilkins' party is days before. I can't let anyone down ... won't," I quickly corrected.

"Angel, sweetheart," Becca said. "They will understand, as I will explain to Dean the problem you are facing."

"No!" Sean growled. "If you tell him what's going on his grandson will figure out we're onto him. We need to catch him in the same act with Jeremy."

Jonah sighed deeply. "Then I suppose that only leaves us with option two."

"Which is?" I urged.

"You remain in the other house with Sean until this is over."

I was shaking my head before he was finished. "As I have already told Sean, Jeremy was able to roam your woods undetected for who knows how long, ergo that is a very bad idea."

I briefly saw Sean and Luke share a look, Sean's lips moved, seeming to answer a question I never heard. I was on the verge of becoming uncomfortable, turning my full attention back to Jonah while fighting to keep it off my face, hoping no one sensed it.

"Besides," I continued. "What am I supposed to tell Kloe? I have to stay with Sean for who knows how long because I have a maniac who may or may not be after me? I don't think so."

"Angelia," Jonah scolded me. "We cannot protect you unless you compromise with us."

"I told you she would be difficult," Sean laughed.

I glared at him.

"We could always lock her in a cellar," Luke offered.

"Hang on a minute," Kelsey called out. "What if we do protection detail?"

"What kind of protection detail?" Jonah asked cautiously.

Every head in the room turned her direction, curiosity burned in their eyes while confusion twisted their features.

"Angel is clearly going to make this hard for all of us" ----- she met my gaze, glaring ----- "so while she's going on with her day we watch her -----." She turned her eyes back to Jonah. "This will also give us a better advantage to know what is going on in town and should John Wilkins try to get close to her again, we'll be there."

"If we're all watching her then how is there going to be anyone to keep watched on the wooded areas?" Luke asked, boredom coloring his tone.

Kelsey shrugged. "We each take shifts."

"And what happens when the sun is out or we need to feed?" Luke asked sarcastically.

Kelsey rolled her eyes. "If Sean can sit around Bobbie's house unnoticed for weeks so can the rest of us. As for our feeding, we trade off, sending two at a time."

That had Jonah and I shaking our heads. A very obvious fact forgotten in this horror entered my mind. I threw my hands out in front of me, like I was trying to stop traffic.

"Wait a minute," I blurted. "Jonah, Mike is very much aware of Jeremy's escape, right?"

"Yes," he stated. "He gets the information when I do."

I relaxed my hands, laying them on the table in front of me. "Okay, so that means I already have protection in town. I'm not going to let all of you do this alone and risk being seen or have to starve."

"Sweetheart," Becca cooed. "our family will not starve or be in any danger."

"Angel," Jonah said, calling back my focus. "Mike will be watching, however he can't keep his attention on recent activities and you at the same time."

I nodded my head in agreement. "But neither can any of you."

"Angelia," Sean moaned.

"Here's what I'm going to do," I said quickly, ignoring Sean's pleading. "I'm going to let the seven of you argue this out. Nobody knows where I am and I certainly don't want them thinking the worst. Especially Bobbie. When you come up with a plan that doesn't involve renovations on my part or hiding in the woods someone can let me know."

Sean glared at me while I stood from the chair.

"Becca, thank you for allowing me into your home."

"You're welcome, sweetheart," she said with a smile.

I pulled my keys out of my pocket while I walked to the door. Sean was there, blocking my way.

"When are you going to accept the fact that this *is* your home?"

"Sean," I groaned. "I don't want to -----"

"You're going to get lost," Luke snickered from behind me.

Startled by the sound I whirled on him. "I have a GPS!" I hissed. Then I turned back to Sean. "Move."

He stared at me for a long second then caught my face between his iron hands. "Be safe." He kissed me, and then released my face.

He walked past me and I yanked open the door, slamming it behind me.

I drove home slowly, carefully, muttering to myself the whole way. I was careful to pay attention to all the curves, I didn't want to take a trip to the emergency room if I crashed or have Sean in my ear, complaining about how I should have been paying attention. But try as I might to stay focused on the dark road my mind was spinning, analyzing what Jonah had said about my having to change. What did he mean, I have to consider it *if* I stay with Sean?

My stomach twisted as I realized that was exactly what he meant.

Sean has promised I would never have to be one of them so how was this still going to work if Jonah says I have no choice? Because I was so preoccupied by the last twenty-four hours I was taken by surprise when I pulled up in front of the house and Bobbie's car was still parked there. I shut off the engine, continuing to sit there, staring out the windshield. I needed to be calm and in control of myself before I went inside. If I didn't Bobbie would immediately pick up on my distress and I'd be in for an even longer night.

I released a slow breath, opened my door, carefully stepping out. I'd only made it halfway up the walk when the front door yanked open.

"Boy, am I glad to see you," Bobbie said, her tone full of concern. "Angel, you had me worried sick. Kyle said the last time he saw you was when you were leaving work last night."

Oy! How much should I honestly tell her? I thought it through quickly while walking up the stairs and onto the porch.

"Um ... I'm sorry. Sean caught me and I went with him and stayed over at his house."

I decided I may as well go with the truth. She knew me too well and would see through any lie I tried. She stood looking at me, a puzzled expression crossing her face.

"I thought he was gone."

"They were," I said automatically. "Their plans got changed so they came back early."

She continued to stare at me, hard. I instantly became anxious, figuring my face gave me away after all.

"Okay," she sighed. "I'm just glad you're all right."

I released the breath I hadn't realized I'd been holding and followed her in the house.

"But next time," she said, turning to face me again. "please call so I'm not getting any bad feelings, wondering if something awful has happened to you."

"You've got a deal," I assured her.

She sent me a nod, and then walked toward the kitchen. I headed up the stairs for a shower and maybe some sedatives to help me sleep.

I didn't sleep well that night. The conversations at Jonah's house raced through my mind. It still swirled dizzily, around the idea they believed Jeremy was on his way back, possibly to clear his insanity defense. The part I couldn't understand or believe was why they believed John would have any part of Jeremy's scheming. As I gradually fell closer to unconsciousness one thing certainly became evident.

Whether John was in it or not I had to protect Bobbie.

The next morning I stood in the bathroom staring at my reflection while brushing my teeth. I don't know how much time passed when my face began to blur, taking on a new image. My hair was brighter, looking more like a flame. My face was hard as stone, my eyes were cold, empty, and no longer green; they turned jet black and wild with thirst.

When it finally sank into my awareness what I was seeing my toothbrush fell from my hand causing a clatter in the sink. I blinked, wildly, shaking my head, and forced myself to look away from the mirror. My hand shook violently as I reached out to pick up my toothbrush. I laid it to rest against the sink, closing my eyes, giving myself a chance to calm down before trying again. After a long moment it worked and I opened my eyes, snatched up the toothbrush; quickly rinsed out my mouth, and then left the room.

The phone rang when I entered the kitchen. I was almost afraid to answer it, but it might have been Brandi, who was probably as worried as Bobbie had been. It was Jen and she was jubilant. Normally I would get excited with her, I wasn't feeling up to hearing the joys of her life when it felt like mine was falling apart. I *mmm'd* and *ahh'd* at all the right places hoping it would keep her pacified. The problem was I was far too distracted to be sure it was working.

"Angel, you sound like you're a million miles away. Are you all right?" she asked.

"I'm fine," I answered automatically. "I just have a lot on my mind."

"Are you and Sean having problems again?" Concern colored her tone.

"We're fine," I said reassuringly. "I'm just worn out from working and trying to get ready for the party."

"Okay," she said indifferently. "School for me is out next week and I'm going to see Mom. Should I tell her to be expecting you?"

I cringed, trying quickly to think of a crafty response. "I haven't really decided where I'm spending Thanksgiving. Sean's family has asked me to attend their festivities."

She groaned, preparing to growl something at me. I heard the front door open and seconds later Bobbie entered the kitchen with Josh right behind her. Suddenly I had a reason to end this conversation.

"I have to go, Jen. I'll call you when I know for sure what my plans are."

"Sean just walked in, didn't he?" she asked, her tone a little irate.

Josh looked at me then sent Bobbie a weary look and sat down at the table.

"No," I sighed, heavily. "Bobbie just got home, she needs to discuss something with me."

I was grabbing at straws by this point, but it was all the hope I had to get free of the conversation.

"Fine," she snarled. "I'll talk to you later."

She hung up without giving me the chance to say goodbye. I shook my head, sadly while I hung up the phone.

"Everything all right?" Bobbie asked.

"Jennifer is mad at me again. I suppose that isn't anything new these days."

She laughed.

"So, what's up?"

Josh flashed his eyes to Bobbie for a fraction of a second before speaking to me.

"We are going to drive up to Salem this evening to catch a movie and have dinner. We were wondering if maybe you'd like to go."

I pictured Sean's pissed expression for a second. "I don't know," I said, hesitantly. "It's going to be kind of late in the day."

"We can stay there for the night," Bobbie said quickly. "I know you have to work in the morning," she added before I could protest. "We'll grab breakfast and still be back before your shift."

I opened my mouth to decline their offer then thought why not? I do need to figure out how to convince Bobbie to leave for Washington a little earlier than she planned and it just might do me some good to get out of here for a while. Remember what it's like to spend time with my *human* friends.

"All right," I said, surrendering. "I'm in."

"Yay!" Bobbie chimed.

I rolled my eyes at her and laughed while I walked out of the kitchen to head up the stairs.

Overreaction

Despite my relaxing night in Salem everything still felt like I was fighting for the same survival I fought for when I left home. Everyone around me seemed more like my rival than my friends. I knew I was crazy, as I was the only one ----- besides the Callengers of course ----- that knew why John was in town now when his grandmother's party was still a couple weeks away or that Jeremy had made himself a free man.

The next morning when we returned there was a note addressed to me attached to the front door. It was from John asking me to call. Bobbie panicked, telling me I should tell Sean. This only added to the guilt I was already feeling, I never got the courage or the chance to tell her about anything. I promised I would, crumpled the note into a ball and tossed it in the waste basket.

I lay in bed not wanting to wake up. I struggled with it as my mind became more alert, focusing on my reality. The week had passed uneventful somehow and still I hadn't seen Sean at all. I couldn't even remember what day of the week I was even in, but I knew work or piano practice or something was waiting for me.

I heard the rain ping against the window and groaned, pulling a pillow over my head, trying to muffle the sound. I squeezed my eyes closed, concentrating on ignoring what I could still hear. The sound of a soft musical laugh made them effortlessly fly open.

"That's not going to help."

I knocked the pillow off my head and rolled over. Sean was sitting in the chair, a half smile crossing his lips.

"Are you trying to cause a heart attack?" I grumbled.

He shook with quiet laughter. "No. You're finally completely awake so I knew announcing my presence wouldn't cause you harm."

"Have there been a lot of false alarms?" I asked, suddenly confused.

He shrugged, lazily. "Just a couple. I thought I had awoken you when I got here, but you only mumbled something and rolled over."

It was then I looked at the clock. It was only six am. I sighed, pushed back the blanket and sat up.

"How long have you been here?"

Sean was careful with his words when he spoke. "Since eleven-thirty last night."

"Oh," I said absent mindedly.

I got off the bed, walking ever so slowly to the closet. I was only in there a second when something finally sank in. I quickly stepped out, looking at Sean.

"Eleven-thirty last night? That was a full half hour after I went to bed."

He rolled his eyes. "I wondered when that was going to catch your attention."

"Yeah, yeah," I hissed. "So Bobbie knows you're here?"

He was shaking his head before I was finished.

"But your truck ..."

"Is still in my driveway." He enunciated on the word 'my' as if I were some kind of moron. That only infuriated me and I walked back in the closet.

"Why have you been here all night?"

I could hear the frown in his voice when he answered.

"I haven't seen you since you took off like a bat-out-of-hell the other night. I figured you were angry with me and gave you a few days to calm down and focus on your conversation with Bobbie and your duties. Which by the way, brings me to another point." His voice wasn't harsh or bitter, yet I knew it well enough to hear the tenor behind the words.

I replaced the hanger back on the rod, and then stepped out of the closet.

"What did I do now?" I grumbled.

"I thought we had an understanding you would only leave town with me? Especially since no one, with maybe the exception of Wilkins, knows for certain where Jeremy is?"

I dropped my head, tossing my uniform on the bed.

"Here we go with the daddy thing again." I turned my body to face Sean, placing my hands on my hips. "Let's get something straight," I growled. "I understand the reasons your family has to take percussions. However, I don't. I've already said this once and somehow it looks like I have to say it again. I'm *not* going to let these creeps have even one ounce of control over my life. I will not be afraid to walk outside alone."

His jaw flexed as he fought to keep from speaking between clenched teeth. "I really wish you would take this situation seriously!"

"I do take this seriously," I hissed. "I know what I'm doing, you have to trust me."

"Please, Angel," he whispered.

I stared into his suddenly burning blue eyes. "Please, what?"

"Please, for me. Please make a conscious effort to keep yourself safe. I promise you I'm trying everything I can to let you do what you need to, but I would appreciate a little help. I've already resorted myself from taking Luke's advice and hold you hostage, that ought to entitle me to some compromise on your part."

He stood from the chair, crossing the room to stand in front of me and wrapped his arms around my waist.

"I would love to stay and finish arguing with you, but I've got to be getting back. Besides, I don't think you would be very happy if I stayed and you were late for work."

"Well if that isn't typical," I glowered.

That slow, cocky grin spread across his face. "What?" he asked innocently.

"You always suddenly have somewhere to be when you're not getting your way."

"Would you prefer everyone, including Bobbie knew I slip out your front door nearly every morning?"

I opened my mouth to make a witty response, he quickly leaned down, shaping his lips around mine, silencing me. I tried to maintain my level of irritation, but between his crystal blue eyes and his satin lips I couldn't. Instead, my hands slid up his chest, resting around his neck. He suddenly tightened his arms, lifting me off my feet. I wrapped my legs around him, crushing my body against his. I half expected him to break my hold while scolding me for such behavior.

I was wrong.

His lips were no longer gentle, urgency taking place of his usual control. His icy cold arms pushed me closer against him. The last time we were in this situation entered my mind, remembering how he had reacted caused my heart to skip an uneven beat. There wasn't much time for me to act. If I waited too long, I wouldn't be able to stop him. I shook my head and his mouth moved to my face, and then down my neck. My blood was boiling under the skin now, my hands were gripping his arms, my head slowly fell back, exposing my full neck. Oh, never mind! my less noble side exulted. He moved back up my neck and I raised my head, carefully till I caught his lips, again.

And then without warning Sean's lips began to move more slowly against mine and I could feel the urgency leaving his body. I tried my best to keep him from stopping, yet he reached up, effortlessly pulling my arms from around his neck, resting them above my head which was now on a pillow. When did we move?

His breathing was as erratic as mine. He kissed my forehead then my nose while releasing my wrist.

"You must never encourage my lack of self-control," he whispered.

"So now suddenly I'm supposed to be the responsible one?" I asked, breathless.

"No," he laughed softly. "but it would help. You could save us both from risking your life should things get out of hand."

My life is doomed anyway, I thought bitterly. So why bother saving it now?

"I'm not going to say I'm sorry."

He gently kissed my lips one last time and in a flash was standing by the door. "That's exactly what I'm afraid of."

I rolled over on my side, watching him open my bedroom door. He stepped out in the hall then looked back at me.

"I love you, I'll see you tonight."

I opened my mouth, but he was already gone. I grumbled at the now empty room, stood from the bed and walked to the door.

"I love you, too," I sputtered sourly.

I wasn't sure he heard me till I caught the faint sound of his laugh from somewhere in the house. I shook my head, turning to look at the clock. It was six-fifty. I had lost more time than I thought. I snatched my uniform off the bed, nearly running to the bathroom.

I pulled into the diner parking lot expecting to see Kyle's Mustang and Kerri's Kia. Instead, the lot only had a few cars on the customers side and Brandi's car was sitting in Kyle's spot. I parked next to Kerri and shut off the engine. The rain was light, but I jogged to the building, anyway.

Kerri was standing behind the counter talking with a customer while stacking jellies in the condiment dispenser. The chime on the door alerted her to my presence and her head snapped up, a smile crossing her lips.

"Good morning, Angel," she greeted me in a chipper tone.

"Morning, where's Brandi?"

"Right here," she grumbled as she entered.

"Not that it isn't nice to see you," I laughed. "but where's Kyle?"

She slightly shrugged. "All I was told was I had to come in this morning because he had some sort of family emergency."

"Where?"

"Montana," Kerri answered.

"Montana?" I gasped. "I guess he's going to be gone a while."

"Yeah," Brandi moaned. "it makes us one man down."

My brows knit in confusion. "Who's taking his place?"

Kerri quickly pointed to Brandi.

I was even more confused. "What about Anna or Marisa? Couldn't one of them trade off with you?"

"Anna doesn't know how to run the kitchen and Marisa took some personal time," Kerri explained.

"So then we're technically two men down." Then I looked at Brandi. "It seems you have a lot of doubles ahead of you. Good luck with that."

"Thanks," she grumbled. "You know, Angel, you could trade off with me until Kyle comes back."

"Oh no," I said shaking my head. I walked past her, slipping out of my jacket. She caught up with me at the time clock.

"Why not?" She sounded like a sulky child.

"First," I said, slowly turning to face her. "I already have a crazy work schedule. Secondly, I still have Mrs. Wilkins' party."

She folded her arms over her chest, a pout look on her face. "That's going to be over soon."

"True," I agreed. "though probably not before Kyle gets back and I am leaving right after the party."

"Leaving?" Brandi repeated, her voice stunned.

I laughed. "That was my reaction, too."

"Does Mom know about this?"

Kerri answered for me. "Yes." She had the dish tub full of dirty dishes in her hands. "Angel told her a few days ago."

I didn't really want to lie to Kloe about a fake trip I wasn't actually going to be taking, I knew if I didn't tell her something Sean or Jonah would and probably end up making it sound worse than what it really was.

Brandi threw her hands in the air. "That's just great! Why am I always the last to know anything?"

"I don't know," Kerri laughed. "but I have an order in the window."

"Ugh!" Brandi huffed out a breath, turning on her heels and walked away.

Kerri and I laughed, and then I went to the prep table while she took the dishes to the dishwasher.

We never got very busy so I left Kerri to run the dining room while I prepped the cooler for the night shift and cleaned up the dish room. I finished everything early and decided to leave and go home to change before going to the banquet hall. I was ready for some quiet time, as well as be alone with my thoughts.

My mind was so perplexed my fingers played mindlessly over the ivory without hesitation. There was so much going on that I was having a hard time sorting it all out. How Jeremy escaped, why John would resort to participating in Jeremy's schemes ----- if he really was ----- and last but not least, how I was going to make a final choice between who I am and who I had to be for Sean. This was by far the hardest of all of it. I mean, it wasn't exactly easy hearing a man escaped prison to settle some sort of debt, but knowing I would soon be forced to choose between the Angel I've always known and Sean's Angel. It was because I was so lost in my thoughts I never heard the door open or anyone's footsteps cross the empty room.

"I guess you really are too busy to return phone calls," came a smooth voice.

My head snapped up at the sound, I stared, wildly at the unexpected visitor. John was standing a few feet away from me, arms folded and was dressed in a dark colored three piece suit, Italian loafers on his feet. His eyes were broody and impatient. I collected myself, determined he wouldn't sense any of the fear now coursing through my body.

"Did you really think I lied to you?" My voice was strong, surprising me.

"Honestly, I did. You have never kept it a secret that you don't like me."

He walked to the front of the piano, gliding his fingers over it. I fought to keep from balling my hands into fist while I closely watched him.

"You are very talented, Angel," he continued. "It's such as shame you're letting it go to waste."

"What makes you think I'm letting it go to waste?" I was trying to keep my voice light.

"That ring on your finger isn't exactly a symbol of freedom. And, aside from you making plans to run off with Sean Callenger I don't hear about you doing anything else."

"Well, then I suppose you're not getting the right information, as I have no plans of running off with anybody anywhere."

He slowly made his way to the side of the piano, stopping a few inches from the bench.

"But you are wearing his ring, aren't you?"

I wasn't sure where he was trying to lead me, but the tone in his voice was beginning to make me uncomfortable.

"I'm guessing you didn't exactly come here to discuss my relationship with Sean so what can I do for you?"

"You could leave all this behind and run away with me," he suggested. "but I'll settle for a simple conversation."

I laughed humorlessly. "Simple has never been your strongest suit, nor has rejection ever been your redeeming quality."

"Ah, yes," he chuckled. "Well, I do have others."

"Then why haven't I ever been impressed by them?" I challenged, raising my eyebrows.

"Apparently you haven't ever been able to see past *Callenger.*" He sneered on his name.

I felt irritation start to surface and fought to suppress it, staying calm. If Sean was right about the possibility John would hurt me there were no cameras inside and because we were the only ones here I didn't want to push him into making snap decisions.

"John, I'm truly sorry if I have ..."

"I am leaving in the morning," he stated, cutting me off. "However, I will be back for my grandmother's birthday. I would like you to join me for dinner and we can discuss our little situation as I have a proposition for you."

I grimaced. "And what proposition would that be?"

"Join me for dinner and you shall find out."

His eyes flashed the same strange distinctive light I'd once seen in Jeremy's eyes. My mind remembered how that ended causing my body to slowly begin to tremble with horror, my eyes flickered away from his face for one second, to the open door. He didn't miss that. He walked behind me, his hand brushing through my hair.

"I'm not going to hurt you, as I never have so stop worrying." He paused, leaning down to sniff the scent of my shampoo. "Coconut, right?"

I had to swallow a large lump that formed in my throat to speak. "Yes." My voice wavered, I cringed internally, hoping he didn't hear it.

"Angel, I'd like for you to tell me something." His voice sounded distant like he was lost in some thought.

"What?" I barely whispered.

My heart was pounding so hard I thought I would pass out. I closed my eyes, trying to focus on keeping my breathing even. I felt his fingers graze the skin on my neck and tried not to cringe.

"Why can you fall for a joke like Callenger, but not give me the time of day?" His fingers softly slid over the skin at the bottom of my jaw, moving to graze across my right cheek.

"I didn't plan to fall for anybody. I told you I wasn't wanting to form any ties to this town, remember?" My voice cracked, reviling the fear I felt.

"But you did form those ties," he said, his tone disapproving. "If you would have bothered to spend the time getting to know me as you had found the time for him then you would have known I could make you happy. Probably even better."

At that I had to laugh, though the sound was shaky. "I doubt that when staying with one women isn't exactly how you work."

"That's true," he agreed. "However, I would gladly give it all up if you were by my side."

I felt a curl of nausea in the pit of my stomach as he spoke and I fought to keep it off my face. He didn't seem to miss that, either.

"I'm going to go before your friends join us, as I haven't meant for this to become a party. I will call you when I return to set a date and time for our dinner."

He turned abruptly on his heels and walked to the door. I tried to sigh in relief, yet every part of me was frozen in place.

My legs were heavy when I finally forced myself off the bench. I turned out all the lights, locked the door, and then walked to the car. The only thing running through my mind was a hot shower and a conversation I had to have with Bobbie; though not necessarily in that order. The night air was chilled, just the short walk from the building to the car had me feeling like I was freezing. I wrapped my arms tighter around my torso trying to lock heat inside my coat.

I nearly screamed in horror when the passenger door opened the same instant mine did. Kelsey's dark silhouette appeared in the light, as she slid easily into the seat.

"For the sake of the human heart, Kelsey," I shrieked. "Couldn't you have at least announced yourself?"

She raised one eyebrow, her voice ominous. "Angel doesn't seem to be as fearless as she wants everyone to believe." She pulled her door closed almost soundlessly.

I tossed my purse in between the seats and climbed in, slamming my door.

"I never said I was fearless," I corrected. "I simply said I wasn't going to let these creeps control my life."

She rolled her eyes, disgusted. "Same thing," she mumbled, mocking my tone.

I adjusted my seatbelt then turned my eyes on her.

"I know you can't be interested in riding anywhere with me so what do you want?"

Now she smirked at me. "Unless you want to run the entire way I have to ride with you."

I shoved the key in the ignition with more force then needed and started the car. Then something sank in. My eyes flashed quickly back to her face.

"What do you mean run with you? I'm meeting your brother, who by the way is probably already waiting for me."

"Actually he's not," she said smugly. "Jonah's got him and Cameron checking perimeters with Luke."

I eyed her carefully before finally backing out of the parking stall. "What are you and your family up to now?"

"We have a discussion to finish and since you just had a visitor the stakes have certainly just got higher."

The stakes just got higher, what does that mean? Buckle up, Angel, you're about to find out, I told myself.

"Ugh!" I groaned. "It is essential for humans to sleep."

Kelsey laughed.

I slowly pulled out of the parking lot, heading the opposite direction of home.

Kelsey changed the stations on the radio numerous times before finding a song she wanted her wind chime voice to sing along with. If I wasn't still so freaked out over John's visit her humanness might have been funny. I always thought Sean was difficult to make happy, but after spending time with his family I quickly learned it was a vampire thing. Jonah was probably the hardest to please.

When I pulled up in front of her house she instructed me to park in the garage. Although this wasn't the normal behavior I kept quiet, following her demands. The only open space was between Sean's truck and Jonah's sedan. I pulled in the spot, careful not to bump either.

I had an unsettling feeling while we walked side-by-side to the house. I expected her to grab my arm at the first opportunity and drag my slow body across the yard. She had her hands in her pockets, seeming content to let me walk my own pace. Paranoia began to sweep over me as thoughts of the last conversation I had with Jonah flashed through my mind. Since John approached me tonight does Jonah believe Sean's right and has changed his mind about waiting to turn me? Is that why he sent Sean so far away?

I fought to banish the thoughts, irritated with myself for even considering such a thing. These are *my* vampires, therefore I should be ashamed for allowing myself to believe they would. I barely got a foot on the stairs and the door opened.

"Angel," Jonah greeted me in his polite tone. "thank you for coming on such a short notice."

"Did I really have a choice?" I asked.

He laughed at my tone. "There are always choices, Angel, as well as compromises."

How do you compromise one's life? I thought sourly.

"We'll see," I said, skeptically.

Jonah held the door open till Kelsey and I entered. They passed me in a flash to join the others standing on the lower platform, nearly forming a circle, talking. They kept the words so low that even ultra-sensitive ears like mine couldn't hear them. For reasons I couldn't understand I suddenly had to fight the urge to turn and run as a panic attack swelled up in my chest, threatening to cut off my air supply.

"Ok ... ay," I said, the word half strangled. "Could someone please tell me what's going on before panic becomes hyperventilation?"

They each looked at Jonah then turned their various colored eyes on me. That certainly didn't calm the panic, they made me feel creepy, too. Jonah sighed, an apologetic look twisting his face.

"It has come to our attention that Jeremy's whereabouts were reported late last night."

I opened my mouth the same time a deep menacing roar filled the room.

"What?" he sneered, his teeth making an audible sound. Sean was already close enough to grab my hand before my eyes could focus on him. "Why haven't you said anything before now?"

"I wasn't going to drag Angel in this just yet, and then she was visited by John Wilkins tonight. Sean, I must say I believe I may have been wrong about his involvement."

My slow human eyesight never saw Sean's movements, but suddenly his arm was slipping possessively around my waist.

"Of course he's involved," Sean snarled. "He's determined to pull Angel away from me at all cost."

"We will not allow that to happen or let harm come to her," Jonah said, reassuringly.

"Where did this information come from?" Becca asked.

Jonah hesitated, eyeing Sean closely. "Colorado."

"Wait a minute," Luke said, sounding confused. "If he was seen, how is he still free?"

"He's free because he seems to be keeping himself in control by not abducting any girls. He stopped for gas in Denver and almost immediately was recognized. The police responded quickly when the gas station clerk alerted them, but by the time they arrived he was gone."

Jonah turned his body and was now facing me. "Angel, I have no doubts he's on his way here," he continued on. "I know you have no desire to formally join our family, but since it has been brought to my attention about your encounter with John Wilkins waiting may not be the best choice. You need to make a decision on which option you're willing to live with; whether it be changing yourself or staying in the other house with Sean until this is over. If you don't …"

"No! No! No!" Sean roared. He turned toward me in a flash, bending over me, his expression twisted in a rage. "I will stand between you and Jonah changing you," he shouted.

I cringed away, my hands over my ears.

"Sean, you know how it works," Jonah insisted. "You saw it with Luke and Mariah. You're choosing not to live without her and that doesn't leave me a choice."

"Jonah?" I asked, under Sean's arm.

He kept his eyes on Sean. "Yes."

"I have done nothing but think about the options you have given me and I've come up with my own compromise. I have already told Kloe I will be leaving, though not before Mrs. Wilkins' party. Once it's over I'll do anything you want."

"No," Sean growled. His jaw was strained tight, his lips curled back from his teeth.

"Angel," Jonah sighed heavily. "Jeremy may already be here by then, allowing these men to carry out their plans."

"It's a chance I have to take. Mayor Wilkins is counting on me, I'm not letting him down. Besides, I've worked too long and too hard for this."

"Are you insane?" Sean snarled. "Have you unmistakably lost your mind?"

That's a question I've been asking myself since I agreed to this relationship.

"Dearest, Angel," Becca breathed. "I so wish there were other options."

"I know, but … I have to do this."

This time it was Luke to snarl in fury.

"Do we have a deal, Jonah?" I turned to look at him.

Sean grabbed my face in his hand, forcing me to look at him. His other hand was out, palm toward Jonah.

Jonah ignored it. "If I go along with your compromise and they get to you before we can contain them I may not be able to do anything more than to change you to save your life." I wished so badly I could see his expression.

I stared at Sean's eyes, despite the fact they were jet black and threatening to burst into flames at any moment, remembering the night I saw them in the cabin for the first time. Then again in the hospital. I had come up with two options for keeping their secret. Insanity or what they would do *if* I had figured them out for myself. Then I thought about the things that had been running through my mind when John interrupted.

The difference between the Angel my friends, whom I considered family, knew and Sean's Angel. The way this future would affect their lives as well as my own and what that Angel would become.

But what if?

"An ... gel -----." My name came out of Sean's lips half strangled.

"Shh," I shushed him. "I'm trying to concentrate."

Fate.

What if there was something more powerful than the forces that turn the planet? What if this was the cards fate didn't want to show? But now the cold hard truth has revealed what it has always known?

Option three: This was where I was supposed to be. This is why I have always looked different from other people; via the emerald eyes, the paper looking skin. I was supposed to be with Sean, no matter the cost. The bond forged between us was not one that could be broken by humanity or vampirism. We were meant to be.

Was that what the vision was trying to tell me?

"Fate!"

"Angel?"

"I get it ----- fate."

"Your need for concentrating?" he asked, his voice uneven and stressed.

"Then so be it." I hoped Jonah understood; it was hard to talk the way Sean held my jaw. And, there certainly was no way of turning my head to be sure he understood. "I've already seen vampire Angel, anyway."

"No!" Sean roared. "Absolutely not!"

"I wasn't suggesting tonight," I said, hastily. "Now let go of me."

"I agree, tonight isn't a good time," Jonah stated. "The humans are unaware of where she is so if she doesn't return to Bobbie's we will have bigger problems than this."

Sean considered that for a fraction of a second. He released my face, grabbing my hand before I could escape.

"I need to speak with Angel a moment," he snarled to his family. Then he glared down at me. "Alone."

He tugged on my hand and in a flash we were across the room. I had to run to keep from getting my arm ripped off. Despite my best efforts to keep up, it felt as if my feet never touched the floor. I tried desperately to think of something I could say to at least slow him down.

Nothing.

When we reached Becca's tower he opened the door, tossing me toward the stairs, and then slammed the door behind us. I jumped at the sound, running up the stairs. I turned, almost unwillingly to look at Sean. For the first time in the months I'd known him, he looked like a true vampire. His eyes were as black as the Kansas sky at midnight.

"Would you care to explain why you never mentioned that little fact to me?"

"You seem to forget I haven't seen you in over a week. And anyways, it was nothing more than a vision, Sean."

He completely ignored me.

"Now all of the sudden you're ready to be a *monster*?" He sneered fiercely on the last word.

"I don't believe that's what I said," I fumed.

"*Dammit*, Angel," he said between clenched teeth. "Your life has more meaning then this."

I inclined my head, slowly, my hands fisted tightly on my hips. When facing a raging bull one must never wave a red flag, instead I had to try easing myself over the fence.

"If you're finished yelling at me, I'll explain everything now."

In a flash he passed me, pacing silently back and forth in front of the high curving window. His expression was calculating. I watched with growing anxiety.

"Are you really ready to spend an eternity with nothing more than a midnight sun?" he suddenly asked.

"Sean," I breathed.

He stopped pacing, his face toward me, a black fire burned in his eyes.

"Are you?" he sneered.

I stared back at him, unsure what answer he would except; even as it would have been the truth. His eyes bore into me, feeling as if they would soon burn me alive.

"No, Sean," I said carefully. "I don't want that. You heard Jonah I have to ..."

"No!" Sean roared. "I meant what I said, I will stand between you and eternal damnation."

I forgot about bulls and red flags, cutting loose.

"Enough!" I yelled. "I have allowed your overreaction long enough. You clearly don't seem interested in coming down off your high horse and let me explain anything."

His jaw tightened. "I told you in the beginning I had no intentions of letting this happen to you."

I tossed my hands in the air, angrily. "So I guess now I no longer get to make my own decisions or decide what's best for me?" I growled.

"I promise, I'll give you whatever you want. I won't give you this." His voice turned pleading.

"From the sounds of it you don't have to. Jonah seems to already have a plan."

"Angel." A growl rumbled from his chest.

I let out a hiss of breath. "You can relax, I plan to just simply stay hidden with you as I clearly don't have any plans to ..." I paused, thinking of a better way of describing what Jonah had planned for me. "... renovate my body nor am I planning to run down the stairs right now and offer Jonah or anyone else my neck."

He snarled something unintelligible, turning back to the glass. Suddenly, before I had time to blink Becca's easel went airborne, crashing into the far wall. I screamed and ran down the stairs, yanking the door out of my way. I never noticed anyone was standing there till a pair of stone, cold arms wrapped around me.

"Shh, Angel," Kelsey's soft voice was in my ear. "It's going to be all right. Luke, get up there and settle him down before he destroys the house."

She waited till he passed us to walk me down the hall to her room. Once we were inside she closed the door and leaned against it. I walked on, wrapping my arms around my torso. I was no longer hysterical, yet my chest felt like it was falling apart.

"That was quite a fight the two of you were having," she said. "Are you changing your mind about being human?" She sounded just as insulted as Sean had.

I pulled in a deep breath, and then turned slowly to face her.

"No, no I'm not. I'm quite happy being me ... most of the time," I barely added. "Despite Sean wanting me to, I was listening to Jonah the other night. If Sean wants to keep me around I don't appear to have a choice."

She frowned, disappointed. "You can stay human as long as it's still safe for you and for us. Jonah was only simply reminding Sean it can't be forever."

"Judging from tonight's outburst he has no intentions of ever excepting it."

She shook her head, sadly. "He'll come around. The question is, is this really what *you* want?"

I opened my mouth to respond, she suddenly held up her right hand, cocking her head to the side. "I'll give you a few minutes to think about it. I need to get downstairs. Just come down when you're ready."

She opened the door and like a ghost she disappeared out of the room, barely closing the door behind her. I stared at it for a long second then walked to the bed, sinking down on it. I felt the tears fall down my cheeks and put my face in my hands.

How do I keep going from one catastrophe to another and how did

I get here? I asked myself. I continued to sit there till no more tears slid down my cheeks. I wiped away the wetness, took a deep breath and lifted my head. I took an extra second to stand, making sure my legs were stable enough to carry me across the room. When I reached the door I shut my eyes briefly on a prayer for courage and strength to stand in a room with Jonah's family; Sean, especially. I carefully opened the door, and then stepped out into the empty hall.

I reached the top of the stairs and could see everyone, with the exception of Sean and Luke, standing in a circle in the center of the living room. They were having an intense conversation, seeming to be careful of my hearing. Becca looked at me then in a move to fast for my eyes to catch, she was taking my hand and walking me down the stairs.

As soon as we were at the bottom she wrapped her arms around me, pressing me gently against her marble body.

"Are you all right, Angel?" Jonah asked softly.

"I will be," I sighed. "Where is Sean and Luke?"

I barely saw Jonah and Becca share a look.

"They stepped out," Mariah said, answering for them. "Sean needed a chance to calm down."

I pulled myself free of Becca's arms ----- with her consent of course -----. "And to think he can lose his mind over nothing more than a vision."

"Sean loves you more than he could ever imagine," Becca spoke softly. "I know he's difficult and ill-tempered at times …"

"*Difficult?*" I gasped. "A two-year-old is difficult. This is nothing but an over dramatic reaction."

"You know my son well," she sighed, heavily.

"He just needs time to process, Angel," Jonah stated. "He will come around once he gets control of his senses."

"He's not the only one who needs time," I snapped. "All of this hasn't exactly been paradise for me." Heavy sarcasm.

"You're right, sweetheart," Becca agreed. "We haven't been in touch with our humanity for so long we often forget how differently things affect you."

"That certainly doesn't make it easier," I mumbled. Figuring leaving was probably the best solution for this situation I reached in my coat pocket for my keys.

Not there.

"Looking for these?" Kelsey suddenly asked, a smirk in her voice.

I looked up and saw my keys hanging from the tip of her index finger. I took a step toward her.

"Yes."

"Are you planning to leave?" Mariah asked, her concern sounding genuine.

I nodded my head. "I've had enough turmoil for one twenty-four hour period."

I reached for my keys and Kelsey quickly moved her hand. It was then I heard an unfamiliar sound.

Cameron laughed.

"It may be very difficult for you to see, as it is so late. Couldn't we talk you into staying until morning?" he asked. This was the first time I've ever heard him talk. I was surprised, his voice wasn't the soft roar like Sean's or as booming as Luke's ... it was more like the sound of a deer when it's calling out for its mate.

My head was shaking before he finished. "I need the space to think. Besides, I haven't been home since this afternoon. I'm sure Bobbie has it figured out where I am, but she still worries when I'm out late."

"She's right," Jonah insisted. "she should go. Angel, keep your doors locked and don't stop for anyreason."

I tried again for my keys, this time Kelsey shot like a bullet to the other side of the room, staying out of my reach.

"Kelsey," I growled.

"You really should stay."

"It isn't in our best interest for the humans to get concerned for her safety, Kelsey," Jonah said, his tone disapproving. "Even more so when Mike knows the danger she faces."

"Then do you think it's a good idea for her to be alone now?" Kelsey contradicted.

Jonah considered that for a fraction of a second. "No," he finally answered. Then he turned to Cameron. "Run behind her until she gets into city limits. If you see anything suspicious do not approach it on your own, come back and get the rest of us."

"Will do," Cameron agreed.

Now that there was no chance of me being alone Kelsey crossed the room, stopping in front of me. I held my hand out for the keys, she dropped them into my palm.

"I know you have already told Kloe, but you need to inform the rest of your humans you're going on vacation with Sean. And, you also need to get Bobbie out of here ... soon," she told me.

"I will the day of the party."

"It's not that *damn* important," she snapped.

"Angel?" Cameron's voice suddenly called. "Are you ready?"

I stared at Kelsey's concerned face a second longer, and then turned to Cameron. "Yes."

He nodded his head at me, heading for the door and I followed him.

I got home and called the hospital. Bobbie was tending to a patient so I left a message for her. Figuring Sean needed time to get here I took a long hot shower, hoping it would relieve my body of all the tensions coursing through me. While brushing my hair and teeth I stared at my reflection. I couldn't help wondering if I would still recognize my own face or if it would transform into something I would never know again. I felt wetness start to form at the corner of my eyes when I thought about Sean's reaction to me becoming someone he would have to keep around. Is that the problem; he doesn't want me around that long? Or is it really about my humanity?

I banished all the thoughts from my mind, rinsed out my mouth, and then tossed the towel in the hamper. I turned off the light and walked into my room. I sat in the center my bed, listening for the faint footsteps to appear downstairs while twirling my ring around my finger, staring mindlessly at the bedroom door waiting for it to open. I thought my problems with Jeremy's escape and John still trying to lure me away from Sean was exhausting; waiting for an angry Sean was far worse.

Time passed and I got up, anxiously pacing around the room. Daylight was a few short hours away and Sean still hadn't come. I tried not to remember the last time he acted this poorly, leaving me to spend most of my time alone. But try as I might the memory of those weeks swirled through my mind. He wouldn't leave me alone like that with John and Jeremy being so close, would he? I knew Jonah wouldn't, but it wasn't Jonah who mattered.

Finally it sank in he wasn't coming. I turned off the light and laid down on the bed. I wrapped the quilt around me, slowly letting out the sobs that had been waiting for hours to consume me. I didn't just feel my heart break; I felt it shatter. Even as I knew this would have more complications then the usual human relationships I loved having an indestructible prince. Knowing that no matter what happened through the course of my life he would protect me. He would love me. Now my fairytale romance was coming to end.

All because I had a vision.

I remembered my ring again when it grazed the skin on my face as I wiped away the tears. Hating the reminder of what I had allowed my life to become I pulled it off, tossing it on the stand beside the bed.

Right and Wrong

The week following that fateful night in Becca's tower was uneasy, tense, and, at first bitter. I knew I should have expected Sean to be gone, as this wasn't the first time something has happened to make him angry. Of course, the last time he was angry at himself, but that certainly didn't make things easier since he was now mad at *me*.

To my dismay, I found myself the center of attention for the rest of the week. I walked in to work without wearing my ring and Brandi was impossible, following me around, obsessed with details of what had happened. I knew she was just being concerned and wanted to be comforting, but I didn't want either. It took repeating the line "I don't want to talk about it" a thousand times before she finally gave up and walked away.

Things at home became awkward. Bobbie was always careful not to discuss Sean or any member of his family. Even Josh was making scarce appearances whenever I was home. The more things seem to change thoughts of leaving would enter my mind. My audition at Juilliard wasn't till January, but I could go on to New York, and then Jeremy nor John would find me. I have enough money saved (thanks to not having to pay for my gas, or my share of the bills) I could get something I can afford, as well as look for a job. Then Sean could be happy that I was not only going on with my human life, but I would no longer be in any danger, and I wouldn't have to become anything … anyone else.

The days passed, turning into another week and Sean still hadn't returned. I cried myself to sleep the first few nights after our fight and he didn't appear in my room, but after a while my body turned numb, my tear ducts dried up, no longer able to produce any moisture at all. I felt so drained physically and emotionally I couldn't even find the strength to get through each emotion.

As though my misery wasn't enough I didn't have much to keep me busy. With the party only a few days away I wasn't playing the piano. Becca was busy organizing the banquet hall, decorators were everywhere. Kyle wasn't back yet so I traded as many of his shifts with Brandi as Kloe would allow. It was when I reached the point of having overtime she realized I was working more than I was having personal time or even sleeping.

That only gave me more time to define the plans I hadn't shared with anyone. Not even Jennifer. She called a couple of days after my last encounter with the Callengers. She knew something was wrong the second she heard my voice. I lied, telling her I was just simply stressed over the party and that I hadn't had time to really think about what I was going to do for Thanksgiving. I *hated* that I was keeping another secret from her, but I knew if I told her I was leaving for New York she would try talking me into staying, at least until it was time for my audition.

Mrs. Wilkins' party was set to take place on Saturday evening. I called the airport on Tuesday, securing a seat on the plane for Sunday morning. Knowing I still had one thing to do before I left I went to my bedroom and sat down at the table to write.

"Sean," I wrote. My hand began to shake almost violently causing me to have to write slower so the letters were legible.

I am very sorry for any pain I have caused you, as I have caused a great deal to myself. I have been struggling as I fumble for the words through the tears, and the hurt, and all the pain while I sit here writing this to you.

I'm going to lay it all out on the line by saying I think it's time we tell this uphill fight goodbye. The future we face together is not one either of us wants so this is the best decision. Tell your family thank you for me. I will always remain in their debt, as I will also always be grateful for what they have done for me.

Please, don't come after me. This is the only thing I can honorably request of you now. Just let me go. Please, for me.

I love you.

Angel

I left the note on the table with my ring resting on it, and stood from the chair. I turned off the light, and then went to bed. A tightness formed in my chest as I felt more pieces of myself crumble. Just when I believed I couldn't shed another tear they fell effortlessly down my face. As I slowly drifted into unconsciousness I promised myself this would be the last time I would cry over Sean Callenger.

The next morning I shoved the note and the ring ----- as I no longer saw it as mine ----- in an envelope, and sealed it. I wasn't scheduled till the afternoon so I drove to his home, with the envelope on the passenger seat. The sun was out, but I couldn't help hoping they were off somewhere feeding, instead of being in the house inside the forest. If anyone one of them caught my scent they would surely catch me, I would be talked into staying. It is impossible to refuse seven vampires. I couldn't help wondering if I really could go through with this, as I was sure I wouldn't be able to survive without him and pondered changing my mind and just wait for Sean to get over this because I knew eventually he would and come back. This is for the best, I reminded myself.

The drive seemed to wound on and on. I started to go faster since there wasn't any moisture on the ground to cause the tires to hydroplane, getting nervous I might not make it out if it took me too long to get there. I forced myself to drive the speed limit, reminding myself the road didn't have to be wet to lose control of the car and run off the road. I didn't want to be lost down in an embankment or wrapped around a tree.

Then there was a break, the road I was looking for and I followed it all the way to the beautiful house. I hit the brakes just before the driveway, looking for anything that sensed their presence. If I saw even the slightest movement I would go no further. I knew it was silly, for they could run faster than any speed of a car, yet I would still give it my best to get away.

But there was nothing.

So I drove down the drive to the house, left the engine running and jumped out on the lawn. I scanned around while I rushed to the porch stairs. I carefully pulled open the double doors, shoved the envelope in between the door and the door jam. I eased the doors closed and ran back to the car. Before getting in I took one long last look at the house built to suit a family of vampires, locking it to memory. And then I got in my car, speeding away as fast as I could.

When I got to work I got quite a surprise; Kyle had returned. He was methodically mopping the kitchen while Anna, Marisa and Sydney arranged the dining room with Thanksgiving decorations. Someone had placed a stuffed turkey on the counter, he had a goofy expression on his face, a cheesy grin under his beak. It took every ounce of control I could manage not to knock him off. Even as I was now walking through my life as nothing more than an empty shell it was still hard to think about how I would be spending this holiday.

It was late when I got home Thursday night. Too exhausted to move right away I continued to sit in the car, staring up at the house. Bobbie was already gone and it suddenly struck me as odd that the house was dark. Not even the porch light was on. A dull nagging feeling began to pulse through me as I wished things could go back to the way they were before I allowed (okay, so maybe *allowed* is wrong ... but still) everything to become complicated. I took a long, deep breath, opened the door and stepped out.

I heard music playing upstairs after unlocking and opening the door. It wasn't loud, but still strange that something would be on when no one was home. Did Bobbie forget to turn off her radio? I tossed the keys in the bowl on the stand next to the door then headed up the stairs. I was already at the top before realizing the music wasn't coming from Bobbie's room. It was coming from mine!

Fear now pulsing through me I quickly went in the bathroom, turning on the light. There wasn't anyone standing anywhere. The hair on the back of my neck made me aware I wasn't alone. I opened my mouth to call out then changed my mind. If there was indeed someone in the house I couldn't be certain who it was. Because Sean hadn't been around I had no way of knowing if Jeremy was now here or if maybe John entered to wait for me. I stood outside my room, giving myself a moment to gather the courage to enter, and then quickly reached around the wall, turning on the light.

Nothing.

I listened to the words of the song while I entered my room and walk to the stereo. It was a tune I'd never heard before, the singer was begging for his love to stay with him. Because I didn't care to listen to anymore I reached out to turn the radio off, and then almost immediately a figure appeared in the open doorway.

"Oh!" I breathed. I backed up to the window, my legs now shaking uncontrollably and slid to the floor.

"I'm sorry," Sean apologized. His eyes and his voice burned with sincerity. "I didn't mean to startle you."

"It's fine," I croaked. "just give me a minute to get my heart out of my throat."

He stood motionless while we listened to the pounding of my heart gradually begin to slow. My body was no longer shaking, I continued to sit there. It felt safer for me to remain where I was.

"I guess it's safe to assume you're the one playing the music?"

Sean leaned against the door jam, crossing his arms over his chest, his legs crossed at the ankles.

"Yes," he admitted. "I heard the song a few days ago. I thought it fit our situation. Don't you think so?"

I didn't answer.

"I mean, I don't have your talent for writing love songs to sing to you, but I can certainly tell you how much I love you and ask you to stay."

There was no doubt he read my note. That had to be the reason he chose to play this song in particular.

"What are you doing here?" I asked, changing the subject.

He lowered his glorious, agonized eyes to mine. "I had to see you, to know you're all right."

The look in his beautiful blue eyes had me fighting a sudden urge to get to my feet and go to him. To wrap my arms around him.

"I get it," I mused. "You found the letter and now you're feeling guilty. Well, as you can see, I'm fine. Now that you know you're free to go."

"Angel," he said, trying hard not to growl. "even had you not left your little note I was already on my way back here once the sun was gone. I need to apologize for hurting you, for how rudely I behaved."

"It's done and over," I said, dismissively. I was trying to sound detached. "But if it means that much to you then I'll tell you you're forgiven. I forgave you days ago."

He uncrossed his limbs and stood upright. My heart ----- though I wasn't sure I even still had one ----- thumped wildly against my rib cage as I watched him cross the room and sit down on the end of my bed.

"*Please*," he pleaded. "I don't want to fight; I didn't come here to fight with you. It's already killing me I hurt you."

The agony burning in his voice had my will to stay away from him crumbling. I closed my eyes briefly, convincing myself it was best for me to stay where I was. As they slowly, carefully reopened I searched my mind for the things I wanted to say. There were a million words I wanted to toss at him the night I waited for him, yet somehow tonight I couldn't find even one.

The distance between us must have been weighing on him. He leaned forward, his arm outstretched, reaching for my hand. I quickly shoved my arms in the space behind my back.

"Don't," I said in a whisper.

His eyes narrowed at me. "Is there a reason you are not wanting me to touch you?"

His gaze unintentionally disarmed me causing me to struggle to breathe. "No ----- well actually there is. The next time I say or do something you don't want to deal with and you decide to walk out again I don't want to be left feeling like I'm standing in a deserted hanger with a plane that can't fly."

He dropped his arm and sat upright, seeming to consider my words. "You're right," he agreed. "I deserve that. So then let me ask you this --- -- what do I have to do to convince you that when I walk out to clear my head, no matter how long it takes I will *never* leave you?"

The expression on his face forced me to swallow a lump I never noticed had formed.

"I don't know," I barely answered. "I do know we are facing a difficult uphill battle and I don't want you here beside me if you're not going to fight it with me. I deserve better than that."

And I started to cry. The tears welled up and ran effortlessly down my cheeks. The sight of my tears made Sean's jaw tighten.

"Angel," he whispered through his teeth. "All I've ever wanted from the very moment I looked at you was to be by your side. I just want you human. Can't you understand that?"

I said nothing.

"I will get down on my knees in front of you right now and beg you to stay with me," he continued. "if it's what you want."

I shook my head, sadly.

Even though the volume was low I noticed for the first time the song was still playing. Sean has once again bought another CD for one song. I wiped away the tears with the back of my hand, slowly inching my way to my feet. I mentally calculated my chances of turning it off and getting out of the room without being caught up in Sean's arms. I had to admit they weren't good. Sean must have guessed my plan because he sat motionless on the bed, his eyes watching me closely.

I pushed the stop button on the stereo, and then took a step toward the door. Sean's movement was so sudden and so fast I didn't have time to blink. He grabbed my arm, dragging me to him.

"Look at me, Angel," he demanded.

I slowly lifted my head, careful not to look at his eyes.

"Tell me what you wrote in the letter is true, that you don't want to be with me and I'll let you go. Just as you asked."

I stared at his face for what was probably several minutes. "I can't," I finally whispered.

He took my face securely in his hands, slowly leaning down toward me. When it began to click in my mind what he was planning I struggled to turn my head. "Please, don't," I begged.

Sean's lips stopped an inch from mine, his eyes scrutinizing my face. "Why don't you want me to kiss you? And I don't want you downplaying the truth."

His breath, thick with the citrus scent caused my head spin, dizzily. I squeezed my eyes closed so I could keep from passing out and have the courage to speak. "Because then I will no longer be able to stay mad and follow through with my own plans." My voice wavered, cracking on the last word.

He waited till I opened my eyes to respond. "After everything you've had to live through, meaning all my unruly behaviors and the fact I have hurt you so deeply that you're ready to leave me, can you still love me?"

I narrowed my eyes. "What kind of crap is that?"

The corners of his lips twisted down into a frown. "*Please*, just answer."

"Fine then," I sighed. "It isn't possible for me to stop loving you. Nothing that has happened or stands to happen can change that or stop it."

A slow smile crossed his lips. "That's all I need to know."

His lips were on mine then and there wasn't anything I could do to stop him. Not that I really wanted to. My will had already crumbled the moment his skin touched mine. I kissed him back with as much passion as I could manage, though my heart was pounding painful rabbit jumps against my rib cage. He pulled away for only a brief second so I could breathe. He whispered my full name, pressing his cold, satin lips back to mine.

No longer able to breathe I was becoming very dizzy. I shook my head and Sean pulled away. He released my face, slipping his arms around my waist, and then lifted me up. He carried me to the bed, gently laying me down, with my head to rest on the pillow. He laid beside me, giving me a few minutes to calm my breathing and slow my pounding heart before lying his head on my chest, above my heart.

The urge to touch his hair coursed through me, I flexed my fingers numerous times trying to fight against it. Try as I might, I couldn't resist the temptation. I slid my fingers through it, letting his natural curls wrapped around them.

"You simply can't imagine what it's been like for me to go so long without this sound."

I didn't say a word. I knew he heard the skepticism in my silence when he lifted his head to look at me.

"Is it safe to assume you have forgiven me enough to stay?"

My fingers froze while I stared at him, confused.

"Why wouldn't it be?"

He didn't answer, lifting up his left hand, shoving it in the space between us. "Then I believe this belongs on your hand."

I hadn't noticed through everything that he had anything on his hand. But there on his left pinky was my ring. I untangled my fingers from his hair, carefully reaching out to remove it. He already had it pulled off and was slipping it back on the third finger of my left hand.

"Do you think we could discuss something without you getting upset with me?"

At that I had to laugh. "We can talk," I agreed. "I can't promise anything else."

He pretended to think about it. "I'll take the deal," he grinned. "We'll talk while you eat."

My eyes instantly narrowed. "What makes you think I'm hungry?"

As if it were on cue my stomach growled, answering for him causing him to raise one eyebrow.

"Fine," I sighed in defeat.

He laughed at my reluctance, nearly flying from the bed. He reached out, grabbing my hand, gently pulling me to my feet. He twined his fingers in mine, leading me from the room and down the stairs. While we were standing in the foyer he kissed my fingers before releasing them and followed me into the kitchen.

I turned on the light and walked on to the refrigerator while he went to sit in a shabby chair.

"What's so important I had to come all the way down here for you to say it?"

I stood looking over the shelves for something that wouldn't take a great deal of effort to make.

"Our last conversation," he said matter-of-factly.

I was about to give up and pull out a package of lunch meat when I finally saw the pizza box sitting on the bottom shelf. I pulled out the box, stood upright and closed the door.

"Didn't we have that discussion already?"

"Angel," he groaned in exasperation. "I was apologizing."

Something in his tone made a coward out me, memories of what happened during that conversation caused my heart to skip a few beats. I fought the urge to look at him, concentrating on putting a couple slices of the pizza on a plate and stick it in the microwave.

"Okay," I breathed. "What about it?"

Images of Becca's easel flashed through my mind as clear as the night I saw it crash against the wall. I quickly squashed them before his sharp eyes saw the reaction on my face.

"I do admit I shouldn't have acted so badly. I should have given you the chance to explain. It's

important to me you understand what made me have a lapse in my sanity."

"I've got a pretty good idea," I murmured. "Sean, I understand, I truly do," I said much louder. "I know you don't want me having to choose the way you did. But I've already spent the last few months walking a serrated edge between your world and mine. I may have been able to keep my balance this far, but you're going to have to realize I will eventually fall."

The microwave dinged, calling back my focus. I opened the door, pulled out the plate, and then closed the door. I set the plate on the counter, finally turning my eyes on Sean's face. Something flickered across his face, before I could identify it he composed himself.

"I do realize it, that's why it's taken me so long to come here. I have done nothing but think about you and the ethics of right and wrong."

"And?" I prompted.

He struggled to conceal the tension behind his serene expression. "The right thing; to keep you safe until after Jeremy is contained and we figure out how to handle Wilkins then exit your life."

"Well …" I paused, biting down on my bottom lip. "… I too, came up with a solution to our problem."

He raised one eyebrow, his voice ominous. "Oh?"

I suddenly didn't feel confident enough to tell him what I meant when I wrote don't come after me in the note. I turned away, taking a glass out of the cabinet and walked to the refrigerator.

"Angel?" he asked.

I pulled out the gallon of milk, slowly filling the glass.

"I made plans to leave for New York Sunday morning." I spoke the words soft and slow.

I barely caught the sound of the chair scrapping the floor and he was grabbing my shoulders, turning me to face. He took the gallon from my hand, shoved in back in the fridge, nearly slamming the door closed then locked a hand on my jaw, forcing me to look at him.

"Angelia," he growled. "you don't seem to understand *you* are the only thing that can destroy me."

"Like that's even possible." The words were on the verge of slurring.

"It is when I can't live without you," he contradicted.

"Then I guess you just sealed my fate."

He smiled, but it didn't quite touch his eyes. "You will have all the time in the world before you have to damn your soul. If you ever do at all."

I tried to twist my head to free myself of his grasp. I failed … miserably. "It's already damned. Shall I give you a recap? Jeremy Corbin, John Wilkins, and last but not least, Jonah Callenger."

"Angelia Lynn," he sighed, heavily.

"We both know I'm right," I argued. "Now let me go."

He glared at me, holding my eyes. "What if we tried this from a different approach?"

I tried again to shake my head, but he wouldn't allow it. He stood motionless, staring directly into my eyes. My mind began to cloud, for reasons I couldn't fathom I was suddenly nervous. My blood began pulsing through me so fast I could hear it pounding behind my ears. I stared back, helpless. I could almost see the wheels turning in his mind.

"Whatever you're planning, forget it," I said sternly.

His eyes widened innocently, a cocky grin crossing his lips. "Why would you think I'm planning anything?"

I rolled my eyes. "I know that look."

His blue eyes began to shimmer. "All I have planned is to simply talk," he said condescendingly.

I opened my mouth to argue, my stomach growled causing him to scowl.

"Go eat your pizza," he demanded me. He leaned down, placing a gentle kiss to my lips, and then released me. I quickly walked to the counter, grabbing the plate and went to sit at the table.

I saw Bobbie's badly worn book laying open on the table and pulled it to me. It wasn't hard to figure out it was her favorite as the binding was so worn out it laid flat against the table. I wasn't really interested in the words on the page, but I needed the distraction from Sean so I could eat without him causing a choking experience.

"Our conversations almost never go quite the way I'm aiming for," Sean said, his voice thoughtful. "so let's try it another way."

I never took my eyes off the book. "Try what?"

"I have nearly lost you twice now trying to force you to do things my way. I would like for us to try a different alternative."

I didn't answer.

"I'm giving you the opportunity right now to tell me what you want," he continued. "It can be anything, anything at all."

His voice suddenly sounded closer causing me to lift my head. He was standing inches from me, arms folded, staring at me with an unfathomable expression.

"I think I already have everything," I replied, uncertain of where he was trying to lead me.

He frowned in disgust. "I'm not talking about what *I* wanted you to have."

I pretended to think about it. "Hmmm... let's see," I said slowly. " ... how about an end to hunger and peace on earth." Heavy sarcasm.

"Be serious, Angel," he growled.

I shook my head. "I want what every other girl wants," I said exhausted. "To live a long happy life with the love of her life."

"Now we're getting somewhere," he said, sarcastically. "What would you be willing to trade for it?"

My brows knit in confusion. "There really isn't anything I could give you unless it's my … humanity." I cringed, waiting for his reaction to my pointing out the obvious.

A wide, wicked smile spread across his lips, exposing his ultra-white teeth. "Oh, my love, there actually is."

Now I wasn't just nervous, I was scared, too. I wasn't exactly sure I liked the course this conversation had taken. He waited for a response.

"All right, I'll bait. What?"

"Marry me."

That didn't sink in right away. I was still waiting for him to say something that made sense and get to the point.

"I'm waiting."

The smile on his face disappeared, a growl rumbled from his throat. "I just proposed and you are treating it as if it were nothing more than a joke."

Now it sank in. I felt the shock on my face before I heard it in my voice. "You're serious!"

Sean dropped his arms and groaned. "I want you to marry me."

"Now who's the absurd one?" I was very close to being hysterical. "I thought you never wanted your fate thrust upon me?" I diverged.

"Honestly, I don't."

"Did you have a change of heart while you were away? Metaphorically speaking, of course," I tacked on when an odd expression shadowed his face.

"What choice have I?" he asked, his voice disapproving. "Even more so when it comes down to swallowing my pride or having to live without you. Truthfully, when I read your note then seen you for myself tonight I thought I was already too late."

"Need I remind you I *don't* want to become someone even I wouldn't recognize?" I hedged.

He slightly shrugged his shoulders. "Then I suppose we will just have to find a way to keep exactly what we have."

"And in the end I'm still the one who stands to lose the most," I said, artlessly.

"How so?" He was puzzled.

I rolled my eyes at him. "As if it isn't obvious," I mumbled. "If I allow you to break your promise I turn into something I don't want to be. If I agree to let things continue as they are then I lose …" My voice trail off. I suddenly felt to embarrassed to finish the sentence.

"You lose what?"

I turned away from him, my cheeks burning and picked up the last bite of the pizza. I hesitated putting it in my mouth, but I forced myself to chew it then swallow, chasing it down with milk.

"Angel?" Sean asked, his tone frustrated. "I need to know what you lose, please, tell me."

The coward in me kept my face toward the window. "Physical intimacy," I whispered.

He didn't answer; I slightly turned my head to peek at him. His expression was calculating, he silently paced back and forth across the kitchen. The memory of the last time I watched him do that flashed through my mind. To keep from panicking I looked back at the table. Bobbie's book reminded me it was still in front of me, waiting for me to finish reading it. I turned the page back to Bobbie's place, pushed the book across the table, and then stood from the chair.

"I'm going to take a shower," I informed him.

"Shh," he shushed me, "I'm thinking."

As if this night needed to get any longer, I thought sourly. I picked up my dishes, crossed the room and set them in the basin. I glanced at Sean once more then walk out of the room.

Sean appeared in my bedroom doorway seconds after I pulled a fresh set of pajamas from the dresser.

"I am determined to try something your way," he said thoughtfully. "so here's the compromise." He paused, his expression was a strange mix of frustration and defiance. "I'll talk to Jonah in the morning regarding my absence. The second the party for Mrs. Wilkins' is over we leave. I'll take you anywhere you want to go."

"Your absence?" I asked, confused.

He rolled his eyes and sighed as though I should have known what he was talking about.

"I won't be part of the group when they contain Jeremy and deal with Wilkins."

I stared at him, waiting ... "Okay, what's the ulterior motive for this decision?"

His face was teasingly outraged. "You really believe there is one?" he asked in a horror struck voice.

Right then my suspicion was confirmed. I tossed my clothes on the bed, fisting my hands against my hips.

"You seem to forget I know you well enough not to believe you would surrender this easily without me sacrificing something. So give it up."

He flashed me a grin, his blue eyes began to smolder. "All you have to do is marry me."

It took every ounce of control I had to look away from him. I was secretly thankful he wasn't close enough to breathe in my face. I can fight one or the other, but never both at the same time. I gave myself a few seconds before turning my eyes back to his face. I kept them low, as not to look at his eyes.

"The party is in two days," I reminded him. "How do you plan to put together a wedding in that short amount of time?"

"Who said anything about productions?" he asked earnestly. "I figure we can go to one of those all-night chapels, as I wouldn't stand out. And, I know how many days there is until the party. I promise, once you are officially mine I will have you back in time to play in the show."

I had a flashback to a conversation I had with Jen about Vegas and laughed. That night seemed like it was a million years ago instead of just a few months.

"So *if* I agree to marry you tonight you'll disregard your rules about intimacy and make love with a human?"

He smiled, flashing a full set of teeth. "I'll get the truck while you're in the shower."

I knew he was calling my bluff ----- dang it!

"Sean," I whined. "I'm only just eighteen."

"And I'm nearly a hundred," he smirked, playfully. "It's time for me to settle down. It has taken me a number of decades to find the one to do that with." He paused and entered the room, walking to me to wrap his arms around my waist. "I finally found the mate intended for me and I want to keep her ... forever."

"Whether I marry you now or later won't make much of a difference. I'll always be yours regardless."

"I don't know if I can really count on that," he smiled, angelically.

"What's that supposed to mean?" I asked, allowing acid to leak in my tone.

He inclined his head toward the table. "On a pad of paper next to the stereo is a boarding schedule to New York."

"Spying on me now, are you?" I accused, icily.

He laughed. "I got curious while waiting for you to get home tonight. And, didn't you tell me you have plans to leave?"

"Merely beside the point," I growled. "You could have told me you knew."

"And ruin the chance of getting you to tell me yourself? Not a chance!"

We glowered at each for a long moment. It was Sean to break the silence.

"If it is true you have no intentions of ever leaving me, prove it. Marry me."

"You're impossible," I hissed. "and truly a monster."

"Isn't that why you love me?" he laughed darkly.

"It seems I need to rethink everything," I groaned.

He shook us with his quiet laughter. "Would you consider all of this more seriously if I produced a ring?"

I felt the panic on my face before I heard it in my voice. "A ring?"

He pulled one arm from around my waist, lifting my left hand up to his face. He kept his eyes on me while skimming his nose over the skin. My heart instantly tried to leap out of my skin.

"This one looks extremely beautiful." He paused, pressing his lips lightly against my fingers. I thought I might pass out from the pounding inside my chest. "However, I think a nice crystal cut diamond would look spectacular." His eyes flashed up to my face. "Or maybe even a princess cut," he mused.

His smoldering eyes scattered my thoughts. I shook my head, both answering him and trying to clear my mind. Now was the time I needed my rational thoughts.

"I think we've had this discussion long enough and I also think you have spent more than enough money on me; such as forcing me to let you cover my bills and that fancy thing outside, in which you pay the gas for."

He released every part of me, folding his arms abruptly over his chest.

"I disagree," he said, shaking his head. "We will keep having this conversation until I finally break through that hard head of yours. Secondly, if I'm not allowed to spend my money on you then what should I do with it?"

"Buy yourself another truck," I suggested. "or maybe get yourself one of those shiny sports cars."

"That's funny," he said, bitterly. "I didn't take you as one of those girls who enjoys riding in something like that. Grow fond of *Wilkins*'" ----- he sneered on his name ----- "shiny car, did you?"

"No," I nearly croaked.

There was a long pause while he stood motionless, staring at me. The look on his face made me wish I hadn't made the suggestion. Then suddenly he laughed, taking my face between his hands.

"Angel, you can be so obtuse! I don't much like sports cars, they're too flashy and I like blending in ----- not standing out. The truck doesn't need replaced, for it is still willing to go any speed I want. Should it ever decide it can't keep up with me I have a personal mechanic to change its mind."

I scowled at him, trying to think of something awful to say. As my luck usually goes, I couldn't come up with anything.

"There is another benefit for you to consider if you leave with me and remain human," he offered, thoughtfully.

I looked at him speculatively. "What?"

"We can keep the plans you have set for New York. You could still attend Juilliard, as I think you should."

"And just what would you do?"

He frowned, his eyes were tight. "I admit my freedom would be limited, but with the death rate I wouldn't have any problem feeding."

And again, all I could do was stare at him.

"Will you marry me?" he asked in a serious tone.

I tried to shake my head, but he wouldn't allow it.

"Sean, please be serious," I pleaded. "I can't let you live like that and what about your family?"

A deep growl rumbled from the back of his throat. "I've had to live in one light before and survived. As far as my family, they'll understand that we want to be on our own for a while."

My eyes narrowed, suspicious now. "You don't want Jonah to know what you're planning."

I watched him fight back a snarl when I mentioned Jonah.

"I'm not understanding you," he growled. "I'm giving you every opportunity to live the way you want and you're refusing. Yet, you are willing to make a deal with Jonah to spend an eternity as a vampire to survive a human attack, you don't even have to be here to risk your life for."

"It seems you still clearly don't see my reason," I accused. "I didn't make the deal so I *could* be like you. I did it because of you and because it beats the alternative."

"What alternative?" he snapped.

"Death," I blurted, hastily.

His eyes narrowed into slits, the color darkening. "If it's really for me then why are you so unwilling to spend an eternity committed to me?"

"You can't honestly believe that," I said softly.

He raised one eyebrow at me. "Don't I?"

"I've already promised to stay with you," I nearly whispered. "Isn't that enough?"

He stared at me for a long moment. "If I could be sure nothing would change tomorrow that could having you running off to Jonah, yes."

"Sean," I whined.

I didn't see even one ounce of compromise on his face or in his eyes. As badly as I wanted what he was offering so I could continue to age and eventually die a human, and still be able to have him I wasn't giving into his idea of marriage. I didn't know much about how it was supposed to work since my parents were divorced by the time I was six, as far as I knew my mother never remarried and Scott couldn't stay sober long enough to even have a relationship, but I did know both people were supposed to be equals. Sean and I were not, nor would we ever be ... even *if* I did become like him.

"It's getting late," I stated carefully. "I would like to be in the shower before daylight."

"Fine," he grumbled, disgusted. "I'll let this go. Keep in mind we are nowhere near done discussing this."

"I never had any doubts," I groaned.

"And, when I leave in the morning I'm canceling that flight. You're mine, Angelia."

He placed a gentle kiss on my lips, and then released my face. I sighed deeply at the relief of being free of his iron grip, my teeth were dangerously close to chattering from the frozen feeling in my cheeks.

When he turned to walk to the chair I grabbed my clothes from the bed and stalked out of the room.

Babysitters at My Age?

Sean planned to drive me to work the next morning. I figured it had something to with making sure I didn't change my mind about the party, or because I was refusing his proposal and sneak off to the airport, anyway. Then Jonah called just moments before we walked out the door, changing everything. So I drove myself, trying not to think about Sean's propitious marriage ideas or Jeremy Corbin. I slept restless, tossing and turning as thoughts of both and John filled my head throughout the night. Sean eventually pulled me into his stone, cold arms and hummed my favorite tune. And, even that didn't help.

The only hope I had now was that my facial expressions were under control before I entered the building. The last thing I needed was for my friends to read something there and become alarmed. It was bad already that I still hadn't said anything to Bobbie.

The parking lot was empty, with the exception of a few cars parked on the employee's side. Brandi's car, nor Kyle's was there. There's hope after all, I told myself. Nobody can seem to read my face better than Brandi. I pulled in and parked next to a small black Honda. I grabbed the backpack I packed so I could change before I left, (I was meeting Mayor Wilkins and didn't want to still be wearing my dirty uniform) opened the door and slid out of the seat. I tossed the strap over my shoulder, closed my door, and nearly ran to the building to get out of the rain.

Kerri was the only person keeping the dining room from being empty. She was sitting at the counter, mindlessly rolling silverware. She looked up when I passed behind the counter.

"Good morning, Angel."

"Good morning." I looked around the empty room. "From the looks of this room we're in for a long day." I made a face of mock horror.

She laughed.

I set my bag on the counter and went for a cup of coffee.

"Do you have any big plans for Thanksgiving?" she suddenly asked.

I cringed. The reminder that Sean wanted me to run off somewhere with him until Jeremy was caught ran through my mind. I pushed it aside, keeping my back to her so the stress wouldn't appear in my voice or on my face.

"Sean's family has invited me to join them." I finished stirring my coffee then turned to face her. "How about you?"

A sour expression twisted her features. "I'm having dinner at my mom's with all five of my siblings and their families."

"Wow," I mouthed. "Your mother had six children?"

She nodded her head. "And, I'm the youngest."

"That must have been hard," I said, thoughtfully. "having to do birthdays six times a year."

"It was," she agreed. "To add even more stress to a single mother, my birthday is in December."

"Twice the presents, not bad," I mused.

"Not really." She shook her head. "She had to divide the gifts for me to have both Christmas and a birthday."

I reached for the strap of my bag and pulled it off the counter. "It's still the best of both worlds."

She considered that while I turned away from her to walk in the back.

"Hey, Angel," Anna's chipper voice called out to me. She was standing at the prep table, lining dressing cups.

"Good morning, Anna."

She looked me over, her eyes zoning in on my ring.

"I see you have your ring on again." She paused to turn her eyes back on my face. "Does that mean you got things worked out with Sean?"

I walked on to the time clock. "Yeah," I sighed. "Yeah, I did." I punched my numbers in, hung up my bag and coat, and then went to join Anna at the prep table.

"Good," she said with a laugh. "Seeing the two of you together gives me hope true love is still possible." A dreamy expression appeared on her face.

True love.

True love wasn't painful, complicated or took anything away from anyone. Life seemed to have a funny way of giving me a true love that *was* complicated, cocky, egoistical, and had a personality disorder. He sounded perfect, except he wasn't exactly normal.

"Don't worry about it, Anna," I said, forcing a smile on my face. "Even if we hadn't worked things out true love is always possible. Sometimes, you find it in the one person you least expected."

No one knows that better than me, I thought sourly.

Since I wasn't in the mood for cheerful talks of relationships I decided to let Anna finish the cups on her own and went to get a start on Kloe's Thanksgiving menu.

I couldn't have known my day could possibly get any worse till I walked out the diner after my shift ended. A sheriff cruiser was parked behind my car, with no one getting out. Figuring it was Jonah waiting to follow me home I continued walking, and then the driver door opened and Mike stepped out.

I instantly froze.

"We have reason to believe Jeremy is here or has been," he informed me. "Jonah and Sean are checking out a hotel room as we speak. You need to start having someone with you whenever you leave anywhere."

I took a minute to answer, giving my mind a chance to think and to keep my voice stable.

"I am planning to leave with Sean tomorrow night after Mrs. Wilkins' party."

"I know, Angel," he said, shaking his head. "In my honest opinion your best bet would be to leave now. It isn't safe for you to continuing being here at this moment."

My head was shaking before he was finished. "I've already had this conversation with Jonah. I'm seeing this through. And anyways, Mayor Wilkins' wouldn't have enough time to replace me. Especially since Derek isn't here," I quickly added when Mike scowled at me.

"He would understand. You don't seem to notice, I'm guessing, but you have a number of people who care a great deal about you and want nothing more than to see that you're safe. I'd hate to be the bad guy here, but if you're going to continue to defy me I will lock you in a cell," he threatened.

"Like Sean would allow that," I mumbled.

I hadn't been aware he even heard me till he raised his eyebrows.

"At this point, Angel, I believe he would. Especially if it's a guarantee Jeremy wouldn't be able to get to you."

I knew he was right and hated it. Sean would happily chain me in a basement somewhere if he thought it would do any good.

"*Dammit*," I muttered. Then I looked at Mike. "Fine, I'll compromise. I'll have someone with me at all times till the party."

"Good," he said, approvingly.

I never noticed how far he had walked to meet me until I watched him walk to his car.

"Mike?" I asked.

He opened his door then turned his head to look at me. "Yes."

"Are you sure it's me he came here for and not just to try to prove his sanity?"

He slightly shrugged his shoulders. "I'm not certain of anything at this moment, but I'm not going to take any chances. Get a chaperone, Angel."

I held my hands in the air, palms forward. "Okay, okay," I glowered. "I'll figure something out."

"See to it you do." He climbed in his car and pulled the door closed.

I watched in awe as he drove out of the parking lot and turned, eventually disappearing out of sight. My legs felt heavy when I tried to walk to my car. It took every conscious effort to force them to move as I fought to put one foot in front of the other.

My heart pounded recklessly when I walked in the banquet hall to meet Mayor Wilkins. John was there with him. I knew it was silly, I couldn't help feeling like I had just walked into a horror movie. I had barely gotten my facial expression composed when they finally noticed me.

"Welcome, Angel," Mayor Wilkins said with a smile. "It is so nice to see you again."

"You, too, Mayor." My voice shook and I suddenly hoped he didn't notice.

"Just call me Dean. I know you have a lot going on right now, but I am glad you could take a minute to talk with me."

Without a conscious decision to do so my eyes briefly flashed to John's face. He saw it and smiled at me. I fought a shiver as it nearly slid down my spine and looked back at Mayor Wilkins. He never seemed to notice any tensions building in the room.

"I wanted your opinion on where you think the piano would best be suited," he continued on.

"Becca has told me the entire town has been invited."

"That is correct," he verified. "Shelia enjoys being in with the community," he laughed.

"Then the piano should probably remain where it is. It is already in the back so it's not taking up any space in the center of the room."

He considered my answer for a long second. "You're right," he finally agreed. "I was just thinking about you being back there unnoticed. You play so well, I'd hate for anyone not to see the talent spilling out the music."

Once again my eyes flashed to John. "Don't worry about it. I doubt I'll be unnoticed."

John shook his head, a wide smile crossing his lips.

"Well then, I guess I'm just being plan silly," Dean laughed. "I suppose you still have a number of things to do before this night ends so I'll just get out of your way. Were you planning to play tonight?"

"I was considering it," I said, weakly. "but I probably should get home."

"Then I'll walk you out."

John said his goodbye to his grandfather then walked out of the building ahead of us. Dean walked next to me, chatting endlessly about tomorrow night's surprise for his wife. I was far too distracted to really pay attention. I was still horrified about seeing John. He told me he would call when he returned, I never heard a thing from him. My skin crawled when I thought maybe it was possible he had some sort of plan of his own.

Dean stopped to lock the door and I walked away.

"Oh, Angel," he suddenly called out.

I closed my eyes briefly, breathing deeply through my nose, trying desperately to clear my face of all emotions before turning to face him. "Yes?"

"I got word this evening about Jeremy Corbin's escape." He paused, an apologetic look on his face. "If you need to leave now feel free to do so. I don't want anything happening to you because you stayed to play the piano to make my wife happy."

I felt my face first turn to shock, then horror now that I was aware he knew the plan. If he knew then odds were John did, too. This was certain to create a bad situation. Dean's expression became anxious while he stared at me.

"Did I say something wrong?"

"No," I quickly blurted. I forced my face clear of all emotions. "Thank you for the concern, Dean, but I've got everything covered. I will be fine."

He looked skeptical. "Okay then, good night."

"Good night." I turned away, fighting the urge not to run to my car.

I almost had a stroke when I got close to the car and saw a tall, dark figure leaning against it. Then I realized it was John.

"Hi, Angel." His voice was friendly.

I swallowed a large lump. "Hello, John."

I walked to the driver door and he moved, giving me room to unlock the door.

"I know I said I would call when I got in town," he said with a sigh. "but unfortunately I was born in politics. I'm free now, how about we get that dinner? I won't drag you anywhere special this time," he quickly added when I threw a glance at him.

"I'm afraid I can't," I said, too startled to be diplomatic.

"Angel, I would really like for you to join me, as there is something important I need to discuss with you."

The tone in his voice alarmed me. I quickly recovered my composure and tried to make my smile warm. "I'm sure you do and I appreciate the offer, but I really do still have a few things to do before tomorrow."

I had been agonizing over the conversation with Mike while I drove here. I kept going over different scenarios in my mind, trying to figure out the best way to explain everything to Bobbie. There was no doubt in my mind now that John knew something and was suddenly desperate to get home.

My dismissal, no matter how friendly I made it caused John to scowl. His hand snaked out, grabbing my arm, and then a dark sedan drove by real slow. His expression instantly turned nervous and he released me.

"Fine," he murmured. "I expect you to meet me tomorrow. Nine am. There's a little restaurant a couple of blocks form here. And, come alone."

I'm going to be lucky if I can even leave the house tomorrow without riding in an armored car, shackled to Sean.

"I'll do my best," I said.

John continued to stare at me, his eyes penetrating before finally nodding his head and walked away. I breathe a sigh of relief, quickly opening the car door and slid into the seat.

Despite the desperation to get home and talk to Bobbie, she was already gone. I felt my heart drop to the pit of my stomach, knowing I was too late. I was putting her in danger with my silence and now that I was too late it sickened me. She had plans to leave for Washington after the party simply because she wanted the chance to hear me play a real piano. Stupid party! I knew I was going to have to tell her in the morning and convince her to leave then.

I got out and quickened my steps to the house. I was near the porch when two dark figures emerged from the shadows. I could feel a scream swelling up in my throat and bit down on my bottom lip to hold it in.

"You can relax, Angel," Kelsey demanded. "it's only us."

She stood beside Mariah motionless, waiting for my rapidly beating heart to slow.

"Are you trying to scare me to death?" I asked when it was no longer painful to breathe.

Her face was incredulous, with a hint of anger. "If that was ever a plan I would have done it months ago before I knew Sean was in love with you."

I scowled at her, wishing she wasn't a thousand times stronger than me or had the ability to incapacitate me so I could slug her.

"Why are you even here?" I glowered.

"Protection detail," she answered hatefully. "You made a deal with Jonah, remember?"

I rolled my eyes and walked past her with a resigned sigh. "Sean will be here soon," I said over my shoulder.

"Not for a while," she announced. She fluttered to my side. "He's still with Jonah."

A second later comprehension came and I gasped in horror. "They found Jeremy, didn't they?"

"They think he's hiding in the motel, but there's no sign of him."

I knew it was silly to fear him being close with two vampires standing beside me. I couldn't help it, I still shoved the key in the lock, turning it and quickly opened the door. I dashed inside and went into the kitchen. It wasn't till Kelsey and Mariah entered I noticed they had bags in their hands. Kelsey walked to the furthest chair, placed one bag on the floor next to it, and then laid the other over the back. Mariah set the brown paper bag in her hand on the table then sat down in the closet chair.

I may have been scared out of mind, but it was still irritating that I couldn't have time to myself without being watched.

"I don't believe this," I grumbled. "I'm eighteen years old and have to be watched by babysitters."

I turned to walk to a cabinet and heard Kelsey sigh, the sound was disgusted.

"You have two choices here, Angel. You can hang out with us until Sean can get here and be available for tomorrow or I can call him and tell him you're being defiant. Bare mind, *if* I do that he will come get you and you'll leave town tonight."

The mentioning of leaving caused me to scowl. Sean told me this morning he canceled my flight plans and he was taking me somewhere right after the party. The problem; he never said *where*.

I pulled a glass out of the cabinet then turned to look at her.

"That is just a bit psychotic, don't you think?"

"It's not psychotic, Angel," Mariah interjected. "It's only an option to ensure you stay safe. Don't think of our presence as babysitting, think of it more like ... a slumber party."

"Right," I moaned. "a slumber party. Shall we play pin-the-tail on the human?"

Kelsey laughed, darkly. "If I thought I could survive my brother, I would."

I glared at her then went to the refrigerator. "Do I dare ask what's in the bags?"

"Sean's clothes, duh." Kelsey's tone sounded offended, like I should have known. "What do you think your neighbors would say if they saw him leave in the same clothes?"

"He's always gone before daylight so they wouldn't know," I said smugly.

I poured tea in my glass, replaced the pitcher on the shelf, and then closed the door.

"Not this time," Kelsey amended. "He's staying with you the entire day tomorrow and driving you to the banquet hall."

Her smugness had my irritation boiling to the surface and I whirled on her.

"Bobbie doesn't know he stays here!" I shrieked. "And, I have a few things I have to do in the morning."

"Then I suppose you have a problem." Her voice was unemotional. "You still haven't told Bobbie what's going on, have you?"

"No," I admitted, shamefaced.

"I guess since you decided to wait so long Sean will tell her in the morning." She stared at me, unhappily for a second. Then her expression changed, her amber eyes began to glow. "I brought something for you to wear tomorrow night."

I instantly became horrified. "Kelsey." I fought to keep my voice calm.

I saw from the corner of my eye Mariah press her lips together, suppressing a laugh while she stood from her chair. She opened the bag she had carried in and was pulling out a container.

"Oh, calm down, Angel," Kelsey growled. "I'm not suggesting committing murder. It's only a dress!"

I opened my mouth to snarl something at her, but couldn't think of anything awful. I closed it. I continued to glare at her for another second before turning my gaze to Mariah.

"What are you doing?" My tone was still harsh, she ignored it.

"Becca thought you might like something for dinner. She was in Toledo a while ago and brought you back a chicken enchilada dinner." She pulled the lid off and held it out to me.

I sent Kelsey one last look while I walked to Mariah. I took the plate from her waiting hand, and then stalked out of the room. I flopped down on the couch and turned on the TV.

It wasn't so bad after a while, with the exception of Kelsey's phone. She had folded herself sinuously on the floor in front of me, Mariah sat at the other end of the couch. I tried to listen to the movie playing on TNT, but with the phone buzzing every few minutes I gave up.

It buzzed again during the second half of the movie and I decided it was time for a shower. The bathroom was the one place I could be without watchful eyes. I stood from the couch, and then Kelsey's eyes were on my face.

"Were you approached by John Wilkins tonight?"

"I don't know if *approached* is the right word," I stated carefully. The look on her face caused me to take slow steps around her. "But yes, he was at the banquet hall with his grandfather."

Her face turned cold, expressionless. "Did he threaten you?"

"No," I lied. "He only asked me to join him for dinner. He said he has something important to talk to me about."

She picked up her phone and I quickly left the room.

I took my time showering. I tried imagining the conversation Sean and I would have. I knew it would be pointless, for I'd have all the right things to say now, but as soon as he starts cheating with those beautiful soft blue eyes I'd forget everything ----- even my name.

The shower wasn't relieving any of the tensions coursing through my body nor was it helping with my resolve. I got frustrated and shut the water off. I dried off, dressed in a matching set of sleepwear, and then fiercely towel dried my hair. I was much too frustrated to put in the time I usually spent brushing my hair and my teeth.

Kelsey was standing in front of my bedroom when I opened the bathroom door.

"How late are you planning to stay up?" she asked.

I suddenly got a bad feeling. "I'm not sure, why?"

"I was thinking we could try the dress ..."

"Ugh!" I groaned.

Her eyes narrowed into slits. "Angel, I thought my brother was just being a whiny jerk when I heard him tell Jonah how difficult you can be. I'm starting to believe he's not so wrong."

I passed her and walked into my room. "I'm not going to need it till tomorrow," I said over my shoulder. "Why is it so important I put it on now?"

"I need to know if it's the right size so I know whether or not I have to spend the rest of the night making alterations."

Her voice suddenly sounded close and I turned around. She was standing only inches from me. It was now Mariah appeared in the open doorway.

I turned my gaze back to Kelsey, glaring at her for a long moment before sighing in defeat.

"Fine," I surrendered, ruefully. "but for the record, this is under complete protest and I'm going to hate every minute of it."

"That's the spirit!" she stated enthusiastically.

She blew past me to my bed. It wasn't till I tried to follow her movements I noticed the gray garment bag laying over the bed. She already had the bag unzipped by the time I reached her side. I felt my eyes bulge when she reached in, carefully lifting the dress out.

It was beautiful, but also a death trap for someone like me. The irony of her color choice had chills running down my spine; it was the same color of Sean's eyes. The top was a V-neck, with wide straps made to sit off the shoulders. The bottom and midsection was slim, fanning out at the waist and the bottom would brush against the floor when I walked. And, it was made of silk. I could feel my stomach turn sick as I thought of the humiliation I was facing.

"It's pretty, isn't it?" Kelsey's high wind chimed voice asked.

"Pretty over-the-top," I grumbled, incredulous. "Kelsey, that dress is designed for a Barbie doll."

"Aren't you close enough?" she sputtered at me.

I shook my head. "I don't think so. Didn't you see how awkward I was in the last dress? I'm clearly not cut out to wear things like this."

"I'll make sure you wear pumps this time," Mariah said from the doorway. "Kelsey, before she puts on the dress I would like to braid her hair."

"Great idea," she answered, approvingly. "I need an extra minute, anyway."

Mariah inclined her head in the direction of the bathroom, and then turned, walking away. I hung my head, moaned then reluctantly followed her.

I couldn't say I have ever been Mariah's favorite person. So it was strange feeling her hands, though they were a feather-light touch, shaping my hair. It wasn't even a minute and she was finished, sending me back to Kelsey.

Kelsey stood in the middle of my room holding the dress in her hands. That part wasn't so bad. It was the long mirror behind her that had my pulse racing.

"You are going to be stunning," she cooed, holding the dress out at me. "I'll give you a minute so you can change."

I very hesitantly extended out my arms and took it from her waiting hands. She nearly flew to the door.

"Call me when you're finished." She stepped out in the hall, closing the door behind her.

I placed the dress on the bed, continuing to stare at it while I slipped out of my pajamas. It's only for one night and a few short hours, I reminded myself. Once the party is over the dress can come off. I took a deep breath, picked up the dress and carefully stepped into it, as not to tear it. After a long struggle with the zipper I gave up and called for Kelsey.

"I was wrong when I said stunning." She paused, crossing the room to stand behind me. "This dress looks absolutely extravagant on you."

She lightly placed her stone cold hands on my shoulders and walked me to the mirror. I stared at the reflection in disbelief. Aside from the eyes, I almost didn't recognize the person staring back at me.

"The dress isn't so bad after all, is it?" Kelsey asked, sounding smug. I barely felt her hands zip the dress.

My eyes narrows in the mirror at her. "Just because I haven't said anything, doesn't mean I like it."

"It's not important if you do or not," she growled. "you'll be presenting for your public. I just have to hope you'll be able to sit in a seat on the plane in it with your fiancée."

"On an airplane with my fiancée!?" I shrieked. I whirled around, my eyes wide with shock. "I'm not ..."

"You most certainly are," she cut me off.

"I don't know what Sean has told you, but I never -----" while I was ranting she put a hand over my mouth.

"You're not leaving to get married, Angelia so relax," she stated firmly.

Her amber eyes narrowed into slits as she waited for my racing pulse to slow. I inhaled as deeply as I could through my nose, fighting to gain control of myself. When I was finally calm she removed her hand from my mouth.

"I'm honestly having a hard time understanding your reaction." She put her hands on my shoulders again and turned me to face the mirror. "When two people love each other as deeply as you and Sean do, the next logical thing is marriage."

"I'm sorry that none of this makes sense," I apologized. "and yes, I love Sean more than I could ever have imagined possible. I'm just not ready for marriage, even more so when it means becoming something that isn't me."

"Angel," she sighed, heavily. Her eyes were on my face through the mirror while she carefully unzipped the dress. "You're always going to be you, just not so fragile. You seem to forget you have already gotten to experience things most of us didn't."

"Like what?" I asked, skeptical.

"Falling in love, feeling that rush the first kiss leaves behind and believing in the promise it all will last forever."

Now I was confused. "You felt all of that with Cameron."

"Yes," she agreed. "but not as a human. Cameron never kissed me until after he had to be changed." Her face turned somber, for a second she almost looked human. "It's getting late," she said, changing the subject. "I'll step out now so you can change. Just call me when you're done."

In a flash she was at the door, pulling it closed behind her. My eyes blinked, wildly as I stared at the door. I had never seen Kelsey be so emotional before. It blew my mind. I finally tore my eyes away from the door, focusing on sliding the dress down my body and step out of it. I placed it on the bed, and then quickly changed back into my comfy pajamas.

"Kelsey," I called in barely a whisper.

She entered my room less than a second later. "Done already?" she asked in disbelief.

I rolled my eyes at her. "It doesn't take long to change out of something you don't want to wear in the first place."

She fluttered to the bed and began placing the dress in the bag. "I don't think trying on dresses would be so bad for you *if* you acted like a girl."

"Just take your *damn* dress and mirror and get out. I'm tired and would like to go to bed."

She finished zipping the bag, and then picked it up, lying it over her arm.

"Sweet dreams," she purred. She blew to the mirror and wrapped her free arm around it. "I hope your upcoming wedding fills them."

She flew out the door before I could find something to throw at her. I turned off the light, growling at the empty room, and then crawled into bed. I laid down, pulling the blanket over me and a quiet knock came on the door.

"For crying out loud, Kelsey," I grumbled. "Couldn't it wait till morning?"

"It's me," Mariah whispered as she opened the door. "I was wondering if maybe we could talk."

Explanation

I stared at Mariah's face, watching the silver light from the moon shining through my window dance across her pale face. She had never taken the time to really talk with me before and suddenly I felt nervous.

"Sure," I breathed. "I'm probably not going to sleep anyway."

I sat up to move to the end of the bed, she already had the door closed and was standing beside the bed waiting to sit down.

"Would it be all right if I sat down here with you?"

Now I was really astonished. My voice came out an octave higher than was expected. "I don't mind at all."

"Thank you," she stated politely. She sat down at the top of the bed, folding herself sinuously and interlocked her fingers, laying her hands in her lap. "Before I get into why I asked to speak with you I'd like to apologize about something."

She wasn't in the room long and was already confusing me. "What could you possibly owe me an apology for?"

She squinted her eyes at me, the purple in them beginning to glow. I swallowed what felt like an extra-large lump.

"It has come to my attention that you believe I don't like you. The truth is, I do. You have made Sean very happy and for that you have my deepest appreciation. We all had given up hoping he would ever find someone. I keep my distance from you for two reasons.

"The first reason is Sean has made it abundantly clear he does not want you hearing how I came to be; the second." She paused, the corners of her mouth curved into a frown, her eyes were tight. "You see, Angel, I haven't been at this as long as the others. Some human scents affect me more than others so I have to fight twice as hard to stay in control of myself. Your scent, unfortunately is one of those I have to fight. For that I am truly sorry."

"I am glad to know now why you seem so ..." My voice trailed off. I searched for a way to finish the sentence without offending her.

She stared at me with unfathomable eyes. "Abstruse," she offered.

"I don't know if that's quite the word I was looking for, but yeah."

I turned my body ever so slightly, putting space between her and I. It sadden me to know my smell was difficult for her. As Sean has never told me any of this. Once I felt I was a safe enough distance away I wrapped the blanket around me, twisting my fingers up in the corner.

"I'd like to tell you it's all going to be fine because I understand, but I really don't. Though with the schemes Sean is clearly planning I soon will."

The mentioning of Sean's plans twisted my face into a scowl. She smiled at my expression, showing a full set of ultra-white teeth and pointed her index finger at me.

"Which brings us back to why I asked to speak with you. I couldn't help over hearing the last part of your conversation with Kelsey. I know you're needing to sleep to be well rested for tomorrow, but Sean never leaves you alone in the presence of myself or Jonah. I figured I should take this opportunity while we have it."

She looked around my room, seeming to be nervous. I wasn't sure if it was because of her unfamiliar surrounding or if it had something to do with my scent. I sat very still, keeping my heart from having a reason to accelerate. The minutes ticked by.

"I don't know how much of my story you've been told," she finally began, softly. "if any at all. I'd like to share it with you now, if you're interested."

I nodded my head. "I'd like that. I've heard everyone else's."

She looked away for a second, and then slid her eyes back to mine. They were clouded and looked closer to solid than liquid.

"I come from a place where legends are as old as time. Bar Harbor is a small town on the coast of Maine and is known for its fishing industry, cobble stone sidewalks, souvenir shops, as it is a place where many tourist visit and the flower gardens at every turn. To this day stories of the rich still fill the silence of nearly every tavern. Some of them are of adultery, stealing, lies and even murder. I can't begin to try to explain to you the countless numbers of times I dreamt to finally be able to escape for good."

Mariah's mood shifted suddenly, her eyes turned brooding. "I'll spare you the details of my childhood. They weren't the greatest aspects of my life."

I kept all emotions off my face, hoping it would encourage her to continue. The seconds passed.

"I don't want you to miss understand me, Angel," she stated matter-of-factly. "Unlike you, I didn't come from a violent family."

I tried to fight my own body to keep from reacting to her words. But, try as I might I cringed, anyway. Her sharp eyes saw it.

"Sorry," she said, apologetically. Her lips twisted into a nervous smile. "That came out harsher than I meant."

"It's okay," I answered sluggishly. "I've heard far worse."

She smiled again, though I don't think it was quite as soft as she wanted.

"The part of the story I want to share with you starts from eight years ago. That is when I became part of the family." She paused for a long moment, waiting for my response. I simply nodded my head.

"My family is actually very rich. My father owned a construction company, as well as a huge part in the fishing industry. He had a great number of boats, in which he would fill with six to eight men and send them out to sea. Sometimes their trip would be for months at a time. Though he employed at great number of men, both from the natives and new ones coming in to look for work, my father would preach, almost constantly to me and my sisters not to get ourselves involved with them. He wouldn't stand for that kind of 'trash' as he so often called them, to enter our lives and disgrace our family. My older sister didn't like that much, for me that was fine. I wasn't interested in any of them, anyway.

"I met Becca first. Her family was one of the new faces to come to town looking for work. She got a job working in my aunt's flower shop and my father had hired Jonah and Luke. Jonah worked a late shift at one of my father's warehouses while Luke was a member of his construction crew. I didn't much like them at the time, of course I knew nothing of the others.

"One of the places my father had Luke working was in what I consider a castle. We were somehow kin to the man that had built it for his beloved wife. It was beginning to crumble on the inside and my father wanted it restored. For weeks my sisters would listen in on our father's conversation while he was on the phone to learn where he would be the next day. When they knew he wasn't going to be anywhere near the castle they would spend most of the morning in the kitchen preparing picnic baskets, and then by the afternoon they'd be at the castle watching the men and eventually feeding them.

"Two weeks after my birthday it had rained heavily, keeping us trapped inside. By the afternoon my sisters decided to return to the castle and play Florence Nightingale to the workers. They each worked on me until I finally agreed to go. I never had before."

She laughed at herself for a moment. "There had to be at least a hundred men working. Everywhere I looked there were ladders and sheets of plastic hanging from the ceilings and on the walls. The room they had been so impatient for me to see was the master-sized ballroom. We had one in our home, but this one was much larger ----- it was at least the size of two, maybe three rooms combined. That's where I really saw Luke."

She smiled fondly, showing off her perfect ultra-white teeth. The purple in her eyes began to glow and shine. My legs were starting to throb from being in one position for so long. The look in Mariah's eyes made me nervous, I couldn't will myself to move.

"He was standing on a ladder," she began again. "installing a new crystal chandelier, wearing only a pair of jeans and a tool belt around his waist. It stunned me how I'd never noticed until that moment how inhumanly beautiful he was. I watched the way the muscles in his chest flexed unable to understand why my heart pounded so hard and why my stomach was so full of butterflies.

"He caught me staring at him and smiled. My cheeks instantly burned from embarrassment. I quickly turned away, fighting the urge to run and went looking for my sisters.

"For the next month I went back nearly every day. I would stand just out of sight and watch him. Once I offered him a sandwich, he kindly declined. Then one day I went back searching endlessly for him. I couldn't find him, my heart heavy with disappointment I turned to leave. I had just stepped out the door and a single red rose appeared inches in front of my face. Startled, I stumbled backwards.

"'I thought maybe this would convince you to talk with me,' came a soft voice.

"I turned my head sharply in the direction it had come from. Luke was leaning against the wall. I was so astounded by his perfect face and his close proximity I didn't know what to say or do. I very slowly reached out and took the rose from his hand.

"Thank you, I said shyly.

"'I've been hoping to get the chance to introduce myself. My name is Luke Bradford.'

"I put the rose against my nose, giving myself a moment to relax so I could speak clearly ----- and calmly. I'm Mariah Maraschino.

"He suddenly raised one eyebrow. 'Maraschino?' he repeated, stunned.

"I completely misunderstood the meaning of his tone, blurting out foolishly. You know, as in the cherries?"

She laughed at herself again, this time the sound was warm and relaxed. She turned her violet eyes on me.

"When I learned Sean had fallen for you I sympathized with you. I've never been attracted to him, he's irritated me from the moment I was changed, but I knew the emotions and confusion you suffer through from the power of those eyes."

Her mood suddenly shifted, her eyes looked distant. "Have you ever noticed Sean's eyes are the same color as a white Bengal tiger?"

I stared at her a long moment before answering. I was wanting to be sure she remembered I was still in the room.

"Truthfully, I've never thought about it. I don't look at his eyes too long, if I do I can't stay coherent."

The pain in my legs was now completely unbearable, keeping my eyes on Mariah I carefully straightened them. They instantly began to feel, as if I were being poked repeatedly with needles. I closed my eyes briefly, fighting against myself to sit still. Mariah never noticed my discomfort, continuing on.

"He looks like a tiger when we're feeding, too," she mused. She was thoughtful for a moment, and then looked at me. "I suppose I shouldn't fill your head with such images."

"I don't dream, but if I did I'd dream of things much worse than a hunting tiger," I informed her.

"This is the first time I've ever gotten to speak of this and despite the constant reminders from Sean I forget how scary some things might be for you."

I almost opened my mouth, telling her it was all too much to handle at times, but the only time it's scary is when Sean throws things faster than the eye can blink. I secretly shivered at the thought and changed my mind. Mariah may have always been the only one to never speak to me much, I didn't want her misunderstanding my statement and lose the chance to know her.

I inhaled deeply through my nose, slowly releasing the breath. "My nerves are great thus far."

She scrutinized my face for a long second. I kept it clear of emotions, waiting for her to continue. The minutes passed.

"Luke and I were together every day," she said, jumping back into her story. "I would lay in bed fully clothed at night waiting for everyone to go to sleep. When I no longer heard anything outside my bedroom I'd tiptoe across the room and carefully crack open the door. The long hallway was dark, there wasn't any lights shining under any of the other doors. I closed my door, crossed the room, and then climbed down from my balcony. My heart would pound as I thought about Luke while I ran to meet him.

"The cliff overlooking Frenchman Bay gave us a great view of the sea-foamed colored water, but the tall grass kept us hidden ---- or so I thought. I remember how I couldn't wait to see the way the moonlight reflected of his skin.

"Of course, I did find it odd that he never touched me or allowed me to be too close. As long as he let me sit on the rocks with him in the summer breeze I could be happy with that. We would talk for hours about where we had traveled and the places we had wanted to see.

"One cool September night we were sitting on our cliff discussing how we were going to meet once the winter set in. We watched a fishing boat as it came in from the Atlantic and thought nothing of anyone being able to see us. The moonlight wasn't very bright, preventing Luke's skin from glowing.

"The next morning my sisters and I were having breakfast with our mother when suddenly our father walked through the kitchen door.

"'Is something wrong, Charles?' my mother asked. She was just as stunned by his presence as we were.

"He completely ignored her, his eyes focused on my face.

"'Mariah,' he said harshly. 'you and I need to talk.'

"At first, I was unable to understand what I had done to make him so angry. What have I done, father? I asked.

"'Never mind that now,' he grumbled. 'We will speak privately in the den.'

"I set my spoon down beside my bowl and stood from the chair.

"'Charles,' my mother called. 'she's eating breakfast. Could it wait until she's finished?'

"My mother was always the one to stand at our side whenever our father showed any anger towards us. I knew early on *I* was her favorite. I was the youngest, the only blond and I was always the one admired the most by other people. My mother was unable to hide her pride when I graduated high school at the top of my class, as *I* was also the only member of our family to ever be valedictorian."

She was thoughtful for a moment and I wondered if she'd forgotten my presence again. But then she looked at me, her expression almost resentful.

"My father never liked it when she intervened.

"'This is not the time for your opinions or request, Cindy,' he snarled. 'She'll have plenty of time to finish up after we talk.' He turned his stormy gray eyes back on me. 'Mariah ... now.'

"Yes, sir, I replied softly. When he turned to walk out I silently followed him."

I knew we had reached the tough part of her story. Her face suddenly turned hard, she ground her teeth together. I sat perfectly still, even breathing with caution. It took her a few minutes to regain control of her emotions. I waited patiently.

"I was so sure I could do this without frightening you with my poor reactions." She shook her head, seeming a little frustrated. I wasn't sure if it was with herself or her story.

"I do apologize," she said a little more relaxed.

"I'm fine," I lied, weakly.

She stared at the window behind me for a long moment. It was a long eerie silence before she finally broke into her reverie.

"When we entered his den he ordered me to close the door. I stood nervously, waiting for him to begin. Instead, he walked to his liquor cabinet and poured himself a drink.

"'Young lady,' he finally spoke, his tone patient. He replaced the top on the bottle, and then turned to me. 'I set rules in this house and I expect them to be followed. You and your sisters seem to think I don't know what you're doing.'

"I was so confused. What could *I* have done that was so much more wrong then my sisters?

"'Dad, I don't under … He raised his hand, silencing me. He swirled his brandy around in the glass, and then took a drink.

"'Do not stand there and try to back sass me, young lady. And, don't try to act innocent. It may work on your mother, but I'm not buying it.'

"I stared at him in complete awe, for I was dumbfounded by his words. I tried desperately to think over my actions. Other than sneaking out to spend time with Luke I'd done nothing wrong.

"'Still confused?' he crowed.

"Dad, I really don't understand, I said.

"'C'mon, Mariah!' he suddenly yelled. 'Are you going to stand in front of me and lie about all the time you're spending with that Callenger boy?'

"I felt my eyes widen in horror, my mouth fell open. The fishing boat ----- they saw us!

"'I don't know how many times I have to remind you girls that I prohibit any of you to fraternize with his kind of people,' he continued.

"I've never been theatrical or had I even defined my parents, but somehow in that moment his words caused a reaction from me I never thought possible. I felt a deeper anger than I could have ever imagined. I could feel, my blood felt so hot it could have boiled the skin."

It was hard to tell in the darkness, but it suddenly looked like her unnaturally olive pale skin got more pale. Especially her face. Her mouth twisted angrily, the words came out through her clamped teeth.

"He is not those kinds of people! I stated hatefully. Maybe if you came down from your high horse and get to know the men that work for you, you might actually find they're no different than you.

"He raised his voice. 'Enough! You may be eighteen years old, however you still live under my roof. Therefore, you *will* obey my rules.'

"The words were out of my mouth before I even had time to think. You know what, Daddy?" ----- her mouth twisted around his name, it came out in a snarl. ----- "You can have your pathetic rules and your house.

"His mouth suddenly fell open, he seemed to be stunned by my outburst. After a few seconds he snapped it shut, composing himself.

"'What did you just say!?' he shouted. He squeezed his hand around the whiskey glass so tightly his knuckles turned white.

"You heard me. I love Luke and he loves me ... that part I wasn't truly sure of but I was too angry at that moment to care ... I'm going to continue seeing him and there's nothing you can do about it!

"'You seem to forget it's my money you enjoy spending. I will cut everything off should you continue on with this nonsense,' he threatened.

"Then I suppose you have to do what you have to do. I turned my back to him and walked to the door.

"'Mariah Nichole Maraschino,' he yelled. 'If you walk out that door there will *never* be any coming back.'

"I glanced at him over my shoulder. Goodbye, Dad. I walked out the door, closing it behind me. I could hear him calling my name as I walked down the long hall. I passed my room, not bothering to stop and pack. I was nearly running, tears falling down my cheeks by the time I entered the kitchen. My mother's expression looked crushed when she saw me. She stretched her arms out in front of her to catch me. I dodged her, running out the kitchen door.

"I ran to the castle looking for Luke. I had barely entered when I was told he had been fired earlier that morning. Deeply crushed I left, hoping what I told my father hadn't just become my biggest mistake. I walked for hours, searching every place I thought Luke might be. Figuring Jonah had been fired as well I never went to the warehouse. Finally, night fall set in and I went to what I'll always consider our cliff. Relief flooded through me when I saw his beautiful skin glowing in the moonlight. I ran to him.

"'Mariah,' he said, sounding relieved at my presence. 'I'm truly sorry if anything I have done caused you any trouble.'

"For the first time in all the months we were together he wrapped his arms around me, pressing me carefully against him.

"Oh, Luke, I whimpered. I'm in such a mess.

"'How?' he asked, earnestly.

"Until then I held all my emotions in, but once his voice showed an ounce of tenderness I fell apart.

"Because I refused to stop being with you my father kicked me out.

"I heard an awful sound rumble from his chest. I stopped sobbing and pulled my head away to look at him. His blue eyes had turned black, his face twisted in agony. It made me nervous seeing him look like that. I lifted one foot to take a step back, never to get the chance. Suddenly, I was cradled in his arms and it felt as though I was flying. The next thing I knew he was setting me on my feet in front of the house he shared with Jonah and his wife. He held my hand and walked me inside. That's when I saw the others for the first time."

She smiled, turning her eyes to me, her expression suddenly amused.

"Sean wasn't happy. I can still clearly remember the look on his face when Luke pulled me inside." Her laughter filled the room, the sound close to a hyena. I tried to shy away from the sound.

"'Luke, you really shouldn't have brought her here,' Jonah said, sounding condescending.

"'I couldn't just leave her without a home because of something I have done,' Luke said quietly.

"'Of course you can't,' Becca agreed.

"'What do you mean leave her without a home?' Kelsey asked.

"'I broke the rules ----- ours and Charles Maraschino's,' Luke admitted, sounding remorseful. 'I've been seeing her these last couple of months.'

"'Have you finally lost your mind, Luke?' Sean said. 'Mariah Maraschino?'" She matched Sean's tone so perfectly I had to press my lips together to suppress a laugh. "'She's not only a human, but also the daughter of a powerful family. The Maraschino's will have a search party out looking for her ----- *if* they don't already.'

"I couldn't believe the way they were discussing me, never seeming to mind I was standing in the room. I also didn't like the way Sean spoke my family's name, like it was something contagious.

"'I know and I'm sorry,' Luke apologized. 'I never meant for any of this to happen.'

"'We understand, Luke,' Jonah said. He walked to Luke, placing a firm hand on his shoulder. 'You're either going to have to find a way to make this right or tell her the truth. Whichever decision you make is going to have to be done quickly. We need to leave while it's still safe.'

"I stared up at Luke, my body began to shake and the only thing I could think was I had gotten myself in a dangerous situation. I wanted to run, but my feet seemed to be planted in place, leaving me to feel frozen.

"'I know the right thing to do is send her back, never knowing anything,' Luke began softly. 'What if I can't let her go?'

"Jonah sighed. 'She learns the truth she just simply may go her own way.'

"His words terrified me. I knew nothing of what my life was about to become, but I knew there was no going back for me. Luke nodded his head once, and then took my hand and we walked out the door. I'm not sure why but that was when I noticed for the first time that his skin was hard and cold.

"Luke took me to a cove, setting me on my feet after we entered. I stood there, watching as he paced back and forth. The minutes seemed to pass slowly. Then finally, he stopped pacing and looked at me. I had never seen his eyes look so troubled.

"'Mariah,' Luke sighed. 'this is by far the hardest thing I've had yet to do. I need you to hear everything I have to say. Once I finish should you wish to return home and make amends with your family I will take you back.'

"He waited for my response, though I was unable to find my voice. I could only nod my head in agreement. Luke took a deep breath, his eyes watching me carefully.

"'What I am about to tell you is going to be difficult for you to believe. I hope you trust me enough to have no fear of me.'

"And again, he waited for my response. When I nodded my head he began.

"'It is important I tell you this first; I love you. I never thought it possible, despite how many times I've seen it happen. For this I hope you choose to save yourself. I'm a vampire, Mariah.'

"I felt my mouth fall open as I continued to stare at him, becoming horrified. He continued on, never showing any distress to my reaction.

"'If you do not choose to return to your life I will have no options but to take away your humanity.'

"I couldn't believe the things coming out of his mouth. Now when I looked at him all the obviousness I'd never noticed before seem to stand out, but it still didn't make me a believer.

"I don't care what you are, I blurted out. I love you, Luke Bradford and I want to be with *you.*

"His eyes widened at my words and suddenly he was pulling me into his arms, his lips feverishly covered mine. At first I was nearly terrified, for I never saw him move, and then in a heated second I responded. I had never been kissed before, it was more than anything I could ever have imagined. A fluttering in the pit of my stomach, so hard it was almost painful. I wedged myself tighter against him, afraid he wouldn't hold me the way I wanted ----- I needed. He responded to my actions, his hands slid ..."

Mariah suddenly looked at me, as if she just remembered I was there. Her eyes narrowed, her expression odd. My face was probably green. It felt green.

"I'll spare you the details," she said quietly.

"That would be great," I said, somberly.

She smiled and laughed, the sound much warmer than it had been. "While we lay together inside the cove Luke whispered an apology in my ear. I tried to understand why he would feel sorry, but then suddenly something sharp was cutting me. First in my throat, and then my wrist, my ankles. I screamed in shock, believing for a moment that he had intended to hurt me after all. Then fire began spreading through me, rushing quickly through my body. It was then I believed what he had told me.

"Luke stayed at my side. He held my hand and apologized over and over, promising all the pain I felt would soon end. Once I was finished transforming he took me back to the others. We left Bar Harbor after night fall. I learned how to quench the thirst and the burning in my throat that would be custom to the rest of my existence."

Her eyes looked distant again, I sat quietly, waiting for her to return to the present. The minutes passed.

"I suppose this is where a long story ends," she sighed.

I couldn't be sure if she was waiting for a response, I wasn't sure what to say.

"Thank you, Mariah, for sharing your story. It's nice to have the chance to know you better. But I'm still confused as to how any of it has anything to do with me."

Now that she was fully alert, leaving no chance of my movements startling her I pushed off the quilt. I was amazed at how much I could sweat.

"You're in the same position I had been. I know and personally understand your reasons for wanting to remain human. However, Angel, this is the point where you have to make a choice."

She saw I was about to argue and stopped me. "Let me say this," she said quickly. "I'm sure there are a great number of things you haven't thought about too seriously. And from what I have seen and learned about you you're much stronger and much more mature than I was. You think you're too young to know what you'll want in ten years, fifteen years ---- and in most human lives that's true. What I'm trying to say is, do you see a future without Sean?"

No one has ever asked me that before; it took me by surprise. I stared at Mariah's perfect, marble face for a long second, and then slowly shook my head back and forth.

"I'm Irish enough to believe in fate. If a future with Sean wasn't my destiny none of you would have been in the woods that night and I surely wouldn't have made the pact with Jonah. But -----"

The mention of that night in the woods brought on flashback images of Amanda. I pressed my lips together in a hard line.

"I know Sean frightened you pretty badly, Angel," she said, misreading my expression. "But it just meant he loves you, much more than he thought possible. He was angry with Luke for years because of what he did to me. Now that the situation is happening again he's learning to understand the hardships Luke faced."

"I get that," I stated sharply. "What I don't get is he *promised* me I wouldn't ever become something or someone else, yet he keeps me facing the fire."

"Angel," she scolded me. Her voice was now more passionate then it had been. "Don't be so hard on him. Just like you he's trying to make sense of all this. He too, has given up his human life for love. It may have been a different kind, but it's still the same principle. If the situation were reversed and he had to make the same decision I know he would walk through the same fire for you."

I stared at her, perplexed. My brain was so dumbfounded I couldn't think of any response. She suddenly stood from the bed and in a flash was to the door. She turned to look at me.

"Just at least think about what I have said. Good night, Angel." She silently opened the door, disappearing ghostly.

"Good night, Mariah," I murmured bleakly.

I turned my body and flopped down on the pillow. It took a long time before I was finally relaxed enough to sleep.

It was still dark when a strange sensation woke me. I was so groggy my eyes barely opened as I reached out to shift the quilt. It didn't move. It took a moment and a few more tugs on it to realize there was something on it. My eyes instantly flew open, trying to see. Somehow it had darkened outside, the too thick clouds covered the moon.

"Sorry," Sean's voice softly murmured. Suddenly, without even the slightest movement on the bed the quilt was freed. "Guess I didn't realize I was lying on your blanket."

"It's not a big deal," I yawned. "and welcome back."

His voice sounded stunned when he spoke. "You're not angry with me?"

"I was at first," I admitted. "but it seems babysitters have their advantages."

Now he was really confused. "How so?"

I rolled to my side, facing him, tucking the quilt around me. "It gave me an opportunity to learn a few things about someone I barely know."

His silence was much too long and it was too dark for me to see his facial expression. I opened my mouth to get him talking when suddenly he grabbed my arm, pulling me to him. He encircled his arm around me, laying me over his chest.

"Mariah spoke to you, anyway, didn't she?"

His tone wasn't bitter, I knew it well enough that I could hear the tenor behind it. I carefully lifted my head and looked at him. The fingers on his right hand were playing with strands of hair that had come out of the braid, his left arm was tucked under his head.

"Don't be like that," I glowered. "You may not believe this, but she's on your side."

I felt my breath catch in my throat when my favorite, slightly cocky smile crossed his lips.

"May I ask what she said to make you believe her? Or is it too confidential?"

I rolled my eyes and playfully swatted his bare chest. "It appears Mariah understands how I feel about what you and your family are asking me to do."

Sean opened his mouth to respond and I quickly placed my fingers against his lips.

"Let me finish," I said sharply. I waited till both his eyes and his face softened to continue. "She told me about her life, how closely it compares to mine and the sacrifices even you have to make."

While I was going on with my rant something she told me that Sean had kept a secret entered my mind.

"Since we're discussing Mariah, why didn't you tell me she finds my scent mouthwatering?"

His face hardened, a resentful expression twisting his features. He trapped my hand in his, kissed my fingers, and then carefully slid them to his chin. And as usual, my heart reacted.

"It is already hard enough for you to fully relax when you're in the same room with each of us at the same time. Why give you one more reason to fear?"

I knew his answer was logical, even truthful, it didn't stop my expression from falling into a frown.

"Moot point," I growled.

Sean laughed.

He released my hand and I rolled onto my back, stuffing the blanket tightly around me.

"Does this mean you've changed your mind about everything and have decided to marry me after all?" he suddenly asked.

"Ugh!" I groaned. "*Please*, don't start this again."

He laughed, this time shaking the entire bed, and rolled on his right side to face me. He lifted my left hand and brought it to his face, lightly grazing his nose over my wrist. Despite how warm I was, a slight shiver ran down my body.

"I was very wrong when I said you smell like a meadow of lilacs," he teased. "it's more like ... spring roses."

I scowled at the darkness. "Just because you find it humorous to tell a girl how good she smells to an extremely arrogant vampire, doesn't mean she will feel all fuzzy inside and agree to marry you."

I heard him sigh heavily. He kissed the inside of my wrist, and then released it.

"It has always been the hard way with you, but I get it. You want me to beg."

I didn't understand his tone or his words. My eyes were widened with shock, watching as he rolled to his back, and then sat up.

"I have never had to beg for anything in my life," he stated, shaking his head. "Since I have met you it has become inevitable. I guess you don't truly believe that if it is really what you want I will oblige."

The pieces to the puzzle slowly began to click in place as he stood from the bed. In a move too quick for my eyes or my mind to keep up with, he was around the bed, carefully easing himself down to his knee beside me. It was then everything became clear and I finally understood. I quickly sat up, reaching out for his arm. I couldn't be sure my reaction would stop him, but to my surprise it did.

"Sean, please," I pleaded. "Could we not talk about this anymore?"

An expression I didn't understand crossed his face. "What am I going to have to do to change your mind? I love you, I want to marry you."

I stared at him for a long second, unsure how to answer his question.

"I love you, too," I breathed weakly. "Isn't that enough to convince you I'll stay with you?"

He was shaking his head before I was finished. "I want to know that no matter foolish I act I'll always have you. Not come home and find a note that you have left me. I want *you* forever, Angelia."

Why did anyone have to tell him my full name!?

I fought off a cringe when he mentioned the note. It seems I may *never* live that decision down. I inhaled deeply through my nose, slowly releasing the breath, through my lips. "What do you say we just call this an agreement to disagree, I really do need to sleep. Just let me have some time to think it all through," I quickly tacked on when a low growl rumbled in the back of his throat.

I gently tugged on his arm to get him to move back on the bed. He complied just as I knew he would.

"Fine," he growled through clenched teeth. "I'll let this be a truce for now, but tell me something."

He laid over me, carefully keeping his weight off of me, though I could still feel his hard, cold body through the quilt.

I couldn't help feeling leery at his request. "What?"

"What is it about spending an eternity committed to me that frightens you?"

Most of the time I pretended to think about his questions before answering them. However, tonight wasn't one of those times.

"Everything," I barely whispered.

He looked in my eyes for a second, and then placed a gentle kiss on my lips. He rolled us, keeping me locked in the bend of his arm and laid me over his chest.

"You're afraid of my poor behavior," he suddenly whispered. "You just need time and then you will see it get better." I felt his lips softly touch my hair. "Sweet dreams, my love."

He began humming our tune and I closed my eyes.

Revenge

I sat, staring grumpily out the window while Sean drove us to the hall. I slept restless the night before unable to get Jeremy and John out of my mind. And worse still, I couldn't stop my mind from turning over my last conversation with Sean. Marriage ----- arg! Then this morning I bounced in agitation every time I looked at the clock, knowing I wouldn't be able to get free from Sean to meet John and was now fearing his rebuttal. I wasn't quite convinced he would ruin his grandmother's party to even the score, the Callenger's still believed he was Jeremy's accomplice. If that is true and he wanted to talk to me so he didn't have to disappoint his grandfather then I just created a more dangerous situation by not meeting him.

Sean got one last detailed called from Cameron causing us to leave the house late so I knew everyone was already arriving to the party, leaving me to mentally calculate how I was getting to the piano without stumbling into anyone or just simply tripping over my own two feet. It wasn't really *that*, that had me feeling so sulky (besides not meeting John's demands, of course). It was the memory of Bobbie's twisted face when Sean broke the news to her about Jeremy.

She was barely in the door and Sean asked her to join us at the table. At first, she was delighted, as I think she thought we were going to give her the news I suspected she believed was coming. But then Sean laid out the story of Jeremy's escape and John's suspicious behaviors. I watched in horror as her expressions changed. They were shocked then slowly turned horrified. Since it was too late for her to leave now Sean requested she put in an emergency leave with the hospital and make plans to get out of Newport as soon as possible. And, to be sure she didn't leave alone. She agreed she would somehow convince Josh to leave with her right after the party.

After that the morning passed, almost normally. I was so close to being a basket case I thought Sean might change his mind about the party and drag me out the door, even if I was kicking and screaming. Instead, he spent the rest of it and most of the afternoon on the phone with his family. Jeremy was somehow managing to stay one step ahead of them. A hotel receipt put him in town the night before, but now there was no sign of him. Sean believed it was because of John he was able to get in and out of town unnoticed. Since they couldn't track him the way vampires would normally track their prey Cameron and Mariah were sent to keep watch over John.

I also couldn't stop thinking about my dress and how humiliating it was going to be when I got my shoes tangled up and tripped over the bottom. I had myself convinced I only had to make it to the piano then I could sit the rest of the night. And then, Sean informed me we wouldn't be leaving till he got *his* chance to dance with me.

Ugh!

That was another thing adding to my sulky mood. Kelsey had been unable to get me any pumps (as Mariah had promised) because they were busy keeping their focus on Jeremy and brought me a pair stilettos. Since they couldn't locate him in town or anywhere around the county line, Mike was insisting they follow everything by the book. Despite Luke's complaining Jonah was happy with Mike's idea, he didn't want his family having anything to do with the capture this time so they could avoid proving Jeremy's theory correct; especially Luke. Honestly, even I was fine with that. I knew it was silly to fear their safety, as I was told repeatedly it wouldn't happen, but knowing they could get too close had me nervous.

When Becca suggested they attend Mrs. Wilkins' party as planned I became anxious. It was then I was informed by Jonah that Cameron and Mariah would be outside watching for any activities from Jeremy or John. I knew Jonah was just trying to comfort me with the idea that Jeremy wouldn't see them nor would any of the townspeople when they came and went, but it worked. Though, only a little.

I grumbled at myself for still thinking about everything and began trying to focus on simply getting through tonight. And then I was reminded of Sean's plans. I didn't have a single clue where he was taking me. I didn't mind that so much. What I *did* mind was the idea I wasn't going to have time to change. Not only was I going to still be wearing Kelsey's idea of a dress, but I was going to have to walk through Portland's airport in my borrowed stilettos. I *knew* because of my lack of sleep and the long hours I was going to have to act like my life was perfect I was going to be much too tired to try to walk. Reminding myself of this caused my irritation to grow that much stronger.

"You seem to be a thousand miles away," Sean noted. "Are you all right?"

"I'm fine," I muttered; my voice was as unconvincing as it always was when I lied. "It's just nerves."

"You're going to be exceptionally brilliant tonight," he said, encouragingly.

That wasn't exactly what I meant. I wasn't nervous about playing for what was sure to be the entire town. I was worried (okay, so *worried* isn't the right word), I was afraid Jeremy would slip through their barrier and sneak inside, ruining everyone's black-tie affair.

At nearly the last minute Dean decided he wanted for everyone to dress formal. He wanted to recreate the night when he first met his wife. It had been their high school senior winter dance. I grimaced while reluctantly admitting the time Kelsey and Brandi had spent trying to turn me into a beauty queen was a good thing.

Through all the haze clouding my mind I couldn't remember if I'd even noticed how Sean was dressed. I tore my eyes away from the window to look at him. He had never worn black before and I was quite impressed with how the contrast of the tuxedo set against his pale skin.

"I have mentioned that you look very handsome, haven't I?" I verified.

"Yes." He grinned.

I fought the urge to look at myself and kept my eyes on his face. "Well good," I stated hesitantly. "I can say with all honesty I'm not going to miss Kelsey and Brandi while we're away."

"Why not?" he laughed.

"Because then they can't treat me like their very own Barbie doll," I griped.

I was forced to spend the afternoon in Bobbie's bathroom, a helpless victim to Brandi playing the hairdresser while Kelsey was the cosmetician. Anytime I fidgeted or complained they would threaten to tear apart everything they had done and start over.

"Angel." He turned the full force of his scorching blue eyes on me.

"What?" I grumbled.

"It's not that bad." His voice was disapproving.

"You'll see," I muttered. "When I'm lying in the hospital with a broken neck you can't blame me."

He rolled his eyes while shaking his head and turned his face back to the windshield. That only added to my irritation. I murmured unintelligibly and pulled up the bottom of the dress, exposing the shoes as evidence.

"I may as well be wearing stilts," I pouted.

His eyes lowered to my legs before he slid them over the dress, staring at it longer than was necessary. The corners of his mouth twitched.

"Hmmm. That reminds me when I see Brandi and Kelsey tonight I need to thank them for doing an amazing job."

I groaned, shuffling the dress down over my legs. Sean chuckled, returning his eyes toward the windshield. Then sighed.

"I'll be right next to you all night. I promise to save you from everything conspiring against you." Then he threw a glance my direction. "Yourself included."

We were at the hall now. I ignored his twisted humor, forcing myself to focus on the building. There were lights strung along the entrance, set to look like stars. The clouds were thin tonight, the rain had stopped hours ago and sky seemed to want to let a few of its own stars shine.

Sean got out and walked around the truck to open my door. He held out his hand.

I sat hesitant in my seat, watching people walk in the building, feeling completely unsure I could go through with this, after all. He sighed, leaning down and wrapped one arm around my waist. I took his other hand and allowed him to lift me from the truck.

"I won't let go until you're ready," he promised, misreading my sudden fear.

It wasn't the thought of trying to walk in the shoes (clearly not meant for someone like me) that suddenly had me changing my mind. I was nearly a hundred percent sure my stubbornness had put everyone in danger. My friends and neighbors and the friendly customers that came into Kloe's restaurant were going to laugh, eat and sway to the music tonight, completely oblivious to the fact that they were about to face horror, maybe even death. All because of me.

He kept his arm tightly around me, seeming to be patient with my slowness.

Despite my sudden fear I couldn't keep myself from secretly hoping the room was big enough for a party the size Dean was aiming for. In a town this size it isn't common to see buildings designed to house thousands of people at once. Maybe he should have worked something out with Derek for his place before he left.

When we got inside, I felt my breath catch in my throat. There were balloon arches, with twisted garlands of pastel crepe paper in blue and white festooning the walls. There were more strings of lights hanging on the walls above all the paper. A mirrored ball hung from the ceiling with lights flashing from it, sending sparkles of light around the room. There were small tables, with four chairs surrounding them lining the walls to the back of the room. In the center of each one was a single burning candle.

Music spilled out of the speakers overhead causing some of the guest to dance. I looked at the dance floor in awe. One couple whirled gracefully around the room, but it wasn't them that caught my attention. Luke stood motionless in a corner, dressed in a tuxedo. His eyes met mine for a brief second and he nodded his head once. Brandi and Kelsey stood beside a long table and were intimidating and flawless in their gowns. Kelsey's scarlet dress was backless, tight fitting to her calves where one side had a mid-thigh slit, with a neckline that plunged to her waist.

And Brandi was … well, Brandi. She was way beyond her usualness. She was striking in a soft pink satin dress with geometric cutouts in the back baring triangles of her tan skin. I couldn't help smiling as I tore my eyes away from her to scan the rest of the room. Many of the faces I recognized, Catlyn and Kyle; Bobbie and Josh. Then there were others I didn't.

"All we need now is a stage and a ballot for prom king and queen and we got ourselves a horror movie," I snickered.

"There are a number of vampires present," he laughed darkly, pointing to the graceful couple. "so I can see how you could easily portray us as part of the scene."

Jonah and Becca flashed us a dazzling smile when they twirled past us. Again, I couldn't help smiling. "Let's just say we get this party over with," I mumbled.

Sean nodded his head in agreement.

He kept his arm around me while I wobbled my feet forward, praying I could get to the piano without being called or humiliated. A second after I sat down on the bench Mayor Wilkins entered the room with his very surprised wife at his side. He like all the other men, was dressed in a black tuxedo while Mrs. Wilkins wore a maroon gown, with the straps crossing over her back. She had a neckless dripping in diamonds hanging from her neck. While she was being greeted by the people now around her Dean walked on, crossing the room to the microphone.

"Could I have everyone's attention please? Thank you," he tacked on when everyone turned their heads. "I wanted to thank all you for coming out tonight to share in this wonderful bliss. Mrs. Callenger, I would especially like to thank you for all you have done to make this evening possible. Shelia, my love." He paused to walk to her and take her hand. "Thank you for the thirty years of putting up with my sulkiness and raising our wonderful children. Happy birthday."

He leaned in, placing a gentle kiss on her cheek. "Now, without any further long winded speeches from me, Angel, would you mind?"

He passed the microphone to the person standing beside him, pulling his wife into his arms. They began their waltz as soon as my fingers played the first note of their song.

Even though I was sitting on the bench in front of the piano Sean kept one arm securely at my waist, pushing himself closer to me if anyone looked like they were going to approach me. So I was instantly suspicious something was wrong when Luke appeared from the crowd.

His eyes met Sean's and a second later he dropped his arm before edging away from me.

"Luke needs to talk," he murmured in my ear. "I'll be right back."

In one fluid move he was on his feet, fluttering to Luke's side. They gracefully passed around the crowd without seeming to touch any of the bodies. They weren't moving with the usual phony human slowness, no one seemed to notice.

I stared after them with horror struck eyes while trying desperately to keep my fingers focused on the melody. I watched them as they reached the dark shadow beside the doorway. I craned my neck over the top of the piano trying to see if they were going to walk out the door. Right then, a speckle of light flashed over them, glinting off Jonah's face. The light only touched it for a half second, but it was enough to let me know something was wrong.

"I have to say I'm truly impressed," came a stunned voice.

I hadn't noticed I was being approached or that my fingers stopped playing and was now curled into the palm of my hands, making fists. I forced them to relax while trying to focus on Kyle's face.

"Impressed with what?" I asked confused.

He gave me an odd expression, waving his hand up and down next to the piano. "Apparently not all of us knew you could play."

"Oh," I laughed, the sound shaky. "I guess I've forgotten to mention it."

I knew the guest were waiting for another song when some of them turned to look at me. I couldn't seem to concentrate on anything but the bodies standing beside the door. When my gaze drifted their direction again I felt Kyle's hand cup around my chin, pulling my face up.

"Why do you seem so distracted?" he wondered.

"I suppose I'm just nervous," I lied.

"Angel?" His brows pulled together, his brown eyes were deep in their shadow. "There's something

going on you're not telling me about, isn't there?"

"Kyle, I ... no, everything is fine."

"She's right, Hesner. Everything is as to be expected." Sean's voice appeared seconds before he did.

Kyle flinched and stared wide-eyed at him. "How do you always mange to appear out of thin air?" he mumbled.

"I suppose you're just oblivious to my presence when you have your attention on the reason for my existing," he laughed bleakly. "If you're still interested in keeping that arm you should let her go ... now."

Kyle released my face and stepped back, waving halfheartedly. "I guess I'll see you around, Angel."

I scowled at Sean for his rudeness. "Yeah, I'll see you when I get back."

He nodded his head at me before walking away, eventually disappearing in the crowd.

Sean sat beside me and wrapped his arm around my waist. His face was hard and expressionless, but I didn't let that stop me from glaring at him.

"What?" he asked innocently.

"I realize you're under a lot of pressure, but did you have to be so rude?"

He wasn't expecting my reaction, that much was clear. He pressed his lips together and his eyes narrowed. "You're right, I apologize. I'm being over protective of you tonight for good reason ... however, I shouldn't be rude to your friends. I'll apologize to Hesner when I see him again."

"Is it really so hard for you to call him by name?" I huffed.

"Do you want to sit here and discuss Kyle or would you like to know why I had to converse with my family?" he grumbled.

"I'm not sure my nerves could take it," I admitted sheepishly.

He stared at me for a long moment before finally deciding to speak. "John Wilkins has been murdered. Mike and the other deputies are at the hotel as we speak and that means Jeremy is here somewhere. I wanted to tell you that we are going to check things out."

"We!?" I shrieked. "You're seriously going to leave me here ... alone?"

He frowned impatiently at me. "You're not alone, Angelia." He paused, extending his arm out at the crowd. "There are plenty of people here."

"You said you would sit out on catching Jeremy," I reminded him. "Were you really going to or was that just talk?" I knew my attempts to change his mind were pathetic, I also knew that if he was right and Jeremy was close I would be in trouble when he saw I was alone.

"Don't be difficult, Angel," he growled. "We would much more prefer not to be involved this time, but since he planned John's death perfectly we have no choice. We cannot allow him to get inside."

"Okay." I closed the lid on the piano, shifted the bottom of the dress and stood up.

He was stunned by my reaction. "What are you doing?"

"Going with you," I stated.

"Angel, it's too ..."

"I go or you stay," I demanded. I fisted my hands on my hips to show him I was serious. "I'm not going to sit here and wait for him to find his way in and watch as he hurts anyone. If you intercept him before he gets close to here and I'm with you then everyone will be safe."

He looked away from me, meeting the eyes of the men waiting for him. "Fine, I'm going to tell Jonah I'm out." Then he turned his scorching eyes on me. "Once I do you're leaving with me right now."

That wasn't exactly what I was aiming for, but if it meant he wouldn't be leaving my side I'd take the deal. "Fine."

He stood from the bench and leaned in to place his cold, marble lips to my forehead. "I'll be right back." A second later he was gone.

My body was rigid as a plank but I forced myself to sit down. I closed my eyes, focusing on slowing my erratic breathing and calm my rapidly beating heart.

"Hello, Angel," came a soft, rough voice.

His voice was friendly, on the surface. I still caught the edge of menace and didn't have to look up right away to know that Jeremy was standing next to the piano. I didn't say anything, continuing to stare down.

"I've been dreaming of our little reunion for months."

I inhaled deeply through my nose, in hopes of keeping fear out of my voice and lifted my head. He looked different from the last time I saw him. His eyes were the same deep blue, but his hair was longer, black instead of blond, and he had grown out a beard.

"You know you were better of dreaming, right?" It surprised me when I heard how strong my voice was.

Jeremy laughed. "I have your sheriff ... busy so if your friends want to even their score then they'll have to prove themselves to the mayor and his wife. How well do you think they'll take it when they find out *what* has been living with them? Or how many of them there really are," he tacked on when I didn't answer.

I felt my insides shiver with fear, but held onto my bravery knowing Sean would soon emerge from the crowd. What is keeping him?

"I'm not sure you should worry about how they're going to fare," I said sarcastically. "What you should be worried about is how well *you're* going to be."

He took a couple of steps forward and leaned over the piano till his face was mere inches from mine.

"You're a lot more fiery than I remember," he cooed. "Does that mean you've missed me?"

"Not particularly." I knew it wasn't a good idea to turn my attention away from him while he was this close, I couldn't help it. I frantically scanned the crowd for any of the Callengers. I forced a smile when I met curious eyes. I knew if they thought something was wrong they would approach us. Once again I was in a dangerous situation that could get someone hurt if I made the wrong decision. Sean was coming ...

"I don't know if I believe that," Jeremy said, calling back my focus.

"And why not?" I challenged.

"You're wearing an amazing dress tonight so you had to be hoping to see me."

"Don't flatter yourself," I said ruefully. "You are truly insane if you honestly believe that."

Anger flashed across his face, hatred burned in his tawny eyes. "I may be a lot of things but insane isn't one of them!" His hand snaked out, grabbing my arm and pulled me from the bench. "It's time for the show."

His grip on my arm tightened as he yanked me around the piano and I whimpered. The bodies standing around us watched in horror while he towed me to the center of the room. Jeremy's speed didn't slow until we were a foot from Dean and his wife.

"I couldn't think of a better way to get your attention," Jeremy snickered to them. "You have things living in your city passing themselves as humans and I intend to show you what they really are."

People were starting to panic and headed for the exit.

"Don't go yet," Jeremy called out. "I don't want anyone to miss the fun." He paused for a second, staring at the door. "I know you're in here so you might as well show yourselves."

Once again I scanned the crowd frantically for any sign of Sean. Nothing.

"Come on fellows," he called again. "You're not going to let me kill her for nothing, are you?"

Mrs. Wilkins' eyes widened in horror as she gripped her husband's arm.

"I don't know who you are and I'm not understanding why you're so angry," Dean said softly. "but you don't have to hurt Angel."

"Don't worry about it, Mayor," Jeremy laughed bitterly. "You will be grateful for my death after you learn what I have done to your grandson. As for her ... well let's just say this is long overdue."

I couldn't tell what direction it came from, but suddenly a deep, menacing growl filled the room. Jeremy shuddered at the sound.

"It's about time," he taunted. "I was beginning to think you were going to let us all down."

I watched anxiously as a dark shadow appeared out of the crowd.

"Sean," I whimpered.

He looked at me for a fraction of a second before turning his attention to Jeremy. Delighted with Sean's reaction Jeremy pulled me against him, using his free hand he yanked on the straps of the dress pulling them further down my arms, and then wrapped his left arm around them. He reached up to stroke my cheek with his thumb while he spoke.

"She really is beautiful, isn't she? I can't help wondering if that's why you haven't killed her yourself. Then again, you look weak compared to the other male."

As if he'd been called for Luke emerged from behind Dean and his wife. He briskly patted Dean's shoulder as he passed him to stand in front of us.

"If you're interested in battling out who's the strongest then let her go and we will settle the matter," Luke suggested.

"And let you screw me a second time?" he snarled. "Not a chance! See, I am very much aware I'm not getting out of here alive, but before my life ends I'm going to get my revenge on all of you."

"Revenge based on what?" Luke challenged.

"I know none of you are *human* and I know there are more than just the five of you."

"Jeremy," Sean's voice was scathing. "You are going to end up very disappointed after you have gone through all this trouble to prove absolutely nothing but pure insanity."

All around us was chaos. I could hear the gruffer of voices, some were trying to figure out who Jeremy was, others were trying to decide if they should leave or call 911. Mrs. Wilkins was frozen in place, her horror struck eyes were focused on my face.

"I can see why she has been so sure of you," Jeremy answered in a patronizing tone. "But, how sure will she be about you while you're watching her bleed out?"

I was beginning to get sick now. This was going to end very badly. I could hear the desperation in Jeremy's voice and even though Luke and Sean were standing close to us they wouldn't be able to stop his plans before it was too late.

"Angel knows she's in good hands," came a soft, yet stern voice from behind us. "It may be true about you hurting her before you are safely contained, but she's a fighter and will survive."

Jeremy jumped at the sound, quickly whirling us to face the voice. Jonah sent him a dark look, his eyes were slowly changing to black.

"Maybe, maybe not," Jeremy countered. "You seem to think you will continuously have your attention on me, but will you be able to resist her blood as the smell floods the air?"

None of us had been aware he had any weapons till he stuck the tip of the knife now in his hand at the base of my throat.

"Now, how about you get the rest of your group in here so I can get on with showing your mayor *what* you really are?"

"My wife and daughter will not be submitted to your little ploy, therefore you will just have to follow through with your plans with just the three of us."

My knees must have started to shake because suddenly everyone around me began to wobble. I reached up, grabbing the arm Jeremy still had around me in fear I'd fall and the knife cut the skin. Whatever his plans were clearly wasn't getting him the leverage he was hoping for. He stared at Jonah for a long second before removing the blade from my neck and placing it against my right side.

"I'll see you in *hell*."

Then I heard the dress rip. It didn't set in my mind right away that I'd been cut. It wasn't till I saw the horrified look in Jonah's eyes and heard the loud roar of Sean's voice I began to realize something was wrong. A second later I felt a warm wetness on my side. There was a sharp, burning pain in my side, my knees buckled.

No matter what Jeremy's original intentions were, he couldn't continue on like this. The faster the blood pooled out my side the weaker I was getting and no one was moving. Then suddenly the entire room went black. I felt my body thrust forward and my eyes closed.

"No, no, no!" Sean's voice cried in horror.

"Someone call 911," Jonah demanded. "Luke, I need you to press this to her side while I keep her body tilted."

"She's losing blood so quickly," Luke noted.

"I know," Jonah answered bleakly. "just hold your breath and it will be all right."

I could hear Sean's agonized pleas and couldn't stand knowing that someone like him should be hurting.

"Sean." I tried to say his name, but couldn't hear myself. My ears were ringing loudly, they heard me.

"He's right here, sweetheart," Jonah whispered in my ear. "Just hang on."

I could feel his hands on the side of my body and his knees against my back keeping me from rolling.

Then my body went completely numb. I tried to focus on the things around me to stay conscious as I knew I was still surrounded by chaos. I couldn't hear anything through the loud ringing in my ears.

I could feel myself slipping further away, as if someone were holding a pillow over my face to stop my breathing.

"No, Angel! Stay with me, *please* stay with me," Sean pleaded.

I tried to answer him but I couldn't get my lips to move.

"Where's that *damn* ambulance already!" he snarled.

"Sean." I wanted to tell him it would be okay, my voice had evaded me.

"Angel, can you hear me? I love you."

He has never said those words to me in front of anyone before. Tears slid down my face and I desperately tried to open my eyes to see his beautiful face, if for the last time.

"Sean," I tried again. This time I could hear his name come out of me though it was more as a moan.

"I'm right here, songbird. Just stay with me, help is on the way."

I could hear the sirens now. "Okay."

I don't know how much time passed, maybe a few minutes and the EMTs were to me. They assessed my wound then lifted me onto the backboard. I managed to get my eyes open when they put the oxygen mask over my face. It looked like the entire town was still there, watching as they loaded me in the back of the ambulance. Sean was allowed to ride with me. When they closed the doors he leaned down to me, touching his hard, cold lips to my forehead.

"I love you, Angelia," he whispered.

My eyes were on the verge of closing again and I managed one last deep breath. "Me too."

Then I heard the greatest sound since this nightmare had started; Sean laughed.

The sound of an annoying beeping somewhere close by and the throbbing pain in my side made me aware of the fact I wasn't dead. I slowly opened my eyes only to be instantly blinded. The white light was much too bright, I quickly closed them. It was then I felt the hardness of the bed and the lumpy pillow. So I did make it to the hospital and I'm still human. What a relief.

I tried to concentrate on pacing myself to reopen my eyes when a quiet laugh interrupted my process. Instead of them opening slowly and carefully they flew open. I turned my head a fraction to the left and found a familiar pair of beautiful blue eyes.

"Hi," Sean whispered, a breathtaking smile on his lips.

"Hi." My voice sounded like I had something stuck in my throat.

When my eyes were finally able to focus clearly I could see the pain twisted in Sean's features. I didn't understand at first, and then images began to flash in my head of the last scene I remembered.

"Oh, Sean," I whimpered. "I'm so sorry."

My heart rate accelerated and I knew then what the beeping sound was. I was wired to a monitor, which was now going wild from the beating of my heart. He shook his head, lowering his hand to my face, covering my mouth.

"Shhhh," he shushed me. "You don't have anything to apologize for. It seems I do."

His words confused me, I stared at him wildly. He waited till both my beating heart and the machine slowed down to pull his hand away.

"What do you have to apologize for?"

"I didn't get back …" He broke off mid-sentence, a low growl rumbled in the back of his throat.

My hands were all twisted up with clear tubes, but I carefully lifted my arm, placing my hand on the side of his pale face. He turned into it, his tormented eyes closed.

"This isn't your fault," I said softly. "I was warned he was close and I still chose to make us attend that party. This one's on me."

He laughed quietly and reopened his eyes. "You're right, you're hardheaded. I should hold you responsible for trying to take yourself away from me."

I glared at him and pulled my hand away. "It's good to see you haven't lost your humor through all of this," I grumbled.

He laughed again.

I sighed and it hurt. I stared down at the sheet lying over me and seen the lump that apparently wrapped around my side.

"So how bad am I?" I asked.

"You have a couple of broken ribs from Jeremy crushing you when he tried to escape. You have a gash in your side and you've lost a lot of blood. They had to give you a few transfusions."

"I'm guessing his plan worked and everyone knows the truth about your family?"

Sean was shaking his head before I was finished.

"Then how did you do it?" I asked quietly. He knew exactly what I meant right away.

"When we realized it was too late and he was already there." He looked away from me, lifting my wired-up hand from the bed and held it gently in his. "We made the women stay outside with Cameron. Jonah instructed him that before things got out of control he was to shut down the power. Then he could slip in and drag Jeremy out unnoticed. The plan seemed flawless at first, but we really had no idea just how far he was going to push us."

I waited patiently for more. The seconds ticked by. And then some unpleasant memories came back to me. I shuddered, and then winced.

He was instantly anxious. "Angel, what's happening? Is something wrong?"

I released a slow breath, relaxing my body against the bed. "I'm just starting to feel the effects of everything. I'll be fine in a minute."

His eyes remained on my face while I focused on the staggering pain coursing through my side.

"What happened to Jeremy?"

"After he threw you into my arms Cameron and Luke took care of him." I wasn't sure why, but there was a fierce note of regret in his voice.

"Then I guess neither of us have to worry about the deal I made with Jonah," I whispered.

He completely misunderstand my statement. His face turned hard, his jaw flexed.

"Were you honestly counting on that!" he hissed through his teeth.

"Of course not!" I snapped. "I am relieved to still be me ... for the most part anyway," I added after I looked down at my body.

I needed a change in direction for our conversation and looked around the room for the first time. That was when I noticed the flowers and the banners.

"How long have I been here?" I wondered.

"I can say with all honesty that you didn't have to fake your way through your holiday ... or run away with me," he added with a chuckle.

That didn't sink in right away. I continued to stare blankly at the words written on the banner as his answer began to click one word at time into place in my mind like a foreign puzzle. I was barely conscious of the sound of my heart accelerating when thoughts of my injuries finally set in. He didn't say anything else; he watched my face warily as reality threatened to crush me.

"I missed Thanksgiving! Oh, no, no, no, Jennifer is going to be so mad at me."

"She knows you are in the hospital," Sean reassured me.

Now I really panicked. "She knows about Jeremy!"

"Just calm down, songbird." He paused. "Bobbie told her that the mayor had some maniac out to destroy his family, but somehow he got you instead. Which I guess I have to tell you about your new found heritage."

"My new found heritage?" I repeated, confused.

"Once everything settled down Dean learned that John was in fact part of Jeremy's plan. He felt so guilty for what had been done to you, he's paying all your medical bills and you have a hefty bank account."

"I don't even want to know."

I stared down at my body under the sheet, the huge lump that was my ribs. Then something else sank in.

"How long is the wound in my side?"

Sean pressed his lips together, his face hard as stone.

"Sean," I said carefully. "how bad is it?"

He shook his head and muttered something unintelligible. "It starts at the bottom of your ribs and ends at just the top of your hip."

I remembered the daydream I had about lying on a beach in Texas with Jen while sunbathing in a bikini.

"Ugh!" I groaned. "So now I have one more ugly scar to hide. That's just great."

Sean folded his arms over the bed rail and rested his chin on them. "It doesn't matter how many you end up with, you're always going to be beautiful to me."

I tossed my hands in the air, instantly regretting it. "Of course it wouldn't matter to you," I growled. "It would sure to be something for someone else to gossip about if they saw it."

I was now aware of the sharp pain in my ribs and the ache throbbing along the wound in my side. It took every conscious amount of control I had not to wrap my arms around my torso.

Sean raised his eyebrows at me. "I wasn't aware you were planning to show anyone things you don't show me."

I rolled my eyes. "That's not what I meant and you know it." Then I looked at him. "Besides, I'm not the one who doesn't want to show anyone anything."

His eyes shimmered and he leaned closer to me. "You know the deal. If you want *me* then you have to marry me."

"Are you kidding me!" I nearly yelled. "I'm lying in a hospital bed cut from here to *hell* and you're bringing this up?"

He shook with his quiet laughter. "I was kind of hoping this would weaken you enough I could just slide the ring on your finger. That's fine, I'll wait. I have forever." He stroked my cheek with the back of his fingers.

"You're impossible," I growled.

I wasn't so lost in my soreness for my body not to respond to his touch. The beeping of the monitor jumped erratically. Sean smiled and leaned closer to my face. His lips stopped just mere inches from mine. A speculative look came in his eyes.

"I wonder what would happen," he breathed.

The citrus aroma from his breath caused my head to spin and my heart to beat wildly. He leaned even closer laughing at how irrational my human reactions were; the beeping noise accelerated. He gently pressed his lips to mine, the machine jumped erratically one last time then stopped all together.

He pulled back abruptly, staring anxiously at the monitor till it reported the restarting of my heart.

"That's a first," he mumbled. "Maybe pushing our luck by kissing you wasn't such a good idea."

"So now you're not going to kiss me? This day just keeps getting better," I fumed.

Sean sat back down in the chair, resting his palms on his knees. "I didn't say I wouldn't kiss you again, I just said it may not be a good idea yet."

And then a nurse walked into the room. Sean sat motionless while she fluttered to my side. She lifted the sheet, looking over the gaze tapped to my side before turning to the monitors.

"Your heart rate was a little high there for a bit. Are you ready for some pain meds,?" she asked, tapping the IV feed.

"I'm fine."

She eyed me suspiciously for a moment. "Okay then," she sighed. "If you change your mind be sure to hit the call button." She threw one last anxious glance at the monitor, and then walked out.

Sean hadn't moved and I tried to turn my body to face him. I barely whimpered and he was out of the chair, his cold hands were on my face, he stared at me with wild eyes.

"If you try that again I will call the nurse back in here to sedate you," he threatened.

"Then sit where I can actually see you and I won't," I tossed back.

"You really should take the medication so you can get some rest."

I shook my head. "I think I've slept enough."

"Angel." He stroked my face nervously.

I didn't budge.

He was irritated, his nostrils flared, and his mouth looked as if it was craved from stone. He released my face and pulled his chair closer to the bed. He sat down in it, lowered the rail, and then folded his arms on the side of the bed and rested his chin on them. His expression was now smooth. Evidently he'd decided he wasn't going to show his irritation.

"I guess since you don't seem to have any interest in resting we can use the time we have alone to discuss when you're going to stop playing hard to get and just marry me."

I was barely able to contain the panic only because I had no strength left to argue with him.

"Why are you still doing this?"

He only just looked at me. He wasn't going to answer, that much was clear.

"Fine," I said exhausted. "I honestly have no experience with relationships but I know enough to understand logic. A man and woman have to be equal and you and I ..."

"We are equal," he said quietly.

"Not even close," I disagreed. "That's like saying Mary Jane has the same abilities as Spider-Man."

Now he laughed. "I'm not actually the good guy in this relationship. So what you're saying is, you're not going to marry me unless I let you make another deal with Jonah?"

"Of course not. Sean, please be rational. I'm just saying I prefer not to be like you, but most importantly I want to age. I know that sounds strange to you," I quickly added when he looked doubtful. "And I have no problem being with you ... I'm just not ready for that."

"This is still about how I feel about trying to make love with you, isn't it?"

I shook my head and yawned.

"That's it," he suddenly said, standing from the chair. "You're still clearly tired." He leaned over me and pushed the button on the wall.

"Yes?" a female voice answered.

"We are ready for more pain relief," Sean informed her.

"Okay, I'll let the nurse know."

"I'm not going to take anything willingly," I told him as he sat back down.

"I'm pretty sure they are not going to ask," he chuckled.

I opened my mouth to respond and a nurse walked in carrying a syringe. Sean picked up my hand, holding it in his while she inserted the needle into the IV tube. She watched the monitor for a few seconds then walked out.

It didn't take long and my eyes began to droop. I vaguely felt Sean's cold, satin lips touch mine.

"Sleep now my little songbird. I promise I will be here when you open those beautiful eyes again."

"Kay," I slurred.

His breath was suddenly next to my ear. "I love you."

"Me too," I breathe.

He laughed, stretching out on the bed beside me. He wrapped his arm around me, gently resting my body against his and began humming our song. I completely relaxed, feeling content and allowed the night to close over me.

Almost a Black-Tie Affair

It had been two months since that awful night and to my dismay I found myself still the center of everyone's attention. I was considered in critical condition and spent my first week in the I.C.U. What Sean failed to tell me when I had asked him about my injuries was the wound Jeremy left in my side was so deep the blade nicked my kidney.

Once my condition stabilized and I began to improve they moved me to another floor where I spent the next three weeks. Sean held to his promise not to leave my side. The entire time, he camped out in a chair by my bed, holding my hand. Whenever I got tired enough to sleep he climbed on the bed to lay beside me. During the second week his eyes were beginning to grow darker as the days passed, and yet he still refused to leave.

A few days after I was out of the hospital Mike had more questions, but also more information about Jeremy's escape. I honestly didn't care about any of it. Jeremy Corbin was dead ----- in my mind, he wouldn't be remembered after a while and the families of his victims could finally get their peace ----- and that was all that mattered. Besides Amanda, of course. I hoped now that Jeremy was forever gone I could get her out of my mind and finally be able to let her go.

The next few weeks passed in a daze. Because of the damage I wasn't able to return to work and since I had more money than I had ever seen in my life Kloe released me from my employment all together. I argued with her to no prevail .

"Angel," she had said. "I understand this is difficult for you and it isn't an easy decision for me, either. You are one of my best girls. However, you don't need the money and quite frankly this gives all the more reason for you to go to New York. You are amazing with a piano and you deserve to spend this part of your life chasing your dreams, not waitressing."

She patted my bandaged hand, and then walked away.

I spent two days at Bobbie's and quickly learned I couldn't walk up the stairs, carry my own laundry basket or just simply drive my car. I began to become deeply depressed and Kelsey pushed for me to stay with her family until I was strong enough to care for myself. Sean was against the idea at first, he worried Mariah wouldn't be able to control herself when she caught the smell of my blood. In the end everyone, including Bobbie felt it was a better idea.

I wasn't able to bend down as it would cause the stitches to break. And, everyone was worried about how I would shower since I had to have help and Bobbie wasn't really able to provide the care I needed. Kelsey helped me with my bathing and changing the dressing still attached to my side. Even as thankful as I was for her help I couldn't wait to get back home. I missed my own bed, but more importantly than that I missed Bobbie and my other friends.

And another week passed.

Finally a break had come for me. I was strong enough to walk up and down the stairs and bathe myself so everyone left to take care of their own nourishments. I felt so alone that I would sit in the living room to try watching TV till I got tired again. That only worked for a couple of nights and the depression began to set in, again.

It was nearly daylight when I got up Friday morning. I knew they would all be home soon so I laid out my clothes for the day, and then packed my suitcase. I went to go eat and get a cup of coffee while I waited for them to come back.

Sean was already there, carrying a bowl of cereal in his hands. He looked shocked to see me, but smiled and held the bowl up.

"You're up early," he said, elated.

"I couldn't sleep anymore."

I walked to him, took the bowl from his hand and headed into the dining room. My reaction to seeing him must have been weighing on him because he followed me.

"I have been gone for the last five days then get blown off when I try to surprise you. Is there something going on I don't know about?"

He was trying to be causal in the way he asked his question, but he often forgets I can hear the tenor behind the words.

I waited another long second to answer. I turned on the light, and then crossed the room and sat down at the table.

"Sort of," I sighed. "I'm thinking about going home today."

Sean groaned in exasperation. "Are you sure you should go back to being alone so soon?"

I was outraged. "Are you kidding me!? I have spent the last few days alone and survived. I missed having Christmas and New Years with my friends. What's the worst that can happen when I have a nurse living across the hall?"

"Angelia ..."

"I'm not spending another day in this house, Sean; I can't. I'm better now and I've been playing by the rules long enough."

He walked to the closest chair and wrapped his hands around the back of it. I cringed when I heard the wood slightly crackle.

"Is this really about being stuck here ----- surrounded by vampires or is it something more and you don't want to tell me?"

I stared at him darkly for a long moment. "I have never given you a reason to be suspicious about anything and after all we have been through you still are. I just want my life back."

The cereal sitting in front of me no longer appealed to me. I pushed the bowl away and stood from the chair.

"What are you doing?" he asked clearly confused by my reaction.

"I'm going to shower since it's something I can now do *alone*."

He stared at me, a wild expression on his face. I stalked past him and went up the stairs.

I barely got my clothes picked up from Kelsey's bed and he was in the doorway.

"Are your feelings about me changing? That would be ... quite fair after what you have been through. I won't contest it as I have told you before humans tend to change after they have gone through a tragic situation. Don't bother trying to spare my feelings, *please* ----- just tell me."

I tossed the clothes back on the bed and fisted my hands against my hips. "Where did you ever come up with this stupid consumption?"

He closed his eyes, shaking his head back and forth. "Since you have gotten out of the hospital and I touch you, you're so ... hesitant, so careful, but still willing to lay in my arms just when I need you to. I want to know why. Is it because I left you alone when you were telling me the danger you faced if I walked away and I didn't listen? Because I couldn't stop him from hurting you?"

He opened his eyes and his face was torn. My words tumbled out as I rushed to get that heartbreak look out of his eyes.

"Listen to me, Sean Callenger," I demanded. "I love you more than I ever thought imaginable and I'm grateful you were there ... both times," I added when the first meeting with Jeremy flashed in my mind. "Jeremy intended to kill me whether you were there or not so I don't want to hear this crap about you thinking I hold you responsible for *his* decisions. Because I absolutely do not!"

He stared at me, his eyes penetrating before finally relaxing enough to walk toward me and speak, again. He stopped inches in front me, folding his arms.

"Then before you run out of here could we converse over a few things?"

"Such as?" I was leery of where he was trying to direct this conversation.

"I know we have had this discussion nearly a thousand times, but humor me. Tell me exactly why you keep refusing to marry me."

My face fell a tiny bit and I stared at him in disbelief. "I cannot believe ..."

"You just said you love me and that you will never outgrow me," he reminded me.

"I know what I said." I exhaled with a loud huff. "I have also said I'm only eighteen. Aren't you supposed to be in your twenties or something before you make these kind of decisions?"

He shrugged. "Didn't Loretta Lynn marry her husband when she was fourteen? In the century I come from it isn't uncommon, you know."

In that moment it was inevitably clear he pays too much attention to *whom* I idolize. It gave him leverage in this argument.

"Sean, please be serious."

"I am one hundred percent serious."

I let him stare into my eyes for a long moment (even as it was making me woozy) while I looked for the slightest compromise in his. There wasn't even one hint of indecision in them.

"*Please*," I pleaded, an edge of hysteria in my voice. "My mother married and had a baby when she was barely twenty years old. It was nearly the kiss of death for her."

"That's an interesting choice of words," he mused.

"You know what I mean. I want more of my life before I'm forced to change it."

"I want you to have that life, too. I simply plan to spend it waking you up just so I can hear what the first thing you say is. I want to watch the sun rise on your sleeping face moments before making love with you. I promise you, marrying me doesn't have to change anything."

"Yes it does," I disagreed. "You have told me repeatedly you won't be intimate with a human and *if* I agree to marry you now then I have to surrender my humanity."

He frowned, irritated now. "That is still something I clearly don't understand."

"What?" My tone was harsher than I meant, but he ignored it.

"Three months ago you were eager enough to make a deal with Jonah to trade your soul to survive an attack from a monster of your own kind, yet so unwilling to spend an eternity committed to one."

I shook my head, my lips set in a stubborn frown. "I have already explained that to you and clearly it didn't happen." I gestured to my body. "I am still *human*."

"Angel, I simply can't believe you are comparing the commitment between a marital union at your age socially unacceptable as opposed to becoming one of the eternal damned and calling that fate ..." He shook his head.

"Make fun of me all you want," I fumed. "No matter what you think I will always believe our union is fate."

"Sensible enough to believe in her own fate, but not brave enough to marry me."

I glared at him through narrowed eyes.

He leaned toward me; his sky-colored eyes melted and smoldered as he took my face securely in his hands.

"Please, Angel," he breathed. "Marry me."

I instantly forgot how to breathe for a long moment. It isn't fair when he cheats like this.

When I recovered, I shook my head slowly, trying to clear my now clouded mind.

"I think -----"

"There you go again," he murmured, brushing his lips lightly over mine. "What if we make a compromise?"

"How?" The word was breathless.

He pulled his head away to look at me. "Say yes right now and I will let you walk out of here to go back to Bobbie's without any interference. We can worry about settling a date later."

I groaned. "That's not exactly a compromise, that's me giving you your way."

He laughed. "In a way," ----- it was clear he was unashamed ----- "but you still get to leave."

He released my face, wrapping his icy cold arms around my waist, pulling me closer to him. His lips were gentle when he kissed my neck.

I was feeling defeated. "You can't be serious."

"That's the deal ----- take it or leave it. As I've said a million times before I don't need a production, I just want you mine."

I looked at the doors of Kelsey's gallery, the sky was growing light.

"All morning you have made it sound like you already have a ring."

His lips were moving up my neck and I felt them form a smile.

"I do," he admitted, unashamed. "It's been ready for me to spring on you at the first sign of weakness. Would you like to see it?"

"Fine," I breathed.

He shook us with his quiet laughter. "You're still not ready. That's all right, you will be soon enough."

"*Dammit*," I muttered, disgusted. "One minute I'm fighting for my own salvation, the next -----"

"You're engaged," he finished.

I made a face. "Must you really say that out loud," I grumbled.

He pulled back, staring at my face, his expression entertained. That only added to my furry.

I clamped my teeth together. "Just show me the *damn* ring already."

"With that attitude?" he asked, sounding appalled.

He was trying to maintain his teasing, but I could see I hurt his feelings with my poor reaction. I took a deep breath to speak calmly.

"Please? I would absolutely like to see it."

It was now suspicion burned in his eyes.

"I'm beginning to think I have met a more dangerous creature than me," he said, amused.

I was about to open my mouth when suddenly he pressed his lips to mine for a quick kiss and in a flash he pulled something from his pocket, and then lowered himself onto one knee.

"Sean," I glowered.

He shook his head. "You have practically agreed already so you can at least allow me to do this right."

He waited for me to protest, but I only remained silent.

"Angelia Lynn Johanson, I vow to spend the rest of eternity making you happy. Will you marry me?"

I stared at him unsure how to answer. It's too late for that psychiatrist, I reminded myself. And, you already told him you never want to live without him.

Fate.

I took a deep breath. "Yes," I said, nearly inaudible.

That cocky smile crossed Sean's lips. He opened the little black box resting against his pale palm. I thought he had been joking before when he mentioned a crystal cut diamond. The rock was extremely large, sending out a cascade of colors and sat on a gold band.

While I continued to stand there speechless he removed the ring already on my finger, replacing it with my engagement ring. Gah. Engaged.

He stood up and wrapped his arms around my waist. "Come home with me." He quickly raised his hand and placed his long, cold index finger against my lips when he could see that I was about to argue. "Give me one night and I promise I will take you to Bobbie's tomorrow."

We glowered at each other for a long moment before I finally sighed. "Fine."

Sean drove me to Bobbie's the next afternoon careful not to pass the banquet hall. My nerves felt like live wires. I knew it was silly to be so nervous, again I couldn't help it. I hadn't seen Bobbie since the day I practically moved in with Sean and his family. I remembered the expression on her face and didn't want to see that same look of sorrow in her brown eyes when she looked at me. I also hoped she wouldn't gawk at the over-sized rock now attached to my finger.

Ugh! My ring.

When he pulled up in front of the house I continued to sit there, staring at the back of my SUV, even after he'd shut off the engine.

"You're turning green," he noted. "Are you all right?"

"I'm fine." My voice sounded flat. Even to me.

"If I asked you something would you be honest?" he asked, sounding doubtful.

"I've never lied to you before so I'm not going to start now."

"What's going through your mind right now?"

I looked up at the house, instantly remembering my last night before the night that changed my life forever. The night I spent with my babysitters.

"The last night before everything changed."

"Listen to your heart fly. Angel, I don't think you're as ready to come back here as you seem to think."

I groaned in exasperation. "Avoiding it isn't the answer."

"Maybe not," he said, reaching for my hand. "but you can't go on torturing yourself, either."

"I know," I breathed. "It's getting cold in here and the rain isn't getting any lighter."

"Would you like me to walk you inside?"

"No." I leaned forward and softly kissed him. Then suddenly his hand caught the back of my head as I pulled away, pushing it to him. His kiss frightened me for a moment. It had too much tension, too strong of an edge to the way his lips crushed mine ----- like he was reliving that awful night, too.

I couldn't let myself think about that if I wanted him to leave. His lips slowly turned gentle again and he pulled away, laying his forehead carefully against mine.

"I'm sorry," he whispered. He lifted his head, his eyes burned with sincerity.

"I love you," I reminded him.

He seemed to be confused by my reaction to his loss of control. I only smiled, and then turned to open the door. I took my time getting out and even more time to walk to the porch.

"Bobbie?" I called as I pushed open the front door.

"In here, Angel."

Moving with caution, I rounded the corner of her kitchen. She was standing at the sink washing dishes.

"I was hoping you would be here today." She paused to point a soapy finger toward the table. "I know it's nearly the end of January, but I picked you up something for Christmas."

"You didn't have to do that," I said, embarrassed.

"I know," she laughed.

I walked to the table and sat down. There in front of me was a box wrapped in silver paper, a bright red bow on top. I tore the paper off then lifted the lid. Inside was three CDs.

"Is this your way of saying you're tired of Luke Bryan?" I asked with a laugh.

"A little," she admitted. "I thought maybe you would like something else, too."

She finished rinsing out the basin and turned off the water. She picked up the dishtowel, drying off her hands as she crossed the room to join me. I took the CDs out, carefully looking them over. I now had Carrie Underwood, Lady Antebellum and Taylor Swift.

"Angel," my name came out in a sigh. "I know you weren't thrilled about staying at Sean's, but I want you to know we made that decision out of love. You were still pretty dazed from the pain medication and because of my schedule now I couldn't give you the attention you needed." Her eyes began to swell with tears.

I quickly placed the CDs back in the box and reached across the table for her hand. "Don't worry about it. Truthfully, it was more comforting having Sean close and anyways, it got me away from discussions with Mike." I pretended to shudder.

She laughed the same instant her eyes zeroed in on the ring.

"Angel!" she said, astonished. "He asked me a few weeks ago if I would be opposed to him asking for your hand, but knowing you the way I do I didn't think it would happen so quickly."

"Why did he ask you?"

She slightly shrugged her shoulders. "He said something about traditions and since your parents are unavailable and you live with me it seemed right."

"Oh." I knew the word was inadequate, but I lacked a better response. "I wasn't ready yet, but even a rock gives away to water after a while."

She laughed at my facial expression. "As I've said before, when you love someone you have to take it by leaps and bounds."

My eyes narrowed at her. "I remember hearing those words and look where that advice got me."

"Oh, Angel," she laughed. "You're never going to find a better soul than Sean's. Besides, not everyone gets lucky enough to find a prince the first time they look and you did."

And again with the prince. She misread the expression on my face and squeezed my hand.

"Just be happy, Angel. You deserve it."

"I am," I barely whispered. "I'm feeling a little tired," I said in a much louder voice. "so I think I'm just going to go up and lie down."

"Okay." She gave my fingers one last gentle squeeze then released them. I stood from the chair, picked up the box, and then trudged to the stairs.

Kelsey made me aware of a horrifying horizon. It was the first Thursday of February and she was standing on the porch waiting for me when I got home. She stood by the railing, with her weight on one leg, arms folded over her chest and a pout look on her face. I'd seen that look before and took my time shutting off the engine and climbing out.

"Are you really going to do us like that after all we have done for you?" she asked as I was walking up the steps.

"What are you talking about?" I walked past her to unlock the door.

"The fact that there's a plan for you to run off with Sean and get married."

I turned the key in the lock and a second later comprehension came and I gasped in horror. I pulled the key free with more force than necessary and whirled on her.

"We're not running anywhere!" My voice was an octave higher than was needed.

She glared at me, not seeming to believe me. I turned away from her and walked inside. She followed me to the kitchen.

"I have to say I'm surprised he hasn't informed you of his plans."

I slipped out of my jacket, laid it over the back of a chair and headed to the cabinet for a glass.

"That isn't anything new, Kelsey. We've only been ----- engaged." I paused as the word felt like it would burn my tongue. I was suddenly grateful she couldn't see my face. "A few weeks."

I walked to the fridge, opened the door and pulled out the pitcher of tea.

"Do you even have any idea what day it is?"

"February seventh." I didn't understand where she was trying to lead me. I finished filling the glass, replaced the pitcher, and then closed the door.

"Then you're aware that next week is Valentine's Day?"

"Yeah, so?" I turned to face her, not understanding the expression on her face.

She shook her head while walking to the table and pulled out a chair.

"Angel, sometimes you're too oblivious for your own good," she said as she sat down. "My brother, your fiancée, has plans for a romantic getaway for two. Ergo, you're fixing to officially be Mrs. Callenger."

I scowled, angrily. "Not if he knows what's good for him. How do you know about this, anyway?"

I suddenly needed something to do with my hands to keep me from doing anything rash. I set my glass down on the table, snatched my jacket off the chair, and went into the foyer.

"We live in the same houses, remember? And, I overheard him talking to Luke."

I froze.

Does that mean he's planning to turn me, after all? Don't be ridiculous, I grumbled to myself. He's too headstrong about keeping you human. I hung my jacket on the hook, focusing on collecting myself, and then walked back in the kitchen. I briefly hoped my voice wouldn't give away the horror I felt.

"I'm still waiting for you to get to the part where this has anything to do with you." It held better than I hoped. I picked up my glass and sat down at the table.

"I came here to propose a deal."

I slightly shook my head back and forth. "I'm going to be honest here by saying I don't like it already. But, I'm listening."

She sent me a dark look. "I figure since we're practically already family that you could let Mariah and I give you a wedding."

My face fell a tiny bit. "I haven't even thought of a date."

She leaned over the table, widening her eyes causing my heart to slow way down.

"If you don't get to deciding something soon, you're going to be an immortal bride in a week. Besides ..." She dropped her hold on me and sat back upright. "... wouldn't your human friends want to be part of your big day?"

I quickly lowered my head, closing my eyes, to give myself a minute to control the burn now in my lungs.

"Why can't the vampires play fair for a change?"

She waited for me to look up to answer.

"We're not supposed to," she said, smugly. "C'mon, Angel, don't you love the rest of us? At all?"

Even though her eyes were still intense I glared at her. "What kind of idiotic question is that? You know I love each of you; I may not always like you, but still."

She shook with laughter. "Is that a yes?"

"I don't know," I grumbled. "I need more than five minutes to think about it."

My eyes were on her the entire time, I never saw her move, but she was on her feet and was pushing in the chair.

"Let me know when you get it figured out. I have come to expect this sort of thing from my brother ... never would I have believed you could."

"*Hump*," I breathed. "Maybe if you hadn't spent the last few months making me your Guinea Pig Barbie I might be a little bit more willing to give into your request."

"If you don't do something soon, you're going to be more than a Barbie," she snickered. "It's your call."

I shook my head while mumbling to myself. Kelsey was gone less than a second later. I continued to grumble at the now empty room and stood from the chair, and then went up the stairs.

That night after Bobbie left I put one of the CDs she had given me in the stereo and went on to the bathroom. I wasn't sure at first I'd be able to hear it with the door closed and the water running. Thanks to my sensitive hearing I had no problems. Once dressed I opened the door, and then walked back to the sink to finish towel drying the chaos known as my hair and brush my teeth.

It wasn't even a minute later and Sean was walking up the stairs. He stopped at the bathroom door, an amused expression on his face.

"Music's a little loud, isn't it?" he teased.

I ignored his sarcasm, keeping my focus on brushing my hair. "Isn't that the whole reason you brought the stereo to me?"

"Soon it won't have to be above a whisper and you'll still hear it perfectly," he laughed.

I flashed him a dark look. "Is someone getting a change of heart about my mortality?"

Because I was now irritated I didn't pay attention to the slight breeze across the floor, warning me he entered the room. And then suddenly his hand snaked out, grabbing my arm and turning me to face him. With his free hand he moved the things on the counter and lifted me up, sitting me down. His eyes were darker in color and held mine, not allowing me to look away.

"Let's get a couple of things ironed out right now," he growled. "First, and most importantly, I don't want your mortality; I want *you*. Second, as I've said before I have a plan to keep you as you are for as long as possible. Third, I'm growing tired of having to spend nearly every night here when we have a perfectly good house. Which by the way, I built you a bathroom and a kitchen."

His eyes were still intense, but they released their hold on me. I looked down to remember what my lungs were for, as well as recall my scattered thoughts.

"You have quite a hefty list to go along with those demands."

He placed a cold finger under my chin, forcing my head back up. "The only demand I have is for you to marry me. Everything else just goes along with it."

My brows knit in confusion. "If you're so bothered by separate housing then why did you agree to me moving back in here?"

There was a defensiveness about his face, a hint of a much bigger secret he was trying to hide behind his casual manner.

"You wouldn't agree to marry me unless you got more time with Bobbie."

He dropped his hand, leaning down to kiss me. I quickly placed my fingers to his lips.

"That does make sense and maybe I knew it. But now I want to know the *real* reason for you trying to speed things up."

He reached up and wrapped his fingers around my wrist, kissing first my palm then my fingers. I knew he heard the irrational reaction of my beating heart when a smile crossed his lips.

"My cold, yet very silent heart has been still for nearly eighty years and has belong to you from the first time you ever looked at me. I have walked amongst your kind and mine never knowing I was missing anything. I never even knew I wanted anything until that night I saw your face." He paused, moving his lips to the inside of my wrist, slowly inhaling my scent. I watched in wonder while giving my heart the chance to slow.

"Now that I know this kind of love exist," he continued. "even more so for me, I just want it to be official ----- to know that you belong to me and no one else."

"I don't honestly think it could get anymore official," I grumbled. "Since we are discussing things being official, is the topic open for negotiations?"

He was shaking his head before I was finished.

"I see," I mused. "You can demand any *damn* thing you want, but I can't ask for negotiations?"

"Angel," he groaned. He kissed my palm then released my hand. "I have already said I'm not looking for attention or any added fans. And, I can't give you a return date as I am not planning to bring you back for some time. I have a great number of things I'd like to show you and ... I wasn't going to say this just yet, I suppose now I have no choice. I was going to give into your request at trying intimacy. If it doesn't work I won't be able to bring you back here at all."

His tone sparked a fuse in me. "I have an FYI for you. I absolutely *hate* Valentine's Day. You may be able to get away with conjuring me into doing things your way, but I swear to you on my life that will not be the day I change my name or my body!"

He glared at me, holding my eyes. "I haven't had the chance to discuss this with you so how are we having this conversation?"

"Have you forgotten you're not the only member of your family I know?" I meant to sound as hasty as he had, my voice wasn't as strong and at the end I ran out of steam.

His jaw flexed. "Kelsey," he said between clenched teeth. "She will do anything she can to make my life complicated."

He lowered his head, pinching the bridge of his nose with his thumb and forefinger. I waited for him to reign in his temper. The seconds ticked by.

"Fine," he sighed, heavily. He lifted his head to look at me. His expression was still furious but the storm in his eyes was passing. "You win ----- this time. I will give you a month to decide on a date you can live with. If you haven't then we will proceed my way."

"And the egotistical jerk returns," I growled.

He laughed once, and then his lips were on mine. All the fury I felt disappeared with the movement of his lips. When they parted mine I felt his cold breath in the back of my throat; my head started to spin.

Just before I was on the verge of passing out he pulled away. His breathing was unsteady like mine.

"You should finish up before your hair dries like that."

He kissed my lips again, and then lifted me from the counter, setting me gently on my feet. He headed to the door as I fought to remember what I needed to do with my hair.

Despite my no longer having a job to keep me busy a month had gone by without my knowledge. Once again it was Kelsey to bring it to my attention. She called me the first Monday in March, complaining.

"Angel, I need to know if you're going to let us do the wedding."

"Calm down, Kelsey," I laughed. "You're going to give yourself an aneurysm."

"As you know vampires are not known for having patience," she growled. "It's the seventh , ergo we have already been waiting a month."

"A month?" I gasped.

I stood in the center of the kitchen floor, frozen. I tried to count back to figure out how I had lost so much time.

"Sometime this century would be great," she nearly snarled.

"Right," I said, still confused. "Fine, I'll let you do the wedding."

"Finally." Her tone was no longer harsh though her voice was still full of sarcasm. "Would you happen to have a date in mind or should I pick it for you?"

I let that turn over in mind. Sean's deadline technically ends today, would it matter if I stretched it for a few more days? I'm including his family in the biggest day of his life so that counts, right?

"Angel," Kelsey growled, impatiently.

"The fifteenth," I blurted out.

"Of?" I have never heard her voice sound so confused before.

"This month ----- March." The words came out in a rush.

"That's short notice for putting together a wedding, don't you think?"

I never heard the door open, but suddenly Sean was entering the room. I could tell by the expression on his face he wasn't listening to my conversation. I wasn't going to make it obvious *who* I was talking to, either.

"I know," I said quickly. "I have to go."

There was a long pause and I worried she was going to ask more questions. Just as I was about to panic she answered.

"I'll be in touch soon." The line was dead less than a second later.

Sean was sitting at the table, looking at me with a peculiar expression. I turned my back to him, rushing my steps to put the phone on the wall.

"Your heart sounds like a buzzing bee. Angel, are you all right?"

"I'm fine," I lied.

It wasn't even a second later and he was turning me to face him.

"I have walked in on many of your conversations and I have never seen you act like this. Tell me what's going on."

I lowered my eyes to look at the floor, not knowing how to tell him. His cool fingers brushed my cheek.

"You're blushing?" His voice sounded deeply concerned.

I knew it was bugging him, knowing that something was wrong, I felt too cowardly to look him in the face and admit to what I had done.

"Angel," he groaned. He finally put a long, cool finger under my chin and lifted my face up. Those beautiful blue eyes were light and full of concern. "I can no longer stand the suspense. Please, talk."

I inhaled deeply through my nose then slowly released the breath. "Today's date caught me off guard. Nothing to panic about."

"Nothing to panic about?" he repeated, sounding doubtful. "Listen to your heart fly, that don't sound like nothing to me."

It was times like this when his perfect hearing was beyond irritating.

"Okay," he sighed. "Let's try this another way."

My eyes widened, but I didn't have time to say a word; he grabbed my arms and lifted me up. He walked to the counter, carefully setting me down in front of him. His lips were next to my ear, sending chills down my spine.

"Unless you would like for me to indulge myself you should start talking," he whispered.

His lips grazed my jaw then along the hollow beneath my ear. I closed my eyes so I could speak.

"All right," I said in a rush. "I was reminded of your pushiness for a date."

I felt his lips form a smile against my skin. "Are we leaving today?"

He moved his lips back to my jaw, taking his time to claim my mouth. My heart pounded so hard I thought it was going to jump out of my chest. His lips were gentle until my hesitation continued. He grew impatient and his kissing got more fierce. Just as I thought I might pass out from the lack of oxygen he moved to the side of my face.

"I kind of want to talk to you about that," I finally answered.

A low growl rumbled from the back of his throat and I froze.

"Angel, I have been more than patient already. Please do not make this harder than it has to be."

"I'm going to marry you," I amended. "It's just ... well, I told Kelsey she could give us a wedding."

"You did what!" he roared. The sound was so loud it echoed off the walls.

In that instant the memory of the night we were in Becca's tower and he lost his temper entered my mind and I was suddenly frightened. I sat completely still, simply breathing with caution. Sean pulled back from me, a black fire blazing in his eyes.

"*Dammit*, Angel! Why did you do that?"

All the fear I felt melted as my own fury began to burn. My teeth snapped together.

"I don't like it when you use that language at me," I hissed. "and furthermore, this is my life, too. What will my friends think of me if I just up and leave without telling them goodbye?"

"And we're back to you focusing on what other people think," he moaned. "When are you going to stop worrying about what they think or how they feel and worry about making yourself happy?"

I glared at him. "I do believe my focus on making people happy includes you. You can correct me if I'm wrong, but I also believe the only reason I've agreed to marry at eighteen is because I'm dating an egotistical, pushy *ass* jerk."

He laughed darkly. "You complain about my language? I don't believe *ass* is considered appropriate."

"Your distractions are not going to work," I warned. "I want to discuss this, Sean. I have earned the right to decide what to do with my life."

"You're right," he somberly agreed.

He stepped backwards, and then turned to lean against the counter. I wasn't ready to see the expression on his face, cuffing my hands around the edge of the counter I leaned forward to stare at the floor.

"I'm sorry," I nearly whispered. "I never meant for that to sound harsh. When you start firing off your demands at me like that I get heated." I carefully turned my head to look at him. "I've spent my entire life doing things someone else's way and forced to pay a price when I didn't. Since I have been here I've learned how to stand on my own; to make my own decisions. Because we don't know how things will turn out for me after we're married I want to give the people who matter something better than me just disappearing and never coming back."

He seemed to ponder my words for a second before suddenly turning to stand in front of me. He placed his hands on both sides of my face.

"I never put much consideration to how you feel about your friends, for that I'm sorry. I have lived so long without having feelings for humans I forget theirs. You are the most important thing in my life and I want nothing more than for you to be happy. I need for you to be happy."

We were both quiet for a minute. I stared at his perfect face wondering why I had been so anxious on my call with Kelsey. I mean, sure my age was still important to me ... but still. I have chosen my life and it only made sense to start living it.

"What made you decide to let Kelsey have her way?" he suddenly asked.

"She had a point about my friends wanting to share this big moment with me. It just wouldn't be fair to keep Jennifer out after all the years she stood by my side. It's my way of letting them know that I have chosen you and when I leave they'll know wherever I go I'll be happy ... and safe. For Jennifer that's the best I can do for her since I've kept so many secrets from her these past few months. If I'm having a wedding anyway, I may as well allow your family to have their fun, too."

Sean continued to hold my face, searching it a long time. Then his mouth was on mine. My heart raced and my hands fisted in his hair before I noticed the intensity of his kiss. I shook my head and he complied, moving his lips to my jaw.

"Sean, no -----"

He brushed his lips over mine. "I have been so focused on what I believe is best for you that I haven't even taken the time to really listen to what you need. You promised to marry me and out of the two of us I'm the one more unwilling to give what the other wants. So therefore ... me first."

His lips captured mine, moving softly, his hands were in my hair. Then suddenly he was lifting me from the counter and cradled me in his arms. I knew human velocity wasn't good enough for him when he flew up the stairs. My mind was racing, trying to figure out how to stop him without upsetting him.

He laid me on my bed, gently pressing me against the mattress. He kissed me again, softly ----- but very seriously ----- before I could find my voice. My hands were already gripping his arms, pulling myself tighter to him. I struggled to clear my head. He finally moved his mouth to my neck, giving me a chance to breathe. Now or never, I told myself.

"Sean, wait." My voice was as weak as my will.

"Not a chance," he murmured against my skin.

He moved his lips back to mine, silencing me. Oh, why not? my less noble side screamed. He parted my lips, my throat was so full of the cool breath. My hands were tugging up his shirt before I realized what I was doing. No, no, no, the voice in my head begged. He slid his lips away giving me an open opportunity. There wasn't going to be much time to act.

"Sean, wait," I tried again.

"Why?" He reclaimed my mouth, preventing me from answering. I pushed against him and he moved his lips.

"I'm not ready to do this now," I breathed.

"From the way your blood is moving I know that isn't true."

He was right, heat coursed through my veins, feeling as though the fire would burn me alive. I forced myself to stay focused, pushing against him again. He pulled away long enough to take off his shirt and toss it on the floor. Because I was speechless he took advantage of it, kissing me. My right hand, on autopilot, trembled as it traced across the contours of his stone chest, and across the flat planes of his stomach while my left pressed tighter against the small of his back. I felt a light shudder ripple through him.

Becoming irritated at myself for my weakness I yanked my hands from him, forcing them to rest on the bed at my sides.

"Stop, Sean, wait," I begged around his lips.

He lifted his head a few inches from mine to look at me. His eyes didn't help me fight to keep my resolve. They were a smoldering black fire.

"Why?" he asked, again. His voice was rough and it stunned me. "Are you changing your mind about everything?"

The butterflies now in my stomach fluttered harder causing it to hurt.

"Are you?" he pressed.

"Don't be ridiculous," I mumbled.

"Then make love with me, Angel. Right here, right now."

I stared at him, dumbfounded and he took advantage of my speechlessness. I couldn't force my lips to stop kissing him back, but I firmly held my arms in place.

"Wait, wait," I tried to say around his lips.

He groaned and pulled back a few inches to look at me. "You better have a good reason for stopping me."

Is he serious? I opened my mouth to state the obvious, and then changed my mind.

"I know for some love and lust don't necessarily keep the same company, for me they do. I want to follow the rules, the right way."

He stared at me with an unfathomable expression for a long second. "You certainly don't play fair."

I grinned at him. "When did I ever say I did?"

He leaned in for one last kiss then rolled on his back, catching me in the bend of his arm, and laid me over his chest.

"I love you and I want you ... I want you more than I could ever believe, but if waiting is truly what you want."

"It is," I said softly.

He kissed my head and began humming our song. I squeezed myself closer to him and closed my eyes.

For the next few days Kelsey immersed herself in the wedding plans. Bobbie got in, too ----- she spent hours on the phone with Jennifer. It was thrilling to know Jen would be coming. It also let me off the hook. Bobbie, along with Sean's family were taking care of all the details and the nuptials, allowing me to do nothing but wonder anxiously around the house.

I left the house early to run to the store for the list of things Bobbie said she needed. I met a lot of curious eyes as I walked the aisles and fought to keep from hanging my head. I felt like someone had turned a spotlight on me to draw attention to the large ring on my left hand. It was really stupid to be so self-conscious and I knew that ... but still. They're not staring at you, I promised myself. They're not staring at you.

Try as I might I couldn't lie convincingly enough to myself to keep from checking. I peeked behind me where Mrs. Stevens was standing with her cart talking to Ms. Johnson. Her eyes bored into mine and I flinched. Wasn't it still considered rude to stare at people? I quickly turned my head, rushing my steps to get out of the aisle.

I couldn't bear to look around anymore. I grabbed things from the shelves, tossing them into the cart and nearly ran to the checkout. I knew it was silly to behave in such a manner, it couldn't be helped. I felt like I was in deja vu all over again. The whispers I would hear when I passed someone after being found in the woods.

"Poor girl," one woman coaxed. "I wonder what will happen to her now."

"I think Jonah's family has taken a kindness to her," said another. "At least I've seen Sean helping her a few times."

Sean's kindness. Sigh.

Moving as if I were running from a burning building, I got the hatch open, set the bags inside and re-closed it within seconds. I rushed to take the cart to the door, and then jump in my car, speeding out of the parking lot.

As I turned onto my street I could see Bobbie's car parked in front of the house. I wasn't sure why, but just seeing it helped to settle my anxiousness. That was the part about my leaving that was the hardest. From almost my first night here just seeing Bobbie calmed every fear I had. She had a way about her that could calm even the most unruly child. Maybe that's what made her decide to be a nurse.

I paused with my hand on the door, taking slow deep breaths. I could still torture myself till I was at the verge of panic when I was alone, but I wouldn't live it down if Bobbie saw even an ounce of it on my face.

"Bobbie?" I called as I pushed open the door. "I think I got ----"

"Hang on just a second, Angel."

My feet automatically planted themselves. "Hang on?" I asked.

"I only need a moment. Kelsey, I don't think that's going to work."

Kelsey?

"Yes it will," she responded. "I just have to get ... there done."

"I'm just going to carry the groceries to the kitchen," I informed them.

It wasn't even a second later and they followed me in the room.

"So what do you think?" Kelsey asked in a thrilled tone.

I set the bags on the counter and turned to face them.

"Wow, Bobbie," I huffed. "Don't you look ... amazing."

She blushed.

Kelsey took her elbow, slowly spinning her to showcase the misty blue dress. Sean's favorite color for me is green. Kelsey didn't think that color would suit any of the bridesmaids so she picked pastel colors.

"It's the final check on fit," Kelsey stated, calling back my focus. "I have one for you, too."

I peeled my gaze from Bobbie to scowl at her.

"I don't want any fits," she scolded.

I sucked in a deep breath and stalked up the stairs to my room. I stripped down to my undergarments while Kelsey unzipped the gray garment bag already lying on the bed.

I held my arms out while she slipped the satin over my skin then turned me to face the mirror. I stared in awe at the white gown. It was extremely beautiful; it had elegant lace on the chest and down the arms. I was relieved when they covered the ugly scar on my forearm. The back buttoned mid-way up, exposing my shoulders.

"And a perfect fit," Kelsey said, her tone approving. "You look absolutely stunning."

I didn't answer. I looked at my reflection a second longer, and then turned to face her.

"Okay, you have seen how our gowns look. Now, where's yours?"

Her eyes widened in shock. "Mine?"

I rolled my eyes at her. "Isn't it traditional for the bride to have a maid of honor?"

"Yes," she agreed. "though mishaps like us don't actually count at the gates, if you know what I mean."

I frowned, unhappily. "None of you are mishaps and if it won't count then why am I having a wedding?"

"Because Sean doesn't want to keep you out, too." She placed her stone, cold hands on my shoulders and turned me back to the mirror.

The next evening Sean and I sat in the shabby kitchen chairs watching Bobbie buzz from one room to another, seeming to be completely oblivious to our presence. She already had a party tray full of cold cut sandwiches on a table in the living room and was now carrying a platter full of cookies.

"I thought bride-to-be's were drug into a bar and paraded in front of men," he laughed.

"Not if they're only eighteen."

He rolled his eyes and sighed. "You really have to let that go."

"Shouldn't you be attending a bachelor party, instead of sitting here watching how they plan to torture me?"

He shook his head. "I have no interest as I'm not saddened by the idea I will no longer be alone."

I opened my mouth to speak, never to get the chance. A loud boom rattled the front door. I didn't have to answer it to know it was Luke.

"It seems your brothers have other ideas," I murmured.

A second later Luke ducked his head in the doorway.

"C'mon little brother. You will have plenty of time to spend with Angel after tomorrow."

Sean glared at him before turning those beautiful eyes on me. "I guess I'll meet you at the altar." He leaned in for a kiss, and then in one fluid move was on his feet, slipping out the door.

I sat there for another long second then stood from the chair.

"Is there anything I can help with?" I asked when Bobbie entered the kitchen.

"I think I've covered everything." She walked to the refrigerator then suddenly stopped, turning around. "I was thinking we could pull out the karaoke machine."

"Great," I groaned.

She laughed, continuing on to the fridge.

Three faint knocks came on the door.

"Good," Bobbie squealed in delight. "They're here!"

I mumbled unintelligibly while I went to answer it.

"You're right on ..." My words caught in my throat when I looked at the person standing there.

The man was tall, olive skinned, with dark hair. His eyes were a dark brown, looking clouded like he might have been on something, maybe even a little drunk.

"I am sorry to bother you," he said politely. "My car broke down out here in front of your house and I was wondering if I could use your phone."

Despite the sudden feeling in the pit of my stomach something was wrong I stepped away from the door. "Okay."

I pointed him in the direction of the kitchen and closed the door. I took an extra minute to control the nausea now burning in the back of my throat. I heard voices within seconds, one sounded terrified. I sucked in one last deep breath and headed in the kitchen.

I saw the gun aimed at Bobbie's head and instinctively froze. Gone from the man's face was the smooth, friendly expression.

"I'm sorry to have to do this, Angel. I truly am. I promise not to hurt your friend if you leave with me right now."

For reasons I couldn't fathom my veins came alive, as if I'd wrapped my hand around live wires. Suddenly all the fear that had been coursing through me just moments ago disappeared.

"I'm not going anywhere with you!"

"Don't be like that, Angel," he said.

"How do you know my name?"

He didn't answer, lowering the gun instead and turned his body toward me. His expression was nearly irrational.

"We should just be on our way. We have quite a drive ahead of us."

I saw from the corner of my eye Bobbie reach for the phone. I quickly flashed my eyes back to him, as not to alert him, keeping his attention on me.

"I've already said I'm not going anywhere."

I hadn't realized he'd stepped closer to me till he grabbed my arm. I flailed in his grasp and felt his fingers dig into my arm. I struggled harder.

"Why are you making this so hard?" he asked with a bewildered laugh.

Because Bobbie was now frozen with fear and he still had the gun in his hand I stopped fighting before one of us, maybe even both of us got hurt.

He towed me to the door and while he was distracted I pulled my ring off my finger, setting it inside the bowl next to my keys. As he drug me across the lawn I looked at the cars parked at the curb.

Will Bobbie alert Jonah before it's too late?

Epilogue: Reflections

The man opened his trunk lid, forcing me inside. I instantly had a flashback of Jeremy laying me beside Amanda's unconscious body. I squeezed my eyes closed, fighting against the tears I felt forming.

I don't know how much time passed when music filled the small space. The song immediately brought on the things I'd rather forget. I covered my ears as Blown Away echoed all around me.

It was based on Oklahoma, yet perfectly described the *hell* I lived through with my father for seven years. The house didn't just have whiskey memories for me, but my mother, too.

As the tears now began to fall noiselessly down my face I tried to banish the thoughts and ignore the song. It took a lot of effort, but I managed, distracting myself over the fact I had no idea where Sean planned our honeymoon. He kept it a secret to surprise me.

I hoped it would be somewhere remote so he wouldn't have to wait for the sun to fade before he could step outside. I couldn't imagine us spending it in some hotel room like most people. It wouldn't be a good thing if something went wrong while we were experimenting with intimacy. Vampire Angel would certainly bring unwanted attention.

Try as I might to drown out the music and focus on what tomorrow would have brought, the song pulled me into the memories I worked so hard to forget:

My mother pulled me from the car and towed me toward the house.

"Angel, honey, it's only for a little while," she had said.

"Mama, please," I begged. "I don't want to stay here."

"Now you dry up those tears and be a big girl," she scorned. "You're almost twelve, it's time to give up this nonsense."

Scott appeared in the doorway a second later, with a can of beer in his hand. From the expression on his face he wasn't happy with this arrangement, either.

Scott looks a lot like me, only his hair is short, balding in the back and his eyes weren't as green as mine.

"He doesn't want me so why do I have to stay?"

"She's right, Samantha," he said, pushing open the screen door. "You wanted to play Donna Reed so you keep her."

"Oh, grow up and be a man, Scott," she hissed. "She's your daughter, too."

She took his free hand, forcing him to hold mine till she was back in the car and driving away.

I squeezed my eyes tighter and that only caused the memories to fast forward to my last night in his house.

I had just come home from being at Jennifer's softball game. Scott was already drunk and stumbling around inside the house.

"Where the *hell* have you been?" he yelled.

"I was at Jennifer's game. I reminded you about it this morning."

"Don't stand there and back sass me, Angelia. And anyways, are you allowed to leave before your chores are done?"

I knew no matter what answer I gave wouldn't have been the right one. I dropped my head, staring at the floor.

"No, sir," I whispered.

"What was that?" he growled. "Young lady, you better *damn* well look at me when I'm speaking to you."

I swallowed a large lump while fighting the tears starting to form and looked up. His expression was so angry his eyes were almost as green as mine.

"Now, what were you mumbling?"

"I said no, sir."

He stepped closer to me. "Does this house look clean to you?"

The house was small, consisting of the standard size living room, a dining room, kitchen, one bathroom and two bedrooms. I looked around, astonished at how he trashed the room in just a few short hours. There were beer cans and cigarette packs all over the floor.

I slowly shook my head back and forth. "No."

He took another step toward me, this time grabbing me around the back of my neck.

"Then I suggest if you want to sleep in that nice comfortable bed of yours, you get this house cleaned up." He tossed me across the room causing me fall into the lamp. It fell with me to the floor. "*Dammit*, Angel! Why can't stay on your feet?" he screamed.

"I'm sorry, Dad." I set the lamp back on the table and tried to stand up.

I barely got to my knees when he kicked me in the ribs. I bit down on my lip, holding back the scream. He stumbled out of the room a second later and I got to my feet. He reentered moments later with a box of trash bags in his hand and threw them at me.

"I want this house spotless and bare mind, I will be watching. It's a crying shame that a seventeen year old girl can't do her chores without being watched." He sat down in his chair as I pulled out the first bag.

When I was finished he followed me to the dining room. This room looked like there had been a wild party. There were cans and bottles scattered all across the table. Ashtrays were full of cigarette butts. I pulled a chair away from the table, tripping over the leg. That only made him more angry.

"Girl, somehow you have gotten to be as worthless as your mother," he sneered.

He came at me and I tried to shield my face. He grabbed a handful of my hair, yanking my head backwards. As soon as my hands were no longer covering my face he backhanded me. I couldn't hold the tears back any longer and they slid down my cheeks. He glared at me for a second then shoved me forward.

"Do you think you can get through the rest of the night without having to be hit?"

I could only nod my head. Scott exhaled a loud huff, and then stalked out of the room.

When he shoved me I hit my mouth off the back of the chair. I felt blood trickle down my lip and wiped it away. Suck it up, I told myself then started cleaning the room.

It was in the kitchen after he discovered he was out of beer he got angry, again. This time he didn't say anything; he walked to me, grabbing my shoulder to turn me around, he punched me in the face. I fell back against the sink, slowly sinking to the floor. That was where I remained till he finally passed out.

I felt the car slow then stop. My heart racing I listened closely for any indication that Jonah or Mike was out there.

Nothing.

The car rolled forward again and I realized he was just stopped at a light. My heart sank deep inside my chest.

To comfort myself I thought over the months I spent with Sean, remembering the way his eyes danced when he laughed. And, the way it felt when his hands would glide ever so gently over my skin. Even better than that; the way I felt while lying in his stone, cold arms. I wondered what tomorrow would have been like. My friends watching as I walked down the aisle to start spending the rest of my life with the man I loved.

As I reflected on where I'd been, I tried to see where I was going. I had no idea who the man was that dragged me out of Bobbie's house. Even as much as Sean loved me, would he find me in time to save me once more?

With no one knowing who this guy was or just where he had gone with the others, I doubted it. Is this the end of everything? My life, my future and my promises to Sean?